A Shift in Night

Lost Legacies
Book 8

Maddox Grey

GREYMALKIN

The Lost Legacies Series

A Shift in Darkness*

A Shift in Shadows

A Shift in Fate

A Shift in Fortune

A Shift in Ashes

A Shift in Wings

A Shift in Death

A Shift in Tides

A Shift in Night

A Shift in Fire

*A Shift in Darkness is available for free download at maddoxgreyauthor.com.

Published by Greymalkin Press
www.greymalkinpress.com

Dev/line editing by Proofs by Polly
Copy editing and proofreading by Rachels Top Edits

Cover Design by Seventhstar Art

eBook ISBN: 978-1-963368-09-3
Paperback ISBN: 978-1-963368-16-1

Quick Note From The Author

Hey there! I just wanted to chat real quick about what you can expect in this book. This is a fantasy novel that contains adult content and situations. If it was a movie, it would probably be rated "R" for violence, language, and sexual content.

For more information, please visit https://greymalkinpress. com/pages/maddoxgrey-faq

Also… quick little note on language. I am a strange, strange person, and I've lived a bit of an odd life. I was born and raised in California, but was mostly raised by my Canadian grandmother and was then unofficially adopted by an Irish family in my late teens. You might be wondering why I'm mentioning this, and the reason is that I have a bit of a magpie approach when it comes to the English language.

Sometimes I like the American English spelling… sometimes I'm really attached to that extra "u" and go for the non-American version. Variety is the spice of life y'all.

Bless the soul of my copy-editor because she just sighs heavily at the start of each manuscript and deals with my eccentricities. So if you're an American and looking at a word and thinking it's not spelt right… it is most likely the non-American version of the word.

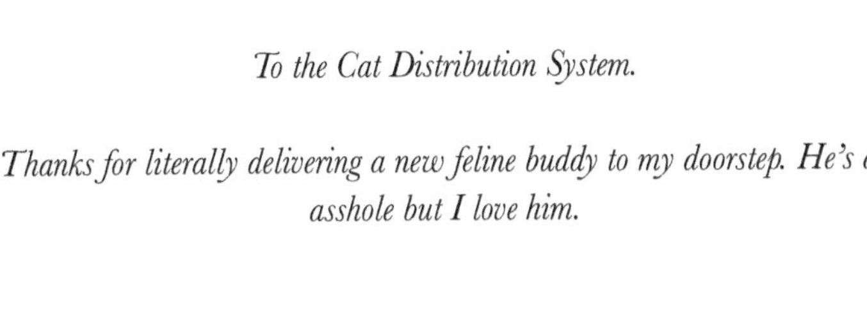

To the Cat Distribution System.

Thanks for literally delivering a new feline buddy to my doorstep. He's an asshole but I love him.

Chapter One

"This is bullshit," I tried to growl, but it came out more like a frustrated whine.

In my four hundred years of existence, the universe had mostly been a giant dick to me. It had clearly forgotten about its standard operating procedure though when it'd blessed me with a gorgeous mate *and* a hot daemon girlfriend.

Recently, Pele—the hot daemon girlfriend—had been spending a lot of time in the daemon realm. Our relationship had been going on for centuries, but it'd always ebbed and flowed. Given that Pele was soon going to be taking over her father's role as Head of the Daemon Assembly, her scarcity hadn't been a surprise.

What *was* a surprise was her suggesting that Mikhail crash our playdate.

So after checking with Mikhail to see if he was cool with it, I gave the only reasonable answer to such a question.

Sign. Me. The. Fuck. Up.

Neither of them had even the slightest interest in each other, which meant I would be the center of attention. In my head, I'd assumed the way it would play out was Pele would tie me up and Mikhail would go down on me, then maybe they'd switch places and Pele would break out some toys.

I may or may not have spent a lot of time coming up with multiple scenarios while sunbathing in my feline form, but there was a fatal flaw in all of this that I failed to take into account. If Pele was the queen of edging, Mikhail was the fucking king.

"Something wrong, shifter?" Mikhail taunted from between my thighs as his tongue flicked around my clit, but not touching. He'd been doing that for the past ten minutes while Pele had kissed and licked my neck and collarbone. The two of them had been getting me worked up for hours, and there was fuck all I could do about it because Pele's stupid magical ropes held my arms above my head and my ankles were loosely tied to the floor.

Thanks to some unfortunate events in my life, I tended to panic when I was bound, but Pele had been helping me work through it over the past few years. On the surface, it looked like just fun sexy times, but underneath was a trust that went both ways.

I trusted Pele not only to bind me but to know how far she could push, and she understood the enormity of that trust and never abused it. She trusted me to be honest about how I felt at any particular moment. The first few sessions had been intense, to say the least.

Being bound still brought on an initial panic, but I was able to work through it now instead of my mind just shutting down. Pele had planned ahead for tonight's event and had made sure there was some give to the tie-downs.

How thoughtful of her.

"You are both the absolute worst," I hissed. "As soon as I'm free of these ropes, I'm punching both of you in the face and burning your houses down!"

"My house is fireproof." Pele snorted, and her breath

tickled my right nipple, which was something she clearly noticed because she breathed on it again and then laughed at my squirming.

"And my house is your house," Mikhail pointed out, his damn head still between my thighs. "And while you might do it anyway just to spite me, you wouldn't risk damaging your weapons."

I let out a long growl and then began listing all the ways I would to get even with them once I was free. It was a long list and very detailed. I was still going when the door suddenly swung open.

Unsurprisingly, it was Asmodeus. We were in Pele's personal playroom beneath The Inferno, and they were the only one who would have strolled in so casually.

What was surprising was the way Pele stiffened for half a second before forcing her posture to relax as she watched Asmodeus stride across the room. She and Asmodeus had been working together for well over a century, and during that time, it'd been a not-so-secret secret that Asmodeus was in love with her. Pele, in all her stubbornness, had been denying her feelings for them because she was worried about not being able to protect them. Her list of enemies was almost as long as mine.

It wasn't that I didn't sympathize; I had the same concerns about Mikhail, but some things were worth it, and Pele was one of the people who'd convinced me that my friends and loved ones made me stronger. The fact that she wasn't taking her own advice when it came to Asmodeus was something I found incredibly frustrating. I could only imagine how Asmodeus felt about it.

Mikhail and I just worked out our issues by stabbing each other. I didn't care what Elisa said. That was a totally valid and healthy way to deal with disagreements in a relationship.

Asmodeus didn't even bat an eye at me tied up naked in the center of the room. As always, they looked professional . . . and hot. Their long black hair was pulled back into a sleek bun, and their lean frame was wrapped in a perfectly tailored black suit. Turquoise eyes met mine, politely staying above my neckline. "Apologies for the intrusion, but there is someone here to see you, Nemain, and I'm afraid it can't wait."

Mikhail said something under his breath before rising from between my knees to stand behind me, slinging an arm around my stomach and tugging me against him.

"Please tell me it's not Unseelie business," I pleaded. "I thought I made it very clear that I was taking a two-week break from all their bullshit."

Mikhail's chest rumbled against my back as he let out a raspy laugh. "I don't think anyone is doubting your declaration after the tantrum you threw yesterday."

"It wasn't a tantrum!" I raised my foot as much as I could with the ties and slammed it down, aiming for his foot, but he moved away just in time and tweaked my nipple in retaliation. Heat flared throughout my body, and I swallowed the moan that tried to escape.

He hadn't let me come once in hours, so the asshole didn't get to hear me moan.

"You set half of the Unseelie Court fae on fire," Mikhail mused as he continued to tease me with his fingers.

Asmodeus arched a dark eyebrow. "Really, Nemain?"

"The vampire is being overly dramatic," I hissed and tried to kick Mikhail away, but he just chuckled and moved to my other nipple. "I only set their clothes on fire. Maybe some hair."

"How responsible of you," Asmodeus replied, a hint of amusement flickering in their eyes at my explanation. "Tonight's interruption is not fae-related. It's . . . your business. He's waiting for you in the meeting room on the third floor. The one with the least amount of furniture to break."

"Quit being cryptic, Asmodeus." I scowled as the barest amount of a smirk appeared on their full mouth. "Who is *he*?"

"You'll find out once you get dressed and go upstairs like a good little shifter."

"Looks like playtime's over." Pele sighed from where she'd been standing off to the side.

"This wasn't playtime." I glared at her. "This was torture. Untie me."

"Now who's being overdramatic?" She glanced at her nails and frowned, holding her hand out so she could further examine the gleaming black polish tipped with a vivid reddish orange.

Fuck this. Blue flames sprung to life along the ropes over my head before frozen ash rained down around me.

"You know I hate getting that in my hair," Mikhail growled as he quickly let me go and moved back.

"I'm not talking to you," I said in a sing-song voice.

"You just did." He snapped his fangs at me before shaking some of the ashy flakes from his shoulder-length black hair.

Asmodeus simply stood there with their hands neatly clasped in front of them. They hadn't so much as looked in Pele's direction since entering the room, nor had she acknowledged them.

"That was my second favorite set of ropes, Nemain." Pele dropped her hand and gave me an annoyed look.

Half a thought from me had the ropes hanging to the far left on the brick wall igniting in crystal blue flames as well. Pele's glare deepened, and I smiled. The red ropes hanging beside the currently burning ones went up next.

It was still hard for me to use my flames like this, but I was getting better. I used to always funnel the devourer fire through my body and then direct it from there. My father, Kalen, had been working with me on that. Although he hadn't been super happy about me using my newfound skill on the fae gathered in the Unseelie Court the other day.

Badb, my mother, had found it hilarious.

"Not the purple ones," Asmodeus said evenly. "Those are *my* favorite."

Pele's head whipped so fast from me to the daemon standing in the center of the room that I was surprised I hadn't heard a snap. "And who exactly have you been using them with?"

Asmodeus' eyes flicked to her. "As you stated last month, we have a work relationship and nothing more. What I do in my personal time is none of your business."

For a split second, hurt shone in Pele's bright eyes before she hid it. "Fine," she ground out. "But this is my playroom. Find your own."

"Of course." Asmodeus bowed their head, not a hint of emotion showing on their beautiful face. "If you require nothing else of me, my shift is over. Also, I compiled a list of replacements for my position on your desk. Let me know who you would like to speak to, and I'll arrange it."

Without another word, they turned on their heel and left the room.

"Pele," I started, pulling my magic back to me and snuffing out the remaining blue fire.

"Don't," she snapped, her tone low and dangerous, before deep orange flames surged across her vibrant red skin as she flung a hand towards the purple ropes Asmodeus had pointed out. Within seconds, the ropes were nothing but ashes.

Then she closed the distance between us, the flames dancing along her skin winking out of existence a second before she wrapped her fingers around my throat and squeezed. Instantly, Mikhail was at my back again, but he didn't seem concerned about Pele's hostility. Instead, he wrapped his arms around me, pulling me snugly against him while his fingers dug into my flesh.

"We're not talking about it," Pele snarled before thrusting two fingers into my hot and aching center. The two of them had worked me up so much that she slid in easily, even as my pussy clenched around her slender fingers.

"Fuck," I said on a strangled moan. "Okay. Not talking about it. Just keep fucking me please."

"Look at that." Mikhail laughed as his fangs dragged across my neck, causing me to shiver. "She said, *please*. Is there something else you want, my violent little mate?"

"Touch me," I pleaded, not having it in me to be my normally bratty self. It was like my mind and body were wholly focused on my building climax. "Bite me."

Apparently, Mikhail was done playing too because he sank his teeth into the space between my neck and shoulder as one of his hands dipped lower to roughly rub my throbbing clit. I screamed, arching further into him.

Every muscle in my body tensed, and it felt like my skin was on fire. Pele fucked me harder while Mikhail's clever fingers created the most delicious friction. Neither of them pulled back, leading me up to the edge and letting me fall over.

My hips bucked forward, and they fucked me through the orgasm, not slowing until I slumped against Mikhail, my legs on the verge of giving out. His arm around my waist was all that held me up as his fangs popped out of my neck and he raised the hand he'd gotten me off with before licking it clean.

It took me a second to realize I was whimpering as tremors still coursed through me.

Pele finally slid her fingers free and used them to grip me by the chin, smearing the evidence of my desire across my skin.

"How are you feeling, Nemain?" Her eyes bored into mine, searching.

"Slightly less mad at you," I panted.

"Good." She smirked. "Now let's go find out what trouble has come your way."

I sighed but set about grabbing my clothes from where they'd landed on the floor hours ago and pulled them on. When I started walking towards the door, Mikhail stopped me and ran his fingers through my hair, a smirk on his lips. "Can't have you going into a meeting with hair that says you've just been fucked."

"Heavens forbid my reputation take a hit like that." I leaned into his touch a little.

"Come on, you two," Pele ordered from where she stood at the door. "You can do your sappy mate bullshit later. I'm leaving tomorrow for the daemon realm, and I'll likely be gone for at least a month . . . maybe longer. I'd like to know what this is all about before I depart."

The hazy satisfaction I'd been reveling in at Mikhail's touch vanished, and I looked worriedly at my fiery friend. "You're going to be gone for that long?"

Pele's expression tightened. "My father is officially stepping down in six months. Most of the factions back me taking his place as head of the Daemon Assembly, but there are others using the transition to make a bid for power. They need to be dealt with sooner rather than later."

"Do you need my help? You're more important than whatever is waiting for us upstairs." I knew she'd say no, but I hoped she'd say yes because I hated sitting on the sidelines while she struggled through things on her own.

Pele shook her head, confirming my fear that she was too damn stubborn to accept help. "You are fantastic at killing but shit at politics, Nemain." The corners of her mouth quirked up into a faint grin.

"She has a point, love." Mikhail snorted.

"Right now, I have a lot of support," Pele continued, "but

that will wither and die if I have the Unseelie Knight swooping in and waving her pointy murder sticks around."

"Rude way to talk about my swords," I mumbled.

The amusement fell from her face, and Pele gave me a tired smile. "I need to handle this myself as much as I can. The Assembly has always respected my father, and most of them respect me. Others doubt my ability to fully step into my father's shoes. I have to prove them wrong."

I knew Pele could handle other daemons, but this still felt like leaving her to fight all on her own. Wanting to prove herself made sense, and I could appreciate that, but still . . . what if some of her enemies just happened to meet unfortunate acciden—

"No," Pele interrupted my murderous thoughts and stalked towards me. As soon as I was within reach, she gripped me by the chin for the second time tonight and forced me to look in her eyes. "Bad shifter." Then she slammed her lips against mine, kissing me hard before pulling back. "No killing my enemies before I say so. Understood, Nemain?"

I stubbornly clenched my jaw, but she continued staring at me unrelentingly. After a tense couple of seconds, I sighed. "Understood."

"Good." Pele released my chin. "I've got this. The second I think I don't, I promise I will let you know." Then she turned and headed up the stairs.

I let out a long, frustrated breath and started after her, Mikhail falling into step behind me, snickering. I stopped suddenly, slamming an elbow back, and was rewarded with a gasp of pain. "Quit laughing."

"I'm allowed to be entertained by Pele scolding you." He slapped my ass. "Now get moving so we can see what this is. The sooner we deal with it, the sooner you can have your thighs wrapped around my head."

My mind short-circuited as a parade of lusty thoughts marched through it, causing my foot to freeze midway to the next step. There were several meeting rooms on the floor we were heading to . . . Maybe we could dart into one real quick and—

"Don't even think about it, Nemain," Pele called from the top of the third-floor landing. "Work first, play later."

I sulked as we made our way up the stairs. Pele waited until we reached her before striding down the hallway, then she went through the last door on the right, leaving it open for us.

Multiple flippant responses were going through my head as I stomped into the room, ready to verbally and maybe physically eviscerate whoever had disturbed my sexy fun times.

Okay, it had been an epic edging fest, but sooner or later, they would have started fucking me.

My fingers pushed open the door that had fallen halfway shut, and I froze as my gaze connected with a pair of beautiful hazel eyes. "Andrei?"

Chapter Two

"WHAT ARE you doing back in Emerald Bay?" I stopped a few feet into the room and stared at my former lover. He was the same as I remembered but different. His boy-next-door good looks hadn't changed, and while he'd added a little muscle to his six-foot build, it wasn't anything drastic.

Slowly, I scanned him and noticed little differences. The way he held himself perfectly balanced like a fight could break out at any moment. There were a few faint scars on his arms and neck, the marks lighter against his tan skin. Werewolves had impressive healing, and he hadn't had those when I'd known him. Only something magic-related could have hurt him that badly.

I'd once told Kaysea that Andrei was a lover, not a fighter. At the time, that had been true . . . but it didn't seem to be anymore.

My gaze drifted back up to meet his stare, but it was a wolf looking back at me. He blinked, and the gold in his eyes retreated until only hazel was left.

What happened to you? I thought.

When we'd been together, Andrei had been more than a

little naive when it had come to everything nonhuman. Hell, he hadn't even known that other realms existed or just how many nasty beasties walked around in the human realm, hidden out of sight. I'd been the one to pop his supernatural cherry.

I'd also been the one to ultimately end things between us. Andrei had loved me . . . and I had loved him enough to let him go, because he was a good person.

I was not.

There was still a lightness to his hazel eyes, but it wasn't as bright as before. I'd hoped that when Andrei and the other werewolves had left Emerald Bay, they'd find somewhere safe to live and stay out of trouble, but either trouble had found Andrei or he'd gone looking for it.

"Nice to see you too, Nemain." He let out a raspy laugh. "You're still as direct as ever."

"Sorry." I snorted. "You just weren't who I was expecting to find. Last I heard, you were somewhere in Europe."

"I was . . ." His eyes snapped over my shoulder to Mikhail, and a golden sheen rolled over them. "I see the vampire stuck around."

"Don't hurt him," I said quickly.

"Wasn't planning on it." Andrei's gaze didn't move from Mikhail, and his hazel eyes turned yellow. Shit. His control over his wolf had never been great, but it seemed to have gotten worse.

"She wasn't talking to you, pup," Mikhail drawled.

A low rumble filled the room, and Pele stepped to the side next to another closed door and crossed her arms, a disinterested look on her face. I would have asked her to help, but she probably would have just set Andrei on fire. She'd never particularly cared for werewolves . . . or vampires, for that matter. Mikhail and the other vampires in my life got a pass because of their connection to me, but even that had taken a while.

Suddenly, Andrei inhaled sharply. "You're fucking him." His wolfish eyes focused on me, and there was a darkness to them that I'd never seen before. That more than his sharp tone had me instantly concerned.

What had happened to my sweet wolf?

"That is usually what one does with their mate," Mikhail answered in a casual tone, like he hadn't just thrown a bomb into the room.

"Not helping," I snapped at him over my shoulder.

"Oh." He grinned at me. "Was *that* what I was supposed to be doing?"

"I hate you," I muttered.

"I love the way you sweet-talk me."

"Mates," Andrei growled, drawing my attention back to the pissed-off werewolf. His nostrils flared again, and this time, his gaze darted to Pele's right hand before cutting back to me and looking at the spot on my neck where Mikhail had bitten me. "So you mated the vampire but you still fuck the daemon?"

"First, Nemain was fucking me long before *either* of you were in the picture, and second, it's called polyamory, wolf." Pele studied her fingernails again. "Try not to be so boring."

Andrei's upper lip quivered. "Is this why you broke up with me? You knew I wouldn't be down with sharing, but the vampire is an asshole, so what does he care, right? Is that what you looked for in a mate? Just a warm body in your bed so you can forget about the fact that you got your last mate killed? Or was Myrna not your mate? Just a fuck buddy like me?"

Shock and hurt tore into me, but I kept it off my face. This wasn't Andrei—or at least not the kindhearted man I'd known. This was the aggression of his wolf manipulating his emotions. His words pained me, but I was more concerned about his mental state. Werewolves weren't as stable as vampires; sometimes their human side and wolf side fought each other until both were driven mad.

Mikhail suddenly appeared in front of me, twilight eyes scouring mine. "You alright, love?"

"I'm fine." I gave him a small smile. "Connor's said way nastier things to me. Helped me build up a bit of a tolerance."

Kaysea's—and Myrna's—older brother didn't like me. We'd come to more of an understanding lately and were almost cordial, but he'd spat all kinds of vitriol at me in the decades after Myrna's death.

"Okay." Mikhail kissed my forehead. "Also, I never agreed to your initial request."

My initial request? *Don't hurt him.* Oh, shit.

"Mikhail," I warned, my hands shooting out to grab him but closing around empty air. Damn it.

A second later, Andrei let out a pained grunt as two daggers sank into each of his shoulders, pinning him to the wall. Before he could pull free, Mikhail was there with his sword against the werewolf's throat, mist still rolling off it.

"I suggest you get your wolf under control, or whatever message brought you back to Emerald Bay is going to die with you."

Andrei's yellow gaze snapped to me as beads of blood formed where the sword bit into his skin. "You gonna let him do this?"

"I don't *let* him do anything," I said tightly. "Mikhail is my mate, not a pet, and if someone had spoken to him the way you just did me, their blood would be decorating these walls right now. I'm honestly impressed by his restraint."

"That's right. I forgot you were both insane." The yellow in his eyes glowed a bit brighter.

"Not so much insane as aggressive and prone to violence." I held his stare. "Although, given how hard your wolf is riding you, maybe you don't have much room to talk."

A bit of hazel bled back into his eyes.

"I don't really care about your control issues," Mikhail said in a low, deadly tone. "The next words out of your mouth better be an apology for being a prick." Then he leaned a little closer, baring his fangs. "And it better be a fucking good one."

I could see the struggle on Andrei's face as he tried to pull his wolf back, eyes flashing rapidly between yellow and hazel. Any lingering hurt was gone, replaced only by concern for my friend. Was this why he had returned? Because he knew he was losing control over his wolf?

That concern erupted into a bonfire. I'd heard of werewolves who had gone insane and lost their grip on humanity. They never came back from it.

"I'm sorry. That was a cruel thing to say," he ground out and squeezed his eyes shut, and when he opened them a few seconds later, they were hazel again. "Truly, kitty cat. I didn't mean it."

His old nickname cut through my fear and helped me calm down. I hadn't lost him yet.

"Apology accepted." I gave him a small smile, and the tension in the room died down.

"Damn," Mikhail muttered. "Was really hoping you'd say something dickish again so I could take your head and be done with you."

Andrei gave him a cool look. "I didn't mean *most* of the stuff I said, but the part about you being an asshole, I stand by."

My mate grinned and pulled his sword away a little too harshly, causing Andrei to hiss as blood leaked out of the shallow cut on his neck.

"Delightful," Pele said flatly. "Now tell us what the fuck you're doing here, wolf."

A flicker of golden yellow flashed over Andrei's eyes at the command, but he pushed the wolf back. "It's probably better if I let her explain." He walked towards the door next to Pele that connected to another meeting room but paused with his hand on the knob. "I need you to not freak out, okay? She's a witch, but you've met her before. No killing."

"It's not like I just randomly kill people for no reason," I huffed and crossed my arms. Mikhail and Pele both stared at me. "Annoying me is a reason!" I snapped. "Open the fucking door, Andrei."

He hesitated for a moment before doing as I demanded, and two familiar faces walked in. I wasn't surprised to see Andrei's sister, Stela, but the witch who followed her was a bit unexpected.

She was exactly how I remembered her. Barely over five feet with warm, medium brown skin and large, dark eyes. Her long black hair was woven into a braid that hung over her shoulder. Age-wise, she appeared to be in her early forties, but the shrewdness in her eyes said she was a lot older.

Lestari, the witch who had helped us once by unlocking Luna's memories. She hadn't asked for anything at the time, which was annoying because it made me feel like I was in her debt.

"Never thought I'd see you again, Lestari." I crossed my arms as Mikhail moved to stand next to me while Pele remained against the wall.

"Why?" Stela asked in a gravely tone. "Because of your reputation as a witch killer?"

I swung my gaze towards Andrei's sister as she moved to stand next to her brother, a few feet behind the witch. Gone was the pretty brunette who'd favored a pinup style of dressing and perfect makeup. She still had her curves but had added a decent amount of muscle to them, and the loose-fitting clothes she wore were similar to what werewolves who shifted frequently preferred. There was a balance to how she moved and held herself that hadn't been there before either.

Looked like she'd accepted her wolf nature entirely and was leaning into it. *I probably shouldn't provoke her.*

Meh.

"Still pissed at me for killing your girlfriend then, huh?" I arched a brow.

Stela bristled and let out a low, rumbling growl.

"Seriously?" I snorted. "Best case scenario, she was gonna ditch your ass without a word, leaving you heartbroken. Worst case, she was planning on killing you and harvesting your parts for a spell. We've all had shitty relationships. Get over it."

"It wasn't your choice to make!" Stela bared her teeth and took a step towards me, only for Andrei's hand to shoot out and grip her wrist.

"Actually, it was." The small amount of amusement I'd been feeling slid from my face, and I gave her a hard look. "She was a threat to me and mine, which meant she had to die. Don't act like you wouldn't have done the same if someone had threatened your brother."

Stela looked away, her mouth tightening in anger.

I looked at the witch. "I get why she's here. They're a bit of a package deal." I waved a hand at Andrei and Stela. "But what brings *you* back to Emerald Bay?"

Lestari held my unflinching gaze. "Sometime soon, likely within the next couple of days, Emir is going to come to you with a request. One you won't be able to refuse because of the blood bargain you agreed to six months ago."

I narrowed my eyes at her. "Keeping track of me, witch?"

The bargain I struck with Emir, the leader of the warlocks, wasn't exactly widespread knowledge. It still pissed me off that I had it, but I didn't regret it.

As part of our bargain, Emir and those he commanded could never directly attack me or those I cared about. Furthermore, he would alert me if he knew of any attacks that my other enemies were planning—if possible. That part of the bargain was a little more vaguely worded so Emir didn't have to act in a way that would jeopardize his alliance with Lir. In exchange, I agreed not to attack him directly and to help him with some unspecified tasks.

It'd been far from an ideal bargain because I'd had to agree to make my enemy stronger, but in the wake of Cian's and Hades' kidnappings, there hadn't been a lot of options. There were too many important people in my life now, and I couldn't keep watch over everyone twenty-four seven.

In the aftermath of the bargain though, Emir had made good on his side of things. We'd avoided two attacks that had been planned by Katrina, the ex-sister of the vamp brats and just all around-bitch, and another by Balor's right-hand douchebag, Lir.

I hated Emir with every fiber of my being because he was the reason my parents were dead, but I'd do whatever was necessary to keep my remaining loved ones safe. To keep Mikhail alive.

Because I knew in my bones that my mate was a target.

Lestari shrugged. "You're a potential enemy, and Emir absolutely is one. I'd be a fool not to keep my eye on you and your dealings with him."

Fair enough.

"What makes you think Emir will be coming to me with a request?" I tilted my head to the side. "Do you have a spy within the warlocks or a very gifted seer in your coven?"

The witch smiled widely. "Neither. The vampires are a product of the human realm; they love technology. We bugged the offices of several Vampire Council members as well as their phones."

I blinked before giving Pele a disgusted look. "This is *exactly* why I didn't want a cell phone. It's bad enough I have to worry about magic bullshit. Now I have to be concerned about someone bugging my phone." I pointed menacingly at her. "I know you're behind Elisa forcing that cell phone on me."

Pele rolled her eyes. "You barely use the thing, and it's protected. Asmodeus created a spell that secures the phone."

"It's a good one too," Lestari mused. "We've tried to break it a few times."

"Asmodeus excels at everything they do," Pele said in a strained tone. I knew it wasn't Lestari's casual admission of prying into our business that had her upset.

Something had broken between her and Asmodeus, and it was hurting her. Hurting them both. But knowing Pele, she'd just stay on course and keep denying what she wanted.

If there was one person in the world more stubborn than I, it was Pele Das'ki.

"Do you know what Emir is going to ask of Nemain?" Mikhail cut in, clearly noticing Pele's discontent and trying to smooth things over.

"He made a lot of lofty promises to get the vampires on board with an alliance," she replied. "They're losing patience, so he's attempting to ease the growing dissent by giving them something major."

"The ability to walk in the sun?" Mikhail guessed.

Lestari nodded. "That and other things, but the magic used to create the vampires and werewolves isn't well understood. He wants to go back to the source of it all: the sorcerer realm."

I whistled. "Even I haven't gone there, and not for lack of trying." I thought about it more. "Okay, my attempts before were half-assed because I was in my twenties and curious, but I think they've done something to make their realm hard to find."

"I've also tried to find it." A crease formed between Pele's dark orange brows. "I think they've used some version of a lookaway spell. So access to the realm isn't blocked . . . you simply can't find it."

"When you were listening in on the vampires, did it sound like Emir had found a way to locate the realm?" I asked

Lestari. "Because if you came here to ask that I refuse to help him, I can't. Not an outright refusal." I held my right hand up with the back towards her and tugged on the blood oath. A slight tingle raced across my skin as the bloodred circle made of chain links flared to existence for a few seconds. "But I truly don't know how to find the realm, so if he wants me to, then Emir's shit out of luck."

I couldn't tell Emir no if he asked, but I didn't have to go out of my way to help him either. Blood oaths operated under the letter of the law, not the spirit, and that often cut both ways. There might come a time when Emir would be in a similar position and choose to fuck me over.

Blood oath or not, we were far from allies.

"He knows how to find it," Lestari replied.

"Fuck." I tilted my head back and stared at the ceiling.

This meant the vampires would be strong enough to wipe the werewolves out of existence once and for all, and then Emir would likely point them at the witches. Between the leveled-up vamps and Emir's powerful warlocks, the witches would be annihilated.

I dropped my head back down and looked between Lestari and the werewolves before holding Andrei's stare. "What have you come to ask of me, Andrei? I can't break the blood oath. If Emir truly knows how to find the realm, I'll have to bring them."

"You will," he agreed. "I know you can't break the blood oath." He briefly glanced at Lestari. "But there's nothing to say you can't bring us as well."

My brows rose. That was definitely not what I'd expected. "Why do you want to go to the sorcerer realm?"

"You might have noticed that my control over my wolf is slipping." He gave me a sad, dejected smile that tugged at my heart. "I don't know how to fix it. I've tried, but it's only getting worse. Something is fundamentally broken between me and my wolf, and I'm not the only one like this. The werewolves were created by the sorcerers. If anyone has the answer to how to fix this, it would be them."

"They might be able to offer us more too," Stela added. "The vampires have additional magic, but we don't. We're fast, strong, and can heal from a lot, but the only other magic we have is being able to shift into our wolf forms. "

"You want to even the playing field." Mikhail eyed Stela. "What makes you think the sorcerers will be willing to help you?"

The werewolf looked towards the witch.

Lestari smiled. "According to someone I know who personally met sorcerers, they make the fae look humble. The war between the werewolves and vampires won't interest them, but the flaws in how they created the werewolves will."

I suspected the unnamed someone was Hecate. I didn't exactly know what their history was, but I knew there was something between the Mother of All Witches and Lestari because Hecate had mentioned her in passing before. And there had been a *tone* when she'd said the witch's name.

Complicated witch relations aside, Hecate had a good read on people. I mulled it over. The sorcerers didn't come to the human realm often, or if they did, nobody knew. They didn't interact with anyone, and the biggest impact they'd ever made here was when they'd created the werewolves and vampires a little over eight hundred years ago. Rumor was the whole thing had been over a bet, but nobody knew for sure because they'd worked their magic and then abandoned their creations.

"What if you're wrong and they refuse?" I looked to Andrei. "It'll be dangerous, and my hands are somewhat tied in how much I'll be able to protect you. If Emir or his allies directly attack me or mine, I'm allowed to protect myself."

When Emir and I had made the blood oath, we'd also signed a contract that Asmodeus had helped me craft. Specific people were named as off-limits; anyone else was fair game. I hadn't put Andrei's name in the contract, though Asmodeus and I had discussed it. Andrei had left town years ago and had seemed to be lying low, and I'd already had a lot of people to name who were in the direct line of fire. We'd agreed that it was better to not draw attention to Andrei because he hadn't seemed like a prime target for anyone.

But now he was putting himself directly in harm's way.

"I need whiskey," I muttered and rubbed my forehead.

Andrei took a deep breath, his nose crinkling, and then walked over to a small cabinet against the wall. He opened it and withdrew a bottle filled with a dark amber liquid. "Still fine with drinking out of the bottle?" He smirked as he walked over to me, completely ignoring Mikhail, and passed me the whiskey.

"Of course." I unscrewed the cap and took a long swig. Much better.

Then I held the bottle out to him, and he took it. "I know it's a risk, but I don't expect you to protect us. We can do that ourselves."

Mikhail snorted. "Pretty sure the last time you went up against a warlock, you ended up dead."

I grimaced at the memory of Andrei kneeling on a beach, bound by the magic of my ex-lover Sebastian. He had died that day. The only reason he was still here was because I'd called on Hades and demanded that he bring back Andrei's soul from the afterlife.

The god of the dead had been less than pleased, especially because he'd barely tolerated my existence back then. We weren't exactly buddies now, but we were getting closer. Something Cian, my brother, appreciated. He hadn't enjoyed playing peacekeeper between his lover and his sister.

"Things have changed." Andrei took a long drink before

giving Mikhail a wolfish grin. "The warlocks and vampires will find me much harder to kill these days."

Mikhail's twilight eyes narrowed. "Don't get overconfident, pup. The ones you and your sister have been taking out across Europe have all been mid-tier at best. You haven't gone up against any Apex vampires yet, and Emir's top warlocks will flay the skin from your bones."

"Been keeping tabs on me?" A raspy growl punctuated Andrei's words.

"I may not give a shit about you, but Nemain does." Mikhail shrugged. "Your death would hurt my mate."

I snatched the bottle back. "What does your intel say about when Emir will be making this request of me?" I asked Lestari before taking another swig.

"Two days from now."

"Alright." I sighed. "We can plan more tomorrow. If I'm going to be out of town, I need to get some things in order first."

"So you'll help us?" Andrei asked.

"Yeah, wolf." I smiled. "I'll help you."

Chapter Three

"So?" I asked casually. It was a few hours after sunrise, and Mikhail and I were still in bed at my apartment. After leaving The Inferno last night, Mikhail had made up for the hours of edging by making me come over and over again until I'd passed out. He'd also woken me up this morning by burying his head between my thighs.

It wasn't an unusual way to wake up. We'd been together for almost a year now, but we still had a hard time keeping our hands off each other. Yet there had been an underlying intensity to how he'd claimed me repeatedly last night that made me suspect my slightly psychotic vampire might have a bit more on his mind than he was sharing.

Ugh. I was going to have to do one of the many things I dreaded: talk about emotions.

"So?" he repeated and continued toying with the ends of my hair.

I turned on my side so I faced him and blew out a frustrated breath.

"Look. I don't really know how to do this. The last time one of my exes rolled into town, he wanted to kill everyone I loved and force me to take him back." Muscles feathered along Mikhail's jawline as he tensed at the reminder. Mikhail and I had met during that perilous time, and we hadn't been friendly to each other, but the pull had been there all the same. "Everything with Sebastian wasn't exactly fun, but it wasn't complicated either. He wanted me. I wanted him dead."

"And this situation is?" Dark, twilight eyes bored into mine. "Complicated?"

"It's definitely more complicated than killing."

And gods, I could use some straightforward killing. I had too many things filed under *it's complicated* at the moment.

Mikhail stared at me for a long moment before dropping his gaze back to my hair that he was still rolling between his fingers.

"If you weren't stuck with me as a mate, would you want Andrei back?"

He was trying to keep his expression blank, but I could read the faint tension in it, and that was nothing compared to what I felt through our bond. The thread that tied our souls together was practically screaming.

Mikhail was genuinely worried that I regretted him. It was true that my magic had sprung the bond on us, and thanks to my weird heritage, it was a bit hard to predict and even more difficult to control.

Normally, fae mate bonds could be dissolved. Ours likely couldn't, not without a lot of pain and the possibility of one or both of us dying.

Yet none of that mattered because I'd chosen him long before the bond had formed. I'd just been lying to myself about it. He was mine, and I was his. Apparently, he needed a reminder.

In one fluid motion, I pushed up off the bed. Mikhail released my hair, his hands falling to my hips as I straddled him.

Then we went completely still, as if the breath in our lungs had frozen.

I'd intended to wrap a clawed hand around his throat and give him a lecture about being an idiot. Maybe draw a little blood. Then he would apologize for voicing such a foolish notion while giving me all the orgasms.

That had been the plan, but it wasn't smooth skin that my fingers were gripping; it was the cool, silver handle of a sword. One pressed against Mikhail's throat with mist clinging to it.

"Umm . . . is this yours?" I pulled the pale, silver blade away and studied it. Faint mist was still rippling across the sharp edges. It certainly *looked* like his sword.

Mikhail stared at the weapon, his eyes comically wide.

A chuckle bubbled up my throat, then another, and soon, I was laughing uncontrollably. Mikhail grabbed the sword before I accidentally stabbed him and dismissed it with half a thought, leaving mist curling in the air where the sword had been a second ago.

"How the fuck did you do that?" he demanded.

"Aww," I cooed between laughs. "Is someone upset that his sword prefers me over him?"

He jerked his hips up, and his hard length ground into me, turning my laugh into a moan. Neither of us had gotten dressed, so I felt every inch of him pressed against me.

Despite being fucked for hours, my body was instantly ready to go again. I wondered if it would always be this way between us. If we'd always be insatiable for the other. I rolled my hips, and we both groaned as he slid through the wetness.

"Nemain," he ground out. "Behave."

I bit my bottom lip hard enough to draw blood, and Mikhail's eyes narrowed before he flipped us so I was pinned to the bed. The tip of his cock was notched at my entrance, and I whimpered. Actually *whimpered* in need. Ugh. Mikhail had turned me into such a hussy.

"Answer my question, and I'll give you what you want." He smirked.

"Mikhail," I said evenly, "if you try to edge me again, I'll summon your sword again and shove it up your ass."

"Kinky." He tilted his head, causing his dark hair to fall over his shoulder. "How'd you summon it in the first place?"

"I don't know," I huffed. "It wasn't intentional, and honestly, I didn't think it was even possible."

His dark brows furrowed together. "It has to be the mating bond, right?"

"Probably," I admitted. "Fae mates can share their magic with each other to some extent. There has never been a bond like ours before though, so it's hard to predict."

"Your parents are bonded," he pointed out.

"But Badb is one hundred percent feline shifter. You and I have devourer blood."

I'd talked to Badb and Kalen about mating bonds, which had been incredibly awkward. It would have been less cringy to talk about sex, but instead, we'd had to talk about a bond that could only be formed by deep and unrelenting love.

Gross.

Magic wasn't truly sentient, but it did react to emotions. Fae were one of the few species that could directly interact with magic without the use of spells or artifacts, and they did it by having an empathic bond with magic, which meant fae bonds were intertwined with our emotions. They didn't have to be romantic in nature, but there had to be a deep love between the bonded individuals for it to happen.

Discussing lovey-dovey feelings that I had for Mikhail with my parents had been painful for everyone involved. The three of us were great at expressing anger and frustration, but not so much undying love.

To add insult to injury, I hadn't even gotten anything useful out of the conversation. Neither Kalen nor Badb could share their particular brand of magic with the other. Kalen's flames didn't protect Badb, and he couldn't open gateways like her. They could share raw magic and give each other power boosts, but nothing more.

So we'd all suffered through a twenty-minute conversation for nothing.

Kalen had suggested I talk to the Unseelie Queen, Elvinia, but I wasn't willing to go down that road yet. I might be her Knight and an official member of the Unseelie Court, but I still didn't trust her. The fae queens marched to the beats of their own drums. For now, our goals were mostly aligned: keep Finn safe and the queens' older brother locked away.

I had no illusions about what I was to them though: a powerful tool for them to wield. The moment I was no longer useful or my existence started to cause them problems, they'd turn on me.

I didn't fault the queens for it because I felt the same about them.

All of this meant that Mikhail and I had no idea what to expect with our mate bond. Up until now, it had been my magic that'd been acting strange. It liked Mikhail and had often gone to him whether I'd wanted it to or not. Blue flames would wrap around him like a protective blanket.

He hadn't been able to summon them yet like I had his sword, but maybe that was coming next? A small amount of dread formed in the pit of my stomach. My devourer flames would never harm Mikhail, but they could harm someone else. Growing up, I'd had almost no control over them, and more than once, I'd hurt my brother, Cian, because of how unpredictable they could be.

Things had gotten better once I'd accepted the devourer part of myself, but the mating bond had been interfering with my control again.

"Stop dwelling on the bad parts," Mikhail purred. I let out

another half-strangled moan as he pushed his cock into me . . . and then hissed when he stopped.

"What did I say about edging?" I growled. "And you don't know what I was thinking about!"

"My love, you've always been terrible at lying to me." He slid in another inch and chuckled when I bit my lip to hold back the sounds of just how much I enjoyed the feel of him. "You were thinking about all the unknowns of our mating bond and worrying about your magic reacting poorly and hurting someone. Elisa. Bryn. Kaysea. Take your pick."

I glared at him. "It's a valid concern."

"It is." Slowly, Mikhail fully sheathed himself, and this time, I couldn't hold back the moan as I stretched around him. Then he held perfectly still and watched me pant beneath him. "But think about all the fun things we can do if we can truly share magic. All the new and creative ways we can slaughter our enemies."

I thought about it. What if I could imbue his sword with my devourer flames? Or figure out how to make my dual blades vanish into mist like his?

"Now you're getting it." He gave me a feral grin. "I'm going to need you to scream for me, because the wolf is outside and I want him to know you're mine."

"Wha—" My question was cut off as Mikhail drew back before slamming back into me at the same moment he sank his fangs into my neck.

An hour later, I braided my damp, ash-blonde hair over my shoulder while we walked down the stairs of our apartment building. I paused at the second-floor landing, and Mikhail went still beside me as we looked at the door. The building was owned by Pele and had a total of three apartments. I'd always lived in the top one because it had the best view of the rocky coastline just outside the building.

For a while, Bryn and Finn had lived on the second floor and the vamp brats on the bottom one. Elisa had typically slept with Bryn in the second-floor apartment, leaving Damon and Misha to keep track of Isabeau and often Finn since he had a bed there too. But Elisa and Bryn had more or less moved into the bottom-floor apartment now that the two teenage boys had moved out.

Men, not boys, I corrected myself. Damon and Misha were both twenty now. Still young, but old enough to make their own choices.

Even if that choice was to get far away from me and Mikhail.

I glanced at Mikhail, who was still looking at the door. His expression was blank, almost tranquil, but I could pick up the little clues as to what he was really feeling: the slight pinching at the corners of his mouth like he was fighting back a grimace and how his fingers were curled as if they were holding a dagger, but there was no enemy to stab here.

"Do you think he's okay?" he asked quietly.

"No," I answered in an equally soft tone. "I think he's far from it."

Guilt hit me hard and fast. We had survived our encounter with the Olympians six months ago, but we hadn't walked away without wounds. I wished it had been me. That I'd been the person who had been hurt. I knew Mikhail felt the same.

Instead, it'd been Magos who had paid the price for defying the gods.

He'd saved me when nobody else could and helped me patch my soul back together. I owed him so much, and there was fuck all I'd been able to do to help him. He was Mikhail's last living blood relative, and more than that, the two of them were bonded in blood and death. They'd been turned into vampires at the same time and had seen the fall of everything they'd loved.

I'd always known the Olympians were cruel and petty, but it was one thing to hear of the fucked-up shit they'd done and another to experience it.

Artemis had seen that Magos was the strength for me and Mikhail. Her prick of a nephew had also enlightened her to the grief he still carried for his beloved wife, who had been killed in the war between the vampires and werewolves.

The bitch had known all that . . . and had used it like a poisoned dagger. Every time Magos drank blood, he would lose a memory of his wife, and it wouldn't simply drift away to nothing; he would know that he lost something vital. Normally, vampires could easily go weeks without drinking blood and months before they started to weaken. Artemis had increased Magos' thirst to ensure he had to choose.

Sacrifice a memory, or sacrifice his sanity.

Recently, he'd gone almost a month without drinking. He'd been so calm about it that none of us had realized how close to the edge he'd been.

Until Bryn had come home five days ago and gone to the second-floor apartment to retrieve something. He'd ripped into her so quickly, the young valkyrie hadn't had a chance to fight him off.

In part because she hadn't been willing to hurt him.

Bryn might not have known Magos as long as the rest of us, but they were both so similar in nature. Honorable. Steadfast. Their friendship had been instantaneous.

It hadn't been enough to stop Magos from almost ripping out her throat though.

The only thing that had saved her was Sigrun and Niall arriving. The two of them had been able to pull Magos off Bryn, who hadn't even been concerned for herself. Instead, she was worried about Magos. We all were. That night, I'd gone to the pocket dimension that was serving as Artemis' prison and threatened to do all kinds of things to her if she didn't reverse the curse. It wasn't the first time I'd promised to rend her flesh from her bones over and over again, but then I'd done something I hadn't done since my parents had been killed in front of me.

I'd begged.

She'd laughed in my face and repeated the same thing she always did. *"A curse cannot be broken, but I bet your friend can be."*

Badb had come to retrieve me hours later after I'd hacked the goddess' body apart multiple times. Apparently, I'd been so unhinged about it that I'd freaked out Nemesis. Maybe one day I'd be proud of disturbing the literal embodiment of retribution who had been born of chaos and darkness, but for now, I just felt defeated.

Magos had refused to leave the apartment since then and had requested that only Mikhail and I enter.

"I'm forgetting what my parents looked like," Mikhail said softly, his gaze still on the door. I didn't exactly know why he brought this up now, but there was so much sadness in his tone that I didn't interrupt. "My father died before our realm fell, and then my mother died not long after Magos and I were turned." His throat bobbed. "For a long time, all I knew was rage and violence. Magos tried to pull me back so many times. Sometimes he did . . . sometimes I laughed in his face and walked away."

My chest tightened because I knew exactly how Mikhail had felt. I'd lost myself too after my parents had been killed, and then Myrna. Magos had helped me too.

"Time is stealing the color of my father's eyes. The way my mother's hair would curl around her face," he continued, a low rasp to his voice. "It saddens me, but what's being done to Magos is cruel. He's held on to his memories of Hasina for so long, only for them to be ripped from him now. He doesn't deserve this."

"I know." I swallowed. "You and I are the villains. Magos is the hero."

Heroes usually died.

My magic churned in my soul, desperate and wrathful.

"They have to be able to help him." Mikhail's eyes latched onto mine. "I'm not leaving that fucking realm until they do."

I closed the distance between us and leaned my forehead against his. "If anyone can fix this, it's the sorcerers. Nobody can manipulate magic like them. This will work, love."

We stayed there for a long moment, breathing in each other's scents. This was the other thing we'd discussed this morning. How we could make this trip to the sorcerer realm work to our benefit.

I was a little frustrated with myself that I hadn't thought of this before. Of all the ideas I'd had for how to get rid of the curse, tracking down the sorcerers had never occurred to me. Like everyone else, I'd accepted it was impossible.

Granted, Emir hadn't made an appearance yet to ask this of me, but Lestari seemed confident he would, and I didn't think anything other than absolute certainty would've brought the witch here to ask for my help. I'd spent a good portion of my life killing witches in the years after my parents had been killed. Lestari had helped us once before, but we were hardly on friendly terms.

"You should stay with him today," I said softly. Ever since our mate bond had formed, we'd both been reluctant to be apart. While I was far from an expert in mate bonds, that much I knew was normal. It usually took a few years for a bond to fully settle. Until then, our magic would be chaotic, something we were very much aware of, and we'd feel an underlying tension whenever we were apart.

It was unpleasant, but we could manage. If Lestari was

correct about Emir asking me for this favor in two days, we had a lot to get done before then.

Mikhail pulled away so he could glare down the stairs at a spot on the wall, as if he could see the werewolf on the other side.

"How do you know he's there?" I asked curiously. Neither of us had actually laid eyes on Andrei, but Mikhail had been confident he waited outside.

Mikhail's gaze slid back to me. "I can feel a werewolf nearby. Not a lot of those in town these days."

My brows rose. "I didn't know you could do that."

"All vampires can, but it does take some practice to attune yourself to it." He brushed a loose strand of hair behind my ear. "The feeling is faint. Just a sense of . . . wrongness. I'm assuming the werewolves get a similar sensation when we're around, but I've never asked."

"Wait." I frowned. "Why couldn't you sense him and Stela at The Inferno?"

"Pele did something to the floor in all the meeting rooms. Hard to sense anything up there." He shrugged.

That did seem like something Pele would've done. I fiddled with a button on Mikhail's shirt. "How do you know it isn't Stela outside? Come to avenge her dead witch girlfriend?"

"She might still be pissy about how it went down, but I'm pretty sure the wolf is more annoyed that she didn't realize she was being used. Besides"—he gave me a pointed look—"you were dead to the world, but before you woke up, a car parked in the lot. I remember the sound of that piece of shit Bronco. It's the pup."

"You've got to stop calling him that." I smacked his chest.

"He's not even forty yet." Mikhail smirked. "I've seen over eight centuries come and go. You're four hundred. Can't believe you fucked him. Cradle robber."

I narrowed my eyes at him. "I will stab you."

Mikhail leaned forward to whisper in my ear, "We don't have time for foreplay, love."

His lips brushed the spot on my neck where his fangs had been buried less than an hour ago, and a shiver ran through me.

When Mikhail started to pull away, I wrapped my hands around the back of his head and kissed him deeply with everything I was feeling: the fear and concern for Magos, the constant stress of keeping everyone safe . . . and the exhilaration about going to the sorcerer realm.

Like Finn and Isabeau, my magic had awoken at a young age. When I'd been a kid, I'd loved the thrill of stepping out of one world and into another.

Into something new and full of infinite possibilities.

Even now, all these centuries later, I was still excited about it despite the circumstances.

When we broke our kiss a moment later, we were both breathing a little hard.

"Tell Magos what's going on." Reluctantly, I released him and stepped back. "We need to convince him to come with us so the sorcerers can examine him in person."

Mikhail's eyes hardened. "He's going with us. His only options are whether he's conscious or not."

Chapter Four

WHEN I WALKED out of the building and around to the small parking lot on the side, Andrei was leaning against his old, beat-up Bronco, wearing jeans and a light grey T-shirt.

His posture was relaxed, and he gave the same lopsided grin he used to wear all the time when we'd been together. We were both different people now, and our relationship was definitely different, but it still made me happy to see that look on his face. To know that, despite everything, he could still smile like that.

"Traded the bike for a car, eh?"

I glanced at the '71 blue Chevelle parked in the spot next to him. "Still have the bike, but the car is more practical these days."

Not that I'd been driving it all that much. I was getting better at opening gateways within the same realm, so there wasn't much point in driving. Elisa used it the most. My Yamaha was parked at Kaysea's small cottage on the other side of town because it had a garage.

Been a minute since I took it out for a ride, I thought wistfully.

There were few things I appreciated about humans, but sushi and fast bikes were at the top of the list.

"No vampire today?" Andrei looked over my shoulder, as if he expected Mikhail to appear out of thin air, which to be fair, was entirely possible.

"Not today," I answered tightly, refusing to look up at the window of the second-floor apartment. If I did, I'd probably march right back inside so I could make sure Magos was alright with my own two eyes. Except he was far from alright, and seeing that would send me spiraling.

I didn't have time to spiral.

Andrei studied me as I closed the distance between us, the grin sliding from his face as his hazel eyes darted to the building before returning to me. "Something happen to the big guy? I don't remember his name."

"Magos," I said quietly, coming to a stop in front of him. "Why do you ask?"

He shrugged. "I was a little surprised last night when he wasn't there. He seemed very protective of you." Again, his gaze briefly flicked to the building. "And I know Mikhail is his nephew. The fact that your pretty asshole vampire isn't here means there's something important keeping him away."

"Well, you've certainly become more observant." I snorted.

"Kind of had to." Andrei smiled again, but this time, it didn't reach his eyes. "The blinders I had on got ripped away pretty fast after I left Emerald Bay."

I bet. Things between the vampires and werewolves were escalating thanks to the warlocks getting involved . . . and Lir. My mouth twisted in distaste. I was getting real tired of that fae prick causing me trouble behind the scenes.

He was the reason the warlocks had been increasing in power and boldness. He'd also played a role in how things had gone down for us in the dragon realm and with the Olympians.

I didn't like leaving powerful enemies like him alive. Unfortunately, I hadn't figured out how to take him out yet. The bastard was hard to track down and usually had enough devourer fae with him to give even me pause.

"So what's our plan for today?" Andrei asked, drawing me out of my increasingly frustrating thoughts.

"Our plan?" I arched a brow at him.

"Look . . ." He sighed. "I love my sister, but I might strangle her if we don't get some time apart. At least until we have to leave for the sorcerer realm."

I huffed a laugh. "She does seem a little . . . intense."

"That's a nice way of putting it." He clapped his hands together. "So, where we going?"

"First stop"—a gateway snapped into existence next to us, revealing a cottage in the middle of a meadow full of wildflowers—"we're going to collect two devil children and drop them off with some new babysitters."

I stepped through the gateway, and Andrei followed after me, blinking when it closed behind us. "You've gotten better at that." He grunted. "Is one of the devil children in question Finn?"

"Yeah." I nodded and started walking around the back of the cottage. "The other is Isabeau. She's a vampire, just so you know."

He grimaced. "Thanks for the warning."

"Don't be an ass."

"Really?" He side-eyed me. "*You* are telling *me* not to be an ass?"

"Being an ass is part of my charm." I grinned at him, letting a feral edge leak into it. "We're a little protective of Isabeau these days. So, seriously, just pretend vampires aren't your mortal enemies or whatever around her."

He rolled his eyes. "I'm not going to be mean to a little kid, Nemain."

I'm almost ten.

Andrei stopped mid-stride and gave me a wide-eyed look.

I smirked. "Did I mention that the brat is an extremely powerful telepath? Like off-the-scales, scary kind of power."

"Great. Another telepath." His eyes narrowed. "Is your asshole cat here too?"

"Might not want to say that out loud . . . or think it," I suggested and resumed walking.

"Why?" Andrei trotted after me but tripped over a rock, then started to catch himself, only to step on the remnants of a rotting log that promptly snapped under his weight. I lunged, trying to catch him, but I wasn't fast enough. His body slammed into the broken pieces of the tree trunk, and one particularly sharp piece rammed its way through the back of his shoulder and out the front.

"That's why," I muttered before mentally shouting, *Jinx! Knock it off.*

The dog will heal just fine. Maybe he'll learn to recognize greatness when he sees it.

"More like I'll kick you across this meadow, furball," Andrei growled while he tore the tree chunk out of his shoulder, a yellow sheen rolling over his eyes as his healing abilities kicked in.

Jinx wasn't wrong. Werewolf healing wasn't quite as good as a vampire's, but it was pretty damn good. The scent of Andrei's rich blood filled the air, yet the bleeding was already slowing. I held a hand out, and he clasped it.

"Don't antagonize him," I warned and pulled the wolf to his feet.

"Has it ever occurred to you that it's possible to be friends with beings who aren't psychopaths?" Andrei rolled his shoulder, wincing a little as the skin knit itself back together.

"Kaysea isn't a psychopath."

Andrei stared at me. "She turned water into a whip and used it to decapitate someone!"

"Did she?" I rubbed the back of my neck. "I don't remember that."

"You were literally standing right there!"

I threw my hands up in the air. "Look, my friends kill a lot of people. It's hard to keep track." My nose wrinkled. "Although sometimes Eddie eats them in his dragon form, and I don't know, that just feels kind of wrong to me."

Waste not, want not, Isabeau chirped.

I snorted and started walking again, Andrei falling into step beside me. As soon as we made it to the small garden behind Sigrun's cottage, I pointed at the young vampire. "And you're not almost ten. You're nine and a half."

Isabeau's brown curls bounced as she leapt off the boulder she'd been perched on. Then she puffed herself up as she glared at me, which, considering she was still small for her age, wasn't so much intimidating as it was hilariously cute. "Last month I was nine and a half. Now I'm nine years and seven months, which means I'm closer to being ten than nine."

"Just go with it!" Sigrun yelled from where she examined a dagger in front of her workshop just behind the garden. Her long braids were wrapped up in a bun, and her golden wings were folded around her like a cloak. "Don't get the little terror all riled up again."

"Aww, but it's so adorable when Little Fangs gets all feisty." Niall laughed before pushing off the workshop wall. His feathery black wings were nowhere to be seen as he strode over to Isabeau, swiping a small sword off a workbench on his way.

"I'm not adorable!" Isabeau stomped.

Niall grinned. "Super. Adorable."

The vampire girl bared her fangs, which only made Niall smile wider. Then he tossed the sword to her—something that made Andrei flinch—and Isabeau snapped it out of the air and spun it around a few times.

It was a flashy, arrogant move. I approved.

Niall pointed at the practice dummy. "Tell Sigrun thank you, and then go practice what I showed you this morning, Little Fangs."

Isabeau's annoyance instantly evaporated as she looked lovingly at her sword before calling out to the valkyrie, "Thanks, Auntie Sigrun!"

I watched with mild amusement as she flounced over to the practice area. Leave it to Isabeau to figure out how to flounce with a sword. That was probably Mikhail's doing.

"Auntie?" Andrei frowned. "They're related?"

"No." I snorted. "We actually don't know who Isabeau's biological parents are, nor do we give a fuck. She's ours. Lately, she's taken to bequeathing us all titles. I think she's up to half a dozen aunties now."

"Are you one of them?" he asked with a smirk.

Niall strolled over and threw an arm over my shoulders. "Nah. Nemain and her unhinged mate got the parent titles."

"You're kidding." Andrei looked at Niall like he was waiting for the rest of the joke.

"Nope." Niall squeezed me. "Don't you think our little stabby shifter is mom material?"

Andrei lost it, laughter pouring out of him until he was bending over with his hands on his legs, trying to catch a breath.

I slid out from Niall's arm and punched the winged fae in the ribs. Hard. Something snapped, but he just chuckled as he danced out of reach. If there was such a thing as a good-natured lunatic, it was Niall.

The fae looked at Andrei, who was just now getting his laughter under control and wiping tears from his face, before glancing back at me. "You brought me something new!" His sky blue eyes lit up as he pondered Andrei again. "What is it?"

Andrei straightened and gave the broad-shouldered man a curious look. "Sorry, who exactly are you?"

I snickered because they'd both been too caught up in making fun of me to bother introducing themselves.

"Niall, meet Andrei. He's a werewolf. They're a relatively new thing. Created by the sorcerers roughly eight centuries ago by combining humans with devourer beasts. Andrei and I used to fuck. He's back in town with a witch because their enemies are our enemies." I gestured towards the fae. "Andrei, meet Niall. He's a sciatháin, a type of winged fae. Mostly extinct now, thanks to the fae queens."

"And Lir," Niall muttered.

"He's over two thousand years old," I continued, keeping my tone even and not hinting at my desperate curiosity about Niall's issue with Lir. It was one of the few things he didn't like to talk about, and Sigrun got grumpy if I pushed him. Something about living in the future, not the past, blah, blah, blah. The valkyrie seriously spoiled all my fun sometimes. "Also, the brave bastard took one for the team and is fucking Sigrun. She almost *smiled* the other day."

It was four centuries of experience that had my hand shooting up to catch the dagger an inch before it pierced my cheek.

"One of these days, you'll realize you're not as funny as you think you are," Sigrun said calmly as she strolled over to us.

"One of these days, you'll appreciate my humor, friend." I grinned at her before balancing the blade on two fingers. "Nice weight. This for me?" I asked hopefully. One could never have too many daggers.

"For Elisa." Sigrun held her hand out, and I reluctantly gave it back with a sigh. "That girl still refuses to learn to fight with a sword, or an ax, or a hammer, but she did promise to practice with daggers."

"Right now, she's enamored with Pele and learning the political machinations of all the realms." I shrugged. All that stuff was boring to me, so if Elisa learning it meant I could shove that kind of work onto her lap, I was all for it. She had Bryn to keep her alive.

Speaking of . . .

"Where are Finn and Her Bitchiness?" I squinted in the bright morning sun as I scanned the meadows, but didn't spot anything. Anger and frustration rose within me. "I told you to keep an eye on her."

"And I told you that you need to let the past go. Besides, you agreed to let the fae queens visit Finn," Sigrun replied smoothly before glancing at Isabeau, who wielded her sword rather expertly against the practice dummy. "Isabeau, you may drop it now."

Between one blink and the next, the meadow I'd been looking at was no longer empty. An enormous tree, which had to be over a hundred feet tall, towered towards the skies, and it definitely hadn't been there during my previous visits. Thick branches stretched out from it, and I spotted two feline forms perched on one, their legs and tails dangling.

Jinx and Luna.

On another branch that was almost as far away from the grimalkins as possible was another feline, this one with a shaggy brown coat. Sigrun's asshole cat, Viggo. Her wolf, Gunnar, was probably around here somewhere too, but my attention fell to the two beings who stepped out from behind the tree.

A boy only a couple of years older than Isabeau walked towards me. He was going through a bit of a growth spurt and was currently all gangly limbs. He also had brown hair that fell well past his shoulders, which used to have a slight curl to it but now was almost straight.

"The wolf is back." Green eyes ringed with yellow looked at Andrei.

"Hey, Finn," Andrei greeted him, reaching out to ruffle his hair. "You've certainly grown."

The fae boy frowned and stepped back, fingers brushing his hair to straighten it. "Growth is to be expected for someone of my age."

"Still as serious as I remember." Andrei snorted before giving me a sideways look. "Would have thought you would have corrupted him by now."

"It'll happen eventually," I murmured, most of my attention on the woman standing a few feet behind Finn.

Not just a woman. The Seelie Queen. And the bitch Sigrun was supposed to be keeping an eye on.

Picking up on the tension, Andrei glanced between me and her. When I didn't introduce them, he took a step towards her. "Hi, I'm Andr—"

"I don't care. You shouldn't deem to speak to me, dog," she sneered.

"Okay, kind of rude," he muttered and moved back to stand next to me.

"Don't take it personally," I drawled, eyes still locked on green eyes that matched Finn's. "The fae think they're better than everyone else, and the fae queens are on an entirely different level of arrogance."

"We *are* better." Áine raised her chin.

"Is she really a queen?" Andrei asked me. "She doesn't look it."

Given that Andrei grew up in the human realm, where royalty usually dressed fancy, I could see why he was perplexed by Áine's appearance. She wore simple brown pants and a light blue tunic, both of which had dirt on them. Her feet were bare, and she wore no crown or other jewelry.

Being a werewolf, Andrei not only couldn't see her power, he couldn't feel it either. Despite the fae blood running through my veins, I wasn't able to see magic, but I sure as fuck could feel it, and even though she was holding it back, it still felt like an electric charge dancing across my skin.

"Perhaps I should give the dog a demonstration?" A wicked light danced in Áine's eyes, and I felt her magic rise.

"You promised to be nice," Finn said quietly.

The building wave of magic instantly died.

"I suppose I did, didn't I?" Áine practically sulked. It was mildly amusing to see a powerful being, who had to be over five thousand years old, pout. Something told me Áine was rarely denied things, but here was Finn, barely past his first decade and doing just that.

It was one of the reasons I continued to let her meet with him, even though I wanted to keep Finn as far away from fae politics as possible. I might have despised Áine because she was a snobby bitch and had likely played some role in the death of my adoptive parents, but she really did love her nephew.

Andrei gave me a confused look. "Why is one of the fae queens here? I thought you hated the fae? And which one is she?"

"Of course you don't even know who I am, you ignorant litt—"

"Nice," Finn reminded her.

I smiled sweetly at Áine when she shut up, but she still narrowed her eyes at me.

"Nemain," Finn warned, "you be nice too."

Áine grinned at me.

"The short version is that I cut a deal with the fae queens so they would leave Finn alone for fifty years," I told Andrei.

"He stays with me and mine and away from political fae bullshit."

Andrei's brows crept up. "In exchange for what?"

"Her freedom," Finn answered quietly before I could. "Nemain sold herself to the Unseelie Queen to buy me five decades."

"Save the theatrical declarations for Isabeau, kid." I reached out and ruffled his hair.

Finn scowled and smacked my hand away. Slowly but surely, he was getting more comfortable with physical interaction. He was still quiet and reserved, but he trusted us enough to push back or stand his ground instead of being terrified we were going to punish him for it.

"It's true!" he insisted. In addition to standing up for himself, we were also discovering that Finn had quite the stubborn streak, especially when it came to taking responsibility for things that weren't his fault.

"Nemain was always going to end up involved in our world." Áine shrugged. "Her landing in my sister's court saved her life because I absolutely would have killed her."

I snorted. "You would have tried, is what you mean."

"Now who's arrogant?" She arched a brow at me.

My fingers curled, wanting very much to draw one of the swords from my back and skewer her with it, but for all sorts of reasons, one of which being that Finn wanted me to play nice, I couldn't do that. So I decided the best course of action was to ignore her because that would piss her off.

The fae queens didn't like to be snubbed, which meant it was rapidly becoming one of my favorite tactics for dealing with them.

"Time to go, Finn."

The young fae boy peered up at me. "But I was supposed to be here until tomorrow."

"I know, but plans changed. Sigrun has somewhere she has

to be tomorrow afternoon, and I expect tomorrow to be a bit hectic."

He studied me for a long moment. "You're leaving me behind again."

I saw the exact moment his expression closed down. Fuck.

"We need a minute," I told Andrei before giving Áine a pointed look to let her know she was included in that request—and that it wasn't really a request.

For once, she didn't have a biting remark; instead, concern shone in her eyes as she studied her nephew before nodding and striding off towards Sigrun. A small form of dread curled in my gut. The fae queens had been ruthless and untouchable for thousands of years, but now they had a weakness: Finn.

Surprisingly, we'd been able to keep the rumors down about Finn's existence. Few in the fae courts knew about him, but sooner or later, it would get out, and then everyone who had a bone to pick with the queens would come after him.

Poor kid. He was inheriting enemies from all of us at this point. Plus, he had the dark prophecy about him dooming the realms hanging over his head.

And I, the person who had happily participated in more than one bloody rampage in her life, was supposed to fix all this. The fates could absolutely get fucked.

"I'm going to say hi to Luna." Andrei jogged towards one of the low-hanging branches and slowed just long enough to spring up. His hands closed around the branch a good ten feet above him, and he swung himself up, climbing towards the grimalkins.

Hopefully Jinx didn't shove him out of the tree. Luna liked Andrei, so that would probably protect him . . . for at least a few minutes.

"Let's go for a walk." I didn't wait for Finn to respond as I strode away from the others. He hadn't reached Isabeau's level of stubbornness yet, so I knew he would follow. It wasn't because he was a pushover; it was because Finn felt indebted to me for keeping him safe and therefore followed my orders.

I didn't feel like he owed me anything, but getting him to accept that was proving to be difficult.

"Did you grow that tree?" Small talk wasn't really my thing, but I'd observed Aki, our resident empath, enough to pick up some tricks. I needed to get Finn out of his closed-off mode before broaching what I was going to ask him to do.

"Áine helped," he admitted quietly.

"Do you like spending time with her?" I asked in genuine curiosity.

He mulled over my question, and I let him take all the time he needed.

"If I say yes . . . would you hand me over to her permanently?" he finally said. "You'd be free of taking care of me, and I might be able to barter your release from Elvinia."

I clenched my jaw hard enough to hurt before forcing myself to relax.

"For someone so smart about most things, you're real fucking dumb sometimes."

Finn frowned up at me. "I don't think you're supposed to say things like that to a kid."

"Don't say foolish things and I won't have to," I snapped before forcing myself to take a deep breath. "Nothing in this realm or any other could make me hand you over to those bitches. I don't care how you came into my life, kid. The prophecy might say our fates are tied together but even if it didn't, I wouldn't give you up. You're mine."

He looked ahead, and as we continued walking, his nose wrinkled slightly. "But you're always leaving."

"I know." Guilt hit me. "But I don't have a choice. Things are complicated right now, and not just because of you, so don't even start blaming yourself again or I'll smack you upside the head."

The corner of his mouth quirked up. "Definitely child abuse."

I decided to go for honesty. While Finn was only eleven years old, he'd been through a lot in his life. I wanted him to understand why I had to leave again.

"Remember how I made that deal with Emir a while back?" I'd discussed it with everyone after the blood oath so Emir's frenemy status was known.

"Yes." Finn nodded. "But we can still kill Katrina."

Finn was generally softhearted but not when it came to Isabeau. Katrina had originally been a part of the vamp brats' little family unit, but now she was a threat. The only thing that made Finn lose his temper, and his hold over his magic, was Isabeau. Specifically anything that endangered her or made her sad.

Which was why he really wasn't going to like the second half of this conversation.

"We can still kill Katrina," I confirmed. "A friend of Andrei's believes Emir is going to be calling in a favor that I can't refuse because of the blood oath. He wants me to bring the vampires to the sorcerer realm to increase their abilities. I'll have to say yes, but I'm planning on bringing Andrei and Stela too because Andrei . . . he needs help. So do other werewolves."

"Do you think the sorcerers will help?"

"I think I'll make them."

We walked a little farther into the meadow, silence stretching between us again. I wasn't always great at being patient, but it was something I'd learned with Finn. Sometimes, he just needed time to collect his thoughts. The trick was not letting himself get stuck in a loop.

"Where are Bryn and Elisa?" I asked to help draw him out while still skirting around the reason we were on this walk.

"They're doing the weekly perimeter check for the wards."

I nodded. We were careful about where we brought Finn. So far, Lir and the other fae devourers who served Balor hadn't tried to capture Finn again, something I was incredibly suspicious about, but that didn't mean we were relaxing our guard. Anywhere he spent a lot of time, we had heavily warded. Bryn was obsessive about checking the wards to make sure there were no weak spots. The young valkyrie was bonded to Finn as his guardian and took his safety very seriously.

Technically, the wards should've easily lasted for years, but if it settled Bryn's mind to check them every week, none of us were going to try to dissuade her.

Finn glanced up at me before looking forward again. "What will it take for you to allow me to go with you on your trips?"

There it was. I'd been waiting for that question.

"You need to show that you can control your magic."

"I already ca—"

"You lost your temper and threw Elisa out of a window, kid," I reminded him. "That's not what I'd call control."

He hadn't meant to do it and had felt horrible afterwards, but that didn't undo the reality of what he'd done—and what he was capable of.

Elisa had come very close to dying that day.

Finn swallowed, his gaze still ahead of us. I could feel the disappointment and anxiety coming off him in waves.

"When I was close to your age, I lost control of my devourer flames," I said evenly as we continued our leisurely walk. "I came into my feline shifter magic first, and that felt natural to me. The fire . . . it was so hungry. Destructive. Cian and I always fought as kids; I mean, we still kind of do now, but we really used to piss each other off back then. He did something, I don't even remember what, and I just erupted."

"What happened?" Finn asked.

"I managed to direct the flames at a woodshed near us. It

exploded, sending chunks of wood shrapnel everywhere. Some of which cut Cian up pretty bad." The memory of screaming surfaced in my mind. Mine and Cian's. We'd both been terrified.

"So what did you do? How'd you learn to control it?"

"I didn't at first," I admitted. "For a long time, I did everything I could not to touch that part of my magic. Back then, I didn't know I was half fae and didn't spend enough time around fae to understand that magic is empathic. By stifling that part of myself, I was only making it worse."

Those perceptive odd-colored eyes of his looked at me. "That's why you want me to practice more with the Seelie Queen, even though you hate her?"

"Yes, and . . ." I couldn't stop myself from grimacing at what I was about to acknowledge. "She does love you. My problems with her aside, I think it's good for you to have a relationship with her. Your parents might be assholes, but your aunts aren't." I thought about it. "Well, they're not assholes to you. The rest of us are kind of fucked."

He laughed softly, his shoulders relaxing a little more, so I decided to drop the other shoe.

"I'd like you to go to Acleonia, the new dragon realm, and help them with their rebuilding efforts. They're starting construction on a new city to ease the housing issues, and you can use your magic to speed up the process."

"Okay . . . Is it alright if I ask Áine to come?" He rushed on before I could object. "At least to help get me started. Her instruction was really useful for the tree."

"Fine." I sighed. "If she's up for it, sure." Cerri and some of the dragon elders had already met the fae queens and they'd actually gotten along fairly well. I supposed it wasn't all that surprising. Both dragons and fae had a lot of magic and thought they were better than everyone else. Now for the tricky part. "Isabeau's not going with you."

Finn stopped, and for a second, I could have sworn the yellow rings around his green eyes burned like fire. "No."

I halted, holding his very angry gaze while I thought about what to say that wouldn't set him off. Around us, I could feel the static charge of his magic in the air. He was upset, therefore, his magic was volatile and dangerous. What would Aki or Bryn have said to calm him down?

Fuck it. I channeled Elisa.

"Don't be a little shit." I booped him on the nose.

His eyes widened, and it felt like his magic froze around us, like it was shocked at my audacity.

"You want to come with me on future excursions, yes?" I arched a brow.

Finn's mouth tightened, but he nodded.

"Then this is part of the requirement for that." I held up a hand. "And before you argue further, I fully expect Isabeau will want to come as well. The two of you are too dependent on each other, which will only endanger you both. You need to trust Isabeau to keep herself safe, and she needs to do the same for you. Otherwise, you're just liabilities and you *will* get each other killed."

The magic around us gained a dangerous edge, but I ignored it. I was happy Finn and Isabeau had each other, and it made sense that they were such close friends because they were similar in age and both had a fucked-up early childhood. But we'd allowed them to become codependent, and that needed to stop now.

"Where will she be while I'm in the dragon realm?" Finn asked tightly.

"Oh, I figured I'd dangle her somewhere as bait for the Vampire Council and see what happened." I shrugged.

"Nemain," he growled.

"Aww." I booped him on the nose again. "It's cute when you try to growl."

"You know, the others strive to keep me calm. You just antagonize me." The magic around us settled a little, losing a bit of its chaotic feel.

"Consider it practice for the real world." I wrapped my arm around his shoulders and pulled him with me as I walked back towards the cottage. "There are a lot of assholes out there. You'll need to learn to deal with them."

"I think there might be something wrong with you," Finn muttered.

"There's no might about it. As for your question, while you're building a city in the dragon realm, our sweet Isabeau is going to be spending some time in the death realm."

Chapter Five

"THEY'VE MADE A LOT OF PROGRESS." Elisa's assessing gaze swept over the beginnings of a city in front of us. The foundation had already been laid, and I could see the general layout. At the center would be a large tower, immediately around it in a ring would be the markets, and then the houses would encircle those. In the week since I'd been here, they'd already built three sides of the perimeter wall.

The dragons had survived the last few centuries by having a strong defense. Clearly, it was something they planned to recreate in Acleonia.

"They're motivated." Bryn raised one of her wings over Elisa to give the vampire some shade, not that she needed it. The sun was no longer an issue for Elisa, thanks to some negotiating on my part with a very grumpy daemon, but Bryn never missed an opportunity to dote on her girlfriend.

"Does it have a name yet?" Isabeau asked as her gaze bounced around, taking everything in. I hadn't told her yet that she wouldn't be staying here.

"Mystrova," I told her.

Elisa leaned forward so she could glance past Bryn. "Are we sure Sigrun and Niall will be okay on their own?"

"Am I sure the two-thousand-year-old valkyrie wielding Mjölnir and her bonded lover, who has over four thousand years of battle experience, will be okay on their own?" I pasted a worried look on my face. "You're right. The poor, helpless lambs will never survive a simple conversation."

Andrei chuckled to my left, and Finn sighed from where he stood in front of me with Isabeau.

Ask a stupid question . . .

Jinx's raspy laugh flowed through my mind, even as he flexed his claws into my shoulder when I shuffled on my feet a little. The stupid grimalkin hated sand, and even though the ground here was sort of sand-like, it was hard and compact. That wasn't good enough for His Majesty though, so he'd immediately leapt onto my shoulders.

Luna had no problem with sand, but Finn was stressed, so the much sweeter-natured grimalkin was curled up in his arms. Both grimalkins ignored the Niflheim wolf and skogkatt sitting at Isabeau's feet.

Sigrun and Niall would be in Heiðra Eilífa, the valkyrie stronghold in Asgard, for at least a few days, if not longer. The Valkyrie Queen Rota, who just so happened to be Sigrun's mother, had a vindictive streak, so my friend hadn't been comfortable bringing her furry companions with her. To my surprise, instead of remaining at her cottage, they'd opted to accompany Isabeau to the death realm.

Well, Viggo had; Gunnar couldn't speak, but where the skogkatt went, the wolf followed.

"The Valkyrie Queen isn't . . . pleasant," Bryn told Elisa. "But Sigrun can handle her."

"Sigrun's mom is a total bitch." I snorted.

"And that's why you've been banished from the Yggdrasil realms," Elisa said dryly.

I wrinkled my nose. "It's not my fault she can dish out insults but not take them."

"What'd you say to her?" Andrei peered at me.

"Don't remember." I shrugged.

"Queen Róta has been stalling on letting the fae queens install protective wards around the Yggdrasil realms. She claims she doesn't want to appear as though she's choosing sides between the queens and their brother," Bryn spoke in an even tone, but amusement flickered in her eyes. "Nemain asked if she'd like a compass and a map to see if she could locate her spine."

Everyone was silent for a few seconds, then the laughter of grimalkins filled my head. Andrei chuckled, and even Bryn broke a smile.

Elisa rolled her eyes. "She's a queen, Nemain. You're not supposed to speak to queens like that."

"I talk to the fae queens like that."

"Can confirm," Áine said in a bored tone from where she stood off to the side, her attention on the construction. She hadn't hesitated in saying yes when Finn had asked her to come. Despite how busy the fae queens were these days, they tried to make time for Finn as much as they could.

"Besides, it worked out well for me because now I don't have to go there anymore. Badb can handle it." It'd surprised me that my mother had volunteered for the task because she hated dealing with political bullshit. Then again, she and Sigrun had become close friends over the past year, so I figured that was why she was doing it.

I was glad Sigrun and Niall had my mom as backup. But between those three going to get the Valkyrie Queen to honor her agreement and my dad being off on some mission for Elvinia—AKA killing someone—it meant we were running low on people strong enough to guard Finn while Mikhail, Magos, and I were away.

Bryn was a strong fighter, but if someone made a move for Finn, she'd need backup, and what better backup was there than a city full of dragons?

"You said this is the *new* dragon realm?" Andrei raised his gaze to the dragons flying far above us before dropping it back to the flurry of activity on the ground. As far as I knew, he'd only been outside of the human realm once, when he'd come with me to one of the fae realms. "What happened to the old one?"

"Devourers. Most of the population relocated to this realm, but there are at least a few thousand dragons hiding in other realms who have thrown their support behind Balor."

Because we didn't have enough looming threats already. Might as well add a small army of spiteful, overgrown reptiles.

We're keeping an eye on them, a voice rumbled.

Andrei started as an enormous blue dragon landed to our right. A second later, a black blur dove through the clouds, not slowing as they aimed directly for where we stood.

Everyone took a step back, but I remained where I was, a bored expression on my face as I watched the dragon approach.

"Nemain . . ." Andrei warned.

Fire rippled over the iridescent black scales before a man landed in front of me, wearing a pair of ripped-up jeans and a Rancid band shirt. Bright orange eyes flickered like living flames as he grinned at me. "This is why we're best friends. You never move."

"And spoil your dramatic entrance?" I arched a brow. "Perish the thought, Eddie."

You two—flames raced along the blue dragon's scales until a woman with bright red hair and piercing green eyes looked at us—"are ridiculous and a bad influence on each other."

Eddie flung an arm over my shoulders. "No more than Vizor is a bad influence on you."

I snorted. Vizor was a distant relative of Eddie's and also the mate of Cerri's best friend. He was firmly on our side but still a bit of an asshole. He and Eddie were locked in what felt like an eternal game of one-upmanship. Despite that, he got along very well with Cerri and Pele because, in his words, *"Unlike most people, they're smart and not complete and utter useless wastes of space."*

Real charmer, that one.

"Hi, Cerri!" Elisa waved before rushing over to the red-haired woman and giving her a hug.

Cerri squeezed the vampire girl back. "It's good to see you again, Elisa. Are you enjoying the journal?"

"Yes!" Elisa released her and stepped back. "Your father was a bastard, but it's fascinating how he used his limited resources to maintain control and th—"

"Time-out!" I held up a hand. "The two of you can continue your conversation later."

Eddie peered down at me. "What's going on?"

"Short version is that I'm likely going to the sorcerer realm in a couple of days with our newfound frenemies." I jerked a thumb at Andrei. "The werewolves are coming too. And a witch."

"Sounds fun." Eddie grinned. "Want me to come?"

"Sure, but you can't eat people until I give the okay."

He pouted. "But the sorcerers must be dripping in magic. They'd be so tasty."

Cerri's brows were bunched together in a way that meant she was scheming. From past experience, I knew she'd say what she was thinking when she was ready, so I didn't push her.

"While I'm away, I thought Finn could help here." I waved a hand at the construction going on. "With his annoying tutor."

A crack formed in the ground beneath me, and I quickly stepped to the side. Áine smiled at me.

"*Bitch*," I mouthed.

"*Mongrel trash*," she mouthed back.

Isabeau giggled, and Finn sighed. Again. The kid did that a lot around me.

"That would be wonderful." Cerri clapped. "One moment. Let me find Iseult."

She returned a few minutes later with a young, pretty, dark-haired woman who looked vaguely familiar.

"Everyone, this is Iseult." Cerri's hands moved fluidly, signing out the words as she spoke. "You've probably seen her around. She's overseeing the construction of the housing district of the city, and I think that's where you would be most useful, Finn."

Hello, Finn signed, giving the woman a shy smile.

Thank you for offering to help us, Iseult signed back with a warm smile on her face. *I've heard about how gifted you are with magic.*

Finn's cheeks turned bright red.

Mom! A telepathic scream ripped through our minds at the same time a loud, panicked sound came from above us. Everyone's gaze snapped up as a small silver dragon tumbled from the sky. Flames rippled, and suddenly, he was a small boy, flailing his arms in a hopeless attempt to slow his plummet.

"Shit," Eddie swore, dropping his arm from around me and darting towards the falling child.

Andrei was closer and faster though. He leapt up and caught the boy midair before landing in a crouch and setting him onto his feet. Tears stained the child's face, and his light blue eyes were wide with fear.

Iseult crashed to her knees next to them, enveloping her son in a hug.

"Young dragons don't always have the best control over their shifting," Cerri explained when I gave her a questioning look. "Sometimes they feel the need to shift suddenly from one form to the next, regardless of the situation. It's why they're not supposed to fly alone."

"Which Erec is aware of, but he thinks the rules don't apply to him." Eddie strode over to Cerri's side. "Iseult has been busy with the city construction, and her piece-of-shit ex-husband is one of the traitors, so it's just the two of them."

Iseult started signing rapidly at Andrei, who looked at me helplessly.

"She's thanking you for catching, Erec," I told him.

"How do I say *you're welcome*?" He raised his hands, a little unsure.

I held my hand up, fingers pointing upward and my palm facing in, then touched my chin with my fingertips before waving my hand forward.

Andrei repeated the gesture to Iseult, who let out a deep breath, finally calming down, and smiled back.

"Finn, why don't you show Isabeau around? Stay where we can see you though. I need to chat with Cerri and Eddie, and then I'll come find you." I kept my tone casual, even as Finn noticeably tensed up. He still wasn't happy about being separated from Isabeau, but surprisingly the vampire girl had agreed to it with only a hint of reluctance.

Too easily. I was suspicious of her motives, and I suspected Finn was too.

"Come." Áine moved closer to Finn and held her hand out. "We need to examine the earth where they want to build the houses."

Finn moved Luna so she was cradled in one arm and slid his hand into Áine's, and they started walking towards what would be the residential area of the city. Isabeau fell into step behind them, Gunnar on her right and Viggo on her left, and Elisa and Bryn went as well.

Iseult rose and gave her son a pointed look. Erec's lips tugged down, but he started after his mom when she turned to follow the others, only to pause and glance at Andrei. Slowly, Erec held his hand out.

Andrei looked at me.

"Go ahead." I waved him on. "I'll be there in a few minutes."

Before Andrei could say anything, Erec's patience wore out as he grabbed the werewolf's hand and dragged him towards the city.

I saw a hint of sadness in Cerri's gaze as she watched the boy and wolf walk away. When she caught me looking, she gave me a tight smile. "Some of the other kids pick on Erec because of who his father is, but like many, Iseult didn't have a choice in who she married. I have no doubt of her loyalty, but that doesn't mean it's been easy for either of them."

"It's part of the reason Iseult volunteered to help here," Eddie added. "To prove her worth and make things easier for Erec."

"Hopefully it helps." Cerri frowned. "It's not easy to be despised amongst your own kind."

"I don't know," a deep voice drawled. "It's never really bothered me."

"Vizor." I bared my teeth at the dark-haired man as he strolled towards us. If I'd been in my feline form, my hackles would have been raised because I hadn't heard him land. Mikhail would have heard it; his hearing was better than mine.

It'd only been a couple of hours, and I already missed my vampire. The mate bond felt like an overdrawn bowstring that got tighter the longer we were apart. I could deal with it, but my magic felt . . . twitchy.

That scheming look appeared on Cerri's face again, and it was enough to distract me from my needy thoughts about Mikhail and the weird vibes my magic was putting out. Because I had no doubt I wouldn't like whatever she was planning.

"It's actually good that you're here, Vizor." She gave him a close-lipped smile.

"Said no one ever," Eddie muttered.

"Nemain is going to the sorcerer realm and will be in the company of warlocks and vampires, plus werewolves and witches." Cerri clasped her hands in front of her.

Crap. I straightened, panic flooding me. That was her politician pose.

Vizor held his standard mask of arrogance-tinged disinterest, but I saw the spark of curiosity in his burnt amber eyes.

"No," I snapped before pointing at Vizor. "He's not coming. Eddie already said he wants to join us."

"My mate is good at a lot of things, but political subterfuge is not one of them," Cerri explained calmly. "You're going to a realm with allies who do not have your best interests in mind. What if they decide your usefulness has run out while you're there and Emir sees an opportunity to get rid of you despite the blood oath? We don't know much about the sorcerers, but what is known implies that they aren't trustworthy and that they love to play mind games. You won't be able to just stab your way out of trouble there, Nemain."

"She has a point." Eddie rubbed the back of his neck while he gave me an apologetic look. "Vizor isn't useful for much, but he *is* a devious bastard."

"What happened to 'besties don't back down'?" I growled at him. "Isn't that what you said just two weeks ago when I was helping you on that heist for that stupid dagger you wanted?"

"First, it wasn't a stupid dagger. It was a very pretty, valuable dagger that helped fund the building of this city." He increased the sad pathetic look on his face. "And second . . . you can't be mad at me. It's against the bestie rules."

"You're seriously suggesting I take him over you?" I crossed my arms, not the least bit swayed by his antics. "He's just as likely as all the other assholes to stab me in the back!"

"I can't, actually," Vizor said in a pained tone. "Lynette likes you. And . . . you've always been kind to her."

"Exactly." Cerri nodded triumphantly. "If there is one thing you can trust, it's that Vizor's world revolves around Lynette." She narrowed her calculating green eyes at me. "And what would you do if anyone ever threatened her, Nemain?"

I clamped my mouth shut. Lynette was Cerri's best friend and reminded me a lot of Kaysea. She was sweet and loyal with a backbone of steel. I vividly remembered her diving from the clouds to rip apart a devourer monster that had been about to kill Vizor.

Cerri's lips curled up in a victorious smile when I caved.

"Anyone who is a threat to Lynette dies," I admitted, albeit begrudgingly. "Preferably out of her sight because she doesn't like violence. Even though I know she's capable of defending herself and others."

"And that is why I would never betray you," Vizor said in a tone that matched my annoyance. "I will do whatever it takes to keep Lynette safe. And you . . ." He squeezed his eyes shut, mouth pinched like he'd just bitten into something sour. "You are unpredictable and quick to violence. But you walk into fights with that insufferable swagger against enemies, who by all logic, should squash you like you're nothing, yet you win. Against all odds. And you do it because you're fanatically loyal to your friends and family and will put their lives above yours every single time."

"You say the sweetest things," I said dryly.

Vizor opened his eyes, and they fell on me. For a second, he dropped his arrogance, and I could have sworn he looked grateful. "Lynette is one of yours now. If something ever happens to me, I know you'll keep her safe or die trying. Therefore, I will do what I must to keep you alive."

"Ugh. Fine. You can come." I threw my hands up and turned my attention to Cerri. "Why can't Eddie come too?"

"Do you really want to listen to them bicker the entire time?" Her eyebrows crept up.

My shoulders slumped. "No."

"Who else is going?" Vizor asked.

"Emir, I'm assuming, and someone to represent the Vampire Council, probably. On our side, it will be me, Mikhail, you apparently, and Magos." I looked off in the distance to where Andrei was with Finn and the others, Erec still standing next to him. "Andrei and his sister are coming. Plus Lestari, a witch."

"And him?" Vizor glanced at Jinx, who was still perched across my shoulders.

Going, Jinx growled. *Like I'd trust you to watch her back, lizard.*

Something so bite-sized should be careful about how he speaks, Vizor's voice rumbled through my mind. Like Eddie, he was a strong telepath. Something that would come in handy in the sorcerer realm but was still a bit annoying.

Careful, Jinx raised his head to glare at the dragon. *We might not be willing to kill you because it would cause Lynette grief . . .*

"But that doesn't mean we can't make you hurt," I finished.

Eddie clasped his hands together before grinning at Cerri. "See? They're going to get along great."

***

"It's time," I said a little reluctantly.

Finn's gaze stayed locked on the earth, where he was coaxing it to flatten out in places to make the construction of the buildings easier like Áine had shown him before she'd left a few minutes ago. I hated to admit it, but spending time with his aunt was good for him. He was learning to control his magic and she was honoring her word about not breathing a word of fae politics.

Isabeau said her goodbyes to Iseult and the other dragons

who were helping out before striding back over to Finn. She was still being oddly cooperative about being parted from him. I studied her face. On the surface, Isabeau seemed like she was easy to read. When she was upset, you knew it. Everyone in a five-block radius knew it. I'd spent enough time around the vampire girl though to know when she was masking her true feelings. Her sunny smile was a little too brittle.

We'd all been shaken up when Finn had accidentally hurt Elisa a few months ago. More than hurt—he'd almost killed her. Even though he'd been the one to throw her through a window, he'd only done it because Isabeau had been upset, which was why she thought the whole thing was her fault.

I rubbed my forehead. Dealing with the emotional problems of supernatural tweens was so out of my comfort zone. We'd all agreed that something had to be done about the codependence between the two of them. Here was hoping Finn didn't completely level the beginnings of this city while we were gone and that Isabeau didn't drive my brother and Hades insane.

"Andrei!" I moved my hand to shade my eyes as I peered up at a section of the perimeter wall that was almost done. Andrei was up there with Iseult and a dragon I didn't recognize, surveying what had been built so far. Erec was back in his dragon form, currently scaling the wall beneath them.

Andrei waved at me and then said something to the other dragon before slowly signing something to Iseult. Even with the distance between us, I could see her amused grin as she signed something back to him. Andrei ducked his head in farewell before jumping off the wall, all the way to the ground, which was a solid forty feet below.

"Well, someone has leveled up while he was gone," Eddie commented.

"Yeah, as much as I adored his innocence, I'm glad he's at

least a little more in touch with his wolf," I admitted. "He looks less like prey now."

For all the differences between vampires, shifters, and dragons, we had one thing in common: we were all predators. Werewolves were predators too, but only the ones that accepted their wolf nature. Granted, doing so was a dangerous thing because controlling that side of themselves didn't come easily, and sometimes it never came at all. When that happened, they descended into madness until they were put down by other wolves or someone else in the magical community. I thought about Andrei's admission that he was losing the battle with his wolf, and my heart clenched.

We would fix this. Find a solution for him and Magos.

"Where to now?" Andrei asked as he strolled over to us.

"Taking Isabeau to my brother," I told him before calling out to Isabeau. "You ready, kid?"

Isabeau looked straight at me and held up her index finger, then turned her attention back to Finn, who was still staring at the ground.

Andrei chuckled. "She's kind of a handful, isn't she?"

"You have no idea," I muttered before glancing at Eddie. "Keep an eye on Finn? Luna and Bryn are going to stay here with him, but they're both a little biased in evaluating where he's at mentally."

"Will do," he assured me. "Vizor is going to bring Lynette here tomorrow. She has a good rapport with Finn, so she'll be able to help out."

We watched as Finn slipped something onto Isabeau's wrist. She smiled, and whatever she said drew a small laugh from him before they both jogged over to us.

"I'm ready now," Isabeau announced.

I glanced at the silver bracelet adorning her slender wrist. Finn had designed it after the climbing roses that grew around Kaysea and Zareen's garden. It looked delicate, but I had no doubt that magic coursed through every ounce of it and that Finn was likely the only one who could remove it.

Eddie cocked his head as he studied the bracelet. "Locator spell?" he guessed.

"Yes." Finn shot me a guilty look. "I just want to know she's okay while we're apart."

"Fine." I sighed, because it's not like we could fix their codependence overnight, and Isabeau clearly wasn't bothered by it. "Remember what we talked about. Keep your shit together, Finn."

"I will." He nodded eagerly.

"We both will," Isabeau added.

"Alright." I opened a gateway to the death realm while Eddie ducked into one of the large tents Cerri had set up as a coordination area to let Elisa know it was time to go. Before we left though, I knelt down in front of Isabeau. *I have a favor to ask of you.*

She arched an eyebrow, exactly as I'd done a few minutes ago. *And you don't want to ask it out loud?*

It's . . . personal, and if it doesn't work, I don't want anyone to let it slip what we tried to do.

Okay . . . She chewed her lip. *What is it?*

Her eyes widened as I told her what I wanted her to work on while we were away.

I've never done anything like that before, she said when I finished.

Will you try? A little hope bled into my question, but I tried to keep a level head. I didn't want Isabeau to feel bad if this didn't work.

For a long moment, she didn't answer, but then, she leaned forward and wrapped her arms around my neck. *Of course. It'd be nice to use my magic to make people happy for once.*

Chapter Six

Less than an hour later, we were next to Andrei's Bronco in the parking lot, and I stared at my apartment building.

For most of my life, I'd been a bit of a loner. Sure, Pele and later Kaysea had been there, but usually, I'd gone to visit them and then left. Even when I'd been with Sebastian, we hadn't stayed in one location long, and there were stretches where we'd spent months apart. The only person I'd truly settled down with was Myrna, and that obviously hadn't ended well.

It had been an adjustment getting used to the chaos the vamp brats brought with them and then the quiet fortitude of Bryn and Finn. I couldn't pinpoint the exact moment, but it had become my new normal.

Magos making me coffee. Mikhail stealing a sip from it and laughing when I threatened to stab him. The vamp brats arguing over if pineapple belonged on pizza, which it absolutely did.

A weary sigh slipped from my lips. Suddenly, going into a mostly empty building, where my mate was trying to keep the man who meant everything to us from slipping into madness, felt like too much.

Everything. Was. Too. Fucking. Much.

Sharp claws dug into my shoulder, and I hissed. Andrei looked at me with a raised eyebrow before glancing at the black grimalkin once again perched across my shoulders.

Stop being a mopey little bitch, Jinx growled.

Tell me again why you're not staying with Luna? I tried to shake him off, but he just dug his claws in deeper.

Unlike you, I'm blessed with a brilliant and competent mate. She's more than capable of handling things on her own for a while, whereas I'm needed here to keep your dumb ass alive.

"Rude," I muttered.

I'm going to nap in the sun. Don't bother me. Jinx leapt down and flicked his tail as he trotted towards the rocky coastline.

"Glad to see he hasn't changed," Andrei commented.

"He's still as grumpy as ever," I grunted, even as I smiled a bit. "I'm going to make some coffee. You're welcome to stay, but it's fine if you need to check on your sister."

"Stela can survive on her own for a few more hours." He paused. "Probably. The witch is with her, and Lestari has a calming effect."

I snorted. "If you say so."

We made our way inside. I started to head up the stairs to my apartment but changed my mind mid-step and entered the bottom-floor apartment instead.

Werewolves had very sensitive noses, even in human form. My apartment would probably still reek of sex to him, and given Andrei's tenuous hold over his wolf, it didn't seem like a good idea to go up there. This apartment was similar to mine and had an open-floor concept for the living room and kitchen. I made a beeline for the coffee maker.

"Holy shit!"

I glanced over my shoulder to see Andrei frozen in the doorway, staring at the far wall with his mouth open.

"Yeah . . . Hannibal has gotten a little bigger." I chuckled and resumed my walk to the beloved giver of life before flipping it on. Someone, probably Elisa, had set it up, so all I had to do was push a button. "I kept telling them to stop feeding the damn thing, but they didn't listen, and here we are."

"Hannibal?" Andrei gaped at me, clearly still having a hard time coming to terms with the enormous fae plant that was easily over eight feet tall now and spanned ten feet, thanks to the creeping vines.

"Isabeau named it after some movie, I guess." I leaned back against the counter and watched with amusement as Andrei cautiously made his way across the room.

He stopped and turned to look at me. "It doesn't have any utensils, does it? Or any other projectiles?"

My lips quirked up at the memory of him getting beamed in the back of his head with a spoon.

"No, but it's probably hungry." I pushed off the counter and opened the fridge, pulling out a whole rotisserie chicken before strolling over to Andrei. "We're well beyond using spoons to feed it now."

The three enormous flowers that had been facing the window to soak in the sun all spun towards me, and electric-blue petals trembled around the bright orange center of each flower.

"Kaysea can't really explain why it's gotten so large." I raised the chicken up and down and smirked as the flowers followed the movement. For not having eyes, they were very good at keeping track of things. "This type of plant doesn't get this big in the fae realms. Our best guess is it's because of all the fast food the kids give it."

"Fast food?" Andrei repeated, glancing at me with a skeptical eyebrow raise.

"It loves greasy fries." I shrugged.

When Kaysea first gave me the plant, it fit in a small pot on my dresser. A year or so ago, we'd replanted it in an old wine barrel and moved it to this apartment. That was when things really got out of control, because clearly, the vamp brats had just been constantly feeding it their leftovers. It was still in the wine barrel, but only because we couldn't figure out how to replant the thing. Roots had overgrown the wood, so we couldn't even see the barrel anymore.

Two other stems had sprouted off the original one. Each with their own flower and dozens of slender green vines that had attached themselves to the wall. Pele hadn't been happy about that.

"Here." I held the chicken out to Andrei. "You can feed it."

Slowly, he lifted the chicken out of the container. The flowers started to sway aggressively as several vines peeled away from the brick wall.

"You might want to hurry," I suggested. "Neither its patience nor its manners have improved."

Andrei threw the poultry, and three vines snapped forward, tearing it apart. The orange center of each flower split open, revealing circular mouths full of jagged teeth that quickly devoured the meat shoved into it by the vines.

Andrei watched with morbid fascination as large bulges slid down the thick stems.

The coffee maker beeped, and I returned to the kitchen, grabbing two mugs from the cupboard. Normally, Magos made my coffee all fancy with steamed milk and sugar, but that was beyond me. The bag for this one said it was salted caramel. I thought that was ambitious and nowhere near what it tasted like, but it was sweet, so I called it good enough.

I took the two mugs over to the couch and claimed a seat before holding one out to Andrei while sipping from mine.

The familiar feeling of a gateway opening pinged my magic.

Andrei paused, his fingers wrapped around the mug, and

tilted his head up to the ceiling. His eyes glowed a golden yellow.

"Are you expecting company? Two vampires just arrived in the third floor apartment." He cocked his head in a purely wolfish manner. "But I can feel another two in the apartment above us, who I'm assuming are Mikhail and Magos."

I raised an eyebrow. "Your accuracy for sensing vampires is that good?"

"I've always been able to sense vampires, but it's only been in the past year that I've learned how to tell exactly where they are. Before, it was only a vague awareness. " His gaze stayed glued to the ceiling, like he was tracking their movement. "They're coming down the stairs."

"It's fine," I said almost tonelessly. "It's two of the vamp brats, Damon and Misha."

Andrei finally looked away from the ceiling to me. The yellow faded from his eyes until only concerned hazel ones peered at me.

"Just . . . umm . . ." I stumbled. "Don't react to anything they say, okay?"

He stared at me for a long moment. "Alright."

I nodded numbly and set my coffee down before getting up and going towards the kitchen, where I leaned against the island and waited for their arrival.

Damon and Misha had been trying to make amends with Isabeau and Elisa, but they'd avoided me and Mikhail. Our paths crossed occasionally, but when that happened, Misha only spoke in clipped words and Damon spoke a little more politely but was still standoffish.

I'd given them a token that would open a gateway to my apartment and told them they could use it anytime. It was carefully spelled, courtesy of Cerri, to only work for them.

They'd never used it before.

If they wanted to talk to Elisa or Isabeau, they had other

ways of doing that. The fact that they'd come to my apartment meant they wanted to speak to me or Mikhail. And I didn't think it was because they'd decided that we were still a family.

Misha had made it very clear that he thought Mikhail and I were monsters. And Damon hadn't disagreed.

A knock sounded on the door.

None of us had ever knocked.

I squeezed my eyes shut before wiping any hint of emotion from my face. "You can come in."

Damon appeared first. Every bit of six foot three inches with a stocky build. He'd been a bit of a late bloomer and had gone through a growth spurt six months ago. His solemn grey eyes and kind face were the same though.

A step behind him was Misha, his exact opposite. Several inches under six feet and lean, Misha stalked into the room. Where Damon had light brown skin, Misha's was pale like Elisa's. He also had the same blue-black hair and dark blue eyes. We'd always suspected they were biological siblings, but we'd received confirmation last year.

"Hello, Nemain." Damon nodded in greeting, stopping three feet inside the apartment, like he didn't dare enter any farther.

A heaviness twisted through me.

I glanced at Misha, who had stopped beside Damon, but his gaze was locked on Andrei. "Who's the wolf?"

"Andrei," I replied. They'd never met, but I knew they were aware of who he was because I'd been a bit of an emotional mess in the aftermath of breaking things off with him and the vamp brats had tried to cheer me up for months.

Within seconds, Andrei closed the distance between us and leaned against the kitchen island next to me. His posture wasn't threatening, but his position next to my side made it clear where he stood.

"Nemain's helping me out with something," he said casually. "She's good people like that."

Misha snorted. "No. She's really not." He reached into his back pocket and pulled out an envelope, thrusting it towards me. "Here."

I stepped forward and took it from him before tearing it open and reading the letter inside.

You really should protect your people better. Or do you not care about these ones?

A growl bubbled up my throat. "Tell me exactly how this letter came to be in your possession."

Misha and Damon exchanged looks.

"Their name was Tadg," Damon said. "I'm guessing sidhe because they had the whole beautiful sort of androgynous thing going on." He frowned briefly. "Actually I think they preferred *he*. Anyway, he came up to us two nights ago when we were grabbing some drinks. Chatted with us for a bit, and then he asked if we could pass this letter to you. That's all."

"'That's all?'" I asked quietly. "A powerful sidhe, a Tuatha Dé Danann, randomly chats the two of you up, and you don't think anything of it?"

Damon shuffled on his feet, glancing at Misha. "He didn't threaten us or anything."

"This"—I shook the letter—"was the threat! He gave you a message to pass along to me to let me know how fucking easy of a target the two of you are. But it could have just as easily been your fucking hearts in a box!"

I slammed the letter down onto the counter and took a deep breath, trying to calm myself. They could have been killed. And I wouldn't have been there to protect them. Hells. I might not have known about it until days afterwards.

Tadg. He belonged to the Soleil family, almost all of whom were members of the Unseelie Court. They'd never directly come after me like this, but Badb had mentioned them before.

The Soleils hated Kalen and his mate. Clearly, that hatred had been passed on to me.

And they thought they could go after my fucking family.

"Do not overreact, Nemain," Misha growled. Apparently, he'd finally deigned to speak to me.

"I told you before: I'll do whatever has to be done to keep you safe," I said coldly.

"No!" He took a step forward. "You don't get to go on a killing rampage and claim it's to defend us."

I took a step forward. "That's *exactly* what it's for."

"Bullshit!" Misha spat. "You're just looking for an excuse to kill some fae you don't like!"

"Enough!" Damon dragged Misha back. "The message has been delivered." He looked at me. "Please do not do anything rash."

"Won't be anything rash about it." I shrugged.

It wasn't a lie. I didn't have time to deal with Tadg now, and he wouldn't do anything to Damon and Misha this soon. He knew I'd understand the purpose of the letter. That he could stroll up to them so easily.

He wanted me to stew over this for a while and gloat about it at the next Unseelie event.

Gods, I hated the fucking fae. How had my parents dealt with their bullshit for so long?

Damon stared at me for a beat before sighing. "Can you open a gateway back to Intira and Gensai's?" He named the supernatural sanctuary where they were staying, run by friends of Magos'.

I waved a hand, and a gateway appeared. Misha strode through it without another word.

Damon paused briefly in front of me. "How's Magos?"

"He's . . . okay," I lied. "We have a lead on a cure."

"If there is any way we can help, please let me know."

I nodded tightly. Damon stepped through the gateway, and I closed it after him.

Silence stretched across the room before Andrei moved to stand in front of me. "Someone told me once that sparring was good for blowing off steam."

"Not sure that's a good idea, wolf," I answered honestly. "Kind of feel the need to break something right now."

"I'm not all that breakable anymore." He shrugged. "Come on, kitty cat."

He grabbed my hand and pulled me over to the sparring mat in the corner of the living room. We removed our shoes before stepping onto the cushioned surface. This one was smaller than the one in my apartment, only fifteen by fifteen feet, but it worked well enough.

I watched Andrei stalk onto the mat. He really had packed on more muscle. The man I'd known had been built like a lightweight MMA fighter; this one wasn't a heavyweight like Magos, but he was firmly in the middleweight division.

"You ready for this?" Andrei gave me a sly look. "I'm pretty good."

I couldn't help but laugh at the memory of him saying something similar to me the first time we had sparred, which no doubt had been his intent. What had he said back then? It came to me after a few seconds, and I grinned.

"Oh yeah?" I started to circle where he stood in the center of the mat. "Did you perhaps dabble in MMA?"

Andrei turned with me, staying balanced on his feet. "I sure did, and I'm now a world champion in shady bar fights."

With no warning, I dropped and swept a kick at his feet. Andrei leapt over my attack and struck at my head with the heel of his hand. I caught his wrist before the hit landed, and we both grinned at each other.

"You can be faster than that." I dropped his wrist and quickly retreated a few paces.

"So can you." A golden sheen rolled over his eyes.

Some of my frustration over the Misha and Damon situation bled out as exhilaration rushed through my veins. I was definitely curious to see what Andrei could do now.

"Show me what you got, wolf." My fingers curled inward several times in the classic *come and get it* signal.

Again, that golden light rolled over his eyes, but this time, some of it stayed, bleeding in with the hazel. Then Andrei *moved*.

One second he was standing in front of me, and the next, I was jerking my arm up to block his roundhouse kick, the impact of his shin against my forearm rattling throughout my entire body.

He hadn't just gotten stronger, he was significantly quicker too. I pivoted my elbow up, and it slammed into his chin. Andrei's head snapped back before he stumbled a bit.

I smiled wickedly at him. "I've been winning bar fights a lot longer than you."

He laughed, flashing teeth stained with blood, and came at me again. We traded blows back and forth. He never managed to get past my defenses, but I had to work to get past his, which was impressive, considering a few years ago, I would have put him on his ass repeatedly by now.

"Gonna tell me what the deal is with you and those vamps?" He jabbed at my cheek, and I pulled back, letting his fist whistle past my nose. "Thought you took them in with Elisa and Isabeau?"

"I did. We had a falling out." I drew my knee up, blocking a kick Andrei had launched at my ribs and taking it on my shin instead. Then I pushed that same leg out, slamming my heel into his stomach.

Andrei caught my foot and grinned. "Now what?"

I grinned back and pushed off the ground with my other

foot, spinning until I was horizontal with the ground, and my foot smashed into his temple.

He let out a sharp grunt, releasing his hold on me and stumbling back. I twisted, landing on my fingertips and toes before springing back to my feet and circling him.

"Stupid feline reflexes," Andrei complained while shaking his head. "What caused the fallout?"

I paused mid-step for a second before continuing to dance around him. "Isabeau is a powerful telepath. She trapped us in a memory loop—it's a long story—but it resulted in the vamp brats getting a front row seat to some of the things Mikhail and I have done."

"Such as?" He snapped a kick out, catching my thigh when I didn't move fast enough.

Ow.

"Me during my witch-killer era. Mikhail at the height of his assassin days." I feinted a punch to his ribs. Andrei moved to block, but I pulled it at the last second and hammered an uppercut to his jaw.

"Will you quit targeting my face?" Andrei shot me a dirty look as he wiped the blood from his mouth.

"Don't worry." I grinned at him. "You're still hot."

"I know." He winked at me. "Didn't they already know about your past though?"

"Seeing is believing." The grin slipped from my face. "They moved out and said they needed time. But you can see how well that's going."

"They'll come around." Andrei's eyes softened for a moment before he launched a series of punches and kicks.

A minute later we were both panting a little. "Impressive, wolf. You really have gotten a lot better."

"Didn't have much of a choice." The muscles along his jaw flexed.

Dread coiled in my gut, but I asked what I wanted to know

anyway. "What happened to you since leaving Emerald Bay, Andrei?"

We moved around each other.

"Pain. Death. A lot of it." More yellow filled Andrei's eyes. "What is it you used to say? *C'est la vie.*"

"I was hoping that wouldn't be your life," I answered honestly. "Besides, I thought you wanted nothing to do with the war between the vampires and werewolves?" I arched back to avoid a punch to my jaw that probably would have fractured it.

A wolfish growl spilled from him when I retaliated by punching him in the side, then we both retreated a few steps.

"It's complicated." He winced and clamped a hand to his ribs, where a little bit of blood stained his T-shirt. "Pretty sure you broke something."

"Oops." I wiggled my blood-tipped claws at him.

"This is why nobody likes cats." He pointed a finger at me.

"Nobody likes us because they're jealous of our perfection." I gave him a minute to heal; maybe next time he'd remember not to leave himself open.

Pain is an excellent teacher.

"After finding out that our parents had purposely left us so we'd grow up outside the pack, I was angry. So was Stela. It felt like our entire lives were a lie." He dropped his hand from his side, but his breath still had a hitch to it. "Back then, in that moment, finding out about the war just frustrated us further, but now I get it. I know why my parents made that choice."

"They loved you." I nodded. "To them, it was the only way to give you and your sister a chance."

And gods, what a heart-wrenching decision that must have been.

Andrei and Stela's parents had been leaders amongst the werewolf packs and very much involved in the war against the vampires, but they hadn't wanted that for their children.

Unlike vampires, who were born with their vampiric nature awakened, werewolves were born essentially human. Unless they were bitten by another werewolf, they'd never turn. Instead, they'd just live out their mortal lives completely unaware of what lurked beneath the surface.

Whether the sorcerer who had created them had intended that, I guessed we'd find out in a few days, but Andrei's parents hadn't been the first to try to give their children a future free of violence and death. Unfortunately, despite their best-laid plans, Andrei had been bitten by a werewolf and turned . . . and then bit his sister.

Once they found out their werewolf heritage though, neither had been interested in pursuing the war with the vampires. Instead, they'd come to Emerald Bay to live in peace and had built up a pack of like-minded werewolves.

"I know they loved us," Andrei said quietly, his voice tinged with grief over the parents he'd never known because they'd been killed by vampires not long after giving up their children.

I picked up on the fact that his breathing had evened out a second before he launched a kick. My body reacted on instinct and muscle memory. I twisted sideways, but not fast enough.

A hiss tore from my lips as he made contact with the side of my thigh, and I staggered back, sharp pain echoing down my leg.

"Move faster, kitty cat." Andrei snapped his teeth at me, his eyes glowing gold.

I stopped moving and yawned.

Andrei narrowed his eyes at me, clearly knowing this was a trap but unsure about how to handle it. I gave him a lazy grin and flicked my fingers in his direction. A few droplets of blood landed on his shirt, and his eyes turned pure yellow.

He charged forward, feigning a punch to my head, only to try to knee me in the ribs. I spun away but stayed close enough to slam my elbow into the side of his head.

"If you're going to walk into a trap, you've got to have a better plan, wolf," I chided. "Tell me what happened after you left Emerald Bay. What changed your mind about getting involved in the war?"

"It's not a war," Andrei rasped, still looking a little dazed from my hit. "It's a slaughter."

I didn't say anything because he wasn't wrong. Throughout their violent history, the werewolves had occasionally managed to hold their own against the vampires, but in the last century, things had solidly tipped in the vampires' favor. The vampires had more going for them. Better organization and numbers, plus the Apex bloodlines that had additional forms of magic, whereas the werewolves had no magic beyond that of shifting into wolves. They were stronger than vampires and almost as fast, but it wasn't enough to combat the unrelenting onslaught.

"We tried to lie low after leaving Emerald Bay." Andrei started circling me, looking for an opening. I spun slowly so I was always facing him. "You probably noticed that the wolves vacated the boarding house outside town after Stela and I left. Most of them followed us to Alberta and settled down there. We found a nice remote town and fixed up some cabins outside of it."

"It was a safe area." I jabbed a punch at his throat and deliberately left my arm extended a little too long. This time, he didn't fall for the trap; he just blocked my attack and kept circling. "The town was completely human, and there were no major populations of any supernaturals in at least a hundred-mile radius."

He gave me a tight, close-lipped smile. "Keeping tabs on me?"

My shoulders raised in a small shrug. "You are and always will be my friend, Andrei. I want you to be happy."

A genuine smile graced his lips. "Same, Nemain." His eyes

darted to the ceiling before falling back on me. "Still questioning your taste in mates though."

I snorted. "Noted. What happened in Alberta?"

The smile slipped, and his pace slowed. "You don't know? Would have thought you'd have heard, even if you hadn't been keeping track of me. They weren't exactly subtle about it."

Shit. Given the disdain in his tone when he'd said *they*, I knew he was referring to vampires.

"You chose a good spot," I said tightly, my own movements slowing to match his. "It was hard for me to get information because I had no contacts in the area. It was isolated and off the supernatural map, so to speak. I was worried that, if I went digging, it would draw the wrong kind of attention."

"Apparently, we did that all on our own." He stopped circling, and I stood still. "They're all dead. Vampires came through one night and slaughtered everyone. Only Stela and I survived, and it was a close call. I thought I was going to lose my sister that night."

"Fuck." I closed my eyes. "I'm so sorry, Andrei."

I hadn't known his pack that well, but I knew they'd all just wanted to be left alone. They hadn't been a threat to the vampires, yet they'd died anyway.

"We only survived because I dragged Stela into a room and barricaded the door till sunrise. We're lucky they didn't set the building on fire."

Probably because they got distracted gorging themselves on werewolf blood, I thought but didn't say out loud.

Andrei could have died that night, and I wouldn't have known for weeks. Months.

"I'm sorry I wasn't there to help," I rasped and opened my eyes again.

"You're not responsible for keeping everyone safe." Andrei gave me a knowing look. "It killed you to make that deal with Emir, didn't it?"

"Yes." My throat tightened. "He played a role in the death of my parents."

Technically, Macha and Nevin were my aunt and uncle, but they'd raised me, and I still considered them my mom and dad even though Badb and Kalen were a part of my life now.

"But you did it anyway." Andrei looked away from me to stare at the mat. "I get it. Giving up a piece of yourself to protect those you love. That's why I went along with Stela's plan of revenge. After Alberta, she wanted to go vampire hunting. If I hadn't gone with her, she would have gotten herself killed. She's so reckless, like she doesn't care if she lives or dies as long as she takes some of them out with her."

I let out a humorless laugh. "Sounds like me after my parents died. At least she has you. It was during that time that I met Sebastian. If I hadn't been so lost, I might have seen the truth of what he wanted sooner. Before it cost me everything."

"It's too bad she hates you because the two of you have a lot in common," he mused, eyes still staring in an unfocused way at the floor.

"Just make sure she doesn't try to stab me or something. I don't really care, she's hardly the first one to try to get a piece of me, but Mikhail will react . . . poorly."

Understatement of the year.

Andrei snorted and gave me a side-eyed look. "You two really mates?"

"Yep."

"Huh." He ran a hand through his hair. "I thought about coming back a few times, you know. To see if things would be different. You were so worried about corrupting me, but it happened anyway. I've got a lot of blood on my hands now."

"It's not the same." I shook my head.

"Killing is killing."

It really wasn't.

"A few months back, I was having a really bad day." I tilted my head as I continued to look at him. "What would you have done to cheer me up?"

He thought about it for a moment before grinning at me. "Take you to the forest so we could run in our fur for a bit. I'd stash a bottle of whiskey somewhere so we could shift back and get a little buzzed, then melt your brain with orgasms."

"Not a bad afternoon," I admitted. "Want to know what Mikhail did?"

"I'm aquiver with anticipation." He held his hands out to the side.

"He took me to the seraphim realm to slaughter a bunch of angels. Sat up on the cliff and watched as I laughed and coated my blades with their blood. I didn't just kill them; I made it hurt." My voice took on a hint of longing at the memory, like I was reminiscing about a delicious piece of cake. "Eventually, he ended it by letting himself get stabbed, which caused me to set my devourer flames on the seraphim. I smiled while they screamed."

Granted, I'd let out my own rage-filled scream too.

Andrei stared at me for a long moment. There wasn't a hint of disgust on his face, more like concern brewing in his kind eyes. "Did it help?"

"Yeah, it did." I grinned wide enough for my fangs to peek out. "*That* is the difference between you and me. You could kill a thousand vampires, but you'll never enjoy it. It's not who you are. You kill to defend and protect, nothing more. Meanwhile, I love it. Whether it's pitting my skills against another and dancing that razor edge of life and death or slaughtering arrogant assholes who never stood a chance. Killing is a part of who I am, and it doesn't bother me one bit."

A slight crease formed between his brows. "I really want to argue that I could have made you just as happy as the damn vampire does, but even I know that's a lie."

"Trust me." I wrinkled my nose. "I tried really hard to fight it. Do you have any idea how hard it is to be with someone prettier than you?"

He laughed. "You're way prettier than him."

"Glad someone thinks so," I muttered before raising a brow at him. "So, no one has caught your eye since you've been away?"

"Not really." He shrugged. "Stela and I were on the move a lot. Plus, I don't trust myself these days around humans. The wolf is too unpredictable, and humans are too breakable."

I grinned. "You know who isn't breakable? Dragons."

Andrei blushed. "I don't know what you're talking about."

"We're gonna get through this bullshit in the sorcerer realm . . . and then you're asking Iseult out to dinner when we get back." I poked him in the chest.

"She may not be interested," he protested.

I rolled my eyes. "She is. Caught her checking out your ass."

"Really?" His eyes lit up a little.

I nodded.

Andrei ran a hand through his hair. "Okay, but you need to teach me some basic sign language while we're away."

"Deal."

I stood outside the door to the second-floor apartment for what felt like an eternity. Andrei had left a while ago to check on his sister and the witch, both of whom were staying at The Inferno. Thanks to the mating bond, I knew Mikhail was still in there, and I had no doubt Magos was too.

The last time I'd seen my friend, he'd looked so dejected. I didn't know what I was going to find when I went in there, but I couldn't just keep standing here.

Fixing my face into a neutral expression, I pushed the door

open. The scent of rich coffee hit me immediately, and I blinked when I saw both Mikhail and Magos casually leaning against the kitchen counter. Magos looked . . . good.

I couldn't stop myself from scrutinizing his appearance. He must have let Mikhail attend to his braids because they looked neater than last time and were gathered in a loose knot behind his head. For the first time in weeks, he wore one of his well-tailored daemon suits and his rich, dark brown skin had a nice, healthy glow. The latter was probably thanks to the blood he'd taken from Bryn; she might have been young, but she was still a valkyrie with a lot of magic coursing through her veins.

It was the hope in his copper eyes that had my own eyes burning. I blinked a few times and did my best to give him a casual smile. "Any coffee left?"

Magos picked up a mug off the counter and held it out to me. "For you."

"Wow. Already had one waiting for me. I like it." I closed the door and joined them in the kitchen, accepting the cup and immediately drinking some. *Mmm. Perfect.*

"You stood outside the door for over five minutes." Mikhail snorted. "Thought I was going to have to open it and drag you in here."

"Would've liked to see you try it, vampire," I said mildly.

A wicked glint flashed across Mikhail's eyes, and he opened his mouth, but his uncle cut him off.

"Everything go alright with Finn and Isabeau?" Magos sipped his espresso. "Mikhail said you were splitting them up?"

"Yeah." I sighed. "Aki suggested it, and I think we're all in agreement that it would be good for them to spend some time apart. Finn needs to learn how to control his magic, and Isabeau needs time to think about how she feels about Misha and Damon leaving without the pressure of worrying about Finn."

"And did you cause any political disasters with the Seelie Queen?" Mikhail grinned slyly.

"No." I rolled my eyes. "We were almost civil to each other. Even I can admit that she's good for Finn. Showed him some things in the dragon realm that will be helpful over the next few days. And Cian is ecstatic to have Isabeau visiting."

"How's Hades handling it?" The corners of Magos' eyes creased in amusement, and it made me so damn happy.

"He asked if I was absolutely sure Isabeau wasn't the spawn of the devil. I told him, as far as I knew, Pele doesn't have any children."

Magos chuckled, and I caught the relief in Mikhail's expression that was probably mirrored in my own.

"So . . . Mikhail told you about the plan?"

I did my best to keep my tone and posture as nonchalant as possible. It had been weeks since I'd seen Magos so relaxed. I didn't want to ruin it but also wanted to make sure he was prepared for what was to come.

"You don't have to worry about me, child." The smile he gave me was so heartbreakingly kind that I didn't even argue about the *child* comment. "I understand there are no guarantees the sorcerers can help me, or that they'll be willing to. I know I haven't been myself lately, and I apologize for tha—"

"You have nothing to apologize for," I said quickly. "Gods know you've dealt with enough bullshit from us." I waved a hand between me and Mikhail. "We've got your back, Magos, and we *will* find a fix for this."

If the sorcerers declined to help us, I'd burn down their fucking realm. Let it serve as a warning to the next group who could help us but refused to do so.

"So now we just wait for Emir to show up?" Mikhail's mouth twisted in distaste. "And then we get to take a fun trip to the sorcerer realm with the werewolves and witch in tow?"

"So . . ." I drew out the word. "One more person will be joining us."

Mikhail liked Vizor even less than I did, and that was saying something. He would not be happy about this.

"Who?" Mikhail asked suspiciously.

"Well, we'll be surrounded by *allies*"—I made airquotes—"waiting to stab us in the back. And we're going to a realm full of beings known for being secretive and manipulative assholes. The three of us are good fighters, but we need someone with a cunning political mind."

"And Pele's busy with bullshit in the daemon realm." His eyes narrowed. "If it was Cerri, you would have led with that."

"We're getting a dragon." I winced. "But it's the asshole one."

"Damn it," Mikhail sighed.

Chapter Seven

"Whas tha 'ound?" I pushed the pillow harder against my ears, trying to block out the persistent melody ringing through our apartment, but then my fluffy defense was brutally yanked from me.

"It's your fucking wolf and his sister," Mikhail growled. "And it's too fucking early. Deal with them, or I will."

I groaned and tried to tug my pillow back, only to squeal when I was unceremoniously shoved out of the bed. My head smacked against the hardwood floor of our apartment, and a litany of French swear words tumbled from my mouth. It had been almost four centuries since I'd lived in France, but they were still my go-to expletives when I was half awake.

"Worst fucking mate," I hissed and stalked out of our bedroom.

Mikhail and I had stayed with Magos for a while after updating him on everything. He'd been in good spirits, which had made both of us feel better. For the first time in months, it felt like having the old Magos back.

After that, Mikhail and I had returned to the top-floor apartment and sparred for a bit . . . which had turned into a different kind of sparring entirely. We'd been up late, and according to my cell phone that I'd grabbed off the dresser, it was just past eight in the morning. Most days, we slept until at least ten.

The majority of the magical community maintained late hours. Apparently, the werewolves hadn't picked up on that fact.

I swiped Mikhail's shirt off the kitchen counter, where I'd thrown it last night, and tugged it on. Since he favored formfitting clothing, it stretched across my breasts and barely covered my ass. Whatever. It wasn't like the werewolves gave a shit about nudity.

After one forlorn look at the coffee maker I had no idea how to use, I jerked the apartment door open and stomped down the stairs.

"What"—I jerked the front door open and glared at the two people next to the doorbell that I was pretty sure had never once been rung until this morning—"are you doing here?"

Andrei grinned at me and thrust a cup of coffee into my hand. "I brought donuts." He held up a large box with a mermaid logo.

"Zareen," I said with a groan of pleasure.

"Does Kaysea know you say her girlfriend's name like that?" Andrei arched an eyebrow and held the box with the answer to life just outside my reach.

"That's how everyone says Zareen's name because she's the fucking god of baked goods!" I snatched the donuts, spun around, and marched back up the stairs.

Don't be so fucking loud, Jinx grumbled from behind the door of the second-floor apartment. I quieted my movements because he was absolutely enough of an asshole to make me drop and smoosh the box of donuts.

I left the door open when I reached my apartment and slumped onto one of the kitchen barstools. Mikhail stumbled out of the hallway as I flipped the box open and drooled at a dozen delicious morsels. My eyes scanned all of them, snagging on the chocolate frosted one with sprinkles. I plucked it out of the box and passed it to my mate, who immediately snatched it out of my fingers and sank his teeth into it.

"Oo doo lurv mee." His words came out muffled on account of his attempt to stuff half the donut into his mouth.

"Yes." I stared at the donut covered in sugar and crunchy cinnamon goodness. "I do love you."

"Umm . . ." Andrei leaned against the doorframe to our apartment. "Are we interrupting?"

Stela shoved passed him. "I don't care. Those donuts smelled delicious and you wouldn't let me have one!"

"I was trying to be a courteous guest," he argued, stepping aside so Lestari could enter. I frowned briefly at the witch, who I hadn't noticed downstairs, but then returned my attention to my beloved donut.

"Gods," Stela muttered. "I hope I find a woman who looks at me the way Nemain looks at that donut."

"Same," Mikhail said around mouthfuls of his donut.

I elbowed him in the gut, enjoying the hiss of pain he let out, before focusing on the three early arrivals. "What are you doing here so early?"

"The sun rose hours ago," Lestari replied while eying our kitchen. "Do you have tea?"

"Yes." I took another bite of my donut. "Don't know where."

She sighed and started opening cupboards.

"I couldn't sleep." Andrei sent me an apologetic look.

"And naturally, he came knocking at my door," Stela said dryly.

Andrei reached into the box and pulled out a chocolate glazed donut and passed it to her. The annoyance instantly vanished from Stela's face as she slipped into sugary bliss.

Footsteps sounded from the hallway, and we all turned to look, except for the witch, who was still scouring in vain for tea. I'd lied earlier, we didn't have any on this floor, but Lestari and the wolves had woken me up early, so I had to take out my annoyance on someone.

Magos walked into the apartment and closed the door behind him, a tin container flashing in his hand. He must have heard us and stopped to grab some tea. Ugh. Even when he was losing his mind, he was still polite.

"My apologies." He held the tea out to Lestari. "I haven't gone shopping lately, so our options are limited."

She took the tin box, opened it, and smelled its contents. "Saffron, orange, and pink peppercorn. This is divine. Thank you."

"You are most welcome." Magos nodded, then pulled the kettle out from the bottom cupboard and set to making tea. He appeared calm and collected. If his hunger was bothering him, Magos hid it well.

Andrei sat on the stool to my left, spinning until he faced me, propping his elbow on the table so he could rest his chin on his palm. "Yesterday was arranging babysitters; I'm genuinely curious for what today entails."

"Pele told me to clear my schedule." I shoved the last of the donut into my mouth and reached for another while silently thanking Zareen for opening a branch of her bakery in Emerald Bay. I knew she'd only done so because Kaysea spent most of her time here so she could support me, but I wasn't going to look a gift horse in the mouth. Gift pastry? Did the hole of a donut count as the mouth?

These were the important questions I had after four hundred years of existence.

"What do you know about the sorcerers?" Stela asked. Today, she sported loose-fitting sweatpants that she'd cut off at the knees with an oversized T-shirt she'd tied into a knot at her waist. Somehow, on her, it looked like high fashion.

I glanced down at my shirt—Mikhail's shirt—that was now covered in crumbs. Whatever. I was still hotter.

"Not much," I admitted. "They rarely visit other realms. Honestly, the only time I know of them coming to this one is when they created the werewolves and vampires."

"Because of the bet?" Andrei dunked his donut into his coffee.

I stared at him in disgust, then confusion . . . then curiosity. Cautiously, I dipped mine into my liquid nectar.

Oh. My. Gods.

Why had I never done this before?!

"Stop moaning," Mikhail growled under his breath.

"Stop being so bossy." I pointed my soggy donut at him in a threatening manner before glancing at Andrei, who was staring at us with a bemused expression. "The rumor is that it was a bet, but nobody really knows why the fuck they came here and decided to make the two species."

Magos passed Lestari a teacup with blue and gold flowers on it. She nodded in thanks, her dark eyes lighting up with delight when she took a sip.

"So we really have no idea what we're walking into?" Stela picked at her croissant, a crease between her brows.

I made a noise of agreement because I was too busy polishing off the rest of my donut and coffee to give her a proper response. Not that I really had one. The sorcerers had just been people who'd existed in some other realm for most of my life. They hadn't bothered me. I hadn't bothered them. It'd been nice while it'd lasted.

Andrei grabbed another donut and passed it to me. I looked forlornly at my empty coffee cup and then at the espresso contraption before making big eyes at Magos. His lips curled up into a small smile before he pushed off the counter he'd been leaning against and walked over to the machine. I listened to the sound of it spinning up while he reached for my favorite mug resting on the shelf above it.

Mikhail loudly slurped his coffee, and Magos grabbed another cup.

"Why?" Stela prompted. When I only gave her a blank stare, she rolled her eyes before clarifying, "Why did the sorcerers make a bet about creating new species?"

"Oh. No idea. Don't even know the names of the sorcerers involved—no one does. I have seen the original devourers they used though." I accepted my cup from Magos when he held it out and took a long sip. Caffeine. Chocolate. Sugar. Perfection.

Somewhere in my appreciation of the absolute best cup of coffee, I'd closed my eyes. When I opened them, I found Stela and Lestari staring at me.

"What?" My eyebrows rose.

"You've seen the devourers that were used to craft the vampires and werewolves?" Stela narrowed her gaze at me.

"Yup." I took another long drink and tried to ignore the painful memories that tried to surface. "In the aftermath of my parents' deaths, I spent the majority of my time in other realms —mostly uninhabited ones."

"I presume this was before you started massacring witches?" Lestari asked pointedly.

Tension instantly filled the kitchen.

"For the most part." I gave her a cool look. "In the early years, I bounced back and forth." A cruel smile stretched across my lips. "Kill a few covens. Vanish into another realm. Rinse and repeat. To be fair though, I slaughtered my fair share of warlocks too."

"Do you think that's why they left? Those young vampires of yours?" she mused. "They saw the truth of your soul and ran?"

I tried to keep the pain from her words off my face, but my

recent encounter with Misha and Damon was too fresh. I couldn't stop the flinch.

"Careful, witch," Mikhail said in a low, dangerous tone.

Lestari's eyes flicked to him and then Andrei before returning to me. "I suppose it's not a surprise you chose the villain over the hero."

"Don't," Andrei warned. "Our history is none of your business. Don't drag your bullshit into it."

Surprise flickered in Lestari's face, but she nodded. "You're right. I spoke out of turn."

"So it's not just witches you hate?" Stela cut in. There wasn't hostility in her words, more curiosity. "But warlocks too?"

I spared her a glance. "Similar to vampires and werewolves, witches and warlocks have been at each other's throats for as long as anyone can remember. Unlike the former, the war between the latter has spilled over to impact the rest of us."

"The witch trials were mostly hate propaganda stirred up by the warlocks," Mikhail drawled. "It took out some of the weaker witch covens, but other nonhumans got caught in the cross fire."

"Like my parents," I said in a hollow tone as the memory of burnt flesh seared my nostrils. Centuries separated me and that day, but the scent was as vivid as ever. Eager to focus on something else, I thought about the realms I'd visited during those times. "The devourers used for the vampires and werewolves don't bear any resemblance to the newly created species. Honestly, the only reason I knew what they were was because I recognized the magic signature." I thought about it a little more. "And the vampire issue with sunlight makes sense, as there is no true daylight in that realm."

"It's always night?" Magos asked.

I shook my head. "Not exactly. There is daytime, but it

never gets particularly light. The sky is dark red during the day, and night is true darkness. No stars. No moonlight."

"And you've never taken me there, shifter?" Mikhail grinned at me. "It's like you don't love me at all."

"Next time you piss me off, I just might." I grinned back. "Monsters truly rule that realm, and at the top of the food chain are the devourers. I only remained there for as long as I did because I didn't run into them until my third day, and I left shortly after that."

The only reason I hadn't fled the realm immediately was because Jinx and I had been separated and it had taken us days to find each other again.

"Werewolves don't have an aversion to sunlight," Stela mused. "What did the devourers look lik—"

A chime rang through the apartment, cutting her off.

Mikhail and I both frowned. Twice in one day. Odd. That doorbell hadn't made a sound the entire time we'd lived here. There were other ways of getting in touch with us. Nobody came here unannounced, and all of our friends and family could just walk right into the building. There was a ward around it that prevented any unauthorized people from entering without an invite, courtesy of Pele.

Given that Andrei, Stela, and Lestari were already here, I couldn't think of anyone else who would be ringing my doorbell.

"Stay up here," I told everyone quietly as I moved towards the apartment door. Unsurprisingly, Mikhail followed in my wake. I grabbed two daggers off the wall, and he did the same, then silently, we made our way down the stairs as the melody sounded again.

Mikhail and I reached the bottom landing, and we both paused as we took in the daemon waiting politely on the other side of the glass door.

"Talia," I said slowly, lowering my daggers. "What is she doing here?"

The daemon with deep red skin politely waved at me. Her silky black hair fell in a curtain to her waist, and four horns spiraled from her head. Similar to Pele, she had bright turquoise eyes, marking her as a daemon from a fire bloodline.

"You know her?" Mikhail's gaze remained locked on the daemon.

"We've met in passing a few times. She works for Ramil, Pele's father," I murmured. "Basically his right hand."

Pele had mentioned she knew of a daemon who might have some knowledge of the sorcerers . . . Had she been talking about her father? Why hadn't she just said that? Unless Talia was here for a completely unrelated reason . . .

"I'm not," Talia said, her words a little muffled through the door as she clasped her hands in front of her. "Ramil has relevant information that will be useful to you in the coming days, and he requests that you meet with him. You're welcome to bring the wolves and witch along."

Great. A mind reader. That was new information. What other fun secrets was she hiding?

"I'm terrified of butterflies, and I can make a really good rhubarb pie. Now will you please come with me?" Talia held up one arm and tapped the watch on her wrist. "I actually have a lot of things on my agenda today."

Mikhail sighed. "I'll get the others."

"Just a moment, please." Talia held up her hand, and we all halted in the brightly lit library. Then she tilted her head to the side, her eyes going a little unfocused. After a moment, she blinked and looked at me, a sense of urgency I didn't like in her expression. *Do not react.*

Before I could figure out what that meant, the heavy ornate door at the back of the room swung open, and two daemons stalked out. One of them was slightly familiar, but I couldn't quite place where I'd seen him before. The other, I didn't recognize at all.

And I definitely would have remembered him if we'd met. Light green eyes shone brilliantly against his bright red skin, and an obsidian black horn, curled like a ram's, protruded from the right side of his head. The horn on the left had been broken only a few inches from the base, which was something I'd never seen on a daemon before, because they could heal just about anything, given enough time.

As he strode closer, I realized the horn hadn't been broken . . . it'd been melted. The edges had a shiny quality to them, like the rocks I'd seen around volcanoes.

The unknown daemon sneered at me as he walked past, slamming his shoulder into mine even though he'd had plenty of space.

Fire rippled down my arms, and I turned in time to see Mikhail palm two throwing knives.

Do not react, Talia repeated, I assumed to all of us.

I kept a tight hold on my devourer magic but parted my lips slightly to inhale the daemon's scent. Badb had passed down three magic gifts to me: the ability to shift into my feline form, the power to open gateways, and the ability to read the souls of others.

For the longest time, I'd ignored that third gift. It wasn't particularly powerful, and I'd deemed it useless, but lately I'd been using it more. Macha, Badb's sister and the woman who had raised me as one of her own, had been much more gifted with her soul-reading abilities. Within seconds, she could see the truth of any person she met.

My magic gave me . . . vibes, and whoever that daemon was, my magic told me he was devious and cruel.

The two daemons didn't spare a glance at Magos, Lestari, or the werewolves, all of whom tracked their exit from the library. A name filtered through my memory. Toci. That was the familiar daemon. I only remembered the young daemon because they were very ambitious and kept popping up in random places. The last time I'd seen them, they'd been running their own tavern, a rare thing for daemons barely past two centuries.

"Who was the daemon with the death wish?" I asked quietly after I heard the doors open and slam shut.

"A problem for another day," a deep, masculine voice said from behind me.

I turned back towards the room and looked at the source of the voice. An enormous daemon filled the doorway. His rich mahogany skin was covered by an elegant navy blue suit that tried and failed to diminish his bulk. Wavy, blue-black hair fell to his jaw, framing a chiseled, handsome face, while sapphire blue eyes that usually held a spark of amusement just appeared tired today.

Pele took after her mother, Lashi, in both looks and magic, but that was where the similarities ended. Lashi had been considerably older than her mate and had passed away when Pele was fifteen years old. Ramil had raised Pele on his own ever since, and the two of them were close. They shared a thirst for knowledge and a love of political machinations.

"You look like shit." I smirked at the leader of the Daemon Assembly. "I'm going to give you the same offer I gave your daughter—who do you want me to kill?"

I thought about the two daemons who'd passed by me. Toci had always struck me as a problem. That daemon he was with was absolutely bad news.

Ramil's eyes shone with amusement. "And I'm going to give you the same response that she no doubt did. No killing." He paused and tilted his head slightly. "For now."

I thought about it. Surely removing Toci and that other troublesome-looking daemon from the playing board would be good for everyon—

"Stop plotting murder, Nemain," Ramil spoke in a smooth tone, but I heard the order loud and clear.

"Spoilsport," I muttered as I passed him and slumped in the dark red velvet chair in front of his massive desk. Mikhail snickered as he took a seat next to me, and the others filtered in to lean against the walls.

Ramil's gaze fell on Mikhail. "You will also stop plotting Samael's death."

"Will I?" Mikhail spun his dagger in his hand.

The dagger flew from his hand and slammed into the wall, burying the blade to the hilt.

"Yes," Ramil said calmly. "You will. Nemain has a long list of enemies, and she continues to make more. At some point, the two of you are going to have to realize it is wiser to not make enemies in the first place."

Magos let out an amused chuckle that he tried to cover up by clearing his throat.

"Perhaps," I acknowledged Ramil's words, ones that were an old argument between us. "But diplomacy doesn't always work, and plenty of the blood on my hands I earned at the request of your daughter—and yourself, if I remember correctly."

The daemons had no king or queen. They ruled by an assembly that was mostly voted into power, but that didn't mean everything was fair and aboveboard. Two centuries ago, a small faction had tried to stage a coup of sorts. When negotiations failed, my well-placed daggers ensured the leaders of that rebellion fell.

Technically, Pele had asked me to do it, but there was no chance she would have requested such a thing without consulting with her father.

Ramil rubbed his forehead, and again, I saw that exhaustion lining his features. "I didn't invite you here to fight or lecture you. I will always cherish you, Nemain, because of the light you bring to my daughter's life. My darling daughter takes after me and can be a bit too serious at times." He gave me a brief smile. "A little chaos is good for the soul."

I waved a hand and leaned back in my chair. "My words were sharper than I intended. You have given me countless wisdom over the years and asked nothing for it. For that, I will always be grateful."

He stared at me for a long moment and then threw his head back and let out a hearty laugh. "You really have been spending too much time with the fae."

"Don't I know it," I muttered.

Andrei yelped, and I spun in my chair to see him flailing his hand around . . . with a book closed over most of his fingers like it'd bitten him. Stela grabbed the book and pulled, her face strained, and then the two stumbled apart, the book dropping to the floor as the werewolves growled at it.

"We need to get a leash for them or something," Mikhail mused. The two werewolves turned to glower at him, but he just rolled his eyes. "Don't touch flowers in the fae realm, and don't mess with books in the daemon realm."

Lestari knelt and carefully picked up the leather-bound book. Gingerly, she placed it back onto the shelf before stepping away and joining Magos, who leaned against the open wallspace a healthy distance from all the books. The wolves stubbornly remained where they were, directly in front of the bookshelves, but neither made a move to touch any of them again.

"My apologies." Ramil glanced at Andrei. "I haven't fed that one lately, so he's feeling a little peckish."

Andrei glanced at the bookshelf. "What exactly does one feed a book?"

"Curious wolves." Pele's father smiled.

"Right," Andrei tugged his sister a little farther from the shelves.

Ramil returned his attention to me, a serious look on his face once again. "I meant to reach out to you sooner, but I was delayed. Am I correct in my understanding that you will be going to the sorcerer realm in hopes of negotiating with them on behalf of the werewolves and other matters?" His eyes flicked briefly to Magos, letting me know he knew what those other matters were. Ramil had been one of the first people I'd reached out to about the curse on Magos. For all the knowledge he'd collected, not even the leader of the daemons knew how to break it.

"Yes," I confirmed. "We expect to leave within the next twenty-four hours, possibly tonight."

"I don't know how useful it will be, but I can provide at least some information on the sorcerers." Ramil propped his elbows on his desk, holding his hands up so his fingertips rested against each other.

"You've met them?" Mikhail leaned forward; his daggers had vanished at some point into the sheaths on his thighs.

Ramil nodded. "Twice. It was shortly after we fled the dragon realm. Before the daemons built up their power base." The corners of his eyes and mouth softened, and he looked almost wistful. "Everything was different back then. There were no factions within the Assembly. It was just everyone working together to survive, to build a new home." Grief tugged at his features, something dark filling his gaze. "I can't help but wonder, if Lashi were still here, would she have held things together better than I have. I've done my best, but she . . ." He swallowed and looked at a rose made of pure flames that burned on the corner of his desk. "She was something else."

I'd never asked about the burning rose, but I was fairly certain Pele's mother had created it, and the man she'd loved more than anything had kept it safe all this time. He'd kept their daughter safe as well.

"It was bound to happen eventually," Lestari said kindly. "People have a tendency to come together in the worst of times; it's peace that tears us apart."

"I know," Ramil said, a hint of vulnerability in his voice. "I've tried but . . . I have faith in my daughter to do better. Pele . . ." He smiled, and the brightness of it chased away the darkness in his eyes. "She is the best of us."

"She is," I agreed softly.

Ramil pulled his gaze away from the rose and focused on me. "In a somewhat random series of events, Lashi managed to make contact with a sorcerer and gain a token to their realm; that's how they invite people there. The first time we went, our goal was to create an alliance between our two peoples. Perhaps have some of our youth visit their realm, while some of theirs could stay with us in an exchange of knowledge. They were somewhat open to this; the sorcerers value knowledge above all else." He grimaced. "The second time we visited them, our goal was to ensure our youth *never* went to their realm and that they never contacted any daemons again. We gave them some of our most prized books and some other items. They seemed disappointed but accepted the deal."

Silence reigned in the small study.

"Why?" I stared at him. Daemons *never* turned down knowledge.

Unease flickered across his face. "I can't explain it exactly. We walked around their city and listened to several sorcerers excitedly discuss different breakthroughs they'd made recently while asking about how many daemons we thought would be interested in coming there. They never threatened us, and we didn't notice anything particularly egregious, but the longer we were there, the more it just felt *wrong*. I've never encountered anything like it since."

Great. Two of the most powerful daemons to ever exist had been so terrified by the sorcerers that they'd bargained to never see them again. Meanwhile, we were about to stroll into the realm and offer just about anything if they could help Magos.

"Is there anything specific you can tell us?" I pushed. "Anything that might help us deal with them?"

"Aside from *don't go*?" He arched a brow but sighed at the resolute expressions on my and Mikhail's faces. "This was centuries ago, so it's possible things have changed, but I can tell you that their cities are similar to daemon ones: large and bustling metropolises. We had to have been the first daemons to ever set foot in the sorcerer realm, and yet nobody reacted to us. So, on the plus side, if that hasn't changed, you will potentially be able to explore unhindered, but I urge you to be cautious at all times. Even if they seem unbothered by your presence, there is something sinister and foul in that realm."

"And the sorcerers themselves?" Mikhail asked. "What were they like to bargain with?"

Ramil pondered it. "We expected them to push back when we told them we were no longer interested in having any of our youth study there, but aside from expressing mild disappointment, they took it in stride. We walked away getting everything we wanted from the deal, and to my knowledge, they never made contact with another daemon. I should feel as though they were pushovers and we took advantage . . . but I don't. To this day, I still believe they pulled one over on us. The only thing that could ever get me to bargain with them again would be if Pele's life was on the line. I know it sounds strange because I can't point to a single thing and say, 'This. This right here is where it all went to shit.' But I'm telling you, Nemain . . . . there is something fundamentally fucked-up in that realm. You shouldn't go."

"I have to." I gave him a tired smile. "For a long list of reasons."

Maybe I could have found a way out of honoring the blood oath with Emir, but Andrei and Magos needed help, and the sorcerers were all we had to go on at the moment.

"Then the best advice I can give you is to trust your instincts, not your eyes, not their agreeable words, and not the beauty of their city. Trust yourself." His shrewd gaze flicked to Mikhail. "Trust your mate, and do what you must to come back alive, because although my daughter will not ask for help, she is going to need it when she ascends to power."

"Like I said earlier"—I gave him a lazy smile—"just tell me who to kill."

He smiled back at me. "Come back alive, and I just might."

Chapter Eight

THAT NIGHT, just as Lestari claimed he would, Emir strolled through the door of the largest meeting room of The Inferno as if he owned it. He looked the same as always. His black hair had silver at the temples and was styled in a short, neat haircut. Between that and the slight wrinkles in his light brown skin, he looked like a human in his late fifties, but I knew he was far older than that because he'd been there the day my parents had been burned alive almost four centuries ago.

Emir liked to appear unassuming to allow people to underestimate him. I wouldn't make that mistake.

He'd arranged for this meeting through one of Pele's underlings, since both she and Asmodeus were in the daemon realm. Apparently, he'd told the daemon in charge of things today not to inform me ahead of time and to wait until he arrived to summon me.

She'd assured him she would absolutely do that and then immediately hung up on him and called me—well, technically, she'd called Mikhail because I never answered my cell phone—which was why we'd all arrived early and had claimed our spots around the enormous circular table.

"So . . ." I drawled. "Sorceror realm?"

I cherished the surprised look that flashed across his face, followed by irritation. He hid it quickly while he took a seat at the table directly across from me, his now-neutral gaze flicking over the werewolves and vampires. Sharp brown eyes scrutinized Vizor, likely trying to figure out who or what he was. The dragon just gave him a haughty, bored look in return. Emir dismissed him, his eyes finally falling on Lestari. "Still sticking your nose where it doesn't belong, I see."

Lestari raised a dark eyebrow. "Still desperately trying to cling to power, I see. How's the Circle these days? Missing anyone important?"

I glanced at her, not sure what she was talking about.

"How many witches did you sacrifice to take out *two* members of the Circle?" Emir scoffed. "Your numbers are looking pretty low these days. Sure you want to keep throwing them away?"

Lestari's mouth tightened.

"Or maybe the witches and warlocks could just wipe each other out without involving the rest of us." I threw back my shot of whiskey, ignoring the thousand-yard stare Lestari was currently giving me, and dropped my glass back onto the table. "How about you tell us why you're here, Emir? I'll put on my surprised face while you explain that you found a way to reach the sorcerer realm and demand that I take you and some of your vampire cronies."

Now both the warlock and the witch glared at me. I thought about pointing out that they could bond over their mutual dislike of me when the door swung open again and two familiar faces walked in.

"Cronies?" A striking man with flawless olive-toned skin and wavy, midnight black hair gave me a hurt look, even as his dark eyes danced with mischief. "Can you believe that, Justina? We've been demoted to mere cronies."

"I instructed you both to wait outside." Emir shot the newcomers an annoyed look.

"We got bored," the woman replied in a husky voice. If the man was good-looking, the woman was stunning. She practically sauntered towards us, the high slit of her formfitting purple dress giving everyone a solid flash of thigh as she moved.

I couldn't help but glance at Mikhail. The vampire who looked like a goddess was his ex-lover. His eyes weren't on her though, they were on the man with the devil eyes.

"Cassius," he said in a smooth tone that usually meant someone was about to die. "Should have known you'd be involved in this."

"I couldn't resist spending time with the pretty shifter who stole your heart after all this time." Cassius winked, and I sucked in a breath as rage filtered down the mating bond. Mikhail's expression didn't betray a hint of what he felt, the mask of bored indifference never cracking.

Justina laughed, the sound deep and a little rough. Of course even her laugh would be sexy. I might have to kill her.

Her golden brown eyes fell on Vizor, and she gave him a sultry smile as she stopped by his chair. "Well, hello. I don't believe I recognize you. I'm Justina." She popped out a hip, which only accentuated her hourglass figure. "And who might you be?"

Vizor gave her a withering look. "Not interested."

"Fuck," I muttered as I took in Justina's shocked expression. "I kind of like Vizor now."

Justina recovered from Vizor's outright dismissal and looked around our table, her cupid's bow mouth turning into a frown when she saw there was space left but that it was next to me. Cassius brushed by her and took the chair before she could, turning it slightly so he faced me. Then he leaned one arm on the back of the chair and rested the other on the table.

"Lovely to see you again, Nemain. You'll protect me from your psychotic stabby lover, right?" He gave me a panty-melting grin, and I pondered him for a long moment. The last time I'd been around Cassius, he'd been bold but not this flirtatious with me. There was some beef between him and Mikhail, and I got the impression he was doing this just to get under my vampire's skin.

I leaned a little closer to him, a conspiratory smile on my lips, and his eyes lit up as he leaned in closer too. "Want to know a secret?" I purred.

"Always." He grinned a little wider.

"Mikhail's sane compared to me." The vampire barely managed to move his hand before my dagger slammed into the surface of the wooden table.

Damn. Fucker was fast.

Cassius threw back his head and laughed. "Gods, you two are so well-matched."

A hand slid around my shoulders, Mikhail tugging me closer to him and away from Cassius. "Fuck off, Cassius."

My curiosity was at an all-time high, but I'd have to wait to grill Mikhail about what the deal was between him and the trouble-seeking vampire later.

That didn't stop me from inhaling deeply and letting his scent roll across my tongue. My soul-reading magic picked it apart. Fresh and earthy. Like the rocks along a riverbank. There was an undercurrent of an inevitable bleakness that left me feeling hollow. It was so at odds with the charming devilish facade he put on.

When I tried to get a read on Justina, I was met with a cool impenetrable wall.

Of course Mikhail would have a history with two complicated vampires.

Magos rose from the table and calmly left the room for a

few seconds, returning with another chair that he placed in the empty spot to Vizor's right. "Here you are, Justina."

"Thank you, Magos." She practically glided over to him. "Courteous and gorgeous. A lady could get used to that."

"Also not interested," he said politely.

Justina rolled her eyes and slumped in the chair in a *very* unladylike manner. "This trip is going to be so boring."

"You could always not come," Stela spoke for the first time. Both she and Andrei had been watching the two vampires with predatory expressions from where they sat on either side of Lestari. "Maybe take a stroll in the sunshine instead?"

"Well, aren't you adorable?" Justina cocked her head, her eyes slowly drinking in the werewolf. "You look sweet enough to eat."

"My blood is off-limits." Stela's top lip trembled in a barely contained snarl.

"Oh." Justina grinned. "I wasn't talking about your blood, sweetheart."

Stela growled as a yellow sheen rolled over her eyes.

"Well, this is off to a great start." I snorted.

The warlock looked at the wolves and the witch. "They're not coming."

"I say they are, and since you need me to open the gateway, it's best you just accept that now." I shrugged. "Let's just get it all out there, shall we? The Vampire Council is at your throat —figuratively for now, but soon to be literally—over the promises you've made them but haven't been able to fulfill. You found a way to get to the sorcerer realm, and your plan was to force me to bring you there. Unfortunately for you, she"—I pointed to Lestari—"found out about your little scheme and got here before you. There is nothing in our arrangement that says I can't help my friends while assisting you, which is what I'll be doing."

A muscle ticked below his eye. "I've been in talks with a sorcerer named Izaak—he's the one who created the vampires. He's not the most welcoming individual, and he won't be pleased about more people coming to their realm than I arranged."

"My heart bleeds for you." I held his stare. "The wolves and the witch are coming."

Emir rapped his fingers on the table, and I gave him a lazy smile in return.

"Fine," he agreed in a clipped tone. "But if they interfere with my negotiations, I'll be forced to take actions to protect my own interests, and don't forget that you can't directly strike against me."

"I haven't forgotten, and they're aware." I poured myself another shot of whiskey.

Emir glanced at Vizor, and I knew he was still trying to figure out who he was. He knew Eddie and Cerri because they frequently visited me, but Vizor only came when Lynette dragged him along, which wasn't often.

"Who is he?" the warlock finally asked when it became clear nobody was going to introduce the mysterious addition to my group.

"A friend of a friend," I said vaguely. "When do we leave?"

Emir tossed a coin to me and I snatched it out of the air. Bluish silver gleamed as magic nipped at my fingertips.

"One hour." Emir rose, sharp eyes locking on Lestari as an arrogant grin spilled over his lips. "Follow the magic trace of the coin."

"Cool." I shoved the coin into my pocket. "Get the fuck out of my bar."

"No more surprises, Nemain." Emir cut me a warning look.

I didn't bother acknowledging him, just poured myself

another shot instead. Emir and the two vampires left, and we all waited a few seconds before speaking.

"Well," Andrei drawled, "this is gonna be fun."

JUST UNDER AN HOUR LATER, we'd all reconvened in the same meeting room, an uneasy tension in the air. It hadn't taken everyone long to gather their things. It brought me a little bit of joy to know Emir was probably still annoyed at us being a step ahead of him.

Unfortunately, we weren't *that* far ahead. I'd tried to open a gateway to the meeting location so we could scout it out beforehand, but Emir had spelled the coin in such a way that I couldn't trace its magic just yet, which meant we were going in blind.

Nobody was happy about that.

Logically, it didn't make sense for Emir to lay any kind of trap for us. He couldn't take any direct actions against me because of the blood oath, and he needed me to get him to the sorcerer realm. But it just didn't feel smart going to an unfamiliar location our enemy had dictated.

That wasn't the only cause of the tension though. Vizor was being even more of an ass than usual. I assumed he'd get worse the longer he was apart from Lynette. Andrei's wolf had been agitated since the meeting with Emir. And Stela was still fuming from all the flirty comments Justina had sent her way. Apparently, she hadn't considered the attention of the pretty vampire flattering.

Or at least she didn't want to admit she had.

And both Mikhail and I were on edge, trying to be a buffer between Magos and everyone else. Although, for his part, Magos seemed to be handling everything okay.

Andrei and Stela had taken the news of Magos' curse

surprisingly well. Given their aversion towards vampires, I didn't think they'd be keen on being around a vampire who could snap at any moment.

But instead, they'd both been . . . kind. I supposed if anyone could relate to Magos right now, it was Andrei. And Stela loved her brother more than anything, so she understood what we were going through. What it was like to watch help-lessly as someone important to you slipped away.

Lestari had been quiet but not hostile. She was hard to read, but I was fairly certain she had no ill wishes towards Magos or Mikhail. It was only me she didn't like, and I was fine with that.

"While we wait . . ." Andrei glanced at Mikhail, a yellow sheen rolling over his hazel eyes. "What's your history with the two vampires accompanying Emir?"

"It's none of your concern, pup," Mikhail answered coolly.

Andrei's upper lip trembled, eyes flashing from hazel to a golden yellow as the wolf tried to claw its way free. Dread coiled in my gut. Magos was slowly losing the battle against his bloodlust, and Andrei was losing against his wolf nature.

And our only hope was convincing the sorcerers to help us save them both.

Mikhail looked at me, no doubt sensing my inner turmoil through the mating bond. He sighed and turned back to Andrei. "Justina and I were in a relationship for decades. It was never particularly serious. We were just . . . convenient for each other. I ended things when she joined the Council because I had no interest in being used for political gain, which she abso-lutely would have done."

My magic churned under my skin. It didn't like Justina and would have loved nothing more than to burn her to ashes. I didn't entirely disagree, but if Mikhail was tolerating my ex traveling with us, I could extend the same courtesy. Unless she tried to touch him again. If that happened, the bitch would lose a hand.

Andrei took a few even breaths, and the tension eased from his posture. There was still a hint of gold in his eyes, but he seemed to be more in control now. "And Cassius?" he prompted.

Mikhail hesitated.

"They were lovers too," Vizor said easily from where he studied Pele's bookshelves. "It ended poorly. My guess is that there was an unequal power structure in the relationship—favoring Cassius."

The way Mikhail carefully wiped any hint of emotion from his face told me that Vizor's assumption was correct. I was more shocked than anything. I knew Mikhail was pansexual because it'd come up in conversation before, and it'd been obvious from my first encounter with Cassius that there was an ugly past between the two of them, it just hadn't occurred to me that it'd been the relationship kind.

Something told me this wasn't just Mikhail not wanting to talk about a previous love; there was more to it than that. Not that long ago, I would have been hurt by him keeping this from me. But I understood now that Mikhail was trying very hard to leave his past with the Vampire Council behind.

Unfortunately, just because we wanted to be done with the past didn't mean it was done with us. I'd learned that lesson repeatedly.

I stepped closer so that our arms brushed, and I felt a wave of gratitude through our mating bond. We'd talk about this later—away from everyone else.

"Well, the dragon definitely lacks tact, but he will be a useful asset in the sorcerer realm," Stela said dryly. "I never would have picked up on that."

"Ignoring the lurid details . . ." Lestari tilted her head and gave Mikhail a thoughtful look. "Is there anything useful you can tell us about Justina or Cassius?"

"Justina wields her beauty like a weapon. She is excellent at reading people and determining their motivations," Mikhail explained. "She'll play the ditzy and naive vampire to get people to underestimate her, the sultry temptress to get them panting after her, or the broken woman in need of saving. Whatever the game is, she'll adjust on the fly. Assume every word out of her mouth is a lie, and do not underestimate her, or you'll get a knife in the back."

Oddly, that description kind of made me respect her a little. The vampires, much like the warlocks, tended to be a misogynistic lot. The majority of the Council were men. Justina was one of two women on it, and there was one gender fluid individual I hadn't met yet. Justina didn't rely solely on her looks, but she didn't ignore them either. As Mikhail said, they were just another weapon for her to use as she cut her way to power.

"What type of magic does she have?" I asked.

Both Justina and Cassius belonged to Apex bloodlines. When the original humans were turned into vampires, some of them had a little something *extra* in their blood—or they weren't human at all, as was the case for Mikhail and Magos. It gave them an advantage over other vampires, which was why everyone who sat on the Council belonged to an Apex bloodline, either first generation or a descendant.

"She can create ice out of nothing and manipulate it however she wants," Mikhail said. "Small amounts are easy, but I have seen her create a ten-foot wall of ice that was at least a foot thick. That took a lot of effort and wiped her out, but it was several decades ago, so she's probably gotten stronger."

"Doesn't seem like that useful of a power." Andrei frowned.

"I'll remind you of that when she jams an ice pick through your throat," Mikhail mused.

"Tell me Cassius has some type of embarrassing power," I said before another argument broke out.

"Unfortunately not," Mikhail replied. "He can teleport."

"Fuck me." I let my head fall back slightly and curled my lip up at the ceiling. Teleporting was a fairly common daemon ability, and I found it incredibly annoying.

"Now's not the time, love." Mikhail smirked before kissing my cheek. "Cassius can easily teleport anywhere in a fifty-foot range. Beyond that takes a little more effort. I'm not sure what his limit is, to be honest."

"Can he take someone with him?" Vizor asked.

"I don't know," Mikhail replied. "He's always downplayed his abilities."

Magic nipped at my thigh, and I hissed. Mikhail loosened his hold on me so I could retrieve the coin from my pocket. "It's time. Everyone ready?"

Magos pushed off the wall and carefully lifted a sleeping Jinx off the desk. He'd been quiet for this conversation, which had me worried, but I kept that off my face as I gave him a reassuring smile. There was no hint of madness in his bright copper eyes today. For better or worse, the blood he'd taken from Bryn would hopefully buy us enough time to fix this.

Jinx yawned before nimbly leaping out of Magos' arms and onto the floor. *Finally*, he grumbled.

I focused my magic on the coin, following the thread back to its origin point. The air split in front of me as a gateway opened and I stepped through.

A starless sky greeted us, the full moon glowing brightly between the clouds. We were on a rooftop . . . somewhere. I could smell the salt in the air, so we were close to the ocean. That was all I had time to take in before my gaze fell on the warlocks and vampires waiting for us, and my entire body went still.

Emir had half a dozen warlocks with him, which wasn't a

surprise. Justina and Cassius stood off to the side with a couple of other vampires behind them. Also not a surprise nor the reason blue flames rippled down my arms.

That reason stood about ten feet in front of the others, his silvery grey hair reflecting the moonlight, making it appear paler.

"Hello, Nemain."

Chapter Nine

In the span of two seconds, I had my dual swords out while
Mikhail and Magos vanished into mist, only to reappear
behind Lir with their own blades brandished. Vizor moved
until he stood far enough away from us that, if he shifted, we
wouldn't be crushed under him. To their credit, Andrei and
Stela moved like a unit, fanning out to cover the side opposite
Vizor.

Jinx dropped his glamour and stood to my left, while the
witch remained on my right.

"So tense." Lir laughed, holding up his hands to show he
held no weapons. "I'm not here to fight you, Nemain. It's not
time for that just yet."

"Are you even here right now?" I pointed one of my short
swords at him. "Or is this more illusion bullshit?"

His grin widened. "In the flesh."

I believed him. Lir had no illusion magic of his own; he
relied on warlock magic when he wanted to project his
consciousness elsewhere, which wasn't reliable. Usually his
image flickered in and out, but the Lir in front of me looked

solid, and there was a cruel glint in his eyes that wasn't there in the illusions.

My fingers tightened around the smooth handles of the swords. In terms of enemies, Lir was almost at the top of the list—only the exiled fae king was above him, but Balor was still locked away in his realm. If I took out Lir, Balor's right-hand man, it would solve a lot of our problems.

"If you're thinking about killing me, you should know that my people have orders to slaughter those two vampire boys should you do so." He tilted his head, causing his waist-length hair to spill over his shoulder. "Pretty mermaid is next. Oh, also,"—he snapped his fingers, and dozens of fae warriors appeared around us—"even if you manage to kill me, it's doubtful you'll make it out of here alive."

Fuck. Mikhail caught my attention and shook his head slightly. We'd fight if we had to, but the odds weren't in our favor. If Lir wanted us dead, he would have attacked right away.

My gaze flicked to Emir. "Explain what the fuck this is. Now."

"Lir is doing us the honor of escorting us to the sorcerer realm." His tone was smooth and unbothered, but I didn't miss his stiff posture or the way his fingers clenched into fists for a split second before he forced them to relax. It was possible he was pretending to be upset, though my gut instinct told me Emir hadn't known about this and he wasn't happy about Lir crashing our party.

Should have been more careful in your dealmaking, asshole.

"Why?" I gave Lir a hard stare.

"I have my secrets and you have yours. Like the blood oath between you and Emir." He chuckled darkly. "It has been a great source of entertainment the last few months, watching him try to suss out which of your friends I would be making a move against and warning you. I would have let the two of you continue on for a bit, but alas, I have business to attend to in the sorcerer realm and figured I would hitch a ride, so to speak."

It wasn't long ago that I'd been sitting smugly at a table, gloating over the fact that we'd been several steps ahead of Emir. Now here we all were, realizing Lir had been playing us this whole time. To what end, I had no idea, but we'd need to figure it out fast before he pulled the rug out from under our feet.

The blue flames dancing along my skin flickered chaotically. My magic didn't like the fact that Mikhail was so far away with an enemy between us. I tried to send it soothing thoughts, but that only pissed it off further. Suddenly, the flames vanished . . . and reappeared on Mikhail, coating him in fiery armor.

Double fuck. It wasn't just that my flames had moved from me to him; I could feel my devourer magic stretching itself between us. If I had to summon it to protect myself right now, I wasn't sure I'd be able to.

"Well . . ." Lir looked over his shoulder at Mikhail before turning back to me, a sly, closed-lipped grin on his face. "Isn't that interesting? Fae mate bonds are fickle things—and that's for normal fae. Can't imagine the control problems you'll be having as it settles."

Triple fuck. Quadruple fuck? All. The. Fucks.

Get back here, I ground out.

Faint mist rolled over my skin, and I felt slightly light-headed. Mikhail's panic slammed into me down the bond before my flames came roaring back and burned away the mist. I sucked in a sharp breath, barely stopping myself from taking a step back.

I did my best to put on a bored expression and pretend like both my and Mikhail's magic weren't going haywire at the moment. "I don't know what you're talking about, Lir," I said a little shakily. "Besides, when I kill you—and I absolutely will someday—it's going to be by ramming my sword through your heart and then watching you bleed out at my feet."

"Sure." He gave me a placating look before turning to Emir. "Shall we?"

Emir nodded curtly, then gestured towards me with his hand. One of the warlocks behind him immediately stepped forward and strode towards me, holding out a single black rose.

I took it from him and was surprised at the weight of it. It was made of glass. Impressive, considering how delicate and lifelike it looked. A faint pulse of magic raced over my skin, and I latched on to it, letting my own magic examine it.

Opening gateways was instinct for me; it came from my shifter side, and other than learning how to shift between my feline and human form, it was the first part of my magic that I'd truly controlled. I'd been working on fine-tuning it lately, but opening gateways between realms had always been fairly easy.

This was not.

The air in front of me rippled as I fought to tear open the gateway. It wasn't so much fighting against something . . . more that I was losing my grip on it. Interesting.

"Any day now, Nemain," Emir drawled.

"Blow. Me," I growled as I fought with the realm that kept sliding out of my grasp.

Suddenly, the gateway snapped open, and I stumbled forward—directly through it. Mist spiraled in the air on either side of me before Mikhail and Magos snapped into existence.

I straightened, and the three of us took in the sight.

"Holy shit," Mikhail breathed out.

I stared in disbelief at the city all around us. It was like someone had taken the skyscrapers of the daemon realm and the natural beauty of a fae realm, shaken it all together in a snow globe . . . and then smashed that globe with glee, letting the contents fall randomly across the landscape.

"Is that skyscraper floating?" Mikhail asked. "And . . . rotating?"

I squinted at the building in question because there was really no missing it. Floating about ten stories in the air was indeed a skyscraper. The steel and glass structure was perpendicular to the ground and rotating slowly within a metal framework against a violet night sky.

There was nothing holding any of it up. At least nothing I could see, and given all the activity beneath it, I didn't think there was an invisible support structure at play here.

"It seems that way," I said slowly, my mind still preoccupied with explaining how the fuck they got a building to just hang out in the air like that.

We stood there as the others followed us through the gateway, Jinx immediately throwing his glamour back on before he leapt onto my shoulders. *Do. Not. Like,* he grumbled.

"Right there with you." I tore my gaze away from the skyscraper chilling in the sky to take in the rest of the city. There were dozens of other tall buildings, all lit up with bright lights, but these looked more like normal skyscrapers and were set on the ground with glass bridgeways floating between them. Little gardens were strewn about between some, though there didn't seem to be any rhyme or reason to where they were placed.

This wasn't what I'd been expecting of the sorcerer realm. Granted, I hadn't exactly known what to expect, but definitely not this.

When I'd thought of the sorcerers, I'd assumed they were obsessive, orderly scholars scurrying around in a stone fortress or something, but most of the buildings here were made of glass with some type of metal either coiled around them or making up the structure. I could feel the magic pulsing from them.

There was also the chaos of the staircases. All around us, people in robes walked with purpose up glass stairs that went nowhere. The people—sorcerers, I assumed—would just get to the top of the landings . . . and vanish.

I examined the building closest to us. No doors. Were the stairs how they got in? How was that easier than creating a fucking door?

Andrei, Stela, and Vizor stood to my left on the other side of Magos, all three looking at the city of chaos. If the wolves had been in their animal form, I'm sure their hackles would have been raised. Vizor looked intrigued.

"Fascinating," Lestari said from where she stood to my right, next to Mikhail.

I looked past her to see Emir with his warlocks flanking him while Justina and Cassius stood between us and the warlocks. Interestingly, the vampires were standing a little closer to us than them.

"Shit." I spun, scanning the area. "Where the fuck is Lir?"

"Did he not come through?" Magos peered at the gateway.

"He definitely did," Vizor said, a deep crease forming between his brows as he searched for the missing fae.

"Great." I let out an annoyed breath. "Love that for us."

"I guess Pele's dad was right about nobody caring about us being here," Andrei noted.

"Guess so," I agreed, watching all the sorcerers walk around us, barely acknowledging our existence. Those who did look our way just looked annoyed at our presence, but not enough to stop and say anything about it.

"What exactly did your contact say, Emir?" I looked away from the chaos to the warlock. "Izaak, right?"

Emir frowned. "He didn't really provide any specific instruction."

"Did he provide *any* instruction?" Justina drawled.

"It took months for me to get him to agree to us coming here, and by agree, I mean I found a note that only said one word on my desk. *Fine.* On top of it was that glass black rose with no instructions on how to use it. I was able to determine that it was created with sorcerer magic, and logic said it was from their realm, so I assumed Nemain would be able to open a gateway here." Emir grimaced. "But I also assumed *here* would be the sorcerer's home or place of business."

"Splendid." Justina rolled her eyes before stepping forward onto one of the pathways next to the grassy patch we stood on.

A sorcerer halted before slamming into the vampire, his crimson robe flowing around him, then light brown eyes narrowed on Justina. "Move."

She smiled and gave him a sultry smile. "Could I trouble you for some help?"

"I don't have time for your nonsense," he snapped.

Justina yelped and leapt back onto the grass, rubbing her arms. "Asshole just gave me the worst static shock of my life."

"I think you're losing your touch." Cassius laughed.

"And I think men should be seen and not heard." Justina snapped her fangs at him.

Stela laughed and then caught herself, but not before Justina heard her. The vampire winked at her, and Stela scowled . . . but I thought I saw a faint blush too.

"Yeah, I'm out of patience." I grabbed Jinx from my shoulders and tossed him onto Mikhail's. Both of them grumbled, but I was already stepping off the grass. This time, when I tugged on my devourer magic, it actually obeyed me. A thin layer of blue flames flowed over my skin and clothing while I planted myself in the middle of the walkway and waited.

It didn't take long before a sorcerer with pretty feminine features and big blue eyes stopped and glared at me. "Get out of my way or you'll regret it, cat."

I was a little surprised that she recognized me as a feline shifter. There weren't many of us kicking around these days, and we tended to keep to ourselves. It meant those who could see or sense magic recognized me as a shifter, but not what kind exactly.

"If you try to zap me, you'll be the one regretting things." I let a tendril of blue flames reach out, and her eyes widened before she moved back a small step. "A sorcerer named Izaak invited us here." I held up the black rose. "Where can we find him?"

Her mouth pinched in distaste as she stared at the rose. "Of course Izaak would've been the one to invite the likes of you into our realm." She pointed a perfectly manicured finger towards two large buildings to our right. "Sixth set of stairs down that way."

Before I could ask for any more specifics, she stepped around me and kept going. We'd been here less than ten minutes, and I already wanted to stab everyone. Shame Lir had disappeared on us, then at least my stabbing could have been productive.

"Let's go." I stalked towards the buildings the sorcerer had pointed to, everyone falling in step behind me. Jinx leapt back onto me and settled across my shoulders. The feeling of his tail curling around my throat helped settle me.

The magic here looks and feels wrong, he said quietly into my mind.

What do you mean? I studied the sorcerers and buildings as we walked. Despite being half-fae, I hadn't inherited the ability to see magic, only feel it, and that was more sensing its level of power than anything. Being a grimalkin, Jinx was far more adept at studying magic around us.

It was Vizor who answered. *They're magic thieves*, he said tightly. *Woven into their own magic is that of others. Fae, daemon, and dragon. I can feel the dragon magic calling to my own—it wants to be free.*

The sorcerers aren't our problem. We need to figure out why Lir is here. The staircases the sorcerer had told us about came into view, and I walked a little faster.

I suspected Lir was here on behalf of his king to negotiate with the sorcerers, but I didn't understand why he hadn't just said that. It wasn't exactly a secret that Balor was making alliances with realms that weren't friendly towards the fae queens.

Wide staircases made of a deep purple stone rose twelve feet into the air before simply ending. I stopped at the sixth one and looked at Emir, gesturing my head towards the top. "Assholes, first."

"Charming," he said flatly before striding up the stairs, his foot hesitating for half a second after the last step before he put it down and stepped into nothing.

The warlock vanished from sight.

Damn. Was really hoping it only worked for sorcerers and he would be set on fire or something. Pity.

Emir's warlocks started up the stairs after him, but Mikhail snapped his arm out, his sword appearing in an instant and blocking their path. "You lot go last."

They glared at him, clearly not liking being separated from their leader but also not willing to go up against Mikhail, whose expression said he very much wanted to kill something right now. The warlocks backed up a step. Magos and Vizor went next, Jinx jumping from my shoulder to Magos' at the last second, the vampires following them. Andrei glanced at me, and I nodded, then he tugged Stela up the stairs. Once they were gone, Mikhail dismissed his sword.

"Ready, shifter?"

I smirked. "Always, vampire."

We walked up together and stepped into the unknown.

Chapter Ten

IT FELT like my body was pulled apart and then slammed back together. Even though I'd stepped into empty air, my foot was very much on something solid right now. I had no idea what that *something* was because my eyes were still squeezed shut on account of me trying very hard not to empty my stomach's contents.

Someone next to me had lost that battle.

"Fuck," Justina gagged before heaving again.

"You good?" Mikhail asked me while he gently rubbed my back, his voice sounding a little rough. Apparently he hadn't liked that teleportation either.

"Mm-hmm." I slowly cracked open one eye and then the other. We were on a stone patio. Directly in front of us, a large archway made of light brown stone led inside. Both werewolves leaned against the wall next to the archway, looking a little pale. In fact, the only one who didn't look bothered by the trip was Cassius.

The four warlocks popped into existence after us.

"Oh shit." One of them—a young man with shaggy blond

hair—bolted for the railing, making it just in time before hurling.

My nose wrinkled at the sight, my own stomach still very much not settled, but then I looked beyond the sick warlock, and my eyes widened. No way. I darted towards the elegant fence wrapped around the balcony and peered over it.

"We're floating," I whispered in awe.

Wispy clouds glided in the dark purple sky around us, and I was pretty sure I could make out the city we'd just been in to the east, although it could be a different one. I leaned forward a little more on the railing, looking down. We had to be a good half mile above the ground.

"Nemain, please step back," Magos pleaded.

Strong arms wrapped around my waist and tugged me away from the railing. "I know you love heights, love"—Mikhail spun me around to face him, the purple in his eyes looking brighter here—"but let's not give my uncle a heart attack."

"Vizor is my stand-in bestie for this adventure." I turned and waved at the dragon, who sat on the railing, one foot planted on it with his knee bent and the other leg dangling off the side. "He's obligated to catch me if I fall."

"You know I hate you, right?" Vizor arched a brow at me.

"You know I wish you were Eddie, right?" I arched a brow back at him.

"Ha!" Justina straightened, wiping her mouth with the back of her hand. "Told you he was a dragon!"

Cassius rolled his eyes at her before turning and frowning at Vizor. "Damn. I really thought you were one of those winged fae."

My interest was piqued as Cassius and Justina continued to argue. The only winged fae I knew of were the sciathán, and that was only because of Niall. He was the first—and only—one I'd ever met. The fae queens had wiped them out in these realms because they were loyal to Balor. It had happened long ago, before my parents had become involved with the queens.

Other than Niall, the only sciatháin left were in the realm Balor was currently locked in. Either Justina was talking about Niall, which seemed unlikely because they'd never interacted and he usually kept his wings hidden, or some of the sciatháin had managed to get past the ward keeping them contained to Balor's realm.

That wasn't good for a whole bunch of reasons. Niall was a lethal fighter, so the last thing we needed was the bad guy version of him complicating matters. The bigger concern was that the ward containing Balor was weakening. It had been for some time now, and the queens had been trying to patch the holes as they formed, but that didn't seem like a long-term strategy for success.

Cassius and Justina suddenly stopped talking, and all four vampires snapped their heads towards the hallway. A second later, I heard the sound of hurried footsteps coming our way.

"Ah, you made it." A man came in wearing a worn robe that had probably been black at one point but was now more of a faded, greyish brown. Deep grooves lined his face, but his green eyes were bright and alert. "Expected you a week ago. What took you so long?"

"Izaak, I presume?" Emir stirred from where he'd been standing off to the side with his warlocks.

"Mm-hmm," Izaak responded in a somewhat dismissive tone as his gaze skipped around everyone gathered on the balcony before stopping on Mikhail. Then his thick eyebrows rose. "Well, aren't you interesting . . ."

He studied Mikhail the way a starved wolf pack looked at a herd of deer.

Creep alert, Jinx whispered into my mind.

No shit, I mentally hissed back.

I felt my magic surge forward protectively and barely

managed to yank it back. The last thing I needed was to put our weird mate bond on display and make the sorcerer even more interested in Mikhail. We'd been in this realm for less than half an hour, and I already wanted out. Ramil had been right; it felt *wrong* here.

We needed to take care of our business, leave, and never return.

"This is the vampire I told you about," Emir said confidently. "He has the ability to walk in the sun, and that is something we would like to extend to other select vampires. Amongst other things." He glanced at me. "Perhaps we can continue this conversation privately inside."

"Yes, yes, yes. Of course," the sorcerer said in a quick, excited tone. "This is my home. Please, come with me." Izaak gave Mikhail one last lookover before striding inside, his long grey hair fluttering behind him. He might have looked like he was in his seventies, but he sure didn't move like it.

Emir followed him, the four warlocks whose names I still didn't know—and didn't really care to know, if I was being honest—went with them. Cassius and Justina shared a look before doing the same, and we walked a few paces behind everyone else, Vizor on my left and Andrei on my right. Behind us were Stela and Lestari with Mikhail and Magos guarding all our backs. Jinx slunk along the wall slightly ahead of us.

The inside of the sorcerer's home was made of a dark mahogany wood that had pearly white lines carved into it, creating an elegant, geometric pattern.

We walked further into the house, and I kept glancing at the walls. Every time I did, the hair on the back of my neck raised a little more, but I couldn't pinpoint exactly what was causing the reaction.

I parted my lips and inhaled a deep breath to better parse the scents. Just as I realized why the walls were causing my instincts to go haywire, Izaak stopped.

"Here we are." He gestured to the two doors on either side of the hallway. "These are the only guest quarters I have made up, I'm afraid. I don't get many visitors."

Emir looked at one of his warlocks, a tall, slender woman with dark brown skin. She looked like one of the characters from the legal dramas Elisa loved to watch. Black hair fell to her shoulders in tight spirals, gleaming against the cream silk blouse she wore tucked into high-waisted navy slacks.

"Aisha, with me. The rest of you, wait in the room." The three warlocks filed in without a word, although the blond man gave Aisha a dirty look on the way.

"Shouldn't we go with you?" Justina politely asked. "After all, we're here to represent our people."

"We both know that's not exactly true." Emir gave her a condescending smile. "I'll handle it."

Justina's expression remained unbothered by the rebuke as she merely nodded graciously before stepping into the room. Cassius frowned at the walls, a faint crease between his brows.

"Something wrong, Cassius?" Emir asked, a hint of impatience in his voice.

Suddenly, an easygoing grin spread across Cassius' face. "Nah, just admiring the beautiful decor. I'll leave you to it." He moved into the room, but not before giving me a weighted look.

Yep. He knew what was in the walls too.

"When you're finished negotiating with Emir," Lestari spoke up, "we would also like to speak with you."

"Fine, but it better not be a waste of my time," Izaak replied shortly before heading up the stairs at the end of the hallway, Emir and Aisha going with him.

We filed into our room, Magos coming in last and shutting the door behind him. After he closed it, he opened it again, just to make sure it hadn't locked. Knowing that we could leave anytime seemed to quell some of the tension amongst the group, myself included.

The room was mostly empty with a few chairs scattered in one corner and two large beds in the others. Not a hint of food or water to be seen. I found myself missing fae hospitality. Sure, they may have been plotting against us the second we strode through the door, but at least the fae were polite about it and fed us first.

Vizor pulled an orb out of his pocket and motioned us towards him. We all took a couple of steps closer, and once we stood in a half circle around him, he held up the light pink glass ball, which started to glow faintly.

"Silence ward," he explained. "This one's fae-made from Eddie's shop."

Even though Eddie was busy helping build the new dragon realm, he still operated his shop in Emerald Bay, selling magical items. Most were rare artifacts or items needed for advanced spellcrafting. It was his way of staying relevant in the human realm's magic scene. He had garnered a reputation for being able to procure hard-to-find items and often requested information for them rather than money.

"Eddie's going to be pissed at you for stealing shit from his shop," I pointed out.

"Don't go snitching on me, and he'll never know," Vizor said snidely. "I don't understand most of the magic in these walls, so I suggest we use this while we're inside as much as possible. Otherwise, speak quietly or telepathically."

"Does anyone else recognize what the white lines are made of?" I looked around, and everyone shook their heads. "Bones," I said with a grimace.

Vizor rubbed the lower half of his face. "That makes sense. Bones can be preserved to retain traces of the magic of whatever being they belonged to. It's not as much as blood or organs, but bones can be ground down, which results in a higher concentration of magic. The magic I see in the walls is a mix. There's definitely fae and daemon there, but at least half a dozen other types as well that I'm not familiar with."

"What the fuck did you drag us into, witch?" Stela growled at Lestari. "You made the sorcerers sound like scholarly mages, not psychopaths who grind up bones and decorate their walls with it!"

"I told you that little was known about the sorcerers." Lestari gave the pissed-off werewolf an even stare. "Nothing has changed. If the vampires grow in power, they will wipe the werewolves out for good."

"And then Emir will use them against the witches," Andrei pointed out. His expression was tense, but he seemed to be keeping his cool better than his sister.

"Look, creepiness aside"—I held up my hands in a placating gesture—"our plan remains. We'll speak with Izaak about both Magos' curse and the werewolves. If he refuses to help us, we'll get the name of the sorcerer who made the werewolves and negotiate with them. With any luck, we'll be out of here in a day or two."

"What're we going to do about Lir?" Magos asked.

Good fucking question.

"I don't know," I said with a sigh and looked out the window to where I could see the skyscraper rotating in the distance. "He sprung this on Emir as much as he did us, and then he vanished as soon as we made it to this realm."

"Didn't bring any backup either," Mikhail added. "He wants to be quiet and unnoticed."

"Since he used you to get here, maybe he'll be stuck in this realm without us?" Andrei mused.

"I don't see Lir going into a situation where he doesn't have an exit strategy." I chewed on my lip before shaking my head. "Whatever he's up to, I doubt it's good for us, but there's nothing we can do about it currently." I turned my attention away from the window and back to the others. "We'll tackle Izaak and the sorcerers first, then Lir."

"So what do we do now?" Andrei asked.

"We wait." I looked at the door. "And hope Emir isn't fucking us over."

We waited for over an hour. I thought about going out to explore but decided against it. Given that Izaak had personally escorted us here, it seemed clear he wanted us to stay in the room. Normally, I wouldn't give a shit about etiquette, but we needed his help, so I remained. The others were preoccupied with the sorcerer's magic.

Both Stela and Andrei were on edge. Werewolves couldn't see magic, nor did they have the sensitivity to feel it like I did, but they still had preternatural instincts, which were telling them to get the fuck out of this place.

The bone pattern from the hallway extended into the room, and both Lestari and Vizor studied it. Like warlocks, witches couldn't see magic without help. She must have either cast a spell on herself or had some type of artifact on her that allowed her to see it, because she and Vizor had been chatting about magical theory nonstop for the last fifteen minutes, and she would occasionally point out spots on the wall to back up her theory.

Oddly, Vizor welcomed Lestari's input and was being at least fifty percent less dickish than usual. Most of what they discussed was way over my head, but the general consensus seemed to be that the magic within the walls wasn't actively doing anything. It merely existed.

Assuming they were correct, that meant the sorcerer wanted a well of power to draw from whenever he needed, and there was a shit ton of magic here to use. We'd only seen a small portion of the structure, but it'd looked like a miniature castle from where we'd been on the balcony. I assumed it was at least three stories and ten thousand square feet. If the bone pattern extended the entire way through that, then the amount of magic just waiting here to be used was insane.

Not to mention *how* he'd managed to collect this many bones, because ground down, bones actually didn't take up that much space. So we weren't talking about the bones of hundreds of magical beings . . . we were talking about thousands.

The sound of someone approaching came from outside our room, and seconds later, the door opened, revealing Aisha.

She walked in confidently, and I couldn't help but be reminded of Pele. The warlock didn't really look anything like my best friend. It was more of the way she carried herself. Confident with a no-nonsense vibe. She even wore a tailored suit like Pele, only hers was human-made, not daemon-made. A colorful red and orange scarf was wrapped around her head.

For half a second, Aisha's honey-brown eyes connected with Lestari's deep brown ones. It was too fast for me to analyze, but I filed it away to ponder later. I'd encountered few female warlocks; most human women who could perform magic joined the witches, either because they believed in the witches' mantra of balance or because they couldn't stomach the misogynistic bullshit of the warlock leadership.

Emir had chosen Aisha to come with him while meeting with the sorcerer though, so somehow, she had risen through the ranks.

Her sharp, intelligent gaze fell on me. "Your presence is requested."

Andrei and Stela took a step forward but halted when the warlock held up her hand. "Just Nemain and the vampires."

"Fuck that," Stela growled. "We're not going to ju—"

"Give us a minute," I said to Aisha, cutting Stela's tirade off.

Aisha simply nodded and left the room. As soon as the door closed, I gave Vizor a pointed look, and he walked towards the center of the room and took out the fae silencing orb again.

"Look, I'm not a fan of us being split up either," I said once everyone had crowded around Vizor again and the magic was activated. "But we don't have a lot of options here because we need Izaak's help."

"Neither he nor any other sorcerers have directly threatened us," Magos added calmly. "I understand that their magic might feel . . . off-putting, but perhaps we should refrain from jumping to any conclusions before we know more."

"What?" Vizor scoffed. "You think Izaak just asked the fae, daemons, and dragons nicely for the bodies of their dead?" The deep amber of Vizor's eyes burned like fire as smoke curled from his nostrils. "And that they gave up the remains of their loved ones so that the magic contained within their bones could be twisted into something unnatural?"

"Vizor, if you want to burn this house down, I'm game." I shrugged, because honestly, I wouldn't blame him. The longer we'd been here, the more the wrongness of this house had seeped into my skin. "But *after* we get what we need from the sorcerer."

"Fine." The smoke dissipated, and the fire burning in his eyes dimmed. "I'll go with you to this meeting. One of the vampires should stay though."

Mikhail glared at the door where the warlock waited on the other side before turning his attention to me. No doubt he was thinking the same as me. It made sense for Magos to come with me so the sorcerer could examine the magic of the curse . . . and because more than once, I'd caught Magos looking at the werewolves with hunger in his eyes.

Bryn's blood might be tiding him over for now, but the presence of the werewolves was chipping away at that. Leaving him alone with them and the witch with only Jinx to keep him under control didn't seem wise.

I pursed my lips together. We might need Izaak's help, but I sure as shit didn't trust him or this freaky house. Not to mention Emir's people in the room across from us.

"We're not defenseless." Andrei crossed his arms.

"I know you're not," I assured him, ignoring the way Mikhail snorted. "But if we have to split up, it doesn't make sense for the strongest fighters to all be in one group." I chewed on my bottom lip. Vizor had to come with me. Aisha wouldn't like that, but he was with me, not Lestari and the wolves, so I was confident she wouldn't push back too hard.

My magic shifted unhappily beneath my skin, small flickers of blue flames blinking into existence across my arms. Everyone glanced at them, but no one commented.

"Jinx and Mikhail will stay." I looked to where Jinx still studied the walls and pushed out my thoughts. *If anything seems even the tiniest bit off after we leave, let us know. We're not going far, so I should still be able to hear you. Vizor definitely will.*

Same goes for you. Jinx swung his head towards me. *If something doesn't feel right, you get your ass back here.*

I gave him a quick nod before heading towards the door. "Let's go."

The crystal blue flames dancing along my arms started to shift in color, losing some of the blue and becoming more translucent. I slowed, frowning at my magic because I'd never seen it change colors before. Suddenly, the fire gave way to mist, and it felt like somebody reached inside me, gripped my spine, and yanked me back.

I blinked, stumbling a couple of steps before steadying myself. I was no longer standing by the door, but back next to Vizor, who hadn't put away the silencing orb yet.

"What the fuck?" I hissed and looked down at the wisps of mist still rolling off me.

"Did you just . . ." Andrei cocked his head in a purely lupine gesture, his hazel eyes darting between me and Mikhail. "Did you just use his magic?"

Mikhail looked at me from where he stood halfway to the door. My magic surged and blue flames erupted between us, wrapping around my wrist and his.

"I don't think our magic approves of us being apart," he said slowly. I could tell he was as shaken up as I was but trying to hide it. His magic might be less destructive and dangerous than mine, but what if I vanished into mist in the middle of defending someone? I could leave Andrei or Stela wide open to attack. What if Magos lost control of his thirst, and before I could contain him, I was ripped away?

The fear of how wrong this could go superseded any excitement I might feel about using each other's magic. We needed time to get this under control.

But we didn't have time.

Mikhail closed the distance between us, and I could practically feel my magic breathe a sigh of relief. Some of the tension bled from Mikhail's face, and I suspected he felt something similar.

"Change of plans," I said reluctantly. "Mikhail's coming too."

We'd just have to hope there was no trap, and if there was, that Jinx would alert us in time.

"It would be unfortunate if Izaak learned about the strangeness of the mate bond between the two of you, given the interest he's already expressed in the vampire." Lestari gave me a pointed look.

Guess I wasn't the only one who noticed Izaak practically drooling over Mikhail earlier.

"I know." I held her stare, but out of the corner of my eye,

I saw my flames die down and felt my magic coil into my chest. For a split second, I considered dusting off the metaphorical chains I'd kept around it for most of my life and putting them to use again, but I squashed that idea almost immediately. Up until the last few years, my magic had been incredibly volatile because of those chains. If I tried to do that now . . . it would react badly.

No. Mikhail and I just had to be careful to mitigate the reasons our magic would misbehave. Right now, we were both on high alert, which meant our magic was hyperaware of any possible danger. We'd need to stick together as much as possible for the foreseeable future.

"There's never been a mate bond such as yours before," Lestari continued as if I wasn't already fucking aware of that fact. "Given the different types of magic stored in these walls, it seems likely that Izaak would be *very* interested in a new type."

"I know," I snapped. "We'll keep it under control."

Doubt shone in her dark eyes, but she didn't comment any further, which was good because my patience was running thin and I had to deal with Izaak and Emir next. Hopefully Vizor could earn his keep by doing most of the talking and just letting me know if I needed to stab somebody.

Gods, I would give Justina's left kidney to stab someone right now.

A polite but firm knock sounded from the door.

"Alright." I let out a long, steady breath. "Let's try this again."

This time, when I walked towards the door, Mikhail by my side, our magic behaved themselves. Magos moved after us, a silent shadow. I was trying not to dwell on how quiet he was being and what that might mean. I felt a small pop between my ears as Vizor turned off the silencer spell and followed us into the hallway.

Cassius and Justina stood just outside their door. They both looked tense, and it made me suspicious about what they'd been discussing with the warlocks while they'd been waiting.

Aisha raised a perfectly sculpted brow at Vizor.

I shrugged. "He's coming with us."

She matched my shrug, turned on her heel, and strode up the stairs. A woman of few words, apparently.

"After you." Cassius gave me a charming smile and made a sweeping gesture towards the stairwell.

As if I would let him at our backs.

"No." I grinned wide enough for my fangs to show. "After you."

"We insist." Mikhail drawled from my side.

Justina sighed and marched up the stairs, but Cassius lingered a moment, pondering us both. "What a pair the two of you make." This time when he smiled, there was a mocking edge to it. "One might even describe it as rare . . . and coveted."

Well, that doesn't bode well, Vizor's voice rasped in my mind.

No shit, Sherlock, I growled back.

Who's Sherlock?

I gave him a withering look before striding after the others, patience officially gone.

Chapter Eleven

"ABOUT TIME," Emir grumbled as soon as we entered. Aisha continued walking and took a seat to his right at the large round table that took up most of the space. Justina had been a step ahead of Cassius, but she slowed just enough that he had to sit next to Emir—something he gave her a dirty look for.

I surveyed the room, mostly to look for exits. There were none. The only door was the one we'd come through, and there were no windows. Between that and the massive table, the room felt cramped.

Vizor took a seat directly opposite Emir and Aisha, his shoulders tense. Dragons constructed their buildings to have a lot of windows and large balconies. Interior hallways and rooms were made wide enough to at least feel more open. Between the creepy magic and being surrounded by walls with not a hint of sky to be seen, he was no doubt a very unhappy dragon right now.

Well . . . unhappier than normal.

I plopped down into a chair next to him while Mikhail and Magos remained standing directly behind me.

Izaak looked at us from where he sat between everyone. His

shrewd eyes studied Vizor as if he was seeing him for the first time, but after five seconds, his gaze immediately went to Mikhail before narrowing and looking at me . . . then back at Mikhail.

I gave him a lazy smile, even as my heart pounded faster. Could he see just how unusual the mate bond was between us? Or did he just think it was odd that a vampire was mated to a half-fae?

"Sorry for our tardiness," I said evenly, my tone not giving away a hint of the stress I was feeling. "Mikhail was doing his hair."

My vampire mate let out a raspy chuckle. "Always so jealous that I'm prettier than you."

"Should we assume that you and the sorcerer have come to an agreement?" Vizor asked Emir in a bored tone. "And let me guess? You require assistance from us on said agreement?"

Emir's eyes narrowed on me. "Letting the dragon speak for you?"

"He really loves the sound of his own voice, so I figured I'd let him have this one." I shrugged.

The corners of Emir's eyes tightened. He'd likely been planning on outmaneuvering me during this negotiation, steering me in the direction he wanted and cutting off other options. I could be clever when I needed to be, but I lacked the patience for wordplay and had no problem admitting it was a weakness of mine. Mikhail was better, but Vizor rivaled Pele for cunningness. And Vizor was a complete unknown to Emir. The warlock was still staring at me, so I smiled widely. *Good luck trying to pull one over on a dragon.*

"There are some things Izaak needs in order to adjust to the original magic that was used to create the vampires. Some of it I can obtain." Emir clasped his hands and rested them on the table, focusing on Vizor. "The rest will be collected by Nemain."

"What precisely do you need Nemain to collect?" Vizor tilted his head. "And where will she be doing this?"

It was Izaak who responded. "I'll need some live specimens of the chimmeris, the devourer species I used for the original spell." He started counting on his fingers, nodding slightly. "A dozen should do."

That's suicide, I told Vizor telepathically. *I've been to that realm. Once. It's crawling with devourers, and they are cunning and vicious.*

Sounds like your kind of place, he noted.

Even I have some sanity left. I held back a shudder. A predator I might be, but I hadn't been on the top of the food chain in that realm. Not by a long shot.

"The blood oath you have with Nemain stipulates that you cannot require her to put her life in direct jeopardy for you. That extends to the people she listed in the contract," Vizor recounted calmly. Pele kept a copy of the blood oath in her desk, and he'd studied it before we'd left.

"I'm perfectly aware of what the blood oath dictates," Emir said evenly. "But while it might be dangerous, the sorcerers managed to capture these creatures. Are you really suggesting that Nemain, who has faced down numerous types of devourers, the Olympians, and Balor's general, is not up to the task?"

"How did you capture the creatures before?" I turned to Izaak, who was staring off into nothing.

"Hmm?" He blinked and looked at me.

"How," I repeated slowly, "did you get the devourers from that realm?"

"Oh." Thick eyebrows bunched together. "I gathered some of the less promising sorcerers and told them I was offering a free seminar. The devourers pounced on them quickly, and while they feasted, I took what I needed." Izaak frowned. "Got in some trouble for that one. Those they were apprenticed to didn't like losing their free labor, so I can't use that approach again. Personally, I don't see what they were so upset about. I did them a favor by getting rid of those who would never amount to anything."

"How considerate of you," I deadpanned.

Izaak nodded sagely.

You were right before, Vizor whispered into my mind. *Eddie definitely should have been here. Could have used his dumb ass for bait.*

Don't talk about my bestie like that. I inhaled deeply before breathing out through my nose. *Just get him to agree to help Magos and the werewolves. Or if he can't help the wolves, at least give us the name of the sorcerer who can. Then we'll figure out how to get the damn devourers.*

What happened to that being a suicide mission?

Unfortunately for us, we don't really have a choice. Because if Izaak needs the original vampiric devourers, then it seems within reason that the sorcerer who made the werewolves will need the same.

You care that much for the wolves? Curiosity laced his words.

No. I care about Andrei. I won't lose him.

So kindhearted. It's going to get you killed one day.

And giving opinions nobody asked for is going to get you killed. Just get the insane sorcerer to agree.

"By the terms of the blood oath, you cannot force Nemain to help you with this." Vizor held one hand up, cutting off Emir's instant rebuttal. "However, Nemain is willing to assist in the collection of what is needed for the vampires, but we request two things in exchange. First, the sorcerer is to remove the curse on Magos. And second, he will correct some of the issues that have arisen with the werewolves."

"The werewolves are a poor imitation of my creation." Izaak's mouth puckered like he'd just bitten into something sour. "It was a poorly thought-out spell, which is why they are lesser beings."

"That's nice," I said flatly. "You're still going to fix them."

"Even if I wanted to, which I don't, it's not possible." He

flicked his hand dismissively, the thick rings on his fingers reflecting the warm light. "I'm able to manipulate the magic of vampires because I created it. It might be a few centuries past, but I can still follow the pathway of what I did. My former apprentice was always chaotic in her spell crafting. I tried to teach her to follow a different path, but she refused to listen, which is why she's no longer my apprentice and why the werewolves are a disaster."

Damn it. I'd known this was a possibility, but I was really hoping we'd only have to deal with one sorcerer.

"So we need to discuss this with your former apprentice," Vizor said, undeterred. "Where can we find her?"

"We don't have time for this," Emir said sharply.

"Allowing them a few hours to see if they can figure something out won't be the end of the world." Justina played with the ends of her silky hair.

Well, that was unexpected. What would she have to gain from speaking up for the werewolves?

She wants something, I said to Vizor.

Look at that. You're not entirely hopeless after all. Vizor chuckled in my mind before addressing Emir. "We've already established that you need Nemain to capture the creatures for the vampires and that she is under no obligation to help you, but if you think you can do this without her, then we're not stopping you." Vizor leaned back in his chair, looking like he couldn't care less, and waved a hand towards Emir. "Have fun catching those devourers on your own."

"Fine," Emir ground out. "Three hours. No more."

"We'll take whatever time we need," Vizor said dismissively. "Now, if you'll excuse us, we need to discuss the first part of our request with the sorcerer."

"Ah, yes." Emir smiled. "That pesky curse. There's no breaking it, but it is amusing what you all so desperately try."

With that, the warlock rose, Aisha and the vampires got up

with him, and the four of them exited the room. Cassius winked at me on the way out, which caused Mikhail to growl under his breath.

If I were a betting woman—which I totally was—I'd put very slim odds on Cassius making it out of this alive if he kept flirting with me.

"Where can we find your former apprentice?" I asked.

"She lives in the city you arrived in, just outside the center." He paused, and for a moment, looked mildly scandalized. "Thaxea considers herself an artist these days. Her front yard is full of sculptures."

Thaxea. I noted the name in case we had to ask around when we got down there. Speaking of which . . .

"How do we get back to the city?" I asked.

"Balcony to the left of the one you came in on." He pushed away from the table and rose. I waited for more information, but apparently, that was all he was giving us. Awesome. Worstcase, if we couldn't figure it out, we could ask Vizor to give us a ride down . . . and hope he didn't do a barrel roll.

"We still have the matter of the curse on my uncle," Mikhail said, smoothly stepping in front of the sorcerer before he made it to the door.

"Mmm?" Izaak looked at Mikhail like he wanted to peel back his flesh and see what made him tick.

My magic stirred, a vicious edge to it, and the bond between Mikhail and me went taut. Oh shit. I practically knocked my chair over as I leapt to my feet and moved to stand next to Mikhail before my magic—or his—put on a display in front of the damn sorcerer.

Mikhail slid his hand into mine, our fingers intertwining, and instantly, our bond settled. My magic, on the other hand, was still tightly coiled, like a snake getting ready to strike.

"Our first requirement for assisting in the capturing of the chimmeris is for you to look at our friend," Vizor explained, drawing the sorcerer's attention away from me and Mikhail. "A powerful being laid a curse on him. We need it removed."

I let out a quiet, relieved breath when Izaak moved towards where Magos stood stiffly next to the table. Mikhail glanced over his shoulder at Magos.

"Curses are tricky." Izaak moved closer to Magos, ancient eyes scanning him like he could see the curse wound around his soul. "This is lovely work," the sorcerer murmured, admiration clear in his tone. "Who did it?"

Mikhail's fingers tightened around mine before he answered, "Artemis. One of the Olympians."

"Ah, yes. It's been so long since I've seen her work, but she always was quite talented." Izaak's gaze seemed to settle on Magos' heart. "So intricate," he murmured.

"Can you break it?" Magos asked quietly.

"It's possible." Izaak snapped out of his admiration and took a step back to fully face me and Mikhail. "I'll need to do some research and gather some things, but I should be ready when you return from the devourer realm."

"And what is your price?" Vizor asked. I hadn't even heard him get up, but he stood next to Magos now.

"A full forty-eight hours to study this one." Izaak waved a hand at Mikhail. "And to examine the mating bond he has with this one." He flicked some fingers in my direction, answering my question about whether or not he could see it.

"No," Magos replied at the same time Mikhail and I said, "Deal."

Since Izaak had already seen our bond and was intrigued by it, it was something we could barter with. I was fairly sure he didn't know just how powerful it was or that we could share magic with each other; otherwise, he would have expressed slightly more interest in me.

We just needed to play it off as a quirky but still normal, boring fae mating bond, and he'd hopefully lose interest.

This is a bad idea, Vizor whispered into my mind. *There is no way that sorcerer will be content to merely study the magic between you two. He'll try to take it.*

So we get him to fix Magos first and then we kill him, I growled.

You're the Unseelie Knight, Vizor reminded me. *It will very likely cause problems with the fae if you do that.*

Then we'll kill those problems too.

"No, Nemain," Magos said firmly. "I won't agree to this."

I bit back a growl of frustration.

Fine.

"Two dozen," I ground out and looked at the sorcerer. "We'll capture two dozen chimmeris for you."

Izaak smiled widely. "You have a deal."

"Fuck, I really don't like that." I clutched at my stomach and swallowed the bile that tried to rise.

I wasn't sure if it was better or worse having no warning about the whole magical transporting thing.

"Same." Stela panted from where she was still bent over, Andrei rubbing her back sympathetically while looking a little pale himself.

"This is not where we were previously." Magos looked around before glancing up at the rotating skyscraper above us. "And that is a different side of the frame. I would guess that the city center is directly beneath it."

"Let's head that way then. We can always ask one of the super helpful sorcerers if we get lost," I said wryly.

There were less sorcerers wandering around than we'd seen on our arrival. I didn't know if it was because it was past midnight or if they just didn't come to this section of the city much. Just like before, the ones who were here completely ignored us, like we weren't even worth their acknowledgement.

"We'll be right behind you," Andrei said as Stela heaved again. Lestari muttered something under her breath and rummaged through the leather satchels she kept tied to her belt.

Jinx, stay with them? We won't get too far ahead, but I don't want to wait around. I felt anxious but couldn't pinpoint why exactly.

Dogsitting duty. Wonderful. So glad I came, he grumbled, but sat on his haunches, away from the puking werewolf.

I'll get you all the sushi when we get home, I promised before heading towards what was hopefully the center of the city. At least the floating monstrosity made for an easy reference point.

"Any idea what Vizor is doing?" Mikhail asked as he fell into step beside me.

"No." I sighed.

The dragon had declared he would be staying behind while we went on this search for the sorcerer's apprentice. I hadn't been particularly happy about that because if he got his ass killed, Lynette would be devastated. Nobody wanted a sad Lynette, but when I'd told Vizor he was coming with us whether he wanted to or not, he'd simply said, *"Strange. Despite the underlying growl in your voice, I don't feel the slightest bit threatened."*

Then he'd strolled off down a hallway.

"Cassius and Justina are up to something," Mikhail said quietly. "There's no way Vizor hasn't picked up on that."

"That would make sense, I suppose." I thought about my next words carefully. Both of those vampires were clearly a sore spot for Mikhail, and while I wanted—and needed—to know more about them, I didn't want to push too hard. "There have always been different factions within the Vampire Council. Perhaps they're making a power play."

Given that the faction with the most power was Magnus and his bloodline, it was in our best interest if someone took them down a peg, or at least weakened their power base.

"They've always hated each other though." Mikhail ran a

hand through his dark hair, his lips pressed into a hard line as he thought about it. "Or at least . . . I thought they did."

"Maybe that's what they always wanted people to think. That they were two factions, when in reality, it was one faction working together towards a common goal from different angles." It would've been a sneaky, underhanded tactic that felt absolutely right for vampire politics, or for the fae . . . or the daemons.

There was a reason I found politics so exhausting.

"It could be a more recent alliance," Magos said thoughtfully. "In which case, their antagonistic history would help with any suspicion."

"I'd be more inclined to believe that idea." A wry smile graced Mikhail's lips. "They've both tried to kill each other in the past and came quite close to succeeding on more than one occasion. I don't think their acting is *that* good. Something must have changed in the Vampire Council to force them to work together."

We made our way through a small patch of garden before walking beside a tall, rectangular building. The wall was made of a dull reflective silver . . . only, our reflections weren't in it. I glanced to my left, where some tall flowers rose on bright blue stems, their yellow petals stretched towards the sky, and then back at the building.

The hairs on the back of my neck rose as I looked at the perfectly reflected flowers. It was as if the mirror-like wall swallowed us whole. This realm was fucked.

"The enemy of our enemy could be our friend," Magos mused.

"We're never that lucky." I glanced over my shoulder and saw Jinx trotting ahead of Andrei and Stela a short distance from us. "We'll have to see if Vizor is willing to share with the class when we get back. If he's an ass about what he learned, I'll tell Jinx to give him bad luck for the rest of his miserable life. Something low-key that Lynette wouldn't complain about too much."

"Such a kindhearted soul you are." Mikhail grinned at me.

"Blow me."

He smiled wider.

Ignoring my obnoxious mate, I turned to Magos. "How are you feeling?"

He didn't answer right away, and his expression turned pensive with a hint of sorrow. "I thought Bryn's blood would last longer, but I think the curse is getting worse, or it's just the presence of the wolves. The pull of their blood is strong. It's more difficult to be around them than I thought it would be."

An icy dread rose in my gut, and I could feel a similar reaction down the bond from Mikhail. Both of us kept it off our faces though.

If everything went according to plan, we'd all be going to a realm full of lethal predators, where our fight-or-flight responses would be on high for the entire duration. Not a good place for a vampire on the verge of losing control over his bloodlust.

But it's not like we could leave Magos behind. One, he wouldn't let us, and even if he did, either Mikhail or I would need to stay with him to ensure he didn't hurt anyone else.

Harming Bryn had shaken Magos to his core. If he killed someone innocent . . . he'd never come back from that.

I had to go to this godsforsaken realm, and if I wanted to survive, I needed Mikhail by my side.

"You don't have to hold on much longer," I promised, even though I had nothing to back that up with other than sheer willpower and a very sharp sword. What was it Misha always said? *Fake it till you make it.* "We'll find Izaak's ex-apprentice, and then we'll get her to hel—" I stopped in my tracks. That damn feeling I'd felt earlier. That strange uneasiness I'd brushed aside. How had I not recognized it for what it was?

Sloppy, Nemain. Really fucking sloppy, I chided myself.

"What is it?" Mikhail asked in a low, dangerous tone.

Nemain? Jinx's voice rumbled through my mind, and I could hear him catching up to us with the wolves.

"I sense devourer magic," I said softly. "Feels like the fae devourers."

Kalen had taught me many things about my devourer nature, one of them was to let tendrils of my magic stretch out around me like a thin web across the ground. It was so faint, the flames didn't manifest, and I couldn't actually do anything with it, but it was great for sensing nearby magic.

The problem was that it was easy to fall into the habit of ignoring it. After a while, it became almost like background noise. It didn't help that my magic was preoccupied with Mikhail and I had a million thoughts swirling around in my head.

"Lir?" Mikhail guessed.

"Maybe . . ." I pursed my lips. "He doesn't actually have that much magic, so it's harder for me to detect him. This feels like too much to be him."

We were lucky this area of the city wasn't busier. There were a few sorcerers here and there, but it was easy for me to skip over their magic signatures. I pushed a little further.

There.

"Got 'em. Definitely fae devourers, and there's more than one. At least thirteen, maybe more I haven't found yet."

"Lir came alone," Magos noted. "And if he were meeting his people here, it stands to reason that he wouldn't have needed to hitch a ride with us."

"I know." I opened my eyes and frowned in the direction I'd felt the magic. "They're not coming towards us. It's hard for me to gauge their exact location, but I think they're maybe a quarter mile away and rapidly putting distance between us." I tilted my head, trying to envision where they were based on their magical imprint. "They're divided into two groups, like they're flanking something . . . and they're moving fast."

"They're hunting," Mikhail said quietly.

"Why have we stopped?" Stela halted a few feet away from us, Andrei and Lestari at her side.

"There are fae devourers here, and we don't think they're with Lir," I explained. Jinx trotted over to me and leapt onto my shoulders. It wasn't like him to be this clingy. I suspected the magic of the sorcerer realm was really freaking him out but he didn't want to admit it.

"Aren't all fae devourers with Lir?" Andrei gave me a puzzled look. "He's Balor's main guy, right?"

"Factions," Mikhail muttered before his midnight eyes cut to me. "Remember Ashling telling us about that other fae woman? Syndra? She seems to have it in for Lir."

"Right." I nodded slowly. "The one whose face I wore."

"Come again?" Stela frowned.

I waited for someone to say "phrasing," but tragically, nobody did. Eddie wouldn't have let that one slide. Nor would Elisa, especially if Bryn was in the room. Elisa never missed an opportunity to make the brawny valkyrie blush.

"We helped out the Merfolk Queen a while back, and to lure out our targets, I wore an illusion that made me look like Syndra." I tried to drudge up everything Ashling had told us about her. Syndra was basically Lir's counterpart. He served Balor, she served Siofra—Balor's mate and queen. We didn't know if it was just a friendly kind of competition between the two or if there was more to it than that. "What if that's the reason Lir came here the way he did? Maybe he was trying to get the drop on Syndra, but her people found him first?" I speculated.

"Do we care about any of this?" Stela looked at Andrei and then at me. "If one of them takes out the other, that's one less enemy overall, right?"

She wasn't wrong. It was to our benefit if Lir killed Syndra or vice versa. We were only in this realm to get the sorcerers help to fix Magos and Andrei—both of whom were on borrowed time..

And yet . . . I couldn't seem to force myself to walk away.

My instincts told me this was something important, and I couldn't let it go.

"They're not far from us. We'll check it out." My gaze bounced around to everyone. "We won't make contact, just see if we can figure out what they're up to."

A yellow sheen rolled over Andrei's eyes before the wolf looked at me. "Let's go hunt the hunters."

Chapter Twelve

"You good?" I gave Andrei a sideways glance. His eyes were still wolf yellow, but otherwise, he was acting normal.

"Yeah." He grinned. "My wolf side likes to hunt, and in times like these, where we're both in agreement . . . it's nice. Feels right."

I nodded in understanding. These days, I didn't get to spend much time in my feline form, but no matter if I was sporting fur or skin, my feline nature was always a part of who I was. There were no two halves, it was just me, and all of me loved a good hunt.

The fae devourers had changed direction a few times, and now we seemed to be heading towards the outskirts of the city. There was no foot traffic here, and the buildings had shifted from tall glass and steel structures to sprawling estates with iron fences surrounding them. Normally, iron was a poor conduit for magic, but these ones vibrated with power. The magic in them didn't feel familiar to me, and Jinx didn't recognize it either.

We gave the iron fences a wide berth.

A few feet ahead of us, Magos and Mikhail froze. Everyone

stopped. This close to the devourers, it was more difficult for me to pinpoint their exact location. I knew they were nearby, but that could mean fifty feet or five hundred feet.

"Lir is definitely here," I murmured. "His magic is faint compared to the others, but it's there."

"Several someones are swordfighting." Magos cocked his head. "I think they're on the other side of this estate."

Mikhail looked over his shoulder at me. "Do you want to keep going? They might be too distracted to notice us, but it'll be harder to stay undetected the closer we get."

I chewed my lip as I stared at the large mansion standing between us and the devourers. There didn't seem to be any consistency with sorcerer architecture other than *weird*. This one vaguely looked like an old English estate from the human realm. Most of it was made up of bright red brick with green ivy growing up its sides, but there were half a dozen towers rising out of it like it really wanted to be a castle.

Just like all the other estates, there were only a few trees and shrubs. Mikhail was right, as soon as we got past the structure, we'd be in plain view of whoever was on the other side.

What do you think, Jinx? I reached up to scratch his head where he was still perched on me.

We've come this far. Might as well keep going. His claws kneaded my shoulder, piercing the fabric of my shirt. *Besides, aren't you curious to see Lir's fighting skills?*

Calling it curiosity seemed too mild of a word. Lir was over four thousand years old. He might be my enemy, but even I could admit he was beautifully lethal with a blade in his hand. How would he fare against a dozen other fae warriors? They were all tainted with devourer blood, which meant they couldn't use magic against each other. It would be a fight based purely on skill.

I had to see it. Sooner or later, I would fight Lir again. We would also battle others like him. The timing of this might not be convenient, but it was too good an opportunity to pass up. We just needed to view the skirmish without becoming a part of it. I eyed the building. It was roughly four stories tall, which meant if we got on the roof, we'd have a pretty good view.

Mikhail followed my line of sight. "Think we can get up there unnoticed?"

"We haven't seen a soul since entering this part of the city." I shrugged. "Maybe they're all in the city center or tucked away in bed."

"Or they're deep in their evil lairs, plotting." Andrei drew his thumb and pointer finger across his chin like he was stroking an imaginary beard. "Probably laughing evilly."

I smirked. "That's definitely a possibility."

"If the fight happening right behind their home hasn't drawn the residents out, I doubt we will," Magos commented.

There is the matter of the fence, Jinx pointed out.

All of us looked at the rather innocuous-looking fence radiating magic.

"Rock, paper, scissors?" Stela joked.

"I got this." I rolled my shoulders. "Maybe step back a bit though."

Jinx leapt off my shoulders, and everyone but Mikhail took five steps away from me before I called on my devourer magic and blue flames spread over my clothing, creating an armor of fire. I took off at a dead run, then launched myself over. The fence wasn't that high, eight feet at most, so it was easy enough to clear. I landed on the other side and turned back towards the others.

"I didn't feel anything." I shrugged.

"Dare you to go lick the fence." Andrei nudged his sister with his elbow.

"Gross." She shoved him away.

"Maybe it operates similarly to the walls in Izaak's home and simply stores magic," Magos said thoughtfully.

"Don't touch it, just in case," I suggested before backing up a bit to give everyone room to land.

Mikhail took a running start and leapt over the fence. Magos scooped up Jinx and did the same. The werewolves didn't bother running. Andrei picked up Lestari before he and Stela strolled up and jumped straight over it from a standing position.

"Show-off," I muttered when Andrei landed.

"Jealousy is a bad look, kitty cat." He grinned.

Stela matched his amused expression. "Aren't cats supposed to be good at the whole jumping thing?"

"I made the jump just fine. I just wasn't all showy about it." I sniffed a little haughtily.

"Love, you covered yourself in blue flames and dramatically ran at a fence dripping with unknown magic," Mikhail said wryly.

"Some might consider that showy." Magos gave me an innocent look.

I glared at Magos. "I expected this sort of betrayal from him"—I flung an accusatory finger at Mikhail—"but not from you. If any of you get zapped by magic while we're scaling the building, I'm not helping!"

Quiet chuckles sounded from behind me as we made our way across the open lawn to the building.

Not a single soul came out to ask us what the fuck we were doing on their property. The vines that grew up the walls had thick stems that made for perfect hand- and footholds, so we were able to scale the building in minutes.

Large, soft purple crystals were lined up on one side of the roof. They stood at forty-five-degree angles in complete defiance of gravity, and a soft glow seemed to hover around their smooth surfaces.

"Same rule for the crystals as the fence—no touching," I

warned, most of which was directed at Andrei because the damn wolf was drawn to anything shiny.

We crossed to the other side of the roof and peered down.

"Damn," Andrei said softly.

"Yeah," I breathed out. "Damn."

Below us, Lir battled six fae warriors in a whirl of clashing blades. Something silver shone on his left forearm. We were up too high for me to see it in detail, but it was like a combination of a gauntlet and shield. The sword he wielded was the same one he'd had when I'd fought him. Even from here, I recognized it. It was a foot and a half long with a slightly curved edge made of a silver so pale, it was almost white.

When Lir and I had battled before, he'd been toying with me. In the back of my mind, I'd known that was the only reason I'd walked away, but watching him at this moment was really hammering that home because Lir definitely wasn't playing now, and neither were the fae attacking him.

Three fae circled around him—a red-haired one with a stocky build wielding a spear and two lithe, dark-haired fae with short swords. The one with the spear lunged forward, aiming for Lir's thigh. At the same moment, the other two attacked Lir's back in a perfectly synchronized move.

Mikhail leaned forward next to me, eyes laser-focused on the battle. Lir twisted sideways at the last possible second. He moved with an impossible grace underlined by ruthless precision. His shield connected with the spear, guiding it behind him in the same breath his sword knocked away the blade angled for his side. The second blade crossed behind his back, just over the spear.

One of the dark-haired fae screamed as the spear punctured them straight through their guts, but Lir was already moving. He swung his sword in a brutal arc, and the head of the spear-wielding fae slid off their shoulders before their body crumbled to the ground.

The entire thing had taken seconds.

Beside me, it felt like Mikhail and Magos had stopped breathing. I knew we were all thinking the same thing: *could we have done that?*

The fae who had been stabbed in the gut was kneeling on one leg, their head bowed as they tried to heal themselves as fast as possible. While painful, that hadn't been a mortal wound. Not for a fae. Only beheading or massive trauma would take a fae down.

Four fae remained on their feet, and they didn't hesitate to go after Lir. He danced across the open field, making it difficult for them to attack him all at once. If he couldn't strike a lethal blow, he went for maiming. One fae wearing a cloak and wielding two sharp, curved knives was a touch too slow in pulling back after a failed strike. Lir hammered a kick to their knee, and even from up here, I could hear the bone crunch. Lir tried to take their head when the fae crashed to the ground, but another fae was already there, blocking him.

A growl of frustration tore from Lir as he backed off. That's when I narrowed my eyes on his gait. He was trying to hide it, but there was something wrong with his right leg. Lir had survived so far, but he must have taken some hits before we got here.

The fae who had been healing from the stomach wound got to their feet. It was five against one.

"He's something else, isn't he? Almost a shame he has to die." A light, feminine voice chuckled.

Immediately, we all spun around, weapons out. A slender fae woman with golden-blonde hair that fell in waves down to her butt hovered over the crystals. Her feet rested barely an inch above the glowing surface. It looked like she was standing on air.

Fuck. I let some of my devourer magic out, and the blue flames formed a half circle around us. I was really getting annoyed with people sneaking up on me like this. She didn't have any devourer blood, but she was sidhe—Unseelie, to be exact. It took me a second, but I recognized her face from court.

Fae could interact with magic directly, but manipulating raw magic was far more difficult than working with the elements. Most fae specialized in one or two elements. The one before us was particularly gifted with air magic, which meant she could tear the breath from our lungs with half a thought.

"Mariam," I said evenly. "Does Queen Elvinia know you're here?"

I was pretty sure the answer was no. Because while the Unseelie Queen didn't tell me everything, she would have mentioned if she were sending someone from her court to the sorcerer realm. It wasn't exactly a common place to visit. Plus she never would have sent someone like Mariam.

Mariam's family belonged to the Tuatha Dé Danann, and they seemed quite content with their position in the Unseelie Court. Her parents were some of the oldest fae in the court at just over a thousand and were soft-spoken and respected by everyone, including the queens. Mariam was their oldest child at almost eight hundred. At court, she was always on the shy side, and her parents were protective of her.

There wasn't a hint of shyness to be seen on her face now. Her bright blue eyes shone with arrogance, and her heart-shaped mouth was curved into a smug smile.

"I'm here at the behest of my queen." Mariam twirled her long hair around a slender finger. "The one true queen of the fae. Not those pretenders."

Behind us on the ground, a fae screamed. Swords clashed, and a second later, I heard a low, pained grunt that I recognized. Lir had just taken another hit.

Mariam's expression changed into one of mock sympathy. "I don't think dear old Lir is long for this world." She rose a little higher in the air so she could see over the building's ledge. "It's a pity. He's so yummy." She licked her lips. "He might be on the losing side, but I was really hoping to get him in bed at least once. I bet he fucks the way he fights, brutal and unrelenting."

"Sounds like someone is desperate to get laid," I drawled. "What do you want, Mariam?"

She'd chosen to reveal herself rather than attack when she'd had the advantage of surprise. We outnumbered her enough that, even with her air magic, she couldn't have taken us all out, but she could have done some serious damage. Instead, she'd chosen to chat, which told me she had no plans to return to the Unseelie Court. And that she was hoping to persuade me to join her side.

Maybe plant another spy in the court since she was out.

Elvinia was going to lose her shit when I told her Mariam was a traitor. She knew Balor had spies in her court, but she had a list of suspects ranging from possible to almost definite—Mariam wasn't on any of those lists. How many others were smiling in the queens' faces right now while their true loyalty was to Balor or his queen?

"I always liked that about you." She smirked. "Your directness. No bullshitting like the fae love to do."

"*You* are a fae," Mikhail pointed out.

Mariam gave him a slow once-over, her mouth curling into a sultry smile before she batted her eyelashes at him. "Yes, but I'm self-aware."

If people could stop hitting on my mate at least until our mating bond was settled, that would be great. Blue flames flickered down my arms and across my blades as my magic expressed its displeasure.

"Not that self-aware if you keep looking at him like that." I raised one of my swords and pointed it at her. "Say what you came to say and then leave."

As much as I wanted to kill her, there was too much distance between us, and air elementals were hard to pin down.

"Even if Lir survives the fight, he will fall eventually." Her gaze slid from Mikhail to me, and I didn't like the triumph I saw in them, like she'd just figured something out. She dropped the hair she'd been toying with; the flirty act was gone, replaced by a cold, hard calculation in her eyes. "Lir's lost his edge. First with his weakness around the second-born and then his obsession with you. He should have killed you and moved on. Instead, he's letting emotions dictate his actions."

Second-born? I had no idea what she meant by that, though I assumed with the emotion bit, she was referring to Lir having a hard-on for tormenting me. All because my paternal grandfather had been his best friend and had left him behind.

"Is this the part where you tell me I should throw my support behind Syndra?" I arched a brow. "And support the return of Balor and Siofra?"

"It *will* come to pass." Mariam moved a little closer to us. "Balor will walk the realms again—this time with his queen at his side—and Syndra will be there, as will I. Lir and those who follow him will not."

"Do Balor and Siofra know their second-in-commands are trying to kill each other?" Magos asked. "Odd way to instill loyalty in your followers."

Mariam glanced at him. "It's only come to this because Lir has grown weak. Balor's too sentimental to order Lir to step down from his position, so he's allowing his queen to handle it. This way is cleaner for everyone."

Another scream rang out from below us, only to be cut off. I hadn't seen who it'd belonged to, but based on the hint of uncertainty that wavered on Mariam's face, I guessed it wasn't Lir.

"Syndra should have sent more people to bring him

down," I sneered. If it were me, I would have gone for overkill and sent a small army after Lir.

"It's not too late for you to change your role in this." Mariam's attention returned to me. "I've seen the way your parents are treated in court. They are feared, not respected. It's the same with you, and I know that, just like your parents, you were left no choice but to swear fealty to the Unseelie Queen."

"Yeah, but I have a fancy title now, so it's all good." I grinned even as her words tore at me. She wasn't wrong. I saw the way my parents were treated. They'd belonged to the Unseelie Court for over a thousand years, and still the fae watched them with scorn in their eyes.

Badb and Kalen may be on friendlier terms with Elvinia now, but that didn't change the fact that they were as trapped in the Unseelie Court as I was.

"Choose the winning side, Nemain," Mariam pushed. "Save who you can." Then the fae woman straightened and tossed her hair over her shoulder. "But know . . . you can't save them all. The boy is a sacrifice. That's all he was ever meant to be."

Finn.

Fire danced down my swords, and Mikhail and Magos took a step forward while the low, dangerous growls of werewolves filled the air. Lestari hung back, but I saw her fingers dip into the pouches on her belt.

Mariam laughed. "Don't kill the messenger, love."

"Not your love."

I flung my magic out, a dozen daggers made of blue flames shooting towards her body. At the same moment, the air swirled around the edges of her pale pink dress before streaming out like a spear. Not at me—at Mikhail.

My magic wrenched itself free of my will. *No!* I screamed. *Stop!*

A wall of blue flame sprung into existence in front of

Mikhail half a second before he vanished into mist. Syndra's magic changed course a hair's breadth away from the flames and slammed into my chest.

It felt like I had been hit with a battering ram. The air violently expelled from my lungs, and I was flung back towards the edge of the building, my swords slipping from my grip. I tried to twist midair to grab on to something before going over but collided with a hard body instead.

"Shit, are you okay?" Andrei set me down as I gasped for air. Mikhail appeared a second later, while Magos and Stela moved to stand in front of us. My hand landed on Jinx's soft fur. The grimalkin had shed his glamour, and a one-hundred-pound pissed-off feline crouched by me.

"New mate bonds can be so unpredictable, or in this case" —Mariam grinned widely—"very predictable. Clock is ticking, Nemain. Do make the right choice."

Then she spun around and dashed off the side of the building, wind swirling around her. I struggled to my feet, my lungs still burning. Suddenly, a punch of familiar magic hit me. Someone had just opened a gateway on the ground below us.

The fae devourer magic had been dwindling as Lir cut them down, but now it flared like a dying flame that just had a bucket of kerosene dumped on it.

Gripping Mikhail's arm, I staggered towards the edge of the roof and peered over. At least forty devourer fae closed in around Lir. Looked like Syndra had decided to send a small army after all. Lir had gone still. I couldn't make out his expression from here, but his stance said that he'd fight until the end—even though he knew the end was coming.

"His weakness around the second-born . . ."

Godsdamn it. We needed to keep Lir alive—at least until I figured out what was going on.

I stepped away from Mikhail, his dark eyes watching me carefully. Half a thought had my blades flying into the air before landing back in my palms. Once upon a time, these swords had belonged to my aunt. I'd never met Badb's older sister, but wielding her swords felt right, especially after the upgrades they'd received, courtesy of Badb.

"We need Lir alive," Mikhail said.

"At least until we can beat some answers out of him," I agreed.

"Sounds fun." Mikhail rolled his shoulders before kissing me on the cheek. "See you down there?"

"Wait till I make a move," I told him. Mikhail nodded, and then both he and Magos vanished into mist. "You three, stay up here," I told Lestari and the wolves before backing up a few paces and focusing my magic where I wanted it. Badb was so much better at this than I was.

"What? No way." Andrei growled before stepping into my path, Stela next to him with an equally determined look. "We can help."

"Don't have time to argue." I gave him an apologetic look. *Jinx? Keep them up here.*

Sure thing. Both werewolves suddenly dropped to the ground like an invisible boulder had fallen on their shoulders.

"Fuck," Andrei ground out as he strained against the unseen force. "I really hate that he can do that."

A grimalkin's ability to manipulate raw magic and turn it into something solid and heavy wasn't all that useful. Fae or anyone with an ounce of magic could counter it easily. Worked great on werewolves and vampires though.

I scooted over to the side a little bit. Here was hoping I didn't go splat.

"Get this the fuck off me," Stela growled.

Steel rang against steel below. The fight was starting. Time was up.

"Sorry, but it's for your own good." I bounced on my feet a few times before taking off at a dead sprint. *"Momentum is key,"* the memory of Badb's words echoed in my mind. *"Trust your magic and commit. Do not hesitate."*

I leapt straight off the four-story building.

For a few seconds, it was just me propelling through the air. My magic streamed out at me, ripping into the wall that separated this realm from the others. Too much, and it would open into an entirely new world, but too little, and nothing would happen. I was threading the needle, and the exhilaration had my heart pumping.

My body straightened into an arrow as I cut through the air. The gateway snapped open in front of me, and I tucked myself into a ball a second before I passed through it. Solid ground greeted me. I let my momentum carry me through a roll before sprinting to my feet, swords in hand.

Lir looked at me with light blue eyes, a hint of surprise showing before resignation settled in them. "Come to kill me too, Nemain?"

My fingers tightened around my sword handles. The fae smiled, probably thinking they were going to get to watch me cut down Lir. Then they could capture me and drag my battered body back to Syndra.

Neither Mikhail nor Magos had appeared yet, both waiting for the right moment.

"You owe me answers." I held Lir's unflinching gaze.

"Do I?" He narrowed his eyes.

"Yes." I nodded. "About the second-born . . . and your intentions towards him."

Lir's mouth tightened ever so slightly but that was the only reaction he gave.

I forced myself to turn so my back faced Lir, something I was only willing to do because I knew Magos or Mikhail could snap into existence and block any attacks.

"Leave," my voice rang out, clear and demanding as I looked at each of the fae warriors in front of me, "or die."

"We take her alive," a tall and broad-shouldered fae ordered. His pale blue eyes slowly perused my body, and his mouth curled into a grin. "Pretty little thing, aren't you? I bet you'll scream beautifully."

"Oof." I let out a raspy laugh. "Definitely shouldn't have said that."

He smiled as he pulled a curved dagger from a sheath at his side. "What are you going to do about it?"

"Me?" I cocked my head. "Not a damn thing."

A crease formed between his dark brows before his eyes widened a fraction in understanding. Not soon enough though.

Mist swirled behind him, and then a sword sliced the fae diagonally from his left shoulder to just above his right hip. I smiled at the blue eyes frozen in shock as his body slid apart, revealing Mikhail standing behind him. My mate flicked the fae's blood off his blade and grinned at me.

Chaos erupted.

These fae had clearly fought as a unit before and were just as skilled as the previous ones that had attacked Lir. Half of them converged on Mikhail, clearly intending to take him down quickly while the other half cut me off from helping him.

My magic panicked, but for once, it didn't try to act on its own, likely sensing the devourer essence radiating off these fae. There was nothing it could do against them. All of us were dripping in magic, but none of us could use it against the other.

This was a fight measured purely in skill with a blade. I relished it. A wicked grin cut across my face as I bent back, letting a fae's sword swing an inch over my body. Another fae tried to seize the opportunity and plunged their sword straight down towards my exposed stomach. I twisted with the grace only a feline shifter could manage. One of my swords blocked an attack from my left while my right sword kissed the neck of the fae who'd struck at my gut.

Warm blood sprayed across my skin, and I whirled away, maniacal laughter spilling from my lips. Briefly, I saw Mikhail vanish into mist and reappear behind two fae. The element of surprise was lost though, because they knew what he was capable of and spun to counter his attacks at the same time two more fae struck at his back. Magos burst into existence, his sword catching both blades and shoving them away.

That was all I had time to see before two more fae were on me. I blocked the strike at my throat and the jab at my thigh but missed the fae closing the distance on my side. *Shit*. I pivoted. The sword I'd caught an inch from my neck slid up my blade, and I whipped it away, trying to block the oncoming attack but knowing I was going to be half a second too late.

A pale silver sword stopped the long dagger a hair's breadth from my ribs. Lir hammered a fist to the fae's face, and bone crunched as his nose flattened. The fae stumbled back just as my sword sang through the air before I whipped it towards his neck.

Lir and I were already moving before the head hit the ground. His back touched mine as five fae circled us.

"I'm still going to kill you one day," he said mildly.

"Samesies." I grunted as two fae attacked in perfect harmony. My swords spun, fending off attack after attack, and I could hear Lir doing the same behind me. We made sure to stay close to each other so that at least our backs were defended.

The blood in my veins froze when I heard Mikhail hiss in pain that was immediately echoed in our bond. I couldn't spare a glance in his direction though, because Lir and I were barely holding our own. Lir had managed to cut down another fae, and I was fairly certain I'd seen Magos take out one as well, but we were still basically outnumbered two to one, and all of these fae were just as skilled as us.

We were on the defensive, and our time was running out. If even one of us fell, it would be over. I just didn't know how to change the odds in our favor. Every time I tried to go on the offense, I was quickly pushed back. Blood leaked from my thigh, and that leg was becoming less responsive. The wound itself wouldn't kill me, but it would start slowing me down significantly in a few minutes, and that would get me killed.

Lir let out a raspy cough and leaned on me for a moment before straightening. In the split second I was off balance from his weight, a fae woman with fiery red hair dove and sliced across my other thigh. I screamed in frustration and struck at her wrist, trying to disable her sword arm, but she danced out of my reach before halting.

"Step away from the dead man, kneel before us, and I'll let one of them live." She jerked her head over her shoulder, where Magos and Mikhail fended off multiple attacks. A cruel smile spread across her beautiful face. "Do it in the next ten seconds, and I'll let you pick which one."

Behind me, Lir stiffened. If I abandoned him, he'd be cut down in under a minute. We both knew it.

Part of me considered it. Even with his death inevitable, Lir wouldn't go down easy. It could be the opening we needed to get out of this alive.

There was something going on in the ranks of Balor's followers though, and I was pretty sure that something was disagreement over what to do about Finn. If Lir being alive increased Finn's odds of surviving, then alive he would stay.

I just needed to figure out how to accomplish that while keeping the rest of us alive, too. As much as I wanted Lir to stay breathing, I wouldn't sacrifice Mikhail or Magos to do it.

"Time's up." The fae woman spun her sword. "Just remember, this could have gone a different way . . ." Her words trailed off as soft pink rose petals swirled around her on a phantom breeze.

A low chant rose, and then several fae started coughing.

"Witch!" the fae who had been speaking roared. "Kill the wi–"

A scream from behind me cut off the rest of her words before it ended abruptly. The deep, distinctive growls of werewolves rang through the night air. I was both annoyed and relieved that Andrei and Stela had disobeyed my order to stay on the roof.

I kept my gaze locked on the fae woman, but her eyes went to the disruption behind me, which meant she missed Jinx creeping up on her. The grimalkin slammed into her back, clamped his jaws around the side of her neck, and ripped out her throat.

For the second time in the past ten minutes, blood coated me.

Her sword dangled from her fingers before she fell to her knees, hands clutched around the wound, desperately trying to staunch the blood flow. She must have come from a strong bloodline because her magic had managed to keep her alive— barely. With enough time and some help, she might have survived.

"Sorry." I stepped forward. "Kneeling before me won't spare your life after you threatened me and mine."

My sword sliced cleanly through her neck. Around me, Magos and Mikhail cut down the last of the fae, although I saw at least two flee. Something told me we'd be seeing them again and they'd be bringing backup, but that was a problem for another day because an eight-hundred-pound werewolf wasn't done killing yet. The wolf with golden-yellow eyes was stalking towards Magos.

Chapter Thirteen

Jinx, I said tightly. *Little help.*

It doesn't work anymore, his frustrated growl rolled through my mind. *That's how they broke free. Both of them shifted into their wolf forms, and they've grown stronger.*

Shit. *Keep an eye on Lir.*

I didn't go through all the trouble of keeping him alive for the asshole to vanish now.

Magos turned to face the oncoming werewolf. His copper eyes were bright, but there was an alien quality to them that sent a shiver down my spine. He appeared the same, but I wasn't looking at my friend right now.

I was looking at one predator getting ready to square off against another.

Mikhail snapped into existence at my side, mist swirling off him. "You take the wolf; I'll handle my uncle."

The two of us slid between Magos and Andrei, our backs to each other. I heard Magos pause but kept my attention on the werewolf, who was still slowly stalking towards me. His jaws opened, lips pulling back in a silent snarl to reveal two rows of massive teeth. The first row were angled down, while the row behind them curved back.

Getting bit by a werewolf was high on my list of things to never experience again.

"Andrei," I said in a soothing voice. "The fight's over."

The wolf halted, yellow eyes dropping to my swords before flicking back to meet my stare. I really didn't want to let go of my swords but could probably summon them back to my hands before the wolf reached me. I eyed the ten feet between us. Probably.

Argh. I knelt down and placed my swords on the ground. Out of the corner of my eye, I saw Stela cautiously approach her brother, still in her wolf form, the witch at her side.

"Keep calming him down," Lestari said softly. "I can help."

Slowly, she reached into a pouch attached to her belt, and the scent of pine mixed with something spicy filled the air. Then she raised her clenched fist to her lips and started murmuring over it.

The wolf's large head swung to her, a deep growl vibrating from his chest.

Stela stepped between the witch and her brother, letting out a low whine but holding her ground, and his growling lessened slightly.

Behind me, I heard Mikhail talking quietly to Magos. I could feel his tension through our bond, but it wasn't getting worse. With a soft sigh, I took a step away from my weapons and sat, crossing my legs.

"What do you say you let Andrei come back?" The wolf's attention swung back to me. "We'll be going somewhere soon where I'll let you hunt as much as you want."

He cocked his head, taking a step closer to me.

I kept talking, describing what I remembered of the realm we'd be going to as Andrei crept towards me some more. There wasn't any aggression in his movements, so I didn't summon my swords. Eventually, he stopped a foot away and settled down in a sphinx-like position. If he went for my throat, there wasn't a whole lot I could do about it. But now that I wasn't triggering his predator instincts I was fairly confident he wouldn't attack.

Those wolf eyes stayed latched onto mine, like my voice was the only thing keeping him from losing it entirely. A slight hitch entered my voice when I felt Magos and Mikhail vanish, but a soothing feeling reached through the mating bond, so I quelled the panic. Wherever they were, they were okay. Mikhail had it under control.

Lestari's chanting became faster, too low for me to understand the words in what I was fairly certain was Bengali, but human languages had never been my strong suit. Whatever spell she was crafting seemed to be working because Andrei's eyes grew heavier by the second, and in less than a minute, the wolf rested his head on his giant paws and closed his eyes. I waited a few beats before getting to my feet, grabbing my swords on the way, and striding towards where Lir waited.

"You care about the wolf. Enough to put yourself at risk. Nice of you to dangle a juicy target like that in front of me." His grey eyes flicked briefly to Andrei. "Although that one seems to already be broken. Who do you think will last longer?" A cruel smile stretched across his lips. "The werewolf? Or your cursed vampire friend?"

"Keep talking, and there's going to be more of your blood soaking the ground," I replied mildly.

I could do it too. The ancient fae warrior was doing his best to keep his stance casual and unworried. His sword was held in a loose grip at his side, feet shoulder-width apart, and his breathing was steady, but I knew what it looked like to cover your pain so you didn't appear weak.

His breathing was too even, like he was counting the

seconds between, and his right foot was just a little too far forward. He was off-balance and didn't even realize it.

"I could never fool him either." He snorted, and his breathing took on a more ragged quality while his left shoulder drooped.

"Him?" I stopped a few feet away. Lir might be injured and damn close to passing out, but I wouldn't put it past him to stab me first.

"Rowan." Lir grimaced and swung his sword over his shoulder into the sheath strapped to his back. "He didn't have a smart mouth like you, but he always saw through my bullshit."

I didn't say anything. Rowan was Kalen's father—my grandfather. Neither of us had ever met him because he'd died the moment Kalen had taken his first breath. He was just this blank spot in our family tree. We knew little about him other than that he'd loved Shayla, Kalen's mother, and the two of them had loved their child enough to sacrifice all of their magic—and their lives—so he would survive.

It was something Lir was very pissed off about.

Lir looked at me for a long moment, his expression unreadable. "Ask what you want to ask, then get the fuck away from me."

"Really weird way to say 'thanks for saving me from getting sliced and diced into a dozen pieces.'" I shrugged. "But okay, let's get to the reason I saved your sorry ass."

"It was a team effort!" Stela yelled from somewhere behind me.

"*We* saved your sorry ass," I corrected. "You want me to suffer, and you've gone to great lengths to make my life a living hell. All because you're pissed off at my grandfather." Something dark and vicious flickered in Lir's eyes, but he didn't say anything. "But what you *haven't* done is try to take Finn from me. Not really."

"I seem to recall chasing you across one of the fae realms doing just that," he drawled.

"That time, sure." I cocked my head and studied him, trying to piece together everything that had happened since Finn had come into my life against this new knowledge. "But you haven't tried since, even though the entire reason you were smuggled out of Balor's realm was so you could bring his son —his second-born child—back to him."

The muscles along Lir's jaw tightened. "I am loyal to my king."

"Sure . . ." My head swung the other way, and I decided to take a shot in the dark. "But you didn't know you would be bringing him back like a lamb led to slaughter when you agreed to find him, did you? You discovered that fun fact later, and since then, you've been stalling. Trying to find other ways to break Balor free that don't require Finn's life. Why, Lir? Why do you care?"

We stared at each other for a long moment before he looked away. "I don't know."

Lie. Lir definitely knew why he was doing this, he just didn't want to share it with me.

Lir straightened, and when he looked at me again, there wasn't a hint of emotion anywhere on his face. "Now that Syndra is here, she'll escalate things. It's what she does. She thrives on chaos and death."

"Don't we all?" I gestured towards the slain fae around us.

He shook his head. "You and I, we love to fight. We need it. All Syndra cares about is death. She was the one who led the seraphim into those backup human realms the fae queens had created. That wasn't a fight. It was a slaughter."

I went still. The fae queens had needed more power to keep Balor and his army contained, so unbeknownst to every-one, they'd been hiding away humans in other realms. Humans were great at two things. Reproducing and generating magic.

No one had been left alive in those realms. I'd assumed Lir had been behind it, but it seemed Syndra had been busy in the shadows.

"Don't you still control the seraphim?" I gave him a sharp look. The seraphim were powerful warriors with an axe to grind with basically everyone. Considering my father had wiped out several battalions of them not long ago and the fact that I was friends with Sigrun—they hated valkyries more than anything, and she was arguably the most infamous one—I was probably high on their hit list.

I needed to know if someone else held their leash.

Lir ground his teeth before biting out one word. "No." Then he stepped away from me, and I let him. We'd gotten some answers, and given the new complication that was Syndra, I couldn't kill him yet. Not if it would make things worse.

Lir started to walk back in the direction of the city center before pausing and turning slightly so I could make out his profile. "Syndra likes plans that are big and showy. She may plot in the shadows, but she'll strike in broad daylight, in a move so bold, you can't help but admire the brilliance of it, even as your world burns down around you."

He started walking again. I hadn't been able to see his face fully while he'd spoken, but I'd recognized something in his voice. It was the same aching pain that coated my words whenever I spoke of how my parents had died and how Myrna had been murdered.

Mist swirled briefly before Magos and Mikhail appeared next to me. We watched the fae warrior cautiously as he strode away.

"What did she take from you, Lir?" I called out.

The ancient fae warrior said something in a low, vicious tone, but he was too far away for me to hear.

"Everything," Magos said quietly. I glanced at him, a question in my gaze as those burning copper eyes met mine. "He said everything."

"SOMEONE'S HOME AFTER ALL," Lestari announced.

I tore my eyes from the direction Lir had gone to look at the witch, but her gaze was locked on the brick wall of the castle. I frowned. During the chaos of the fight, I hadn't noticed that there were no doors or windows on this side.

A seam split down a section of exposed wall close to the ground before parting like curtains. My mind struggled at seeing solid stone move as if it were made of soft fabric, and clearly, I wasn't the only one.

"Did somebody slip me some drugs?" Andrei slid between Magos and me, still buttoning his pants while gaping at the newly formed door, a gravelly undertone to his voice, courtesy of his recent shift.

"Watch the vines," Mikhail murmured from where he stood at my other side.

I squinted. It was subtle, but the vines attached to the wall were definitely moving. Slithering. That unsettled feeling I associated with this realm raised the hairs on the back of my neck.

"Let's go," I said under my breath.

Before we could move, a wizened old man shuffled through the large opening. He was wearing what I could only describe as a red flannel nightgown with a matching hat. The end of the hat had a fluffy ball attached, and it swung with each step, most of his weight leaning on a thick cane.

He stopped a few feet past the doorway, his slippered feet sinking into the grass. Deep wrinkles carved through his face, and a busy white beard stood out brightly against his deep brown skin.

"Did we just find Santa?" Stela shoved between Andrei and Magos, causing both me and Mikhail to tense up, but Magos simply moved several feet away, putting more space between him and the werewolves.

"Not Santa," I said evenly, my gaze continuing to monitor the vines.

Our group collectively took a step back as some of them peeled off the wall and crept a few feet out onto the grass.

"How much?" The sorcerer pointed with his cane at the various fae corpses littering his lawn.

Everyone looked at me, and I met each of their bewildered stares, matching them with one of my own before returning my gaze to the old man.

"Just to be clear . . ." I said slowly. "You want to buy these from us?" I waved a hand at a decapitated body lying next to me. Wait. Was it a decapitated *body* or a decapitated *head*? Had I been saying it wrong all these years?

Mikhail elbowed me, a dark eyebrow raised, and I realized I'd missed whatever the sorcerer's response had been. "He says he'll give us ten gems."

"Gems?" I frowned. "What the fuck do I want with gems?"

"Technically, this was a team effort, so we'd all get some gems," Andrei added.

"We should ask for more." Stela's gaze darted around, counting up all the bodies.

"They do have a lot of magic." Lestari toed what I was pretty sure was a spleen. "Very useful for a variety of spellwork."

"Forty gems," Mikhail countered on my behalf—or I guess the group's behalf. "And you'll tell us how to find a sorcerer named Thaxea. She was Izaak's old apprentice and lives somewhere near the city center."

"Bah." He waved a hand. "I know who she is. Izaak

wouldn't shut up about his wayward apprentice for centuries. Twenty gems, and you can use one of my portals that lets out a block away from Thaxea's house. Half of them are missing body parts because those stupid wolves decided to have a snack!"

Andrei and Stela looked innocently up at the sky, avoiding the sorcerer's accusing stare. Ugh. *It would be great if my friends could stop eating people.*

"Fine," I agreed smoothly.

The vines that had been slowly creeping through the grass moved faster. Each of them reared up, their ends sharpening into points before spearing into the bodies. The dead fae jerked like puppets on a string, and then large bulges started sliding down the thick stocks.

Gradually, the dark brown color of the vine stems gained a red edge, and the green leaves became tipped with red as well. My eyes followed one back to the house, slightly mesmerized, and I startled as I took in the now almost solid red wall of plants, all swinging slightly in a phantom breeze.

"Here you go," the sorcerer called out gleefully. I snatched a bag out of the air on pure reflex and passed it to Mikhail. He opened it and peered inside before tying it to his belt. The sorcerer patted one of the vines before pointing his cane at the opening into his home. "Simply go inside and follow the hallway until it reaches the dead end. There is a door on the right, which leads to my interior garden. The first short set of spiral stairs on your left will take you to the city center. It's only a block until you'll reach Thaxea's place. Just look for the yard full of giant metal atrocities."

Exactly how bad did Thaxea's place have to be for him to call her decorations *atrocities?* We all stared at the vines that were now making slurping sounds. We'd have to step over several of them just to get into the house, and gods knew what he had in the interior garden.

So who wants to go first? Jinx asked. *I nominate the wolves.*

"How about I pick you up and throw you?" Stela offered. "Cats always land on their feet, right?"

One of the vines dropped a body, and it fell onto the lawn. We stared at the dried-out husk that used to be a fae.

"Yeah, you know what, we'll just walk," I announced, taking a small step back. "Everyone okay with walking?"

Everyone nodded.

"Suit yourselves." The sorcerer shrugged and looked down at his vines like a proud parent.

We hightailed it out of there and made it to the city center without any further distractions or problems, other than the few sorcerers who grumbled at us for moving too slowly. Andrei and Mikhail both got zapped, which was something I found incredibly entertaining. I had no doubt Mikhail would make me pay for laughing at him later, and I was very much looking forward to it.

"Huh." I stopped at the end of a lawn full of purple and pink flowers with a modest cottage sitting behind it. "This wasn't what I was expecting."

"It's got to be a trap, right?" Stela peered suspiciously at a metal sculpture of a duck leading a line of ducklings through some taller flowers. Her eyes narrowed further. "I don't like it."

I glanced at Lestari, an eyebrow raised, but the witch just shrugged. "I don't sense any magic in them. I think they really are sculptures."

Mikhail chuckled. "Maybe that's why the sorcerer was so offended by their existence."

Taking a few steps onto the lawn, I laid my fingers against the cold metal of what seemed to be a unicorn, although the equine creature had ram horns instead of the single horn in the center of its forehead, and there were spines running down its back. There were a dozen or so sculptures like this, most ranging from six feet to twenty feet tall. Some of the creatures I recognized, others I didn't.

"Beautiful work," Magos commented as he scanned the sculptures.

We approached the worn wood door of the cottage, and I raised my hand to knock when Lestari gently placed her hand on top of mine. "Perhaps I should lead this conversation?" Her eyes dropped to my clothing, and I looked down. Dried blood stained most of the dark material, some mine, some not.

Mikhail and Magos had some blood on them too, but not nearly as much as me.

"You're so messy." Mikhail tugged on a piece of my ash-blonde hair that had come loose from the braid and was now more of a rusty red color. "I don't know how you do it."

"It's truly one of her gifts," Magos said dryly.

"You're both just jealous that I killed more of those assholes than you." I sniffed but stepped back, letting Lestari move closer to the door.

The witch knocked politely, and we only had to wait a few seconds before it opened. The woman before us appeared to be in her early twenties, but assuming it was Thaxea, she had to be at least seven centuries old. Curly brown hair that she had tried and failed to contain in a bun floated around her head, and freckles decorated her nose and cheeks. Streaks of vibrant orange paint dotted her pale skin.

"Hello, new friends!" She beamed at all of us.

It was fortunate that Lestari had taken point on this conversation, because if I'd been standing in front of the sorcerer, I would have stabbed her out of principle. People who smiled like that at complete strangers were evil incarnate until proven otherwise.

"Hello." Lestari smiled back kindly. "We've come to speak with Thaxea. Are you her by chance?"

"I am! Come in!" She made a sweeping motion with her arm while she moved back. "I just made a fresh pot of tea!"

Lestari glanced over her shoulder at me, and I gave her an encouraging look. The witch rolled her eyes and stepped inside with only the smallest amount of hesitation. When nothing happened, the werewolves followed after her, and I did the same, Magos and Mikhail falling in step behind me.

Jinx leapt onto my shoulders. *I don't trust her. Why is she so happy?*

That's what I thought!

I bet she steals souls or something.

Lestari exchanged pleasantries while we moved through the cottage. Nothing about it gave off creepy vibes. Bright paintings of flowers and sunsets decorated the walls. Everything had a light, homey feel to it.

Maybe she was a serial killer?

"Please, take a seat and tell me what I can do for you. I don't get visitors all that often," Thaxea said as we stepped out onto a light grey stone patio at the back of the cottage. Wooden barrels filled with fluffy white flowers lined both sides, and directly behind the patio was clearly where she worked. Several in-progress sculptures were scattered towards the back, along with an easel that had a large canvas of a breathtakingly beautiful sunset.

Stela frowned. "You're the sorcerer who made the werewolves, right?"

"Werewolves?" Thaxea scrunched up her nose while she poured each of us a cup of tea. "Oh, yes! My final project before finishing my apprenticeship with that impossibly arrogant curmudgeon." Her eyes widened. "You're one of my creations! Delightful! How are you all doing?"

"How"—Stela ground her teeth together so loud, I winced—"are we doing?"

Some of the cheer bled out of Thaxea's face as she took in

the fury on Stela's. Andrei tried to put a calming hand on his sister's shoulder, but she shrugged it off.

I sipped my tea. Mmm, tart and sweet.

"You created a brand-new species, and then you just fucking left!" Stela spat out. "Did it ever occur to you, even once, to come back and check on us?"

"I thought . . ." Thaxea glanced around the table and met a wall of stony faces. "You seemed fine that first week," she finished lamely.

"'That first *week*'!" Stela shrieked. "You only stayed one godsdamned motherfucking week?!"

Lestari leaned forward, folding her hands on the table. "Please forgive her," she said calmly, regaining control of the conversation from Stela, who was now slumped in her chair, arms crossed and glaring daggers at Thaxea. "She's simply worried about her brother, which is why we're here, actually. We're hoping to get your help in correcting some . . . issues with the werewolves."

"I don't really do much in the way of spellcasting anymore." Thaxea chewed her bottom lip. "After my fallout with Izaak, I struggled to find a purpose. Magic is everything to us—to sorcerers. We're supposed to dedicate our lives to increasing our understanding of it. Pushing what we can do that much further." She stared at her sculptures and let out a bitter laugh. "It took me centuries to realize it was all bullshit. There's so much more to life than that."

"Your sculptures are beautiful." Magos smiled kindly at her.

"Thank you," Thaxea said quietly before clearing her throat and focusing on Stela and Andrei. "I admit that it never occurred to me that something could be wrong with the spell. I was young and egotistical when I created the werewolves, and then I simply"—she winced—"forgot."

"What's done is done," Lestari told her in a firm but not

unkind tone. "Now is your chance to save the future of the werewolves. Their magic has never been as strong as the vampires', who have been slowly annihilating them, and for some wolves, like Andrei, there is something seriously wrong with their connection to their wolf nature."

Thaxea rose and moved around the table to crouch next to Andrei. A yellow sheen rolled over his eyes as her hand hovered a few inches from his chest. "May I?"

He blinked rapidly, eyes flashing between yellow and hazel. Perhaps it was the wolf reacting to the presence of its maker. Thaxea waited until Andrei gave her a curt nod and then laid her hand over his heart and closed her eyes.

"I can see the flaws . . ." Her brows bunched together before a wide smile spilled across her face. "But my work truly was beautiful. Far more ambitious than Izaak's."

None of us commented until she let out a long breath and dropped her hand from Andrei's chest, rising to her feet.

"What do you mean by ambitious?" Andrei asked. His eyes were hazel, but there was more of a growl to his voice than normal.

"Do you know why werewolves and vampires were created in the first place?" Thaxea asked as she returned to her seat.

Andrei glanced at me. "Someone said it was because of a bet?"

Thaxea snorted. "I suppose that's not far off." She picked up her teacup and leaned back in her chair. "Am I correct in assuming none of you know much about sorcerer culture?"

"Yes," I spoke for everyone. "Given how little sorcerers have intermingled with the other realms, pretty much everything we know is based on rumor and speculation."

"We're encouraged to limit our time in the realms," Thaxea explained. "Our government is made up of six political branches. I won't bore you with the details, but they're elected positions and represent different factions amongst the sorcerers. They disagree about almost everything—except that our realm should never involve itself with the politics of others."

"Given that . . ." I frowned. "It's odd that no one has reacted to us being here."

"Other than zapping us for merely asking questions," Stela muttered.

"Locating our realm isn't easy. Rather than blocking entry, we focus on obscuring it. It's rare for outsiders to come here but not unheard of, and it's always because they've been given a token." She gave Stela an apologetic smile. "Sorcerers are only curious about magic, not people. They saw you and likely assumed you were here at someone's bidding, and they didn't care beyond that—unless you got in their way. Most sorcerers are cranky."

"Not you, apparently," Stela pointed out before grunting when Andrei elbowed her. "I wasn't being rude." She scowled at him. "Just pointing out a fact."

"This is why you're single," Andrei replied solemnly.

"Yeah. That's why." A yellow sheen rolled over Stela's eyes. "Not the fact that I've been hunting vampires all over Europe while crashing at shady motels with my brother. Or the fact that I'm a little wary after my last girlfriend turned out to be a witch plotting my death."

"Actually, she was just planning on leaving you without any explanation," I helpfully offered. "And probably wouldn't have given you a single thought after that."

Stela glared at me.

"Just trying to stick to the facts." I gave her an innocent look.

Magos politely cleared his throat and focused on Thaxea. "Have you heard of or noticed any other outsiders in the city?"

She shook her head. "No, but I honestly don't leave my home much other than to go down the street to my gallery."

I took another sip of tea. "So how did you and Izaak find yourselves in the human realm all those centuries ago?"

Thaxea sighed. "All sorcerers are required to apprentice under an elder. That lasts until either the elder deems them ready to strike out on their own or the apprentice challenges their mentor."

"Let me guess," Mikhail said dryly. "You challenged Izaak?"

"You've met him." Thaxea scrunched her nose like she'd just bitten into something rotten. "It wasn't my choice to have him as my mentor. Izaak is a little eccentric, even by sorcerer standards, but he was the most gifted of his generation. My parents pulled some political strings to get me an apprentice-ship with him, and I had no say in the matter."

"Your parents . . . are they high-ranking?" Lestari asked.

A humorless smile flashed across Thaxea's face. "They're heavily involved with the government—Praephis faction. Me being an artist is highly embarrassing for them."

"That's their loss," Andrei told her, waving a hand at the sculptures. "Magos is right; your artwork is beautiful, and we can always use more beauty in the world."

Pink stained Thaxea's cheeks, and she ducked her head. "Thank you. I think so too." Then she cleared her throat before continuing, "Our competition was to see who could make the best creature from a blend of devourer and something else."

"Why those devourers in particular?" I asked, curious if it was just a random choice or if there was something more to it.

"The chimmeris and hyaenir are . . ." Thaxea's brows furrowed as she seemed to search for the right word. "Primordial. We believe they were some of the first devourers to be created. Their magic is *old*. It allowed the essence of their being to be manipulated easier and to be merged with that of another."

A chill ran up my spine. My experience with the devourers in question was limited, but there had been something about them that had freaked out my instincts more than any other creature I'd ever come across.

"Izaak used chimmeris," Stela said. "And you used hyaenir?"

"Yes." Thaxea nodded. "Izaak only used humans and chimmeris, modifying his creation as he saw fit. He wanted the appearance to remain mostly human but take on some of the characteristics of the chimmeris. I wanted to take it a step further—to create something that could shift between two forms while maintaining a sense of self. I added wolves into the mix because I saw them while I was in the human realm and thought they were beautiful." She sighed. "Looking back, I can see I was too ambitious. Blending two beings into one is far simpler. By adding the third, I complicated things."

"Do you know what's wrong with me and the other were-wolves?" Andrei asked quietly.

Thaxea let out a long breath and set her teacup down. "The blending of the wolf and devourer worked perfectly, but that new creature only partially bonded to your human side. The other two parts on their own are not a complete being; they cannot exist without the human side, but they're not a part of it either. It's created an imbalance where neither side can thrive."

"That's how I feel most days," Andrei admitted. "Like there is this valley between myself and my wolf, and it's only growing larger."

Thaxea's brows bunched together, and she glanced inquisitively at Stela. "Do you feel the same?"

After a beat, Stela shook her head. "No. I sometimes feel a disconnect with my wolf side, but I've never experienced a loss of control."

"It'll be helpful if I can study you as well," Thaxea said hesitantly. "If you're okay with that."

"Whatever it takes to help my brother," Stela answered immediately. "Do you think, while you're fixing whatever is wrong with us, that you can make our magic stronger? Or give us additional abilities like the vampires?"

"I'm not sure." Thaxea frowned. "It's going to be a somewhat delicate process, correcting my previous mistake."

"But you think you can?" I asked evenly. "Fix it?"

Thaxea stared at Andrei's chest, where she'd laid her hand, and chewed on her bottom lip. "Yes, I believe so."

The relief on Andrei's and Stela's faces was almost palpable, and a small amount of tension bled out of me.

"Aside from studying Stela and possibly other werewolves, what else do you need? Name it, and we'll find it."

"Blood," she said instantly. "From a human, a wolf, and the original devourer species."

"You can have my blood," Lestari offered.

"And we can get the wolf blood easily enough," I added. "And it just so happens that we're going to the realm of the devourer in question, so we can get theirs."

"You only need the blood?" Mikhail studied the sorcerer. "Not the whole specimen?"

"Yes." She frowned. "If I were creating something entirely new, I'd need more, but to simply adjust my existing spell, blood will be sufficient."

Mikhail and I exchanged suspicious looks.

"Let me guess." Thaxea let out an annoyed sigh. "Izaak asked you to bring back some live specimens of the original devourers?"

"Yes," I confirmed. "We have to capture two dozen of them."

"He's using you." She looked to the sky in the direction of Izaak's flying castle. "My old mentor was pissed when he was forbidden from collecting any more devourers from that realm after he sacrificed all those young sorcerers."

"Any idea what he wants them for?" Magos asked.

Thaxea shook her head. "We're not exactly on friendly terms, and even if we were, Izaak doesn't share his motives with anyone. All I can tell you is that he's a self-serving asshole and no good will come of it."

Chapter Fourteen

"Well, the house might be creepy as fuck, but you can't knock this view." I admired the night sky from a balcony on Izaak's floating house—one that didn't teleport us anywhere. Some stars peeked through the clouds, and we were far from the light pollution of the city. It made me happy I'd gone looking for Stela and Lestari ten minutes ago.

If I hadn't, I probably would have punched Vizor in the face.

He had learned nothing concrete while we'd been away. Just that Izaak and his house were sketchy as shit and that Emir and the vampires were up to something.

Shocking news. Truly. Nobody could have predicted that.

Vizor was in a very pissy mood, and I'd been making it worse, so Mikhail had been the one to suggest I take a walk. We'd been cooped up in our room for hours after returning from Thaxea's, waiting for Emir to tell us it was time to go to the devourer realm. I could have walked around Izaak's house, but I really didn't like how it smelled.

Luckily, when Mikhail had practically shoved me into the hallway, I'd followed the scent of Lestari and Stela, who had already grown tired of me and Vizor sniping at each other, and found them on this balcony.

One of them had snatched the silencer from Vizor so we could talk freely without worrying about being overheard.

"I could do without the height." Stela warily looked at the stone railing that bordered the balcony from where she sat against the wall of the house. "But it is pretty. Not bad for my first time in another world."

"Ugh." I made a face. "There are definitely better worlds. Stick around for a few weeks when we get back, and I'll take you to some."

"Really?" Pretty hazel eyes fell on me.

"Yeah," I told her honestly and leaned against the outer railing so I could face them both. "New dragon realm is pretty nice. Daemon cities are cool. There are some weird ones we could pop into for a bit. And I guess there are always the fae realms."

Stela let out a rueful laugh. "You act like going to those places is nothing."

"For me, it is." I shrugged. "Some people have referred to me as a realm walker, and I suppose that's true. I've been to hundreds at this point." I glanced at the witch, who was sitting a few feet from Stela. "What about you? Have you been anywhere besides the human realm?"

"The fae realms a few times," Lestari answered. "And the daemon realm twice. That was a long time ago though."

I thought about her wielding her magic during the fight with Lir and the other fae devourers. "Did Hecate take you there?"

"Yes," she said after a beat, her eyes narrowing on me. "How did you know?"

"Earlier, you used dried flower petals and herbs; it smelled exactly the same as concoctions." A smirk played across my lips. "Plus, despite being a witch, you're still human. Neither the daemons nor the fae would have welcomed you into their realms. But with Hecate at your side? Even they wouldn't have questioned it."

Stela gave me a confused look. "Who is Hecate?"

"She's a god . . . sort of." I tilted my head back and forth. "Hecate is from the same realm as the Olympians, but she's not exactly the same as them. Her magic comes from a different place. Humans worshiped her as a god for a long time, and she has a close connection to the witches. One of her titles is the Mother of All Witches."

Lestari snorted. "She always complained about that title. On one hand, she didn't want the responsibility that came with it, but on the other, she couldn't stop herself from meddling."

That was definitely Hecate. I'd listened to more than one speech from her about how she was never getting involved in witch business again, only to hear a month later that she'd done exactly that.

"What happened between the two of you?" I asked curiously.

The dark-eyed witch sighed and leaned her head back against the stone wall. "We were close friends once upon a time."

"Roommates?" Stela asked while she wiggled her eyebrows suggestively.

Lestari looked at me. "This is a young person reference that I don't understand."

I chuckled. "She's asking if the two of you were sleeping together."

"Oh." Lestari laughed softly. "No, nothing like that. We truly were friends. Maybe even more like sisters. We had a kinship that is hard to explain."

"And then?" Stela prompted, leaning forward slightly.

A hint of sadness showed on Lestari's face. "I might be a witch," she intoned, "but I'm also human and, more importantly, I was born and raised amongst humans. Which means I experienced things differently than Hecate and those supernaturals who live in the human realm but keep themselves apart. Racism, colonialism, sexism. I experienced all of that. On what felt like a never-ending loop. I watched my friends and family suffer over decades, centuries. It wasn't something I could turn away from." Her lips pressed into a hard line. "Hecate couldn't understand that."

"Her entire realm fell to devourers," I said softly. "Everything that you care about in the human realm—everything you fought for—she'd already lost. Hecate was born anew in this realm, and while there are parts of it she loves, it'll never be hers."

I understood this because I'd met countless beings over my existence who had fled from fallen realms. Their homes were overrun by the devourers Balor had unleashed. Entire histories, cultures, and civilizations gone forever.

Lestari sighed. "I know. And I tried to respect Hecate's decisions on how she wanted to live, but it caused a rift between us."

"There was a time when she was different. It was long before I was born, but in the early days of her being in the human realm, she cared. It's why she taught some humans magic." I smirked. "And earned herself that title she so hates."

"What changed?" Stela asked.

"What always changes for immortals," I replied. "She tired of watching them die. Of investing so much into beings who are so breakable. She decided it was easier to close herself off from the human realm and let the witches seek her out."

"It wasn't easier for me," Lestari said softly. "After a while, all we did was fight. So I left. I waited for her to come and apologize, but she never did." She looked out towards the sky, a wry, close-lipped smile on her face. "She's probably doing the same, but here we are, four centuries later. Two stubborn women unwilling to budge."

Stela blinked. "Four centuries? How old are you?"

"Seven hundred thirteen."

"I mean, you're a witch . . ." Stela's eyebrows crept up. "But as you said, you're still human, and you barely look over forty. How are you still alive?"

Lestari didn't answer right away, and I chuckled. "What's the matter, witch? Worried about losing that moral high ground?"

"There are spells," she said mildly, glancing at Stela, "that can extend a witch's life. Any human's really."

"How?" Stela watched the witch, as if she suddenly realized that a predator had been walking beside her this whole time.

Now you're getting it, I mentally cheered. "Yeah, Lestari. Educate our young wolf here on how it's done."

"It's not like I steal the souls of children." Lestari gave me an exasperated look before returning her gaze to Stela. "At the root of all witchcraft is balance. Life for life. There are different ways to achieve that. A single human life. Blight a crop. Plenty of options." Her lips parted in a smile. "Just as there are lots of wicked humans who the world is better off without."

"There it is!" I slapped my thigh gleefully. "And yet you make all these snide comments about me killing witches as if y'all are so innocent."

"Some of the ones you killed were!" Lestari snapped.

"I was barely twenty and had watched my parents get burned alive because the warlocks decided they were tired of taking shit from the witches." I leaned forward a little from my perch on the railing as my temper surged. "We both know things were brewing between the witches and warlocks for a long time, and the witches did nothing to put out the fire. And when it was too late, they saved who they could and left the rest of us to burn."

Stela's eyes widened by the second as her gaze bounced between me and Lestari.

Lestari opened her mouth but closed it before surprising me with her next words. "You're not wrong. Mistakes were made. I'm not much older than you, Nemain." She let out a harsh breath. "I remember what it was like to be young and angry at the world."

The anger I'd been feeling faded at the sincerity of her words. "For what it's worth, I hold no grudge against you or any other witches anymore, and . . . I'll try to choose my words more carefully in the future." Even I could admit that I'd baited Lestari more than once in the time I'd known her.

"And I will do the same." She dipped her head in acknowledgement. "There are plenty who deserve my wrath; you are not one of them. Not anymore."

Stela slow clapped. "Look at us! Bonding and all that shit!"

The witch and I looked at each other and laughed.

"Might as well do it now before we go into the devourer realm to die," I said dryly.

"Is it really gonna be that bad?" Stela wrinkled her nose.

"No . . . Maybe." I raised my hands, palms up. "We'll survive, but it definitely won't be a walk in the park."

A crease formed between Lestari's brows. We'd decided earlier that she, Vizor, and Jinx would stay in the sorcerer realm to monitor things here. While the witch had demonstrated that she had offensive magic, it wasn't exactly quick to wield, and it would be useless against the devourers, just as Jinx's magic wouldn't work against them either.

Dragonfire was trickier. Magic was woven into it, making it stronger than regular fire—but it was still fire. Sometimes it worked against devourers; sometimes it didn't. The main reason Vizor couldn't go was that he would attract too much attention. A dragon setting foot in that realm would be like ringing a dinner bell for every devourer in the area.

We needed to fly under the radar. So only those of us with devourer magic of our own were going. The devourers would still happily kill us to strip the flesh from our bones, but we wouldn't be any more attractive of a meal than anything else in that realm.

"So, was Aisha one of your witches who turned into a warlock spy? Or was she a warlock who you flipped to your side?" I asked casually.

"Aisha . . ." Stela frowned. "That woman who was with Emir?"

Lestari snorted. "The dragon suspects the same, but he didn't ask me."

I shrugged. "Vizor likes to figure things out on his own and have concrete proof before doing anything with that knowledge. I'm a little more direct."

"That's one way to put it." She smiled faintly. "And Aisha actually turned on her own. Or at least that's what she claims. Says she fell in love with a witch who was later murdered under Emir's orders."

"You don't believe her?" Stela guessed.

"I want to believe her." Lestari tugged her shawl a little tighter around her body as the cool breeze kicked up. "But this could just as easily be a ploy by Emir to get a spy on my inner circle."

"You should talk to Queen Ashling," I told her. "Ash might be able to determine if your warlock spy is too good to be true. I'll introduce you when we're back."

"Thank you," Lestari said after a beat.

"You both know what you're going to work on next when we return." Stela stared off into the night sky. "I have no idea what I'm going to do. When Andrei is safe, I mean. He followed me to Europe to hunt the vampires, and I love him for it, but . . ." She looked back at me. "I understand why you ended things with him. I've never felt more alive than I have in the past couple of years. Given the chance, Andrei would happily accept a life of peace and calm tomorrow. But if I tried to stay with him . . ."

"You'd hate it," I finished for her.

Stela nodded, almost sadly. "His dream is to have a family. Settle down and raise a bunch of kids with dinner at the table every night. My brother is a sweetheart, and I want that for him. I really do. I don't know what I want exactly . . . other than not that."

"Some people's dreams are another person's nightmares." I spun on the railing so my feet rested on it and lay down, stretching my body across the smooth surface and letting the cool night breeze wash over me. "We'll fix your brother, Stela. Andrei is going to have the life he deserves. And then you'll have a chance to figure out what you want. I promise."

***

"Do we look like pack mules?" Justina arched a brow at the bag I held out to her.

"You look like deadweight." I stared back at her. "Either carry the pack, or you'll be upgraded to bait."

"Just carry the bag," Cassius said absently to Justina. She cast him a dirty look before snatching the backpack that held our meager supplies and shrugging it on.

Cassius took a similar pack from Mikhail without complaint. The two of them had knocked on our door an hour after Lestari, Stela, and I had returned to the room, announcing that Emir had said it was time to depart.

We'd grabbed our stuff and followed them to a room where they'd said Emir and Izaak would meet us. Cassius had been oddly quiet and agreeable compared to Justina, who was tense and snappy.

I moved to where Magos looked out the window. It seemed like he was merely admiring the view, but I knew it was really because this was the farthest he could get from the werewolves. The tension in the room was eating at his control.

Andrei and Stela had already shifted to their wolf forms at my behest; they might have improved their fighting skills in their human skin, but their wolves were stronger and faster.

"You ready?" I asked quietly, my gaze out the window as we stood shoulder to shoulder.

"Yes." There was a finality in his tone that I didn't like one bit.

Aside from Mikhail, I rarely touched people—outside of fighting of course—but I found myself reaching for Magos' hand and wrapping my fingers tightly around his. "If you falter, I will catch you."

After a long moment, he squeezed back. "You might have to let me go."

"No," I said simply. "I will not." Still gripping his hand, I pulled him towards the center of the room just as Izaak and Emir strolled in.

"Are you not coming with us?" I dropped Magos' hand as I eyed the warlock. He wore dark slacks and a button-up shirt. Not really monster-hunting attire.

I'd assumed he'd make us do most of the heavy lifting in the devourer realm, but I'd thought he'd be there to help at least. He didn't give a shit about the werewolves, but he was under pressure to make good on his promise to the vampires.

"The chimmeris are just one piece of the puzzle," Emir replied smoothly. "I will be handling everything else while you collect the specimens."

Mikhail and I traded a look. Between this and the weird

way Justina and Cassius were acting, all of my instincts were blaring a warning.

"Here." Izaak shuffled forward and set a small box on the table. "These will transport the chimmeris to a holding area I've designated for them." He reached in and held up a thin gold token. It reminded me a little of a coin, but it was larger, almost the size of my palm, and had no markings on either side. "It needs to be pressed to the top of the spine of a chimmeris long enough to attach." He did something to the object, and dozens of barbs shot out from one side. "It'll do this automatically when it makes contact with the chimmeris, so you don't need to do anything to activate it."

"How long does it take to teleport them?" Mikhail asked as he plucked one of the gold tokens from the box and studied it.

"Eh . . . ten seconds or so?" Izaak tilted his hand back and forth.

Great. We had to get up close and personal to a chimmeris, stab it with a weird coin thing, and then try not to die while it expressed its displeasure.

And we had to do that two dozen times.

"Anything else we should be aware of?" I sighed.

"It'll only work on chimmeris," Izaak said.

That was fine. Thaxea had given us a crystal thing to draw blood from a hyaenir.

"Alright," I said slowly. My instincts were still screaming that something was off, but I didn't know what. "Let's get these into the packs, and we should keep some on hand as well. If we lose them, we can restock and try again."

The vampires and the wolves started disseminating the tokens.

Emir glanced around. "Where is the rest of your group?"

"Like you, they have other matters to attend to," I answered mildly.

Thaxea had offered rooms for us to stay in if we didn't

want to remain at Izaak's. Vizor, Jinx, and Lestari had already left for her place. It got them out of this creepy house but also meant they could protect Thaxea if Emir or any of his people went after her.

The warlock stared at me for a long moment. "What is your plan for collecting the specimens?"

"There are a few hours of night left. We'll do some scouting and see if we can track the chimmeris to wherever they roost during the day. If things get bad, I'll open a gateway back here, and we'll try again." I glanced over his shoulder at Aisha and the other warlocks, who waited by the door. "None of your warlocks are coming with us either?"

"You'll have those two." He pointed at Cassius and Justina. "Surely four Apex vampires, two werewolves, and yourself will be enough?"

"The warlocks would have made good bait." I shrugged, only half kidding, before turning to face Mikhail. Tension rolled through our mating bond. Like me, he was suspicious of this whole situation. But there was no turning back now.

"Ready?" he asked.

I nodded.

"Ignore everyone else." Mikhail rested his forehead against mine. "Remember not to fight it. Let it flow over and through you."

"Tell that to my magic," I murmured before taking a deep breath and letting it out, mist coiling around me.

My devourer flames had a biting cold to them, but while Mikhail's mist was also cold, it felt more like rainfall on a cool night. Following Mikhail's guidance, I welcomed the magic into me while it swept over my body. My own magic was actually helpful this time and practically rolled out the red carpet for it. Our magic mingled, coiling around each other before settling in my soul.

Now for the part we had been practicing while waiting to

leave. With a gentle mental nudge, I sent Mikhail's magic outward again, and a thick mist formed over my clothing and weapons.

"Now focus on the thread between the magic and your possessions," Mikhail said quietly. "Then will them away. Do not let go of the thread."

I closed my eyes and concentrated on that link. This was the tricky part. It was second nature to Mikhail and Magos, although Mikhail had put a block on his for a long time. I inhaled, feeling that thin but resilient thread, and still holding onto it, I exhaled.

My clothes and weapons vanished along with most of the mist; only a few wisps fluttering over my skin remained. "So convenient." I let out a satisfied breath as I felt the small thread to where my belongings existed in a pocket dimension, waiting for me to retrieve them.

"Good, shifter." Mikhail brushed a kiss across my lips before stepping back, and I immediately missed the warmth of him against me.

"Damn, Nemain." Cassius let out a low whistle. "You are stunning."

Was he trying to get killed before setting foot in the devourer realm? Because that's what it sounded like. I turned my head to find him gazing at me, bright blue eyes slowly roaming up and down my body. Even Justina looked at me, her delicately arched eyebrows raised.

Magos politely averted his gaze, and I was pretty sure the werewolves didn't even register my nakedness as something to react to. Only the vampires and warlocks were outright staring.

It didn't particularly bother me, because like the wolves, I'd gotten used to being naked before and after shifting. Plus, Cassius wasn't wrong. I *was* stunning. Couldn't fault the vampire for having good taste.

Well, I couldn't, but apparently, my mate felt differently.

"She is," Mikhail agreed smoothly before stepping in front of me and blocking everyone's view. "She's also *mine*."

"Just looking." Cassius held up his hands.

Izaak and Emir had also been looking at me, but there had been nothing lecherous about it. Emir appeared mildly surprised while Izaak practically hummed with curiosity.

I could have waited until we were in the devourer realm to use Mikhail's magic but Cassius and Justina would have reported it back to Emir anyway. Besides, based on how Izaak had been able to examine Magos' curse earlier, I didn't think there was much point in hiding this from him. Mikhail and I agreed that all that mattered was that they didn't know how unpredictable the bond could be.

My being able to stash my swords and clothes in the pocket dimension would come in handy because I likely had a lot of shifting in my immediate future.

Mikhail growled something at Cassius, but I tuned it out as I called on my shifter magic and dropped to all fours. A steady burn raced through my body as bones snapped and reformed. There was no pain to shifting, just an uncomfortable pressure that didn't release until it was done.

A few minutes later, I arched my back and stretched out my front legs, three-inch-long claws jutting out and scratching the wood floor. Like the wolves, I was faster in this form and my senses were more acute. I didn't like not being able to wield my swords, but this would serve me better—at least in our initial entry into the realm.

Andrei trotted over and bumped his head against mine.

If I tell you to run, you run, wolf, I reminded him.

It's hard for werewolves to roll their eyes, but Andrei gave it his best effort. I smacked his head with my paw, claws tucked away, and he mockingly snapped his jaws before returning to Stela's side.

Werewolves weren't telepathic in their wolf forms, so

neither could communicate with us, but when I was rocking fur, I got a slight power boost to my mostly weak telepathic abilities, which was enough for me to push my thoughts to them.

If Damon were here, the young vampire could have linked all our minds together. It would have made things a lot easier, but like Misha, Damon wanted little to do with me these days. A deep pang hit me when I thought about them.

Get ready, everyone, I pushed the thought out. *If something nasty appears, I'll slam the gateway shut and try again in a different spot. Otherwise, we'll go through. Worst-case, we can pop in and out of the realm to find what we need.*

I concentrated on opening a gateway to the specific realm we needed. Mikhail had asked me once how I knew where I was going when I did this, but it was impossible to explain, because it was a feeling more than anything else. Every time I went to a realm—however briefly—I forged a connection to it. I'd only been to this realm once, so it took a few moments for me to find it, but when I did, I just instinctively knew it was the right place.

The air in front of us rippled before splitting open to reveal a pitch-black sky. We waited for several beats, and when nothing came out of the darkness to attack us, Mikhail and I stepped forward as one, making Cassius and Justina the last ones to step through.

The seven of us hovered a few feet away from the gateway, ready to dive back through if needed.

According to the daemons, realms were alternate realities. They varied in terms of landscape and climate, but many of them were at least somewhat similar, like the human realm, daemon realm, and most of the fae realms. Occasionally though, they would be drastically different. So much so, it was hard to believe we weren't looking at an alien planet.

This realm was one of those. I was fairly certain it was never true daylight here. When whatever passed for a sun around here rose, the sky lightened slightly and took on a red haze. The realm was always dangerous, but nighttime was when the nastiest monsters came out to play.

Those monsters were why I suspected that sunlight was a long forgotten concept in this world, because all the creatures I'd encountered during my short time here had obviously evolved to not only survive but thrive in low- to no-light situations.

Both the vampires and werewolves could see in absolute darkness. I couldn't, which put me at a disadvantage. For now, light from the other side of the gateway illuminated our immediate surroundings.

It wasn't just the animals that had adapted but the plant life as well. Giant, tree-like ferns surged to the sky around us, and dark green moss covered their thick trunks, only ending where leaf stalks fanned out twenty feet from the trunks in all directions. The leaves that made up the blades stemming from the stalks were a crimson red. I'd learned from experience that the ones with purple edges were razor sharp.

Luckily, most of the leaves were ten feet above us, so we didn't have to worry about them while running, but if I opted to jump into the trees later, I'd need to watch out. The same moss that raced up the ferns also covered the ground, making it slick. Even with my claws, it was difficult not to slip.

I breathed in the cool, humid air. There was a certain beauty to this realm; it was just hard to appreciate when you were running for your life.

With Magos and Mikhail in front of me and the wolves flanking me, I closed my eyes and let my magic reach out, searching for the familiar feel of devourers. I had to go out fairly far, at least a few miles, before I began to sense them.

"We're good," I said quietly, because while the devourers were the worst of the creatures, there were others prowling this realm that I'd rather not encounter.

Just as I started to close the gateway, Izaak flicked his hand towards me. A white disc shot through the air, passing through the gateway and slamming into my chest. Mikhail hissed and whirled to face me. He'd struck at the object with his sword but had been half a second too slow.

What are you doing? I growled as I felt whatever Izaak had thrown pierce my flesh in half-a-dozen places.

"Just making sure all of our interests align." Emir shrugged. All his warlocks had moved to stand next to him.

They already do, you asshole! I let out a low whine as the burning sensation in my chest turned cold. My magic. This fucking thing was going after my magic!

I tried to summon my devourer flames, but nothing happened. *No, no, no,* I cursed.

Mikhail crouched in front of me, and I felt him carefully part my fur to look at my chest. "Bone," he murmured before I felt his fingers brush along the edges of the foreign object, only to pull back when I hissed in pain.

"It won't cause any harm as long as it's not tampered with," Izaak said mildly.

Mikhail pulled his hand away, fingers curled into a fist like it was all he could do to keep from ripping the bone out of me.

"This wasn't part of the plan," Cassius said tightly from where he and Justina stood to the side, both looking pissed off and nervous.

Emir gave him a cool look. "As I told you earlier, I'm not sure you bargained in good faith because I have my doubts about your abilities. Consider this an opportunity to prove yourselves."

"Get fucked," Justina growled, and I was in full agreement with her for once.

Emir looked at me with a mocking smile. "This is in your best interest, Nemain. Nothing matters to you more than family."

I took a step forward, a deep growl rumbling from my throat.

One of the warlocks held up a hand with a purple ball of flame hovering above his fingers. He looked pointedly at Andrei.

Fuck. They couldn't attack me, Magos, or Mikhail directly—but Andrei and Stela were fair game.

The blood oath will blow back on you for this. I turned my attention to Emir. *This was a foolish move, warlock.*

"I may have failed to mention earlier that going to this devourer realm is strictly forbidden—for anyone," Izaak said. "I had to call in several favors to get permission for you all to go there—but only once."

"As you've said several times, that realm is dangerous. In the heat of the moment, you may have decided to give up and return before retrieving everything we—and you—need." Emir gave me a mocking smile. "You would blame yourself later, of course, as you watched your friend"—he glanced at Magos—"descend into insanity. So I'm really doing this for you, Nemain. Removing that temptation."

Another growl of frustration tore from me. That was the problem with blood oaths. Breaking them came with serious, often deadly, consequences, but there were always loopholes. Asmodeus had helped craft the blood oath between myself and Emir, but it's not like they could have foreseen a situation where I would be monster hunting at the behest of a sorcerer in an ancient realm.

"The bone enchantment will disengage once I've received all two dozen specimens and your magic will be accessible to you then," Izaak explained. "Best of luck." He snapped his fingers.

I felt the last block slide into place between me and my magic. Without me holding it open, the gateway slammed shut, trapping us in the realm of monsters.

Chapter Fifteen

"*FUCK!*" I internally screamed.

"Nemain?" Magos asked in an even tone as he scanned our surroundings. "What is the status of your magic?"

I forced my rage down until it was a simmering force beneath my skin and focused. My shifter magic was partially intact. Izaak hadn't blocked everything. Shifting was a go, but opening gateways wasn't possible. Likewise, my devourer magic also wasn't accessible, although that part didn't feel as closed off as my ability to open gateways. Maybe because that magic was linked to my fae heritage, which was also responsible for the mating bond?

Mikhail. I peered at my mate. *Can you summon my fire?*

He tilted his head, vibrant purple eyes narrowing in concentration as he held up a hand. Several moments passed, during which I held my breath, then crystal blue flames erupted from Mikhail's hand.

Okay. I let out a deep breath. *That's something. Not sure what we're going to do with it yet, but at least we know you can access it. I can't open gateways, but I believe I'll be able to shift back when I need to.*

"Should we try to get that"—Magos pointed at the bone in my chest—"out?"

I'm not sure how Izaak's spell will react to that. I'm guessing badly, I answered honestly. *We need to wait until we're somewhere safer and not out in the open before we attempt to tamper with it.*

"We should probably consider doing something about that too." Mikhail nodded towards Stela and Andrei, who were stalking towards Cassius and Justina with their ears flat against their heads and lips pulled back in silent snarls. "Although, honestly? Kind of indifferent to how it turns out. There's no way those two didn't know Emir was plotting something."

"We didn't," Cassius said tightly, not taking his eyes off the wolves. "Despite what you think, Mikhail, I don't want to hurt you . . . or your mate."

"And despite what *you* think, I'm not going to fall for your bullshit again." Mikhail's gaze hardened.

Now isn't the time. We will get our answers, I told him. *But right now we need to find somewhere to lie low until sunrise.*

A muscle on Mikhail's jaw ticked before he vanished into mist and reappeared between the pissed-off werewolves and the vampires.

Magos remained perfectly still by my side. "I can't get involved," he said tightly. Something cold and distant flashed in his copper eyes before he squeezed them shut. "Don't let them spill any blood. Please."

My heart hammered when, twenty feet away, something large moved through the ferns. It wasn't one of the devourers; this was bigger. It was likely trying to determine what we were before attacking, or maybe it was a pack hunter and waiting for its friends to arrive.

It's okay, I assured Magos with a confidence I didn't even remotely feel. *Mikhail and I got this.*

He nodded tightly, and I darted forward to stand next to Mikhail, placing Cassius and Justina behind me—something I really didn't like. Sensing my discomfort, Mikhail moved so his back was to mine and the vampires were in front of him.

Moving like a unit, Stela and Andrei split apart, putting several feet between them and making it hard to keep both wolves in my line of sight.

Stop, I ordered. Both wolves growled but didn't attack. *I'm pissed too. I don't know what the fuck just happened—and we will find out—but now isn't the time to fight. This realm is full of underground cave systems, some of them are interconnected, but most are just isolated pockets. We get to one, secure it, and then we can figure out what the fuck to do next.*

The wolves stared at me for a long, tense moment. Then Stela finally dipped her head in agreement, but Andrei's yellow eyes remained locked on the back of Mikhail's neck.

Shit. Andrei wasn't home right now. This was the wolf in control, and if he attacked Mikhail, blood would definitely be spilled. Magos would lose the tenuous control he had, and then we'd all die when the monsters descended.

My thoughts spiraled as the panic grew. I couldn't watch anyone else I cared about get hurt or killed. They were counting on me, and I couldn't let them down.

I kept my gaze on Andrei but spoke to the others. *Follow us. Do not intervene.*

"Don't do anything brash, shifter," Mikhail said harshly.

I let out a chuffing sound.

"Nemain." Mikhail stiffened next to me.

Sorry, love. Brash is my middle name.

I leapt, slamming my bulk into Andrei. He outweighed me by several hundred pounds, but all his attention had been on Mikhail, so I easily caused him to stagger. Before he had a chance to recover, I smacked him with my paw, keeping my claws retracted so as not to draw blood.

He let out an enraged growl, but I was already moving.

My goal had been to break the predatory focus he'd had on

Mikhail and redirect it to me. Mission accomplished, because I now had an eight-hundred-pound pissed-off werewolf hot on my tail.

Mikhail's rage burned through our bond. I'd definitely be paying for this later, but we needed to get somewhere safe, and with both Andrei and Magos on the verge of losing it again, this was the best solution. Mikhail would realize I made the right choice once he got past his anger, and he'd be reasonable about it.

Probably.

I leapt over a large mass of twisted roots, my paws slipping a little on the landing because of the stupid moss, but I surged forward just before Andrei's jaws snapped on my tail. We raced through the primordial fern forest, leaping and winding our way through the fauna. I heard something large charging us.

Apparently, whatever had been stalking us had decided to join the hunt. Awesome. I had to trust Mikhail and the others to deal with it because I didn't exactly know what would happen if Andrei's wolf caught me. On one hand, his wolf liked me, but I also suspected it was his wolf side that had been descending into madness and pulling Andrei's human half with it. He might very well rip me to shreds only to mourn me afterwards.

Werewolves were stronger than me, but I was faster and more agile, especially in my feline form. Staying ahead of Andrei wasn't difficult. What was tricky was maintaining just the right amount of distance that I was in no danger of those jaws but also kept his interest. I was also doing my best to scan for cave entrances.

We needed a safe place to regroup.

There was a particular type of moss that grew around the caves; it was a bright shade of violet that stood out against the green moss covering most of the floor. I hadn't spotted it yet, and I was really hoping we hadn't had the unfortunate luck of landing in a part of the realm that didn't have any fucking caves.

Behind me, Andrei howled.

Godsdamn it, I mentally swore. That would *definitely* attract attention.

A roar echoed in the distance from a creature that sounded far bigger than whatever was chasing us.

Something purple flashed in my peripheral vision. *Cave. Safety. Fuck yes.*

My paws skidded across the slippery forest floor, claws shooting out, digging for purchase as I abruptly turned right. Andrei's bulky form couldn't make the sharp turn, and he crashed into a fern tree hard enough to cause the entire thing to shudder. Enraged growls filled the air as he scrambled after me.

Stela, I ground out, *get ready to help me secure your brother. Everyone else, stay out of the way.*

What I didn't say but knew Mikhail would understand, was that I needed him to keep Magos calm. Because I was about to guide us into a likely small underground cave, and if Magos lost his shit, we were so fucked.

Well, extra fucked.

A high-pitched shrill rang out. It'd been centuries since I'd heard it, but I recognized the hunting call.

We were officially out of time.

I sprinted towards the cave entrance as fear pounded in my chest.

Darkness awaited me, but I didn't hesitate, just dove inside. If there was something else in here seeking shelter, we'd deal with it. The opening was narrow and had a steep downward pitch to it after ten feet. The small amount of light winked out of existence, and suddenly, I was running blind. Sharp rocks dug into my paws as even the resilient moss was choked out by the lack of light.

Still, I kept running.

Behind me, Andrei struggled to find his footing, and I heard the werewolf slip several times. The ground leveled out, and I slowed my mad dash. Instinct screamed at me to turn, and I did, but not fast enough. I slammed into the cave wall, my shoulder taking the brunt of the impact.

Oww. That was one way to stop.

Andrei growled, only for it to end in a sharp yelp, and I heard the distinctive sound of fighting. Blue flames sprung to existence in front of me, revealing a very pissed-off Mikhail with blue fire flickering down his arms. He glared at me as I shook my head, trying to shrug off the lingering pain of hitting the cave wall at almost full speed.

Not safe yet, the thought broke through the haziness of my mind.

I whirled towards the entrance and found that Justina had already done what I'd been about to order her to do. A crystal-clear wall of ice blocked the ten-foot-wide tunnel entrance. On the other side, dark shapes moved, a collection of eerie clicking sounds echoing through the cave before the creatures vanished.

It was unlikely they'd leave entirely, at least not for another hour. Even though they were towards the top of the food chain, they weren't immune to being attacked by the other predators here, especially if they were in a vulnerable position like a cave entrance that would hinder their movements.

No doubt they would find a place to safely watch and see if we came out.

"What the fuck was that?" Justina panted. The back of her shirt was torn, and I could make out several deep, bloody grooves in her back.

I glanced to where Stela still had Andrei pinned to the ground with Magos' and Cassius' help. Alarm shot through me at Magos being so close to the werewolf, but he seemed in control and Andrei was calming down, so I let it be.

What? You didn't see the family resemblance? I turned my attention back to Justina, who glared over her shoulder at me, her hands still outstretched towards the wall of ice. *You just met your ancestor.*

A FEW MINUTES LATER, I was back in my human skin, fully clothed and holding my swords. It was odd to call on Mikhail's magic but also right. His magic was much more obedient than mine. Ghostly blue flames still hovered over his skin, and nothing he did could get them to go away. I suspected it was freaked out over being essentially cut off from me and so it was being extra protective of Mikhail.

I didn't entirely hate that notion. Unfortunately, it wouldn't be able to defend him against the devourers, which were our biggest threat in this realm.

Mist still clung to my swords. As soon as I'd recalled them, I'd examined the blades and confirmed that they still contained some of my devourer magic. It was nowhere near the amount I could call from my soul, but it was there in case I needed it. I'd also done a more thorough internal check of the rest of my magic but only confirmed what I'd told Magos earlier: my ability to shift was still possible, but I was completely blocked from opening gateways.

The gateway thing made sense, but I didn't entirely understand why Izaak had taken away my devourer magic. My best guess was that he'd done it to protect himself so I couldn't have retaliated before he'd closed the gateway. He'd likely keep it locked away even after he allowed us to return. He'd be in for a surprise when Mikhail called on my flames or I used the magic stored in my swords.

I was very much looking forward to the look of shock on

his face, especially right before we forced him to fix Magos and then killed the bastard.

Speaking of brutally killing people . . .

Mikhail was still scowling at me, but when I tilted my head ever so slightly to where Justina frowned at the others getting Andrei under control, I felt his acknowledgement through the bond.

He was definitely not done being pissed at me but was willing to transfer his wrath to someone else. For now.

As one, we moved. In half a breath, I had Justina pinned against the wall, the sharp edge of my sword pressing into her throat enough to draw a thin line of blood. Cassius blinked into existence next to us, only to be slammed against the rocky surface right next to Justina. Blood gushed from his throat where Mikhail dug his dagger in a little too hard.

"We need him conscious, baby," I told Mikhail, although my tone made it clear I didn't particularly care about Cassius' well-being.

They'd been acting strange before we'd come to this realm —before we'd been betrayed. Clearly, they hadn't been aware of exactly what Izaak and Emir had been scheming, but they'd known *something*.

And they hadn't warned us.

Justina went still beneath my blade, so I briefly glanced over my shoulder to confirm that Andrei wasn't going to start ripping into us now that Cassius wasn't helping keep him under control. Instead, the werewolf had started transforming back to his human self as Stela watched over him.

Magos hovered a few feet away, his bright copper eyes fixed on the cave floor. The blood Mikhail and I were spilling probably wasn't helping his control, but we needed answers.

I locked eyes with Justina once more.

"In one minute, I'm going to shatter your kneecaps and slit your throat." I kept my tone light and casual, like I was discussing options for lunch. "Then we're going to break through your ice wall, chuck your body outside this cave, and wait for the devourers to come back. We should be able to grab at least a few of them while they're ripping you apart."

Her face went bloodless as she tried and failed to keep the fear off her face. "We didn't know anyth—"

"Forty-five seconds." I leaned in until my face was an inch away from hers. "I suggest you don't lie."

Cassius let out a hiss of pain. Out of the corner of my eye, I saw blue flames dance across the blade Mikhail still had digging into the vampire's throat. He must have sensed Cassius getting ready to teleport again. We'd both spent enough time around Misha to recognize the subtle tells.

"Thirty seconds," I said mildly. "Perhaps you need a little more motivation."

Justina screamed when I stabbed her with my other sword, sliding the blade between ribs and stopping just short of her heart. The wound was far from fatal, she'd heal pretty quickly if she drank some blood, but in the meantime, the pain would be excruciating.

"Fifteen seconds." I twisted the sword a little more. "My patience is running out. Maybe we should just skip to the end and I can do what I've wanted to do since you walked into my life?"

She gasped as I slowly slid my sword across her neck, blood spreading over the silver blade. Her sharp nails dug into my wrists, trying desperately to prevent me from slicing her throat completely open, but between her wounds from the devourers and the ones I'd dealt her, she didn't have the strength to stop me.

"Emir knows Justina has a child!" Cassius shouted.

Shock ricocheted down the bond so fast and hard that I gasped and had to pull my sword away from Justina so I didn't accidentally behead her.

Mikhail stumbled back from Cassius as if he'd been struck, his eyes wide as he stared at Justina. My brain caught up to the fact that the shock I'd felt hadn't been mine; it'd belonged to him . . . because he'd been in a relationship with Justina for almost a century.

My gut churned. This couldn't be happening. We seriously didn't need this right now. Plus I really wanted to kill her, but I couldn't kill the mother of Mikhail's child . . . right? Then again, she was really annoying. The kid might be better off.

"It's not Mikhail's," Justina rasped, her hands clutching at her throat, trying to slow the bleeding until it finished healing. "Although the look on both of your faces right now is priceless."

Oh good. I could kill her.

I started to move, only for Cassius to slide between me and Justina. I narrowed my eyes at him.

"Please," he said quietly.

"Don't think I've ever heard you say that word," Mikhail drawled, silently moving to stand beside me.

The vampire glanced at him. "Then that should tell you something about how important it is that you hear us out."

Argh, now I was curious.

"Fine." I dismissed my swords into mist—I was really loving this new trick—and crossed my arms. "Explain why we shouldn't kill you."

Cassius' gaze slid from Mikhail to me and scrutinized my face for a long moment, like he was trying to determine if I would attack again.

Justina stepped around him, dropping her hands from her throat so she could place one on his forearm and wrap the other around her ribs. The cut across her neck was healed, but I could see the blood leaking out between her fingers where it was clasped against her side. If we decided not to kill her, she'd need blood to fully heal.

I looked over my shoulder at Magos, in the same spot, leaning against the wall, but his eyes were closed now. Vampire blood wasn't nearly as alluring as werewolf blood, but it was no doubt pulling at him.

"I'm fine," he said evenly, as if he sensed me looking at him. "Please allow them to explain."

"So polite," Justina gave me a withering look. "Pity it didn't rub off on either of you."

"You're still alive," Mikhail told her. "That's about as polite as we get."

I didn't say anything, just waited for Justina to start talking. Tension still rolled down the bond; Mikhail's expression was cold and closed off, but inside, he was a whirlwind of emotions. I'd thought I'd let him come to me to discuss Justina and Cassius, but maybe that had been wrong. Mikhail and I were alike in so many ways; we both tended to shove any complicated feelings down until they erupted.

Only now, we couldn't hide those feelings from each other.

"What does your child have to do with this, Justina?" I prompted when it seemed like the vampire was struggling to find the words to explain.

A freshly shifted Andrei stepped to my side, wearing only a pair of dark sweatpants. A thin sheen of sweat clung to his chest and arms, fresh from shifting. Stela stood next to him. Neither said anything, just loomed ominously.

I had to give it to them; they were good at it.

"The Council doesn't know about Liam." Justina whispered the boy's name, as if, even here, in a forgotten realm of monsters, she was worried they would hear it. "Even if I didn't have a seat on the Council, the offspring of any Apex bloodline vampires must be disclosed. Typically, those offspring are raised in environments where they can be observed . . . and controlled."

"We're aware," I said, my words sharp enough to cut.

Elisa and the rest of the vampire brats had grown up in such a place. None of them had ever interacted directly with their parents. They'd lived in a compound, where their every move had been watched. Either their parents hadn't cared . . . or they'd been silenced by the Council.

"Right." Justina jerked her head in a nod. "You have Marius' kids."

"He has no claim on them." My fingers curled as if I was holding my swords, and I felt the cool mist coiling around them, only for Mikhail to slip his hand into mine.

"Elisa and Misha have never known their father," Mikhail said smoothly. "They're our family, not his."

"Even though the boy turned his back on you?" Cassius asked.

"Yes," Mikhail ground out, pointedly not looking at Cassius. "When some of us give our loyalty, we actually mean it."

I winced at the sharp stab of pain in my chest, drawing Cassius' attention. That vampire saw too much, and I didn't like it one bit.

"Liam was an accident," Justina continued, a hint of softness touching her face. "It happened five years ago. I used protection, but for whatever reason, it failed." She let out a humorless laugh. "For the first time since I'd become a vampire, I'd experienced true fear. I might hold a seat on the Council, but I knew it wouldn't be enough to protect my baby. Trust isn't something that exists amongst vampires, definitely not between those on the Council. Even Liam's father wanted to use him before he was even born." She scoffed.

"What happened to the father?" Stela asked.

Justina flashed her a vicious grin. "I carved him apart and set the remains on fire. Liam is *mine*. There is nothing I won't do for him."

"So that's why you betrayed us," I surmised. "Emir

somehow found out about Liam and threatened to tell the Council?"

She hesitated before nodding. "Yes. Although it wasn't supposed to happen as it did. Emir told us to make sure the wolves died." Justina glanced towards Magos over my shoulder. "And him."

"We weren't going to do it." Cassius stepped closer to Justina before halting at the look Mikhail gave him. "We told Emir what he wanted to hear, but the plan was to tell you once we were in this realm and then we could figure out a way to trick him into thinking we'd done as asked."

"Why?" I tilted my head as I pondered him. "What's your role in all of this?"

Cassius was definitely protective of Justina, but for some reason, I didn't think they were together. Something about the way he acted felt more brotherly than romantic.

"My mother was one of the original vampires. She was kindhearted and quiet. Grew up in the human world when women didn't have a lot of rights." He held my stare, his eyes revealing nothing and his tone completely even. "She was also very pretty, something that caught the eye of a powerful vampire. My mother became his mistress, and I was the result. Shortly after my birth, he lost interest in her and became distant. He was never my father, just someone who had donated his DNA. I took after my mother in terms of magic; she could teleport too, which is probably one of the reasons he never bothered with me. He wanted a child who took after him. But twenty-four years ago, he told my mother he wanted to try again—to have another child."

Fury darkened Cassius' eyes before he squashed it.

"My mother agreed—she didn't truly have a choice—and my sister was born." Cassius swallowed. "To increase the chances of a child being born with the proper magic, a brother followed a couple of years later. My brother took after our mother, like me. But our sister . . . she could shift into a wolf. Just like our father."

"No." It was my turn to stagger back like I'd been struck. A sister who could shift into a wolf and a brother who could teleport.

Elisa and Misha.

Cassius finally looked at me. "I'm glad you're still so fiercely protective of my brother even though he rejected you, because if you ever became a threat to him or my sister, I would rip out your heart."

Chapter Sixteen

Five minutes later, we stood in several different groups with as much space between us as the cave would allow.

Mikhail had taken Cassius' warning as a direct threat against me and had buried his dagger in the vampire's side before I'd even realized he'd moved. Cassius had grunted and responded by headbutting Mikhail. The two of them had ripped into each other after that. At one point, Cassius had yanked the knife from his flesh and stabbed Mikhail in the exact same spot, but other than that, they'd kept to their fists.

Which was why they both sported a black eye and numerous cuts and bruises.

If we were going to survive, we needed to work together. Something Magos was currently trying to get through Mikhail's thick head because my way of doing it would have been slamming his aforementioned head against the wall. Even I had to admit that more violence was probably not the answer right now.

"How are you two doing?" I looked away from the vampires to check over both Stela and Andrei. It was the latter

I was concerned about, but I didn't want to risk upsetting his wolf by pointing out his loss of control.

"It's strange being here," Stela admitted. "Part of me is terrified, but another part feels like it's finally come home."

Andrei nodded. "I can feel the divide between my human side and the wolf side even more here."

"Is that going to be a problem?" I asked mildly. We'd gotten lucky in finding this cave so quickly. If Andrei's wolf took over again, we might not be so fortunate. Worse, if the wolf ran away from us, we'd probably never find him again.

He opened his mouth and closed it before finally saying, "I don't know."

Great. "If you feel like you're losing it, say something." I gave him a hard stare. "This isn't the time or place to try to deal with it yourself. The more notice we have, the faster we'll be able to contain you if the wolf takes over again. Got it?"

"Loud and clear, kitty cat." He gave me a solemn nod, even as a small grin played across his lips. "You'll be the first to know if my wolf side decides it wants to play with the other monsters."

Mikhail and Magos strode over to us. The corners of Magos' eyes were tight, but otherwise, he seemed in control of himself. I scrutinized my mate, but the worst of his cuts and bruises were barely visible now. I suspected the stab wound on his side was still sore but mostly healed.

Let's test that theory.

My fist connected with Mikhail's ribs, and he let out a sharp hiss as he glared at me. "What the fuck was that for?"

"For letting yourself get stabbed!" I snapped. "With your own fucking dagger!"

Andrei and Stela snickered, earning an annoyed look from Mikhail.

"Nemain," Magos said calmly, "perhaps you could refrain

from attacking my nephew—your mate, who you love by the way—while we sort out what we're going to do next?"

"Fine," I grumbled but pointed a warning finger at Mikhail. "Do not let yourself get stabbed again."

Mikhail's eyes flashed. "I didn't let myse—"

"I no longer sense those creatures outside," Magos interrupted.

"They won't have gone far. Let's wait until 'morning.'" I made air quotes, because it wasn't like there was really a morning here. "Then we can go exploring."

"And then what?" Justina asked harshly from the other side of the cave. "We're fucking trapped in this realm! Emir knows about Liam! What if he tells the Council about him? What if they fin—"

Something slammed against the ice, and we all jumped.

Cassius tried to pull her away from the wall, but she yanked her arm out of his grasp and placed her palms against the ice. Blood smeared on the surface as she pushed her magic into our only defense against the beasts outside.

The piercing sound of claws scraping against ice filled the cavern, and the beast let out a low rumble before ambling back out into the night.

"What the fuck was that?" Justina whispered.

"No idea." I sighed. "But that's why we're staying here until daybreak. Don't get me wrong, it'll still be dangerous as hell, but at least some of the monsters will be sleeping."

Justina dropped her hands from the wall. Slowly, she crouched until she practically fell on her ass and scooted to sit against the ice wall. "And then?" she asked tiredly.

"And then, we'll track down a hyaenir and grab its blood before embarking on the task of capturing two dozen chimmeris." I held up one of Izaak's gold tokens between my fingers. "Then we go home and beat the shit out of a certain sorcerer."

"Can't kill him though," Mikhail added. "Not until we get what we need from him."

"True." I tucked the token back into my pocket. "But after that, he's fair game."

"How do you know we'll even be able to get out of here after capturing all the chimmeris?" Justina grimaced as she placed a hand over her abdomen where I'd stabbed her.

"The blood oath," Cassius murmured. "Emir might have found a way around it, but it's still in effect. They have to honor their promise that Nemain will regain the ability to open gateways once all two dozen chimmeris are captured."

"The asshole speaks the truth," I said reluctantly.

"I do that occasionally," Cassius said dryly.

"That remains to be seen." I gave him a cool look. We'd be doing some digging into his claims about being related to Elisa and Misha once we got out of here. "Your mother . . ." I trailed off.

"Is dead." His voice was completely devoid of emotion, as were his eyes as he stared at Justina's wall of ice. "She couldn't handle having her children taken away from her and tried to find them."

I closed my eyes for a moment. She must have loved them if she defied the Vampire Council and looked for them.

"For now, we need to survive the night." I opened my eyes again. "We'll go hunting in a few hours. The chimmeris can be out in this realm's 'daylight,' they just don't prefer it. But that means you two will be fine." I waved a hand at Justina and Cassius.

"How long can you keep that up?" Stela asked Justina as she gestured at the ice.

"As long as it takes." The vampire closed her eyes. "I will survive this place. I will see my son again."

Stela's eyes softened for a moment before she settled down

next to Andrei and leaned against the cave wall. She looked at me. "So we wait?"

Somewhere in the forest, a cacophony of howls and roars sounded.

I took a seat between Mikhail and Magos. "We wait."

"For now, I'm going to stay in my human skin," I said several hours later. "The chimmeris should be returning to their roosts soon, but the hyaenir will be active. I think it makes sense to target them first because they're solo hunters, whereas the chimmeris are always in groups."

"My brother needs to stay in his human skin because the wolf is too close to the surface, but I can shif—" Stela's offer was cut off by a low growl from across the cave. We all looked to the vampires.

"You're being stubborn!" Cassius hissed at Justina where they stood in front of her ice wall.

Even with the dim lighting, I could see the beads of sweat on Justina's forehead. And now that I thought about it, the scent of her blood still permeated the air. My brows pinched together. She still hadn't healed?

"Do you need blood?" I called out.

Cassius' and Justina's heads whipped towards me.

"No," she said at the same time Cassius ground out, "Yes."

I rolled my eyes. "We don't have time for this. You can have mine." I took one step forward, only for a hand to grip me by the throat and yank me back against a hard chest. Mikhail's other arm wrapped around my stomach, a low growl vibrating up his chest and throat.

Okay, then.

"Vampires are territorial over those they regularly feed from." Cassius gave me a patient look. "As tasty as you no doubt are"—Mikhail growled even lower—"you're off limits to us," Cassius finished.

"Oh, for fuck's sake," Stela snapped and stomped across the cave. "Drink." She shoved her forearm out towards Justina.

Cassius smirked, a sly glint in his gaze as he glanced at Stela and then back to Justina before moving to stand next to me. Something that made Mikhail stiffen behind me. "Relax, Azuris. I just want to have a better view."

It was my turn to stiffen at Cassius so casually using Mikhail's birth name. Few people knew it. Justina was one of them, and apparently Cassius as well. Which meant that at one time, Mikhail had trusted him enough to give that to him.

It was possible that Cassius had slipped in using it, but I doubted it; he wielded truth and lies like carefully crafted weapons.

Justina sighed, a put upon expression on her face. Then, between one blink and the next, she stood behind the pretty werewolf. The arm Stela had extended was pressed diagonally against her chest, pinned there by Justina's hand as the vampire tugged the wolf closer.

"You sure?" Justina trailed her lips against Stela's neck. She had a couple of inches on her, but I had no doubt that Stela was strong enough to break out of Justina's hold if she wanted to. Despite the wolf yellow that flashed in her eyes, she didn't try to pull away. *Interesting.* "You might grow to enjoy my bite, wolf."

"Not a chance," Stela said evenly. "But you're not biting my brother, and I'm tired of smelling your blood in the air. Try not to get wounded next time, vampire."

Justina struck, her fangs sinking into Stela's flesh, eliciting a groan from the werewolf. Out of the corner of my eye, I saw Magos go completely still.

"How about Magos and I go check outside and make sure

the coast is all clear," I said lightly. "Justina can you, uh, maybe do something about that wall?"

A crack formed in the ice and started to spread.

Mikhail moved to stand in front of me. "Why don't you stay here? Magos and I can mist outside so Justina can leave the wall up, just in case."

The memory of monsters howling and clawing at our safe haven all night was fresh on my mind.

"No," I said quickly. "It'll be good for me to familiarize myself again with the realm. Maybe it'll help me remember more useful things."

"Nemai—" he started.

"I said I got this," I snapped. Justina's ice wall collapsed, and I stalked through it. "Come on, Magos."

A dark, hazy, red sky greeted us as we exited the cave. I flipped it off and started walking off with no particular purpose in mind other than getting Magos away from the cave and Justina feeding.

Based on the soft moans Stela was making, the werewolf was enjoying it quite a bit.

"You've been pushing Mikhail a lot recently," Magos said calmly as he and I explored the woods immediately outside the cave. "It's hard for him to watch you put yourself in harm's way."

I peered at a fern tree that had a wide hole in the trunk about six feet up. "Yeah, well, he's just going to have to accept that I'm every bit as protective of him as he is of me."

"Are *you* though?" Magos peered at the tree with me. "Accepting it? Looks a little one-sided to me. You'll do anything for him but won't allow him to do the same. I thought you moved past trying to do everything yourself."

That was before I fucked up, and you got hurt, I thought bitterly. "Mikhail and I are figuring things out," I said instead. "We both have a lot going on right now."

There. A sufficiently vague response. I narrowed my eyes at the tree. Did something just move in that hollowed-out part?

"The two of you are worried about me," Magos said quietly. "Both of you hold yourselves responsible. Mikhail is drowning in guilt. And you're dealing by trying to envelop him in bubble wrap instead of allowing him to fight by your side."

My fingers coiled into tight fists before I forced myself to release them while I turned to face him. "What happened to you is my fault. I left Hades' knife in the dragon realm. I'm the reason the Olympians found out he was still alive. And I dragged you all along to help save him and my brother. You were only in harm's way because of me, and I will never forgive myself for it."

I let out a long breath. There. Got it all out. On some level, Magos had to know what I said was the truth. It was for the best that we all acknowledged it.

"Foolish child." He gave me a small smile. "I kept you safe. That's all I ever wanted."

"That's not what I wanted!" I screamed, not even bothering to argue with him referring to me as a child again. Hot tears burned down my cheeks. "You've already lost so much. I hate that your love for me has cost you your memories of Hasina." I angrily wiped at my face.

Magos grabbed me by the shoulders and pulled me away from the tree just as a long, vibrant blue tentacle snapped out and wrapped around the empty air where I'd been standing.

"See?" I choked. "You never stop taking care of me. I only had to protect you the one time, and I failed."

The tentacle silently slid back into the tree.

Bright copper eyes looked at me for a long moment. "Let's walk around some more," he finally said.

I nodded with relief as I frantically tried to pull myself together. A realm full of monsters was really not the place to have an emotional breakdown.

Magos and I meandered through the trees, staying close enough to the cave entrance that we could make a run for it if we needed to. What passed for dawn around here was starting to break so I wasn't too worried about running into anything nasty. There were a lot of large predators here, but as long as we made it back to the cave, they wouldn't be able to follow. I was fairly confident Magos and I could handle anything else.

For a few minutes, we just walked through the ancient forest, avoiding a couple more tentacles and warily keeping an eye on something with a long, scaled tail jumping around in the canopy before gliding away.

"About eight months ago, something happened to me at The Inferno that I didn't think would ever happen," Magos said quietly. "There was a woman there, fae I think, and I found her attractive. More than in just a general observation type of way. Like I . . . just me . . . thought she was pretty."

"Oh . . ." I bit my lip as I ducked under a vine.

Periodically, Kaysea and I had thought someone would pique his interest over the years, but it'd never happened. He just politely turned down anyone who flirted with him. Someone had caught his eye though . . . two months before he'd been cursed.

Fuck. Had I screwed up Magos' second chance at finding love?

"Nothing was to come of it, Nemain," Magos said, clearly reading everything in my expression. "She was meeting someone—romantically, that is. But it was the first time I felt that way about someone and didn't immediately get hit with guilt." He shook his head, a mournful smile tugging at the corners of his mouth. "I know Hasina wouldn't have wanted this for me. She would've wanted me to be happy. And if our situations were reversed, I would want the same for her. But there is a difference between what the mind knows and what the heart feels."

"If you're telling me this to alleviate some of my guilt, you're failing," I rasped. "Because all I'm hearing is that you were close to moving on before Artemis cursed you."

Magos placed his hand on my forearm, and I stopped, my eyes on the trees around us because if I looked at him again, I would cry. I'd already done that once since we'd left the cave, and I really didn't want to do it again.

"That isn't why I told you," he said gently. "You and Mikhail thought I had it all together, but I didn't. Nobody truly does. You blame yourself for what happened, but don't you see that I hold myself accountable too? That I'm disappointed in myself for not being stronger? I should be able to let go of my memories of Hasina. To not let that loss torment me the way it does. But here I am"—he spread his arms wide—"losing my mind over some dark spots in my memory."

"It's more than that though," I argued, finally meeting his gaze. "The curse will torment you regardless of whether you accept the loss of those memories. You won't know what you lost, only that something is missing. Artemis designed it as a lose-lose scenario."

Work-arounds like writing down the memories didn't work either. For one, that was a tedious task that would take a long time. Magos and Hasina had been married for decades. The curse might steal a small moment of him bringing her flowers one random morning. It wasn't something he'd necessarily remember to write down, but once it was gone it would be a hole in his memories that would weigh on him.

So many small moments would add up. And the curse made sure he could never let it go.

"That's my point." Magos rested a hand on my shoulder. "I need to come to terms with my guilt around the curse and how I'm handling it, as do you. This is not my fault. Nor is it yours."

"I don't know what to do with that," I rasped. "It's

Artemis' fault. But I've killed her a dozen times already. It doesn't fix anything."

"Sometimes, there is no fix." Magos gave me a sad smile.

"Don't give up on me." Desperation coated my voice. "We've beaten the odds before. We can do it again."

Magos wrapped his arms around me, hugging me tightly. "I won't lose faith in you, Nemain. I'm just asking you not to take on everything yourself. Knowing that you and Mikhail have each other gives me so much peace. Please let him help you."

The thought of anything happening to Mikhail opened up a dark void in my soul. Even though I was blocked from my devourer flames, I could have sworn I felt them flicker in rage.

"I'll try," I lied.

Magos leaned his head on top of mine and let out a long sigh. "Losing the two of you would destroy me faster than any curse." He hugged me tighter. "Try harder."

Chapter Seventeen

"Alright. In theory, vampires should be more sensitive to the presence of hyaenir, and werewolves should be more sensitive to chimmeris." I scanned the shadows in the forest around us. We were a quarter mile from the cave now, but so far, we hadn't encountered anything. "If anyone detects anything, let everyone know immediately, okay?"

A chorus of quiet agreements sounded. On either side of me, Andrei and Stela in their wolf forms looked at me and let out soft woofs.

Only Mikhail didn't respond because he was still mad at me for insisting on going out with Magos. Although now, it was more frustrated annoyance burning through our mating bond than the raging bonfire it'd been when Magos and I had returned to get everyone.

"Alright. Let me see if I can find us a general direction to go," I murmured before jogging over to the nearest tree, crouching down, and then leaping straight up. My fingers grasped a branch ten feet off the ground, and I pulled myself up. As long as I stayed close to the trunk, the branches were thick enough to support my weight, so I continued my upward trajectory until I reached the top.

It was hard to see because a thin mist hugged the tops of the trees. Plus, the light cast from the deep red sky wasn't particularly useful. Still, I could make out at least the general landscape. Which was . . . an endless forest. There were a few dips and rises, but no mountains or breaks in the trees that I could see. Nothing stood out as useful as I slowly spun around.

Wait.

"What the fuck is that?" I breathed and leaned forward slightly. In the distance, there was a glow, too intense to be from something like the luminescent moss of the cave. If it was this bright from here, it had to be even more so at the source.

Maybe bright enough to keep the chimmeris and hyaenir at bay?

Out of the corner of my eye, I saw giant fern trees tremble in the distance, like something huge was passing by them.

A second later, mist swirled next to me, and Mikhail appeared on the branch. "Something is headed our way. We can only faintly hear it, so probably half a mile, but it sounds large."

I pointed southeast, to where the trees still swayed. "Probably the same thing that roared when we first arrived." I swung my hand northward. "That's where we need to go."

He squinted. "Are those trees . . . glowing?"

"No idea." I shrugged. "But let's find out."

Mikhail looked down before returning his gaze to me. "Do not fall." He glanced at the trees snapping in the distance. "But also hurry up."

Some of the mist clung to my skin where Mikhail had vanished.

I wonder . . .

I glanced at a branch ten feet below and pulled on the mist.

Coldness spread through my veins, and it felt like the air froze in my lungs. I gasped, eyes squeezing shut.

"Oh shit." My eyes snapped open, and I spun my arms, trying to regain my balance on the branch beneath the one I'd targeted. This one was way thinner.

It wasn't going to hold my weight much lon—

Snap.

That same cool mist wrapped around me, and then I was on another branch. I grinned. Fun.

In small bursts, I made my way down the tree until I landed directly behind Mikhail. "Boo!"

Magos smiled, shaking his head at my antics.

"You're using my magic," Mikhail said wryly before vanishing into mist and reappearing behind me. "I can feel it." He slapped my ass. "Now, how about we run before the enormous monster arrives and has us for an appetizer?"

"Something that large will be slow." I tilted my head back and forth. "Probably." I looked at the others. "We're heading away from it anyway. North, to be exact. There's something glowing about five miles away, bright enough that we could see it from up there."

"Lead the way." Magos looked north. "I'll guard our backs."

"If anyone senses chimmeris or hyaenir, we'll stop to investigate; otherwise, we'll keep heading to the potential safe zone." I raised my eyes to the sky peeking through the trees. "We should make it there with plenty of time to spare. Any questions?"

"Nope," Cassius drawled. "Onward, shifter."

"Don't call her that," Mikhail snapped.

Cassius raised his brows at my mate's outburst. I didn't want to explain that Mikhail and me referring to each other as our species was a thing, so I grabbed Mikhail's hand, and we took off at a steady jog.

The wolves flanked us, running on silent paws. Behind us, Cassius, Justina, and Magos followed just as quietly.

Fern trees towered over us, and other fauna filled the forest floor. One of the most prevalent was a red vine with a bright green flower blooming every six inches. The petals were slightly luminescent, but what really stood out was the viscous yellow liquid dripping out from the center. It reminded me a little of the filling of a lemon pie.

A memory of Andrei trying to taste a flower in the fae realm popped into my head. He seemed to have more sense now, but still . . .

Andrei, don't lick any of the flowers, I pushed the thought out. Mikhail laughed quietly under his breath, and I heard Stela snort in amusement.

Creatures occasionally moved above us in the trees, and I caught glimpses of things racing along beside us, clearly trying to figure out if we were worth attacking. One rumbling growl from the wolves had them all deciding to find easier prey elsewhere.

Mile after mile, we ran, and just when I thought we would make it to our destination without encountering a single devourer, Mikhail reached out, his fingers brushing my forearm. "Hyaenir," he said in a low tone as we drew to a stop.

We'd been keeping a good pace but not all-out sprinting. I wasn't even close to winded, nor was anyone else. Andrei and Stela sat on their haunches, noses in the air as they tried to catch the scent. But all the vampires looked dead ahead, a predatory focus in their gazes.

"Can you sense how far?" I asked quietly, trying to do the mental calculation. We couldn't be more than a mile from our destination.

"Hard to tell." Magos' lips pressed into a hard line, his copper eyes peering through the trees, as if he could see his target. He pointed just slightly to the left of the direction we'd been running. "Half a mile would be my guess."

Half a mile. I could work with that. Now I just had to get Mikhail to agree to my plan.

"You all need to hang back," I said casually, rolling onto the balls of my feet and cracking my neck from side to side as I loosened up my body.

I didn't have to turn to know Mikhail was giving me a frustrated look. The one that said if I were anyone else, I would be experiencing a painful death right now, but he loved me, so that wasn't an option. Instead, he just had to bottle up all his rage and wait for a different target to present itself.

Tension filled the air as he remained silent.

Magos cleared his throat. "Why do we need to 'hang back'?"

Based on his tight expression, he didn't like this either.

"Because if we can sense the hyaenir, then it stands to reason they can sense us," Cassius pointed out. "The wolves are too inexperienced to take it down, which leaves Nemain as the best option."

"Exactly," I said almost reluctantly because I really didn't like that it was Cassius in agreement with me. But it was the best plan; I just needed Mikhail to see that. "It'll be infinitely harder to get the blood we need if the hyaenir gets its armor up. I can sneak up on it, stab it, and run to the glowing patch of forest. Easy peasy."

The side of my face burned from Mikhail trying to stare a hole through it. I stubbornly didn't look at him. Fingers grabbed my chin and twisted my head in his direction.

"You will take Andrei and Stela with you," Mikhail said in a calm tone that meant he was on the verge of losing it. I opened my mouth to argue, only to snap it shut when his grip tightened and six feet of pissed-off vampire filled my vision.

"You will take the lead. They'll be there as backup or a distraction. This is not up for debate."

"Not the boss of me," I reminded him half-heartedly.

In my peripheral vision, I saw the wolves trot a few feet away while Magos sighed.

Mikhail chuckled darkly before releasing his grip and closing the distance between us. His mouth crashed against mine in a brutal kiss that he broke off all too quickly. "Run, shifter," he breathed against my lips. "And be prepared for me to catch you later."

"Looking forward to it, vampire," I whispered back before taking off in a dead sprint.

The werewolves melted into the trees as if they were ghosts. I knew they were there, but for the life of me, I couldn't spot them. My feet flew through the forest as I cut a path to where Magos had pointed, only slowing when we got close to a half mile.

I slunk forward and quietly withdrew Thaxea's doohickey.

"Push the end with the glyph while the other side is against the creature's hide. Five seconds should draw enough blood," her instructions echoed in my mind.

Five seconds. An eternity in a fight.

Sneaking up on the hyaenir would've been easier in my feline form, but I needed opposable thumbs to use Thaxea's device. I would get only one chance at this, and who knew when such an opportunity would present itself again.

The distinct sound of flesh being torn from bone filtered through the trees. I crouched a little more as I slunk through the underbrush. The thick foliage parted enough for me to get a glimpse of the hyaenir, and the devourer was exactly as I remembered.

A stout body on four legs, the front two longer than the hind ones, causing its spine to slope downward. The joints of the front legs were angled so they could run fast but also twist their forearms enough to hug trees. And they did that nearly as fast as they ran. It was a trait passed on to the werewolves. Thaxea might have used wolves to pretty up her creation, but she'd kept the lethal, predatorial characteristics of the hyaenir intact.

The hyaenir raised its blunt head that sat on a thick, powerful neck, a foot-long piece of bone in its massive jaws. *Crunch.* Two bone halves thudded to the forest floor as the devourer crushed what remained in its mouth before swallowing it and tearing off another chunk.

Coarse, purple fur coated the devourer's body. There was an oddness to the texture that wouldn't make sense until the hyaenir went into defense mode. And then, every single one of those hairs would rise, each one razor sharp not only on the tips but the sides as well. I'd made the mistake of tackling one once, and it had been like dragging my hand across broken glass.

I needed to be fast enough to stab it before it raised its fur and agile enough to avoid those bone-crushing jaws when it retaliated.

What had I done the last time I'd gotten into a fight with a hyaenir? I tried to tug the memory free, but my time in this realm had been a mix of awe and terror. Jinx had been with me then. Our normal tactic was to stage a distraction . . .

Can one of you make a small noise? Like step on a twig or something? I pushed the thought out to the wolves. I need the hyaenir's attention to be somewhere else but also not in full defense mode.

I paused behind an enormous fern tree fifteen feet from the hyaenir. The slight breeze was in my favor, putting me downwind of it, and I didn't dare try to sneak any closer yet. Instead, I waited for Andrei or Stela to do as I requested. Not for the first time, I wished werewolves had better telepathic abilities so we could coordinate better.

Every muscle in my legs tensed as I prepared to sprint forward, my fingers tight around the spelled crystal device in my right hand.

Get the blood. Run to the glowing sanctuary. Hope that the very pissed-off monster won't follow me into it.

Something snapped in the trees on the other side of the hyaenir. Instantly, its head whipped up, bits of flesh dangling from its teeth as it peered into the dark trees.

I bolted forward, closing the distance in a flash. My thumb pushed down on the end of the crystal, and I stabbed downward, straight into the space between the beast's shoulder blades.

An ear-shattering roar punched me as I counted to five in my head and yanked the device away. Not fast enough. I screamed as the hyaenir's hair rose. It felt like hundreds of needles pierced my right hand and wrist. Still, I didn't let go of the crystal, leaping back just as the beast whirled and swept a claw-tipped paw forward. I sucked in my stomach, the razor-sharp edges snagging pieces of my leather vest but missing my flesh.

The hyaenir lunged towards me, its maw gaping wide and showing off two rows of sharp teeth, but I was already running.

I held my bloody arm to my chest, the crystal clutched in my fingers, and ran like a hound of hell was chasing me.

Actually, I wished it were a hellhound. It would have been slower.

On four legs, I could outrun a hyaenir, but not on two. I weaved and ducked under low-hanging branches, forcing the devourer to dodge as well. But the damn thing was immediately back on my heels, and if it landed a bite, I was fucking done.

Mist swirled around me, but I shoved Mikhail's magic away. *Not the fucking time!* I wanted to scream at it. But it wasn't like it would understand. Mikhail's magic was merely reacting to fear-laced adrenaline pumping through my blood and down the bond. It wanted to help, but my control over the mist magic was tenuous and required too much concentration on my part to attempt to use it now.

Suddenly, the trees thinned a bit, and there was nothing to hamper the devourer's movements. *Shit.* I threw myself to the side on nothing but instinct, a sharp cry spilling from my lips as my shoulder slammed into the earth and jostled my wounded arm.

The hyaenir sailed through the air, landing where I would have been, and spun as soon as its paws hit the dirt.

It really wasn't fair that something so big was fast and agile too.

Three pairs of eyes running vertically down the beast's face watched me. Its purple fur was still raised, and I suspected I could have spotted my blood on it if I looked closely enough. The hyaenir didn't growl or make any noise; it just studied me. I wondered if it sensed my devourer magic and didn't know quite what to make of it or was wondering if I had any nasty tricks up my sleeve.

It didn't really matter because I likely had seconds before it decided to just go for the kill. I didn't know if I'd be able to summon my swords in time to counter its attack, and even if I could, it was unlikely I could do enough damage quickly enough to keep it from ripping me to shreds.

Time seemed to slow as I became aware of every breath, watching the monster and waiting for it to make a move so I could do the same. Part of me was terrified, but another part— arguably a larger one—felt exhilarated. There was nothing quite like dancing on the knife's edge of life and death.

The hyaenir's eyes narrowed ever so slightly. Just as I was about to twist to the side and summon my swords, its long ears swiveled, and a deep, warning growl rippled from its throat a second before Andrei slammed into its hind legs, aiming for the devourer's knees. A second after he hit, Stela rammed the devourer's other side, and it went down hard.

I didn't wait to see what happened after that. Once again, I took off at a flat-out sprint. *You better be running*, I mentally screamed at the wolves. Twin howls echoed through the forest, and I heard them racing after me.

The sharp, angry scream of the hyaenir rang out.

Run faster, I urged as the brightly lit area filled my vision. One hundred yards. We could do this. I wrung every last drop of speed out of my body. Stela blew past me, a deep crimson streak on her side. Andrei paced himself next to me. I had to make it because the foolish werewolf wouldn't leave me behind.

Behind us, the devourer roared. It was entirely too close for comfort.

If it kept chasing us into the glowing forest, we were fucked. Maybe we'd be able to hold it off long enough for the others to get here. But if the hyaenir ventured into that area, there was a decent chance the chimmeris would too.

A brilliant blue glow momentarily blinded me. It was so at odds with the dim red sky, I had to close my eyes for a second, opening them only to blink several times as I hoped I didn't run into anything. I slowed, Andrei doing the same next to me until we both stopped, Stela appearing in front of us.

All three of us breathed hard.

I turned to look back in the direction of our mad dash, and I could just barely make out the large, dark form of the hyaenir pacing outside the boundary. It let out a frustrated whine before melting back into the dark forest.

"Oh, thank fuck." I bent over, one hand pressed against my knee while the other clutched the cylinder to my chest, and gulped down breaths for a minute before straightening. "You two, keep watch while I get this"—I gingerly raised my shredded arm—"cleaned up before Mikhail gets here and see—"

Mist shot to the area in front of me, and a second later Mikhail snapped into existence. His eyes immediately went to my blood-soaked arm.

"I got it!" I held up the cylinder and gave it a little shake.

His twilight eyes darkened before he glanced at Andrei. "The others will be in momentarily. Don't go wandering off. I need to have a little chat with my mate."

"I'm actually kind of tir—ow! Watch the arm, vampire!" I hissed as Mikhail threw me over his shoulder.

"Shouldn't have let yourself get hurt," he replied gruffly and stalked further into the luminescent sanctuary.

Chapter Eighteen

"Damn it, Mikhail!" I glared up at him from where he'd unceremoniously dumped me onto the ground. For someone who had been so pissed off at seeing my bloody arm, he didn't seem all that concerned about injuring me further. "We can't just leave them alone! Just because the devourers can't enter this area doesn't mean other predators can't."

"I heard you the first three times you said that." He snorted.

"And yet you didn't answer." I spread my arms to the side, wincing a little. The wounds had already healed, but my right arm was still sore.

I drew my arms back and rubbed the enchanted bones Izaak had embedded in my chest. A small spark of magic bit at me, warning me to stay away, and I let out a frustrated exhale as I dropped my hand.

Some of the anger faded from Mikhail's face, and he settled on the ground next to me, crossing his legs so our knees brushed as he leaned back onto his palms.

"Magos and the others weren't far behind me; they'll take care of the pups." He crossed his arms and gave me a hard stare. "No more going off on your own, Nemain. I don't give a shit what reasons you come up with."

"Well, I'm not going to stand there and watch you get hurt when I can prevent it!" I screamed in frustration.

"I'm going to get hurt!" he yelled back. "You're going to get hurt! We're all going to get fucking hurt, Nemain! We just might get hurt *less* if we're together!"

"We were all together when Magos got hurt," I rasped. Suddenly, all the fight drained from me, and I just felt numb. "I'm almost healed anyway." I shook my right arm around, showing that it was still attached to my body and functioning normally. Mostly. It still tingled a bit. Did the hyaenir have toxins in the stabby bits of their fur?

I wiggled my arm a little more. Eh. The numbness wasn't spreading and seemed to be lessening.

"Nemain."

"Yes?" I blinked at Mikhail and slowly lowered my arm back down.

He sighed and rubbed his face before nodding towards my pants pocket, where I'd tucked away the hyaenir's blood. "Did you get what we needed at least?"

"Of course I did. Should be enough for Thaxea. Now we just have to deal with the chimmeris." I mirrored his position and leaned back on my hands. I was tired, and standing was overrated. He'd carried me out here, and I fully intended on making him do the same on the way back. "We lucked out with the hyaenir. What do you think the chances are of our good luck streak holding out?"

"Honestly?" He glanced suspiciously at the tree behind me. "I'm a little worried that tree is going to topple over on us just for you suggesting such a thing."

I let out a low, raspy laugh. He wasn't wrong.

Silence stretched between us, and I studied my mate, who still stared up at the tree. During Mikhail's rough handling of me on our walk here, I'd gotten a good look at the trees. They were the same fern trees that grew throughout the forest, but the luminescent glow came from some type of fungus growing on them. Small critters raced across the treetops, leaving behind little footprints. It felt almost whimsical and definitely out of place in a world of darkness and death.

Our mating bond was suspiciously quiet, which made me think Mikhail was doing his best to keep his emotions locked down. But he must have dragged me out here for a reason, and this weighted silence wasn't exactly our usual foreplay . . .

Pain flickered inside my soul.

It wasn't mine though.

"Tell me about Cassius."

The pain erupted into a bonfire, and a muscle beneath Mikhail's eye twitched. "He's an asshole."

"I gathered that much." I gave him a sad smile.

We sat there in silence for a couple of minutes before Mikhail sighed. "He was my first . . ." A humourless laugh spilled from his lips. "Everything. Cassius was my first everything."

Suddenly, I wanted to kill the tricky, handsome bastard even more.

"Feeling murderous, my love?" he asked, a touch of amusement driving away some of the darkness in his tone.

"Yes." I didn't bother lying because I was sure my vindictive emotions were screaming down the bond. The rational part of me knew Cassius was no threat to me and Mikhail, nor was Justina and her obnoxious flirting, but that didn't stop me from wanting to carve out their hearts and offer them as a present to Mikhail.

That was a good mating gift, right?

"I like when you get all territorial." He bumped his shoulder against mine.

"In my defense, I am trapped in a realm with not one but

two of your exes." I bumped him back. "I think the amount of restraint I've shown is truly remarkable."

"Let me get through this story, and I'll reward you appropriately."

Heat pulsed through me, and I turned to find Mikhail's twilight eyes on me, full of the same wicked desire. "Explain quickly."

He laughed and intertwined his fingers with mine. Blue flames sprung into existence and wrapped around our joined hands as I laid my head back on Mikhail's shoulder.

"Cassius' magic might allow him to teleport, but his true power is his ability to read others, to see what makes them tick. He's even better than Justina at it. I suppose they're both equally good at keeping secrets," he mused. "She's kept her son hidden from the Council all this time, and I had no idea that the man I'd been in love with was the son of my enemy. Hell, I didn't even know Marius was alive back then. I'd believed the Council's lies about his death."

"They wanted you under their control and to harness your rage for their benefit. You never would have become their assassin if you'd known Marius was there, pulling the strings the entire time."

"I was their pet assassin for thirty years before I met Cassius."

I tried to do the math in my head. "So he was, what, mid-twenties?"

"Twenty-two."

My eyebrows raised. "And you were . . ."

"Fifty-two."

"Ha!" I grinned. "Who's the cradle robber now?"

"First, you are *centuries* older than Andrei," Mikhail said wryly. "And second, Cassius was the one who pursued me. I rebuffed him several times because I had a bit of a reputation and was used to the attention of self-serving vampires."

"And just what kind of reputation was that?" I flipped our intertwined hands so mine was on top, watching my flames joyously dance across my skin. "Gorgeous, broody assassin?"

"Close. Gorgeous, broody, *virgin* assassin."

"I don't even understand how that's possible." I shook my head. While I teased him all the time, Mikhail really was gorgeous. Prettier than me. I would never admit that out loud though. "I mean, you never . . . not once? With anyone? In fifty-two years?"

"I told you before that I was quite shy in my home realm before it fell," he reminded me. "Then my people came here. I became a vampire. My people died. Magos and I went our separate ways. For a while, I was so consumed by grief and rage that I had no interest in anyone like that. By the time I started to come out of that haze, I found myself surrounded by beings who wanted to use me or brag about being the one who finally got me into bed."

My fingers tightened around his as I thought about how isolating that must have been. To be surrounded by others but know you couldn't trust any of them, and that while you all may share a similar purpose in life, none of them actually gave a shit about you.

Like Mikhail, I'd lost myself after my parents had died— pushed Cian away and shunned everyone but Jinx.

Eventually, I'd met Pele, and she'd pieced my soul back together without asking for anything in return. I hadn't even known she'd been doing it until years had gone by and it'd suddenly felt like I could breathe again.

But Mikhail hadn't found a Pele to help him; he'd gotten Cassius instead.

I raised my head, sitting a little straighter so I could look at Mikhail, but his gaze was once again focused on the tree.

"What did he do to you?"

"The original members of the Vampire Council were

elders from the village. They'd had power as humans, and that'd carried over when they'd become vampires, but it didn't take long for others to rise into power and demand a seat. To claim one, they had to prove they belonged there. That they could be cunning and ruthless." Mikhail tilted his head towards me, his dark hair falling across his face. "And what better way to do that than to seduce the vampire assassin, twist him around your finger by making him fall in love with you, and then convince him to kill your political rivals?"

It was probably for the best I didn't have access to my devourer flames right now, because I was fairly certain I would have burned the forest down.

"I found out it had all been a lie when I was summoned before the Council and Cassius detailed exactly what he had done. He told them intimate details of our time together, the key moments he had seized on to win over my trust, and how he had manipulated me into killing others. It's not just that it was humiliating or that I'd had my heart ripped out." He drew in a deep breath and let it out. "I'd walked away from Magos. It was bad enough that I'd left the one person who'd actually cared about me, but he'd had no one else either. I'd thrown all that away, only to find myself surrounded by vipers." Mikhail shook his head, his dark brows bunching together. "Part of me has to give Cassius his due; he truly had me fooled. I may have been inexperienced when it came to relationships and sex, but I wasn't naïve. I knew Cassius was ambitious and wanted power, but I still fell for his bullshit."

"Sounds like he and Sebastian would have made quite the pair," I said tightly. "Took me almost a century to realize that asshole had been using me."

"At least some part of him actually loved you," Mikhail grunted. "It was twisted, sure, but it was there. After earning his seat on the Council, Cassius acted exactly as he does now.

He'd flirt and tease me, as if he hadn't publicly ripped my heart out."

I wanted to march back through the forest, find Cassius, and bash his head in, but I also remembered the bit of insight my magic had given me into his soul. That scent of a raging river, barreling on because it had no choice. That feeling of desolation and how all his flirtation with me felt empty, like he was only doing it to get a rise out of Mikhail. All of which I just didn't understand. Cassius had gotten his seat on the Council, and Mikhail had walked away from the vampires years ago, so why continue the act?

"Did he ever tell the Council your birth name?" I asked.

Mikhail blinked. "I . . . don't know. If he did, it wasn't in front of me, and nobody has ever brought it up."

Great. A complicated villain. Ally? What even the fuck was Cassius?

For all we knew, he was lying about being Elisa and Misha's older brother. Maybe all of this was a setup to get into our good graces. We'd need to figure out how to validate his claims once we made it out of here. Then we could figure out what category to put him in. And Justina. And maybe Lir.

"We need a murder board," I muttered. "But like for Do Not Murder, Maybe Murder, and Definitely Murder."

"I knew it was only a matter of time before you'd want one after you saw the one Ashling put together." Mikhail sighed. "Given everyone's shifting loyalties and connections, I suppose it would be useful."

"We can set it up in the second-floor apartment and invite Kaysea over. She loves to color-code shit, so she'll . . ." I trailed off as a familiar-but-not feeling hit me.

In an instant, I was on my feet, mist swirling off my dual swords. Mikhail's muscled back was pressed against mine as we scanned the woods.

Six feet in front of me, the air rippled. It reminded me of

when a gateway opened, but not exactly the same. This felt . . . weaker?

A dark form took shape.

"Mikhail," I warned.

He moved to stand at my side, and we watched as the shape coalesced into a six-and-a-half-foot man. A worn cloak covered most of his body but failed to hide his warrior build. From beneath the hood pulled up to hide most of his face, dark brown hair spilled to his shoulders, framing a square jaw that would probably break my hand if I punched it.

He was more visible now, but not entirely solid. "Throw a dagger at him," I said under my breath.

Mikhail didn't question my request, and a second later, one of his throwing knives hurtled at the stranger's face—and passed straight through it, embedding into a tree trunk behind him.

"Projection?" Mikhail asked.

"I don't think so." I shook my head, puzzling over what I felt. When I opened a gateway, I tore a hole between two realms. "I think we're looking into another realm and our friend is on the other side."

"You're more clever than I've been told." A deep voice chuckled, and slowly, as if he didn't want to startle us, he reached up and drew his hood back. My eyes darted to his ears. Tapered. Fae. They weren't the only ones with pointed ears, but my gut told me that's what he was, even though I couldn't sense a lick of magic off him, which further confirmed my suspicion that, somehow, we were looking into another realm without a gateway being open. Something I hadn't known was possible.

I glanced back as a small smile flashed across his handsome face, and the breath froze in my lungs.

I'd seen that smile. Just like I'd see the green of the stranger's eyes that reminded me of spring grass. It'd been on a smaller and more innocent face, but it was all the same. This man was related to Finn, and there was only one person it could be, even if it should be impossible.

"Balor." Dread coated the name as it passed my tongue.

"I thought we were overdue for a chat." His bright green eyes skimmed the trees behind me, a wistful element to them. "This was one of the first realms I sent my devourers to. My sisters' spell keeps me locked in my current realm, but it's weakening—just as they are—and they're having to choose where they reinforce it. This is a lost realm that no one cares about, and my connection to it is old. It won't be long before I can walk in it." Those sly eyes slid back to me. "How fortuitous that you ended up here."

"Only it's not, is it?" My voice remained steady despite feeling like the rug had just been yanked out from under me.

The exiled fae king gave me a placating smile. "Do you really think the sorcerers would have bothered speaking with a warlock?"

"You went through all of this just to speak with me?" I asked numbly.

"Technically, all I did was ensure the sorcerer responded to Lir and then monitored the situation from there to make sure you ended up in this realm. Do you not think you're worth it?" His stare turned curious. "From a magical standpoint, you're one of a kind. I'm a warrior by trade but a scholar at heart. Your unusual heritage alone would make you of interest to me, but you've also put yourself at the center of an ancient war and taken something of mine."

"Finn's not yours." I pointed one of my swords at him. "If you ever step outside your realm, I'll kill you."

"We'll kill you," Mikhail corrected me. "We've killed gods already. A fae king would be nice to add to the tally."

"It's always important to have goals in life," I agreed.

"Ah." Balor smiled widely. "The infamous banter I've

heard about. That smart mouth of yours irritates Lir, but I admit that I find it entertaining. Almost as entertaining as the idea that you could ever defeat me."

He stretched a hand forward as if he were touching an invisible wall. I sucked in a breath as he tracked his fingers through the air, like he was skimming them over water. The empty space between us rippled, and the landscape around us completely changed. Gone was the beautiful forest of dancing starlight. Instead, a massive citadel rose in the distance within a sprawling city. Thick trees decorated the landscape with patches of wildflowers springing up here and there.

And tens of thousands of fae wandered around me. All with weapons strapped to their bodies, as if they were just waiting for the order to go to war.

The air rippled again, and the city vanished.

I understood in that moment why the fae queens had locked their brother away and were practically killing themselves to keep the ward in place. Because if Balor and his army ever got out, there would be no fighting it.

There were plenty of powerful fae who followed the fae queens, but they relied on magic to fight, not steel. What would they do if Balor's army of tens of thousands marched on them? Warriors who had been training for thousands of years and were immune to magical attacks?

"Good." Balor nodded. "You understand how foolish it is to oppose me."

"There are worse things than being a fool." I raised my chin, meeting his eyes. "My statement stands. You step out of your realm, and I—we will kill you."

Balor tilted his head, genuine curiosity brimming in his eyes once more. "Why?"

"Because you're a threat to our family," I said simply.

"And threats are neutralized," Mikhail finished.

"I see." Balor walked along the barrier separating our

realms. He raised a hand and let his fingers trail across the invisible boundary once more. It rippled and moved beneath his touch again, and I felt the echoes of it.

I closed the distance between us and walked next to him, Mikhail a silent, deadly force at my side. The barrier remained, but I believed Balor when he said it would fall soon.

The exiled fae king glanced at me. "What if I wasn't a threat to you or your family?"

I stopped dead in my tracks. "Please tell me you aren't about to start a speech about how you're just misunderstood and that you see me, the true me." Mist swirled around my swords before they vanished, and I crossed my arms. "You have nothing to offer me. I will never join you."

Balor stopped and smoothly spun to face me. "My dear, I have everything to offer you, and I'm not here to tempt you with pretty words. I'm sure my sisters have told you about me. The evil conqueror of realms. The unjust king. They're not wrong. Left to their own devices, people will turn on each other. It doesn't matter the species or the world, they're all the same. I mean, look at the current state of the fae realms. Two fae queens fighting with every ounce of their power to keep their realms free, yet their own people seek me out, begging me to return."

I shrugged. "There's no shortage of stupid people, and the fae have more than their fair share."

He tipped his head back and laughed. There was something menacing in it that had me desperate to bury my swords in his chest and keep cutting until he was no more.

Balor started walking again, still chuckling to himself. Mikhail and I exchanged a look and followed him. Anything Balor told us, we'd have to pull apart and examine. I had no doubt he'd fill our heads with lies to further his agenda, but just like with Lir earlier, this was an opportunity to collect information.

"Lir has told me all about you," he said casually. "Dead parents. Dead first love. It seems death follows you wherever you go. How much longer do you think before it visits you again? Who will it take this time?"

"If I wanted a philosophical conversation about death, I'd talk to my necromancer brother and his lover—the actual god of death."

Balor smiled, undeterred. "You're not a hero. Not even a good person, really. People whisper about you, and they do it with fear and hatred in their hearts. They will rejoice when death claims you. You spent your life in hiding, and when your secrets came out, you had to sell yourself to my sister." He chuckled. "I might despise my sisters, but I respect their cunning. Elvinia, no doubt, saw your potential. You are a weapon to be pointed, but while my sister blackmailed you and the warlock before her trapped you with love, I am offering you something else entirely."

"Unlimited power to smite my enemies?" I drawled.

"No." That small smile that reminded me of Finn's flashed across his face. "You already have the power. I'm offering you permission to embrace the monster you were meant to be with no repercussions. Do you want to wipe out Emir and the warlocks once and for all? All the fae who plot behind your back to not only kill you but your birth parents as well?"

"I don't need your permission for that."

"No . . . you need the permission of my sister. The queen you sold your soul to." His fingers pushed harder against the invisible boundary of our realms, and my magic shifted uneasily within me. Balor's green eyes latched onto mine. "Aren't you tired of being leashed?"

He wasn't wrong, and I hated him for it. Elvinia rarely asked anything of me despite the fact that I was her Knight. She still used Badb and Kalen for most things, something that frustrated me even though I was also grateful for it. I didn't want to be at Elvinia's beck and call, but Kalen had served the fae queens his entire existence, and Badb had willingly given up her freedom to serve beside her mate.

They'd paid their debt and deserved to be free of it.

But I wasn't buying what Balor was selling. He'd have me on a leash too, and while he might not tug on it often, the second I stepped out of line, I'd find myself choked.

The question I really wanted to know the answer to was why he would even offer this to me in the first place.

"What is it you want from me, exactly? We both know you could just take my magic, so that's not it." Balor's magic was unique amongst the fae. He had the ability to steal the magic of others. Absorb it into himself and make it his own.

"I admit it would be very convenient to open gateways as easily as you do, but once I'm out of this realm, I can easily build gateways. I have no need for the rest of your magic. Shifting into a feline doesn't hold any particular interest to me, and trust me when I say I wield devourer magic far more destructive than your flames."

Ghostly blue flames flickered down Mikhail's arms, there and gone in a flash, but Balor still saw them. His lips curved upward slightly. "Congrats on the mating bond, by the way. Enjoy a few years of chaotic magic."

I ground my teeth together. Despite Mikhail and me trying to hide it, I was fairly certain the entire world would know soon that not only were we mated but that my magic was unreliable. Balor's comment about the fae in both courts plotting my demise wasn't exaggerated. Even the ones who were loyal to the queens and not him didn't like me being the Knight. They hated Kalen because of what he was, and that hatred filtered down to me.

Even more so because while Kalen was tainted with devourer magic, he was still pure fae. Whereas I was half fae, half shifter. They didn't mess with Kalen because of his lethal devourer magic, but if they learned my control over my magic was tenuous, they'd view it as a weakness.

And despite all their elegant clothing and pretty words, the fae were predators. They would seize the opportunity. Suddenly, I felt so tired. We were fighting enemies on all fronts, and the very people I was trying to defend would stab me in the back at the first opportunity.

Mikhail's hand slipped into mine, and blue flames flared back into existence. They raced up my arm and across my shoulders to trail behind me like a cloak, an identical one flowing behind Mikhail.

I wasn't alone. My magic might be on the fritz, but if the fae struck at my back, they'd find my mate there with his very sharp daggers.

Balor's gaze flicked over my flames—he seemed amused by them more than anything—before meeting my eyes once more.

I raised my chin. "My enemies will find that I thrive in chaos. If I was hard to kill before, I'm a hell of a lot harder now with my mate standing beside me."

The amusement in Balor's eyes grew. "I think I like you, but you cannot stop what is coming, Nemain." He pushed a little harder against the realm boundary, and a wave seemed to roll through the air. Glimpses of his realm broke through here and there, reminding me of the massive army waiting for us on the other side. "This has been in the works for thousands of years. You might win a minor victory here and there, but we have more plans in place than you can possibly imagine. You are merely plugging cracks in a dam that is about to get obliterated entirely. I am offering you and your mate a chance to stand with me, because I can always use more ruthless and cunning people."

If I were Ashling or Pele, I could have pretended to be mildly tempted or at least entertaining the idea to try to get information out of Balor. Mikhail could have pulled it off too, but I had never been particularly good at subterfuge.

I turned to Mikhail. "He's fucking with us, right? I mean, he's actively planning on betraying most of his allies."

"He probably needs to fill in the ranks since his own people seem intent on killing each other." Mikhail shrugged.

"Right." I snapped my fingers and pointed at Balor. "Does Lir know you're here, chatting me up? Or are he and Syndra still busy trying to off each other? That's why you want Mikhail and me, isn't it? You're about to lose two of your best people to a pissing contest."

For the first time since our encounter started, a hint of annoyance showed on Balor's face. "I'm not loyal to the vampires or warlocks because they're not loyal to me. We all entered the agreement knowing we would betray one another. That's how these games are played." He dropped his hand away from the invisible boundary. "My queen and I long ago stopped getting between Lir and Syndra. They're stubborn and set in their ways. Ordering them to leave each other alone simply resulted in them trying to kill each other behind our backs. I have no interest in micromanaging their personal differences. As long as it doesn't interfere with their work, we let it go."

"And when one of them dies?" I pushed.

Balor shrugged. "Then they weren't worthy of the position."

I shook my head. "You're not worthy of your crown, and I look forward to slicing off the head upon which it rests."

"So you can become the new queen?" He arched a brow. "You don't strike me as someone who would want the responsibilities of a crown."

"You're right, I don't," I said honestly. "Finn will make a good king one day if that's what he wants."

And if Balor's sisters ever wanted to give up the throne.

They'd talked about him becoming king like it was an absolute, but they'd been ruling for thousands of years. Neither of them seemed like the type to retire.

Given the confrontation we were marching towards against Balor, it seemed likely not all of us would survive, but why would they think their deaths were a foregone conclusion? They were two of the most powerful beings in existence. If anyone survived, it would be them.

"Finn . . ." Balor sighed. "It isn't a child. Hells, it's barely fae. It's not even a weapon. It's just a piece of fruit that we were waiting to ripen. Now, it's been on the tree too long, and soon it will rot and poison everything around it. You know we didn't even name it. That was the caretakers doing. We should have removed them. It was clear they were going to become attached, but somebody needed to take care of it. Unfortunately, our concerns proved to be true when they smuggled it out of the realm. Siofra took out her rage on Lyra for months before handing her off to Syndra. Last I checked, she could barely speak. Syndra likes her toys, though she has a habit of breaking them."

Mikhail's fingers tightened around mine, and I struggled to hold back the rage I felt at Balor's callousness. Lyra . . . was alive. Two beings were responsible for Finn escaping: Luna, one of my grimalkins, and a fae woman named Lyra. We'd all assumed she'd been killed, considering Luna had barely survived.

And this whole time, she'd been at the mercy of Balor, Siofra, and Syndra.

Once again, I stopped, released Mikhail's hand, and turned to face Balor, who had also halted. He casually lifted his hand to mess with the realm boundary, sending ripples through the air like it was water. I shifted my nails into claws and swiped them across my left palm, opening up a deep, three-inch gash.

"I swear on my blood, magic, and soul that you will never get Finn back. He's ours."

Opening gateways might be out of my reach right now, but I was still sensitive to realm boundaries, and every time Balor had messed with it, I'd become a little more attuned to its location. I slammed my bloody palm against the rippling air and felt the magical resistance of two worlds overlapping.

I pushed harder.

The forest around Mikhail and me fell away, replaced by a massive fae city. We remained in our little sliver of the devourer realm, but the surrounding fae paused, looking at us with raised eyebrows before turning to their king.

Balor said nothing, just tilted his head as he pondered me.

"We will never kneel." I pulled my hand back and slammed it against the border again. A few of the fae jolted, but Balor's expression gave nothing away. "You will never have Finn." My hand slapped the boundary again. "I don't care how many realms you conquer or how large your army is. Come after me and mine, and I'll fucking end you."

The exiled fae king raised his hand, a broad smile on his face, and pressed his palm against the boundary on his side, right over my hand. "I look forward to meeting you in person." The air rippled one more time, and then Balor and his realm vanished.

Chapter Nineteen

"We just spoke to the four-thousand-year-old exiled fae king."
I stared at the healing cut on my palm. Magic burned across
my skin. I was bound by my word. It wasn't exactly a blood
oath, but something akin to it. This was why the fae were
careful with their words. Because their souls were so intertwined with magic that sometimes, whatever they spoke
became binding.

I'd spent so much of my life believing I was just a feline
shifter that I wasn't used to taking in my fae side.

"Actually, I think he's more like five, maybe six thousand
years old," Mikhail said calmly.

"And I threatened him." The cut finished knitting itself
back together, leaving a dark red line as a reminder of what I'd
sworn.

"I don't think he saw it as a threat, more of a challenge,"
he helpfully added, still using that same easygoing tone.

I whirled towards Mikhail. "How are you not freaked out
about this? Because I'm a little freaked! The fucking fae king
orchestrated events just to have a chat with me. He has an
army of tens of thousands, made up of some of the best

warriors to ever walk any realm, and they have been planning for thousands of years." I dragged my hand down my face. "And I just threw down a fucking gauntlet."

"Did you not mean every word you said?" Mikhail cocked his head, twilight eyes staring into me with an intensity that had stopped me in my tracks the first time we'd met.

"Of course I fucking did! That asshole"—I jerked my thumb to where Balor had stood moments ago—"is never getting his hands on Finn. He never thought of Finn as his child. He's ours now. Finders fucking keepers."

Mikhail grabbed the front of my leather vest and yanked me to him. Strong arms wrapped around me, and he kissed the top of my head. "We will find a way to survive this. He won't hurt Finn. He won't hurt any of them."

The fear my anger had been suppressing surged. Maybe before we'd gone up against the Olympians, I would have shared his confidence. We might have defeated them, but I wouldn't say we'd won. Not with Magos slowly slipping away.

"You can't know that," I said softly. "We might actually be out of our league on this one."

"It'll be oka—" A roar tore through the forest, cutting Mikhail off. It came from the direction where we'd left Andrei and Stela.

"Can we not catch a fucking break?" I snarled.

Mikhail and I took off, running all out and ducking under low-hanging branches and vines. The roar sounded exactly like the one we'd heard when we'd first arrived in this realm. The rapid beat of my heart had little to do with my sprinting and everything to do with my friends being in danger and my not being there to protect them.

I couldn't lose Magos or Andrei, not now. Even Stela, I wanted to keep safe. The vampires, I wouldn't shed any tears over. In fact, if the opportunity arose, I'd probably push Cassius into the mouth of whatever beast was attacking.

The forest flew past us. Mikhail could have vanished into mist and made it there before me, but apparently, he took his declaration of not leaving my side seriously, and I'd have to stop to concentrate on using the mist to travel. It was faster for me to just run.

In no time, we made it back to where we'd left the werewolves and skidded to a stop just outside the small clearing.

Before us, an enormous monster battled against a pack of smaller ones. My gaze quickly went to the tree behind them, where a disc of ice had formed halfway up the trunk. Two of the smaller creatures were trying to find a way around it. They vaguely reminded me of scorpions, only six feet long, and they had three tails instead of just the one, all of them ending in a stinger.

I chill ran up my spine at the sound they made as they moved. Bugs were not my thing. Especially when they were oversized.

Movement in the trees caught my attention, and I glimpsed Stela's brunette hair. For whatever reason, she must have shifted back while we were gone.

Relief hit me. They were safe. At least for the next few minutes.

We just needed to figure out how to get them out of here or lure the monsters away. The small ones were thwarted by Justina's ice shield, but the big one certainly wouldn't be.

"Is that . . ." Mikhail's eyes were wide with shock, and his mouth hung open slightly. "Is that a fucking dinosaur?"

"Don't be ridiculous," I replied in a somewhat dazed tone. "Dinosaurs are a human realm thing; it'd be called something else here."

Mikhail pointed a finger aggressively. "That looks like a T-Rex!"

I continued to stare at the beast. "It's just a bipedal creature with a blocky rectangular head and a thick neck. And kind of tiny arms. And a big-ass tail."

"It's covered in scales!"

Two smaller monsters tried to dart underneath the one we were debating about, only to get crushed when it raised an enormous, taloned foot and stomped down on them.

"T-Rex didn't have spikes!" I announced in victory as the monster turned, giving us a better view of its back.

Mikhail rolled his eyes. "So it's a spiny T-Rex. Still a dinosaur."

"You're just making stuff up now."

"Stop trying to ruin my fun." Mikhail glanced at me, his eyes bright with a feral insanity. "I want to fight it."

"We can't fight the not-dinosaur monster, vampire," I replied half-heartedly. Because I totally wanted to fight a dinosaur and was willing to ignore the semantics. It looked like it belonged in the dinosaur movies Isabeau made us watch, which was good enough for me.

I just refused to let Mikhail be right on principle.

"Pretty sure we can fight it, shifter," he argued. "And we have to do something because they're trapped in that tree, and as soon as it kills all these smaller creatures, it's going to notice some snacks that are basically eye-level with it."

I quickly but efficiently scanned the dragon-sized creature. There was no way our swords would do any significant damage. We could blind it maybe, but I didn't want to seriously hurt the thing. It was just trying to survive, and it was pretty fucking cool.

We did need to get it away from here though; otherwise, we'd have no choice but to kill it, assuming it didn't just stomp us into the ground or swallow us whole.

Mist swirled next to me, and Magos appeared. His expression was serene as he watched two of the small insectoid creatures climb up the leg of the sort of T-Rex. The large carnivore roared as they reached its body and buried their stingers into its flesh. It flung itself against the tree all of our friends hid in, crushing one of the scorpion monsters. Bright green ichor flew through the air, some of it landing only ten feet from us, and the smell immediately punched me.

"Gross." I covered my nose and mouth.

The second scorpion went flying when the T-Rex's tail slammed into it. It crashed to the ground and jerked a few times, trying to rise. Three of its packmates saw its struggle and gave up on trying to climb the tree to rush over to their fallen comrade . . . and promptly tore it to pieces.

Cannibalistic giant scorpions. Awesome.

More pungent odor filled the air.

"We need to lure the big one away before it knocks that tree over," Magos said calmly as he reached into his pocket and pulled out a slim phone.

"What are you doing?" I stared at him.

"Taking some pictures and videos for Isabeau. I couldn't get a good angle from the tree." He smiled brightly at me. "It's a dinosaur, Nemain. You know she'll be overjoyed by this."

"It's not a fucking dinosaur." I pursed my lips. "And she's going to want to come here and see it in person. There is zero chance of me ever coming back to this fucking realm."

"Nemain and I will lure the big one away." Mikhail tore his eyes from the fight to glance at his uncle. "Will you and the others be able to deal with these scorpion things?"

Magos nodded. "We were fighting them off and doing quite well—they have several weak spots along their spines where the body joins together—but then that thing arrived and we had to climb the tree."

"Kill them or scare them off." I looked east. "Then find a safe spot to rest until we make our way back."

"How do you want to do this?" Mikhail leaned forward on

the balls of his feet, mist swirling off the sword he'd summoned.

I glanced at Magos. "Can you clear us a path to the big spiny thing?"

"Yes." Magos gave me a small smile. "I can clear a path to the T-Rex for you."

When I narrowed my eyes at him, he just smiled a little wider. "Then we'll do the tried-and-true method of stabbing the definitely-not-a-T-Rex enough to piss it off. And then we'll run away. Fast."

"Your strategy skills are truly inspiring," Mikhail said dryly.

"Don't fix what isn't broken." I flipped him off. Mist curled around my fists and down my fingers as I concentrated. A second later, my swords appeared. "Let's play tag with the not-dinosaur."

Magos sighed. "I'd tell you both to be careful, but I don't think it'll do any good."

"You be careful." I wrinkled my nose. "And try not to get any of their blood or ichor or whatever it's called on you. That stuff reeks."

"Any other requests?"

"Whiskey," I said instantly at the same moment Mikhail said, "Salted pretzel."

Magos and I looked at him, and he shrugged. "Zareen made some two weeks ago, and I've been craving one ever since."

A crack sounded, and we looked to the tree our friends hid in. The thick trunk still stood, but now, it had a lean to it, courtesy of a deep fracture running straight up its center. Large chunks of ice littered the ground. The scorpions were regrouping, and now half a dozen of them were between us and the wannabe dinosaur.

"Little help would be nice!" Stela called out.

"I'm too cute to be eaten!" Andrei added.

Ice raced down the tree, reinforcing the splintering trunk. Justina wouldn't be able to keep this up for much longer, and one more solid hit would probably take the entire tree down.

"We'll come find you," I told Magos.

He nodded and stepped towards the scorpion creatures. His sword swung through the air before they even realized he was there. Mikhail and I sprinted towards the spiny monster as ichor spurted from the stump of one creature where Magos had sliced its stingers off.

The enraged scorpion charged Magos, and the rest of the creatures keyed in on him too. For a second, despite Magos' skill, I worried about him being overwhelmed. But then a spear of ice flew down from the trees and pierced the stinger-less one. It let out an earsplitting shriek as it tried to tear its way free.

Two shaggy bodies fell from the trees and tore into the scorpions, and in the blink of an eye, Cassius was there too, wielding two axes.

"Mikhail," I yelled a warning as the T-Rex-looking monster focused on the chaos and all the tasty treats just waiting to be snatched up.

Mist swirled around Mikhail, and he vanished, appearing right by the beast's huge foot and stabbing his sword straight down. It threw its head back and roared before raising its bleeding foot and stomping. Mikhail vanished a second before he would have been flattened.

I pumped more speed from my body, flipping my swords so I held them at a downward angle. The dinosaur swung its head around, bright yellowish-brown eyes searching for Mikhail. Its gaze latched on to me as I charged straight for it. I leapt up and to the right. My feet made contact with a tree, and I bent my knees before pushing off.

Just as the creature opened its maw to snatch me out of the air, Mikhail appeared again and stabbed its other foot. Its head twisted down, trying to spot him, and my swords sank into the tip of its nose.

"Boop!"

The monster shook its head from side to side, trying to shake me loose as it let out a low grumbling scream.

"Mist, mist, mist," I chanted. A cool mist wrapped around me, and then I was weightless.

I staggered on the ground, trying to orient myself. A very pissed-off roar came from behind me, followed by several short, high-pitched sounds.

Then Mikhail was there, grabbing me by the elbow and tugging me forward. "Time to run again!"

"I hate this fucking realm!" I hissed as Mikhail and I took off at a dead sprint. "We never stop running!"

"You're the one who booped it!"

"It worked on the werewolf!" Something bright and serpentine-shaped lunged from a branch above me. I slapped it away from my face and kept running. "And that might have been my only opportunity to boop a dinosaur. Now I have bragging rights."

"I thought you said it wasn't a dinosaur!" Mikhail hissed.

"I want the bragging rights!" I shrieked. Eddie would be so jealous.

Mikhail and I just needed to avoid becoming dino food for the next few minutes.

I cackled as we ducked and weaved through the trees. We didn't have to look behind us to know the quasi-dinosaur was still on our tail; the sound of snapping tree limbs and earth-shattering footsteps made that very clear. At least the thing wasn't super fast. We weren't expanding the distance between us as much as I would have liked, but we weren't losing ground either.

Unfortunately, both Mikhail and I were bleeding from several open wounds thanks to the denizens of this forest taking a swipe at us any chance they had. My right arm had gone a little numb when one of those serpents had practically fell on me from a tree above and sank its fangs into my biceps. A strange creature I could only describe as a mix between a porcupine and a raccoon had lashed out at me with six-inch claws that had torn through flesh and muscle across my thigh.

Everything in this fucking realm wanted a piece of us.

I'd dismissed my blades because I couldn't stop to fight anything, and running with them was difficult. It's not like they would do a lot of good against the giant monster chasing us anyway. Other than piss it off, which I'd already done.

"Water up ahead!" Mikhail shouted from slightly in front of me. "Maybe it'll be deep enough that we can lose it there!"

With our luck, it was a muddy pond that would trap us or have electric eels in it or something. The monster let out more of those short, rumbling sounds in quick succession. I finally heard the water Mikhail was racing towards. We weren't far, and it sounded like a fast-moving river. Fortunately, both of us were strong swimmers. All we had to do was make it there, and we'd be fi—

Trees to my right snapped, and the twin of the beast hunting us lunged for me.

"Fuck me!" I screamed and dove forward, straight through the monster's jaws, clearing them a second before they snapped shut. I tucked my body in just before I hit the ground, rolled, then leapt back to my feet all in one smooth motion. "They hunt in pairs!"

"No shit!" Mikhail doubled back for me, only to swerve to the side when the first monster caught up to us.

We both ran flat out towards the water.

The trees had thinned out in this section of the forest. Slender mushrooms grew up from the ground, glowing with a neon green luminesce. They were pretty, but I very much missed the trees right now. Mikhail and I had been staying ahead because, while they hadn't provided much of an obstacle, the trees and undergrowth had been just enough to keep the giant predators from getting up to their top speed.

That was no longer the case, and they covered an annoying amount of ground with each stride.

My breathing hitched as my footing slipped, causing me to stumble and put too much weight on my injured leg. The ground shook beneath me as the second predator closed in.

Mist swirled to my left, and then Mikhail was there, shoving me out of the way. I crashed to the ground, and he misted a second before jaws snapped shut around the now empty air. Pain laced up my side thanks to my poor landing, but I shoved it down, leapt to my feet, and kept running.

Twin roars shook through the night air, so loud, they were like a punch to the gut.

Mikhail appeared six feet to my right. He bled heavily from a wound on his arm. We wouldn't make it much farther.

The ground gained a downward slope. I couldn't see the river yet, but it sounded closer. *Please be closer.*

I angled my direction enough that Mikhail and I reached the edge of the slope at the same time. The ground suddenly gave way to a raging river below. I slipped my hand into his, neither of us hesitating as we leapt forward.

For a few seconds, I free fell, and then icy cold water stole the air from my lungs. Mikhail's hand tightened around mine for a few seconds before he released me so we could swim to the surface. I sucked in a deep breath and caught a glimpse of the two monsters standing on the bank. They both let out another earth-shattering roar before the river carried us away.

"Fuck. This. Realm." I shivered where I sprawled on the riverbank. My clothes were plastered to my skin, but I just didn't have it in me to struggle with peeling off wet leather despite how much I hated the feeling.

"If we never come back here, it will be too soon," Mikhail agreed. He tugged a hand through his dark hair, grimaced when he hit a tangle, and let it drop. "The fae might periodically try to kill us, but at least they offer room service."

"Right!" I snorted. "I had the same thought earlier."

I squinted at the sky. It was difficult to tell the time, but I figured we still had a few hours left of this sort-of daytime.

"If we have to spend another night in this realm, we should come back to this spot." I reached out and flicked a glowing mushroom. "The luminescence here is even brighter, and those briars would likely keep out a lot of the predators." I waved to where ten-foot-tall bushes grew in a semicircle around us. Bright purple thorns almost three inches long covered most of them.

"I'd prefer not to spend another night here," Mikhail said dryly.

"We just fought a dinosaur. Okay, we mostly ran from it. But still." I let out a strangled laugh. "A fucking dinosaur, Mikhail." More hysterical laughter poured out of me. I couldn't help it. Everything was so absolutely fucked, and it had been for a while. I could roll with a lot, but it felt like the goalposts kept getting moved.

A few years ago, my sole purpose had been getting revenge against Sebastian. Now, I was the Knight of the Unseelie Court and worked directly with the fae queens. I was at the center of an end-of-the-world prophecy. And I had two young children who I felt responsible for—plus some teenagers who hated me but I still cared about.

Weirdly, it was that third one that disturbed me the most.

I loved Mikhail. He was my everything. But we hadn't even had a chance to stop and take a breath, to come to terms with this unpredictable mate bond between us. And now, the lives of

Magos and Andrei were in the hands of sorcerers; one of whom we definitely couldn't trust and the other who I wasn't entirely confident could really help us.

The fact that we'd just encountered—what I was now willing to accept as—a fucking dinosaur was just too much.

It was all too fucking much.

More laughter poured out of me. Was this what it was like to lose your mind?

"First." Mikhail vanished into mist and reappeared, standing above me, holding a hand out. "You said it couldn't be a dinosaur because we're not in the human realm. Second, I need you to keep your shit together for a little bit longer."

"Really?" My unhinged chuckles faded, and I rolled my eyes before letting him pull me to my feet. "You couldn't even be bothered to get up? You had to mist?"

He flashed his fangs at me. "Helps the clothes dry faster. You should try it."

I scanned his clothes. Still wet, but they did look a touch drier. He was right that I needed to not lose it right now, so I pounced on the prospect of a distraction. Plus, dry clothes sounded really fucking nice. I concentrated, searching for the cool, rain-scented magic in my soul. Between one blink and the next, I was ten feet away, closer to the trees growing along the riverbank.

"It's going to take a while to get used to that." I plucked at my shirt. It was now damp instead of soaking wet. "Nifty."

Blue flames erupted across Mikhail's shoulders, causing him to flinch before rolling his eyes at the fire as it cleared the distance between us and circled around my waist. "I think your magic is jealous."

"Miss you," I murmured to the flames. "We'll get this bone enchantment out of me soon, and then you can feast on that asshole sorcerer. After he fixes Magos' curse."

Mikhail stepped towards me, wincing as he rotated his left arm.

"Are you hurt?" I stopped coddling my flames, and they winked out of existence. Most of my wounds had already healed, although my arm still felt a little tingly where that viper had bitten me.

"Some centipede thing fell out of a fucking tree and tried to burrow into me." He displayed his arm so I could see where his shirt had been torn and a nasty gash festered. Clean bites and cuts healed fast, but whatever creature had attacked Mikhail had shredded not only his skin but the muscle beneath it.

I moved closer to better examine it. "It must have had some type of necrotic toxin."

He pulled his arm back. "Another ten minutes or so, and I'll be completely healed."

A frown tugged at my mouth. Vampire healing was impressive, but that wound looked nasty. I didn't like seeing him injured. Luckily, there was an easy solution to this problem.

"Or you could drink so it'll heal faster." I brushed the loose strands of hair that had fallen out of my braid away from my neck.

Mikhail narrowed his eyes at the move before shaking his head. "You were hurt as well and had to use a fair bit of your magic to heal. I'll be okay."

"Please." I snorted. "I've been wounded far worse than that. I feel fine. We're going to have to backtrack several miles to rejoin the others, which will be more difficult if that rot on your arm spreads." Tugging the collar of my shirt down, I stepped closer, invading his space. "Just drink, Mikhail."

His eyes darkened, and a slow grin spread across his face as he deliberately took a step back until he was up against a tree. "Like I said, there's no need."

A memory slowly floated to the forefront of my mind.

We'd done this before, the first time he'd drank from me. Even the situation had been similar. Only, it'd been a flying monster instead of whatever the fuck those two things were. But we'd been in a forest and separated from our friends, and Mikhail had refused to drink from me despite being wounded.

What had I said back then?

I grinned and moved forward until only inches separated us. "I mean this in both the literal and nonliteral sense." Mikhail's eyes darkened as I planted my hands on either side of him against the tree, boxing him in. "Fucking bite me."

In a flash, our positions were reversed, and I was pinned to the trunk. Mikhail had one hand possessively on my hip and the other gripped my hair. He didn't hesitate, just struck, and a low moan slipped from my lips as his fangs sank into the soft skin of my neck.

The hand in my hair tightened, and his other one moved from my hip to grip my ass, lifting me up so I could wrap my legs around his waist. Adrenaline still coursed through my body from that mad dash through the forest plus the lingering shock of meeting Balor.

I needed something to ground me for just a few moments and block everything else out.

"Harder," I demanded, my fingers tangling in Mikhail's silky dark hair and pulling him closer.

He growled in response, his hips pushing against mine. Suddenly, I was desperate for less clothing between us.

Cool mist kissed my skin, and I got my wish. Our clothes vanished, and I felt Mikhail's thick, hard length push against me.

There was no foreplay or teasing. Mikhail just lined himself up with my slick heat and sheathed himself in one brutal thrust.

"Fuck." I let out a strangled scream even as I squeezed my

thighs around him so I could rise and slam back down on his cock.

Mikhail groaned, his fangs sliding from my neck before his mouth crashed against mine in a kiss that was more a claiming than anything else. I slipped my tongue into his mouth, enjoying the coppery taste of my blood.

The mating bond between us hummed like a live wire.

More. I needed more.

I dropped my hands from his hair to his shoulders and shoved. Mikhail staggered back, still clutching me to him before smoothly dropping to the ground with me beneath him.

"Something you want, shifter?" His fingertips dug into my legs and yanked them from around his waist. I growled and pivoted up, only to arch my back and scream when he pinned the top of my thighs to my chest and hammered into me.

The scent of my blood filled the air as it dripped down my neck and legs from Mikhail's grip. He was usually intense when we fucked. Like it was his sole mission to wring every ounce of pleasure from me and then demand more. He was methodical, thorough, and loved to watch my face as I unraveled.

This was not that. There was a desperation and anger to his movements now.

"You were giving up earlier," he accused, pulling back until his head was notched at my entrance. "After we talked to that arrogant prick."

"I wa—" My protest ended in a scream when he slammed back into me all the way to the hilt before withdrawing. I hissed my protest but Mikhail flipped me over onto all fours and I barely had time to brace myself before my pussy stretched around his cock as he rutted into me.

"You were," he snarled. His fingers roughly tugged on my braid, and then my hair fell loosely around me, only for Mikhail to wrap it around his fist and pull back, forcing me to arch even more. My thoughts scattered as Mikhail kept up the fast, unforgiving pace. A delicious pain spread from my hips, where he gripped me tight enough to bruise as he claimed me over and over again.

My claws dug into the earth as the orgasm ripped through me so intensely, I saw stars for a moment. Only towards the end did Mikhail start to slow, and that was when I made my move. I timed it so I could slide out from under him, then twisted to shove him onto his back.

It was Mikhail's turn to let out a pissed-off growl that morphed into a moan as I straddled his hips and sank onto his cock.

I wrapped my left hand around his throat, claws piercing his flesh, and rested my other one over the deep purple flower magically tattooed across his heart that was a twin to the one on my back. "I was having"—I ground against him hard—"a moment. I'm allowed to have a small freakout, Mikhail."

He opened his mouth to argue but groaned instead when I picked up the pace. His head fell back against the earth. Strong hands clutched my ass as I fucked him every bit as hard and fast as he'd done me. The rich aroma of his blood mingled with mine as I clawed at his skin.

"Nemain," he rasped. "Don't stop."

I rolled my hips and released Mikhail's throat so I could throw my head back and give myself over to this feeling. My hair fell around me in a tangled wave. Pleasure built and built with every thrust until I thought I couldn't take it anymore.

Then one of the hands on my hips glided across my sweat-soaked skin and Mikhail rubbed his thumb roughly over my clit. A scream tore from my throat as I climaxed. My pace faltered, and Mikhail flipped us again so he was over me, but this time, he caged me in with his arms, and I wrapped my legs around his waist as he fucked me through the orgasm before pouring himself into me.

A few minutes later, he collapsed onto the ground next to me, panting.

Reality started to creep in almost immediately. Between how much noise we'd made and the blood in the air, predators would come to investigate, and they'd eventually find a way around that thorny barrier. Plus, we needed to get back to the others.

"We'll beat Balor," Mikhail said quietly. "I don't know how yet, but don't lose faith in us."

"I won't," I promised him, and I meant it. My head flopped to the side so I could look at him. "You might have to fuck some sense into me in the future though if I ever falter again."

Mikhail sighed. "As your mate, I suppose that is my burden to bear."

I scooted closer and rested my head on his chest, just over the flower, listening to his heart beat in sync with mine. "One more minute, then we need to go back."

His fingers ran through my hair, untangling it. "As you wish, my love."

Chapter Twenty

Less than thirty minutes later, we reunited with the others in a tree on the boundary of our luminescent forest. We'd made good time back because I'd practiced vanishing into mist to cover more ground. There were definitely limitations in what I could do. Mikhail could stay in mist form for as long as he wanted; for me, it was a max of ten seconds before I poofed back into existence, whether I wanted to or not.

We'd also discovered that Mikhail had to be physically present for me to call upon his magic, which I thought was totally unfair because we found out he always had access to my devourer flames. Although, currently, he couldn't really do anything with them. My flames would flicker whenever they felt like it, and the few times he'd tried to direct them to do something, it hadn't worked as intended.

Which was why there was a tree covered in frozen ashes somewhere in the forest, and why both Mikhail and I had had to mist away from some very enraged hornets.

On the plus side, Mikhail and I had managed to avoid the pseudo-dinosaur monsters on our way back, but we'd heard them several times.

Aside from some torn-up clothes, Andrei and the others had made it through their fight just fine. Apparently, Cassius had been stung several times by the scorpion monsters, but tragically, he hadn't died. Justina had also been stabbed . . . while defending Stela. Something the werewolf was having trouble with, based on the way she kept giving the vampire perplexed glances.

The thick branch creaked as I adjusted my much heavier feline form. I'd shifted once Mikhail and I had made it back, because as convenient as disappearing into mist was, I found it strangely tiring, like a muscle I wasn't used to using. My feline form was faster than my human one, and I could still mist in it if I needed to.

Did you see where the chimmeris went? I scanned the dark forest stretched before us. The sky was taking on a hazy red hue and growing lighter by the minute.

"Yes," Magos said from where he crouched on a branch to my left. "They landed about a mile that way." He pointed northeast. "It was difficult to get an accurate count of their numbers because they were tightly packed together, but I'm guessing more than twenty, less than sixty."

My claws shot out, digging into the textured tree bark as I thought about our options. The original plan for tackling the chimmeris had relied on us being able to escape through a gateway. They occasionally strayed from their pack, like the one that had attacked us when we'd first arrived, but we needed to capture twenty-four of them.

The chances of us successfully luring twenty-four chimmeris away one at a time seemed slim, and if the entire pack focused on us, we were fucked. There was no way we'd make it back to this forest. Even if we did, the commotion caused by the chimmeris chasing us would draw the attention of other predators.

Actually . . . maybe that wasn't the worst plan.

"Gods, even in her feline form, you can tell when she has a crazy idea." Justina sighed.

It's not crazy, I growled. *Just . . . chaotic.*

"If it gets us out of this realm sooner, I'm all for it," Stela said lightly. "We've been here less than twenty-four hours, and I've lost track of how many times we've almost died."

Separating the chimmeris one by one will be almost impossible. Their instincts drive them to swarm their prey, but we can use that to our advantage. We just need to give them prey big enough to distract them that also won't immediately die. In the chaos, we can pair off, and each pair can work on snagging as many chimmeris as possible, I explained. *We might get lucky and get all two dozen in one go.*

Magos pursed his lips thoughtfully. "They're one of the apex predators in this realm, so what could last in a fight against them?"

"Maybe two dinosaur-like monsters that are pissed their meals got away from them," Mikhail drawled.

You're reading my mind again, vampire. I let out a distinctly feline chuff as I turned away from our quarry to meet his twilight eyes. *Think we can lure them?*

"You're not going to argue that you should do this on your own?" He arched a single dark brow.

Rising from my branch, I nimbly jumped over to the one he was crouched on and butted my head against his. *You and me, baby. It's like a date.*

Mikhail stared at me for a long moment. "One of these days, we're going to go on an actual date that doesn't involve running away from monsters or killing."

"That seems unlikely," Justina muttered.

She wasn't wrong.

Let's track down the chimmeris. I leapt my way down the tree. *Once we locate them, everyone can get in position while Mikhail and I find our wannabe dino buddies. We'll be coming in hot, so everyone will need to be ready to go.*

Once everyone was on the ground again, we stepped out of the relative safety of the luminescent trees. Mikhail stalked silently to my left, and I was a little surprised when Justina appeared on my right. "I could be mistaken, but I thought I felt a hyaenir in the area shortly before you two got back," she warned quietly.

If you sense it again, let us know. The hyaenir would likely avoid the chimmeris—unless it sensed one of them was wounded. Then it would come to investigate and see if it could drag it away without the other chimmeris noticing. And I really didn't want the wild card of a hyaenir joining our party.

Justina nodded and dropped back to walk next to Stela, who was in her wolf form and just behind me to the right. A low, rumbling growl came from Andrei, who was on Stela's other side, but the vampire ignored it. I couldn't see where Cassius was, and the fucker was quiet enough that I couldn't hear him either, but I trusted Magos to guard my back.

Not that I really expected Cassius to fuck us over, but given how quickly allegiances were changing, I found it difficult to trust anyone or their motivations outside of our circle.

It didn't take long for the darkness to set in as we put more distance between us and the glowing trees. The red haze from the sky beaming in through breaks in the tree canopy was the only light, and it did little to brighten the shadows. I was still grateful for it because it provided the bare minimum for me to see.

Which was why I stopped when I caught something large moving through the underbrush ahead of us. Everyone went perfectly still behind me, and we watched as a herd of what looked like deer trotted past us . . . if deer had six legs, were eight feet at the shoulder, and had what looked like bone protruding out of their bodies in sharp points like armor.

We waited until they passed and then carried on. After a half mile, Andrei and Stela took the lead, their uncanny sense of chimmeris helping to narrow in on where they rested for the day. The forest changed the farther we went. Tall, slender trees with skeletal branches and hardly any leaves replaced the fern-looking ones.

It was good in some ways because there would be less underbrush for us to deal with once the party started, but until then, it made us very exposed.

"I'm really happy we don't take after them in appearance." Cassius grimaced as he looked at the creatures perched along the trees in front of us. They blended in almost perfectly, thanks to the pale white skin stretched over their skeletal frames.

"I don't know what you're talking about," Justina breathed out, her eyes locked on the creatures. "You're the spitting image of them."

"Quiet," Mikhail ordered.

I watched as a chimmeris on the tree closest to us took a swipe at another one. They really were ugly bastards. They stood mostly upright on two muscular legs, but their arms were freakishly long, reaching almost to their knees. I knew from experience that they were fast climbers and that their favorite thing to do was to scale a tree and leap off the top. Once they were airborne, they'd snap open those spindly arms, extending the thin leathery membrane attached to their sides.

They were excellent gliders and completely silent when they did it.

On the ground, they would drop to all fours and sprint. Flying or running, they were fast as fuck. The hyaenir relied on their brute strength and bone-crushing bite, but the chimmeris were all about speed and slashing their prey open with their fangs or the long claws that adorned each of their fingers.

One-on-one, they weren't fun to fight but manageable. My eyes scanned the trees. Ten. Twenty. Thirty-five. Fifty. I stopped counting.

Stela and Justina. Magos and Andrei. I turned my gaze to the pairs I'd just announced. *It'll be the job of the werewolves to pin the chimmeris down and the vampires to get the tokens on.*

"What about me?" Cassius glanced between me and Mikhail.

As soon as Mikhail and I get back, we'll zero in on a chimmeris. You slap the token on it once we have it pinned, and then we'll move to the next one.

Justina shrugged her backpack off and passed around the gold tokens.

I hesitated. This was the part when we left them. It was my plan, and I thought it was our best chance, but I still hated the idea of leaving them alone this close to the chimmeris. If they were detected, they'd never make it back to safety.

"We'll be fine." Magos gave me a calm, reassuring smile.

Andrei bumped his head into mine and then licked the side of my face.

I pinned my ears back and gave him a silent hiss, but he just sat on his haunches and let his tongue hang out the side of his mouth.

If you have to make a run for it before we get back, just remember, you don't have to be the fastest, and sometimes people trip. I looked pointedly at Cassius.

"Forgot I can teleport?" He gave me a wry smile.

I took a menacing step towards him, but Mikhail rested a hand between my shoulders. "We need to go."

Mist rippled over my fur, and I gave Cassius one last warning look before disappearing into nothing. Exactly ten seconds later, I reappeared, only staggering slightly before taking off at a steady run. Mikhail appeared at my side, easily keeping pace with me.

We headed towards the last place we'd heard our monster friends. Hopefully, they hadn't gone too far—or found a meal. If they were happily munching away on something, it would be difficult to convince them to give it up and chase us.

It didn't take long for us to reach the luminescent forest. I misted one more time just to cover more ground and then stuck to running. Given that the more I misted, the harder it got, I didn't want to burn myself out and then have nothing left when the angry wannabe-dinosaurs tried to stomp me out of existence.

"When we find them, let me handle it." Mikhail side-eyed me. "Do not boop them again."

Don't tell me what I can and cannot boop, vampire.

"Shifter," Mikhail growled. "Don't you fucking dar—"

A tail slammed into Mikhail, sending him flying. I started after him, only to abort when the second dino monster lunged out from the trees and snapped its massive jaws at me.

How the fuck are things this big so godsdamn quiet? I growled and darted around a tree. Mist swirled, and Mikhail appeared, clutching his ribs.

"I don't know," Mikhail grunted, blood leaking out between his fingers. "Bloody magic, maybe!"

Oh. Right. That made sense.

We dove forward just as jaws closed around the trunk and cracked it before yanking it out of the ground.

Can you run?

"In a minute," he rasped.

Okay, you mist, I'll run. Then we'll switch. We need to keep their attention.

"Yeah, I think we have that!" We weaved through the forest, trying to slow down the enormous predators, but they barreled through the trees like it was nothing. "Run faster, shifter!"

Mikhail hung back just enough to draw their attention while I ran as fast as I could. I looked back over my shoulder in time to see him mist before monstrous jaws snapped shut around the air he'd just vacated. The two of us hauled ass back to where we'd left the others, each taking turns vanishing into mist to avoid getting eaten.

I'd really only needed the one time of running away from dinosaurs for bragging rights. I darted through two narrow boulders, earning myself a brief reprieve as the monsters were forced to go around.

Twin roars sounded from behind me. At least this part of my plan was working well. Now, we just needed to not die for the second part, and then I could gloat about how brilliant I was.

Soon enough, we were out of the luminescent forest, and the trees gradually changed to the skeletal ones.

We're almost there! I mentally shouted as loudly as I could.

Mikhail appeared at my side, and we raced into the small clearing below the trees, where the chimmeris rested. Solid black eyes that were freakishly large latched on to us, and I saw the hunger in them flare. Then we vanished into mist and reappeared with the others, watching as the not-dinosaurs skidded to a stop.

Mikhail was right; they definitely had some low level of magic to help silence their movements. This made them even more of a temptation for the chimmeris, who immediately forgot about the small snacks that had disrupted their sleep and focused on the large, magic-laced meal before them.

Wait for it. I crouched, my muscles bunching, ready to move.

High-pitched clicking sounds filled the air as the chimmeris stirred, and then they launched themselves from the trees.

Chaos erupted.

Now! We split into three groups, each targeting a different chimmeris. As much as I wanted to see how the others fared, I needed to stay focused. The chimmeris swarmed the two dino monsters, but their fangs weren't long enough to pierce the beasts' thick hides, and the wounds from their claws amounted to paper cuts.

Meanwhile, the larger predators were snapping chimmeris out of the air but were also getting annoyed at having to constantly bat them away.

It wouldn't take long before they left, and then it'd be seven of us against close to sixty hungry and riled-up chimmeris. We needed to be gone before then.

For the first few minutes, our plan worked amazingly well. The chimmeris were frenzied in their attacks, which resulted in a number of them getting bitten in half or stomped on. We were able to grab a dozen and slap Izaak's transportation tokens on them before they perished.

The rule was we had to send him live specimens—with no specifications about what state they had to be in. I could play by the letter of the law but not the spirit.

Unfortunately, the chimmeris started to get a little more cautious in their attacks, so our easy targets dried up. Extra unfortunate was the fact that Magos' original estimate was wrong. More chimmeris poured from hollowed-out trees, putting their numbers closer to a hundred, not including the dead or dying ones.

Six chimmeris converged onto the dino monster's tail, only for it to slam them against a tree before flinging them off. Justina and Stela were there in an instant, slapping tokens on each of them. They got four before they were forced to retreat.

I surveyed the clearing, trying to pick out our next target. Mikhail was on my left and Cassius to my right, the latter holding the gold token.

On silent wings, a chimmeris glided above us, landing directly in front of me with its back to us, all its attention on the fight. Seizing the opportunity, I leapt, aiming for its back, only for it to sense the attack at the last second and spin. Pain exploded down the side of my face and neck as it backhanded me.

I landed on my feet, crouched and snarling. Blood soaked my fur where its talons had torn through flesh.

Eyes that were nothing but pools of darkness focused solely on me. Even on all fours, the chimmeris was easily six feet at the shoulder. Thanks to the curve of its spine, its head hung low, completely blocking its throat. A direct frontal attack was out of the question. It'd cut me to pieces.

In my peripheral vision, I saw Mikhail and Cassius flanking it. I needed to keep its attention to give them a chance at pressing the token against it long enough to activate the magic.

I took a step forward, and the devourer opened its mouth, displaying rows of long, thin teeth with two curved fangs and letting out a bone-chilling shriek. Several other chimmeris swiveled their heads away from the large monsters and looked at us.

Shit. Stupid frontal attack it was.

I darted towards the chimmeris, and the devourer lunged forward to meet my attack. It struck at me with one arm, its talons raking my chest, not enough to do serious damage but enough to draw more blood. My body slammed into it, knocking it onto its back. I threw myself onto its right arm, claws shooting out from my paws to pin it down, and in a flash, Mikhail gripped its left.

The monster flailed, trying to dislodge us, while letting out a mixture of shrieks and more of those strange clicking sounds. I hissed as it kicked me. The talons weren't as long as the ones on its hands, but they were every bit as sharp.

Any day now, Cassius! I growled.

The vampire staggered towards us, blood coating the left side of his face, and based on the shredded state of his vest, he'd come very close to getting disemboweled. One of the looky loos must have gone for him while Mikhail and I had been distracted with this one.

"This plan is insane," he ground out as he eyed the chimmeris snapping its jaws in my direction. I was trying very hard to keep my body away from those teeth, but every time it kicked me, I got a little closer.

"Nemain!" Mikhail shouted in warning, but it was too late. The chimmeris gave up trying to dislodge Mikhail and put all its effort into me. Both its hind feet slammed into the side of my ribs. I couldn't stop the back half of my body from pivoting directly onto the beast's mouth.

A pained scream tore from me, but I refused to let go of the chimmeris' arm. If I did, it would disembowel me in one strike. Dozens of sharp teeth ripped into my flesh as the devourer gulped my blood down.

Cassius was swearing up a storm. I saw a flash of gold and felt a strange magic brush against my senses. He must have activated the transport token. Thank fuck.

My vision dimmed around the edges. Too much blood loss.

Why did ten seconds feel like an eternity?

"Don't pass out on me, shifter!" Mikhail shouted.

Don't. Tell me. What to do. Vampire. Suddenly, the devourer disappeared, and I fell onto the forest floor. Pain exploded from what felt like every inch of my body. On the plus side, it sent a wave of adrenaline through me that chased away the darkness pulling at my mind.

I tried to get to my feet but stumbled a few times before succeeding. We'd managed to nab one chimmeris, but all three of us looked like we'd gone through a meat grinder. Despite the attention we'd briefly drawn, most of the devourers still swarmed the two large predators. The temptation of a magically rich meal was too much for them to ignore, despite the dozens of broken chimmeris bodies littering the ground.

Across the clearing, a werewolf went flying and slammed

into a tree. Another werewolf ripped into a chimmeris with Justina darting in with a gold coin. Stela. Which meant the blood-soaked one lying limply in front of the tree was Andrei.

My heart seized, and it felt like it only started beating again when the wolf stirred and struggled back to his feet.

Three chimmeris peeled off from the others and stalked towards Andrei, who shook his head like he was trying to clear it. Magos appeared in a swirl of mist, standing between Andrei and the devourers. Blood coated every inch of his skin and clothing, and his copper eyes practically glowed.

All this blood and mayhem had to be hell on his control, but there he stood, defending a werewolf against certain death.

I needed to get to them.

Before I took a step, Justina screamed, and my head jerked towards her just in time to see a chimmeris yank its claws from her gut. It raised its gore-covered hand to strike again, only for an eight-hundred-pound werewolf to slam into it like a freight train. Stela's jaws closed around the back of the chimmeris' neck, and she shook it like a rag doll. Even from where I stood forty feet away, I could hear the snap over the chaos of the battle.

Justina staggered back a step, her hands clamped over her stomach, likely holding in her guts.

Two chimmeris crept towards her.

I glanced back at Magos and Andrei. The chimmeris flanked them, getting ready to attack, and an entire clearing full of monsters battling it out separated me from them.

Okay, maybe my plan hadn't been the best.

Cassius, get to Justina. Try to nab as many chimmeris as you can. Mikhail and I will help the others and do the same. Hopefully, that will get us the remaining ones we need and we can get the fuck out of here. I concentrated on drawing Mikhail's mist magic.

"Fine." Cassius tossed Mikhail another token. "Let's do this.

In a blink, he was next to Justina and shoving her back. Stela rose from her kill to stand by her side, blood dripping from her jaws as she growled at the oncoming chimmeris.

I let the mist pull me away, and then I was staggering next to Magos . . . and I was on two feet. And clothed. *What the fuck?* Mist swirled around my wrists, and my swords materialized.

Mikhail appeared a second later. "Did you mean to do that?"

"Nope." I rotated my wrists, spinning my swords a few times. "But I'm not going to try switching back now." Blood leaked down my neck and side. Apparently, shifting via mist didn't heal me as well as the old-fashioned way did.

The three chimmeris went completely still and cocked their heads in unison as they tried to figure out how their prey had doubled.

"Creepy fuckers," I muttered when their heads snapped the other way.

"You good, pup?" Mikhail kept his gaze laser-focused on the chimmeris, and Andrei let out a low growl in response, which was underlined with pain.

"How many more do we think we need?" I tried to count in my head. Six more maybe? "Did you get any, Magos?"

No response.

"Uncle?" Something in Mikhail's tone had me risking a glance away from the chimmeris. My eyes fell on Magos, and a chill ran up my spine. He stared at my neck—right where my pulse was beating—and he very much didn't look like my friend right now.

"Magos," I said tightly, turning my attention back to the chimmeris that were creeping closer. "I need you to hold it together for just a few more minutes, okay?"

Again, he didn't answer, but he didn't attack either. Good enough.

Instead of waiting for the chimmeris to come to us, I went

for the one closest to me, executing a fast, horizontal strike aimed at the side of its neck. The devourer sprung back, preternaturally fast, and shrieked at me before going on the offensive. Its long arms swiped at me, forcing me to back up because its damn reach was better than mine.

Out of the corner of my eye, I saw Mikhail and Magos each battling their own chimmeris. They'd mist to get behind them, but somehow, the devourers sensed where they'd be. I let out a sharp cry when talons ripped through Mikhail's neck before he misted away. All I saw was him standing several feet away, a hand wrapped around his neck, before similar talons cut through my thigh and I let out a strangled scream.

I took a step back, but my weight was off, and my wounded leg gave out.

"Nemain!" Mikhail rasped.

The chimmeris was on me in an instant. Talons dug into my flesh as it pinned me down and struck at my neck, only to shriek when Andrei slammed into it.

Another scream ripped from me when the chimmeris dragged its claws through my flesh as it hit the ground next to me. Andrei tore into it, but the beast kept its neck protected and doing far more damage to the werewolf with its dagger-like talons.

"Token!" I screamed, blood coughing up and spilling over my lips. "Fucking token!"

With one hand still clutched around his throat, Mikhail leaned down, swiped something gold off the ground, and threw it at me. I dropped my swords and snapped the token out of the air before practically falling on the chimmeris.

My blood-slicked fingers almost dropped it, but I managed to slam it against the chimmeris' skin. Magic nipped at my fingertips, and I let go, falling away. The chimmeris let out a litany of clicking sounds before vanishing.

The enchanted bone in my chest burned and crumbled

away. Instantly, the block that had been between me and most of my magic was gone. My devourer flames would be of no use here, but I was more than ready to open a gateway and get the fuck out.

"Time to go!" I yelled.

Magos appeared in front of me. Blood coated his sword, and his movements were . . . off, but he held out a hand and helped me to my feet. Copper eyes lingered on my neck for a few seconds too long before he stepped back.

I searched for Mikhail and found him staggering towards me—not misting. Shit. He must be tapped out. Now that I focused on it, it wasn't just pain I felt through our bond but exhaustion.

Andrei slowly got up, his yellow eyes dim. His right front leg was severely mangled, and he had to hold it off the ground.

"We just need to get to the othe—" I flinched along with everyone else when one of the dino monsters roared before stalking off into the woods, its mate following it. "Oh, fuck," I breathed out.

Some of the chimmeris chased after the retreating monsters, but at least thirty remained.

And they were all looking at us.

Chapter Twenty-One

So close. We'd been so fucking close to pulling this off. Now, forty feet separated us from Stela, Justina, and Cassius. While Cassius was still in the Might Need To Get Murdered column, Stela definitely wasn't, and Justina . . . well, I didn't quite know what to make of her.

But Andrei would never leave his sister behind, and I wouldn't abandon him, which meant we needed to figure out how to survive the next few minutes so we could reach each other and I could open a gateway. Despite getting my magic back, I was exhausted, and opening a gateway to the sorcerer realm would be difficult. I only had it in me to do one.

Blue flames flickered down my arms as my devourer magic surfaced, and some of the chimmeris close to us jerked back.

"Can your flames hurt them?" Mikhail narrowed his eyes as more chimmeris shrank away.

"No," I murmured. "If I hit them with it, the flames will just splash harmlessly over them. Devourer magic wielded against another devourer just cancels out." I called on my magic more, and the flames grew a little larger, but it felt like I was drawing from an empty well. The chimmeris hesitated, making clicking noises to each other. "It's the light that's keeping them at bay."

I flung my hand out, sending a blazing line of fire straight through the clearing to where Stela and the others were and letting it circle them. Darkness crept into my vision again, and Mikhail steadied me.

"You good?"

"Yeah," I panted. "That's all I can do though."

Enraged snarls bounced off the trees as the chimmeris leapt away from the flames. They didn't flee though, just put more distance between them and the fire. The problem with my blue flames was that while they were brighter, their light didn't go far. The chimmeris seemed to tolerate it just fine five feet away. There was another problem too.

"If they touch the flames, their devourer essence will snuff out the fire where they make contact." I took a deep breath and instantly regretted it when a sharp pain had me gasping. Apparently, I had a punctured lung on top of everything else. The fact that it hadn't healed already told me how bad of shape I was in; my magic was prioritizing healing based on severity and hadn't gotten to the lungs yet.

Based on the way Mikhail leaned against me, he wasn't in much better shape. There was zero chance of us fighting our way out of here.

Cassius snapped into being next to me and froze at the dagger Mikhail had at his throat. Injured or not, my mate was lethal.

"Once an assassin, always an assassin," Cassius said lightly before turning his gaze to me. "We need to get Justina out of here. What's taking so long?"

"I was just about to open a gateway, but I can only do one, so it'll have to be in the center of the clearing. Get the others ready to move. We need to do this before the chimmeris touch my flames and realize the fire can't hurt them," I told him, reaching for my magic to prepare the gateway.

Something flickered in Cassius' eyes. It was too fast for me to interpret, but it instantly made me put my guard up. He gave me a shallow nod, not the least bit concerned about the blade to his throat, and teleported back to the others.

"He's up to something," Mikhail said warily.

"Agreed." I watched as he slung both his and Justina's packs on before bending down and lifting the unconscious vampire. Justina looked like a broken doll in his arms. Stela watched him closely before moving next to him but a little behind, so she could monitor him.

It seemed we were all wary of Cassius and his intentions at the moment.

Andrei limped towards us, his feet almost collapsing out from under him several times. I tried not to panic at how much blood stained his coat.

"You all go first," Magos said tightly. "I'll follow."

My heart thudded inside my chest as I took in Magos' burning copper eyes that were affixed to the ground in the center of the clearing. As if he feared that so much as looking at us would snap the last strands of his control.

I maneuvered Andrei between me and Mikhail, and we slowly walked towards the center of the clearing. Cassius did the same from the other side, with Stela following. Twenty feet. Just that short distance, and then we'd be out of this godsforsaken realm.

The chimmeris moved closer, and their chittering sounds grew louder.

"Shut up," I growled as I tried to concentrate on opening the gateway and keeping the flames going. Normally, this wouldn't be difficult for me, but between the blood loss and explosion of pain every time I took a breath, it was hard to focus on multiple things.

Kalen and I would have to add this to our training regimen. He'd balk at hurting me, but Badb would have no problem stabbing me in the gut if it made me a stronger fighter. Her idea of motherly love was . . . unconventional.

"Where are you opening a gateway to?" Mikhail asked, his eyes on the chimmeris, who were growing more and more agitated.

"Thaxea's," I replied. "Hopefully Jinx, Vizor, and the witch are there; if not, we'll need to find them and then figure out what to do about Izaak. And Emir."

Mikhail nodded, his expression grave. We were going from one dangerous realm to another, but we needed to collect our friends, and there was still the matter of fixing Andrei and Magos. We didn't have a choice.

The air rippled six feet in front of us, and I poured a little more of my magic into it. The chimmeris crowded in so that less than five feet separated us from them, and they were still inching forward. I doubted they understood what the gateway was, but they clearly knew we were doing something to escape, and they didn't like it.

Andrei stumbled, and a piercing shriek tore from a chimmeris to my right before it launched itself into the air and glided a few feet to stand between us and the gateway. Mikhail steadied Andrei as we came to a stop.

"There's one behind us too," Magos said with a calmness I didn't feel at all.

"Stay close, Andrei." My fingers tightened around my swords. The other chimmeris hadn't attacked yet. We just needed to convince this one to move, and then we'd be in the clear.

Just as I was about to lunge forward and stab the devourer, it swung its arms open wide and brushed my flames. Like a stone dropped into a pond, my flame faded away where it made contact. The beast swung its head towards the vanishing fire, and clicking sounds poured out of its mouth, echoed by the other chimmeris surrounding us.

"Run!" I screamed.

Mikhail and I darted towards the chimmeris blocking our way. Three-inch talons swiped at my neck, and I sliced at its arm with my sword. It reeled back with a high-pitched scream that was cut off as Mikhail's blade carved through its neck.

More chimmeris swarmed us. Mikhail and I parked ourselves in front of the gateway. We needed to keep this area clear so the others could get through.

Claws tore at my left thigh, where I'd blocked too slowly. I slammed my sword straight through the chimmeris' face and pulled it free to stop another attack.

Magos charged through the gateway with Andrei slung over his shoulder, only to return a second later without the wolf.

"Cassius!" I yelled. "Get through the fucking gateway!"

He had Justina, and I suspected Stela wouldn't leave without her.

"I'll get them," Mikhail growled and darted around me. Magos instantly filled his space, and we did our best to hold back the horde of devourers.

My world shrank to a two-foot radius. Nothing but pain and death existed.

Stab. Block. Scream when I was too slow. Repeat.

Fangs sank into my right forearm, and I cleaved through the chimmeris' spine with my other sword. Spots appeared in my vision, but I kept fighting.

Then Mikhail was dragging me back and demanding something of me. It took several seconds for me to process the words.

Close the gateway.

I grasped the magic thread that connected me to the

gateway and pulled, the realm of monsters falling away, and I finally let the darkness claim me.

"Why isn't she waking up?"

Stela. It was Stela who asked that question. My mind felt hazy and sluggish. She sounded far away. Was she asking about me?

Slowly, I opened my eyes. It felt like someone had superglued them shut, so it took a few tries. Dull pain echoed throughout my body. Clearly, I hadn't been out that long, because I was still healing. Then Mikhail's beautiful face appeared over me.

"Hey, shifter." His tone was light, but I could see the concern in his eyes.

"Nemain's awake?" Stela asked, and I raised my head enough to see her sitting on the edge of a bed across the room from me. I didn't recognize the room, but the paintings and odd decorations were familiar enough. We were definitely in Thaxea's home.

"I guess that answers my question of whether you were asking about me a moment ago." I grimaced as I pushed myself up into a sitting position with Mikhail's help. He settled in to sit next to me, like he was afraid I would shatter into pieces. Given how I currently felt, he had reason to be concerned. Was there any part of my body that didn't hurt right now? I wiggled my toes. Ow. Even my pinky toe hurt. Stupid fucking realm.

"She wasn't asking about you, but don't take it personally," Andrei said dryly from where he rested on the ground a few feet away from me in his human form. "My own dear sister barely spared *me* a glance."

"Oh, quit your whining." Stela rolled her eyes. "I did check on you, but your dumb ass was still passed out after swooning like a southern belle and making the vampire carry you."

"Sisterly love." Andrei sighed. "Isn't it grand?"

I laughed and instantly regretted it when pain laced up my side. My breathing was better though, so at least my punctured lung had healed. I could feel how drained my magic was. The serious wounds had been prioritized, but now I didn't have enough juice to finish healing things like torn ligaments and muscles. The next few days were going to be super fun.

Gradually, the fog lifted from my mind, and I took stock of the room. Stela was perched on the bed of a very unconscious Justina, who looked pale, but all the blood had been cleaned off her. Cassius leaned against the wall on the other side of Justina's bed; he also looked cleaned up.

I raised the sheet someone had thrown over me and glanced down. I'd been redressed in a loose-fitting shirt, no pants or anything else, and my skin was covered in bruises, but all the blood was gone.

Frowning, I let the sheet drop, and my eyes landed on Magos, who was as far away as he could get from us without leaving the room. He sat on the floor with his back against the wall and arms resting on bent knees. Copper eyes burning with hunger stared into nothing.

The pain I felt in my chest had nothing to do with my lingering injuries.

It felt like I was underwater as I slowly turned my head to look at Mikhail.

"He hasn't spoken since we got here," my mate said softly. "Thaxea was able to scrounge up some clean clothes for us. I cleaned you up, and Stela cleaned up Justina." His throat bobbed as he swallowed. "We thought maybe once the blood was gone, he would . . ." Mikhail trailed off, and it broke me to see how lost he was.

My gaze drifted back to Magos, and I grabbed hold of the

fear I felt and shoved it down. We'd survived the monster realm and brought back everything we'd needed. I wouldn't give up now. Magos was stronger—stronger than all of us; he could hold on a little longer until I tracked down Izaak and forced the sorcerer to remove the damn curse.

"Where is Thaxea now?" My voice sounded like I'd been gurgling rocks. I cleared it, and my next question came out stronger. "And did she mention where Jinx and the others are?"

"She's going to get them now, actually. She was waiting for the sun to set and the area where they're stashed to be less busy," Mikhail answered. "Apparently, Vizor trashed the hell out of Izaak's flying house before he grabbed the witch and escaped." Mikhail smirked slightly. Thaxea worried that someone would find them if she hid them here, but she has a vacant place nearby.

I chewed my bottom lip. "Have Izaak or Emir bothered her directly at all?"

"No." Mikhail shook his head. "But she's fairly certain they're watching the house."

Andrei grunted. "Emir definitely is. When I was getting cleaned up, I carefully went to an open window in the front of the house. I caught his scent on the breeze . . . and also some people who smelled like those devourer fae we fought."

Not great. I wasn't all that surprised, but that meant we couldn't stay here much longer. If they didn't already know we were here, they would when Thaxea came back with the others. Unless she had some sneaky way of getting them into the house. Assuming she didn't, we'd need to be ready to go as soon as they got here.

"What's your next move?" I gave Cassius a hard stare.

He shrugged. "Same as always."

"So, whatever benefits you then?" Mikhail's lip curled, and I saw the same disgust echoed on Stela's and Andrei's faces. I kept my expression blank, even as my certainty that Cassius was up to something built.

"Precisely." Cassius shot Mikhail a bright smile. "I'm not exactly a fan of Emir or his pet sorcerer, but I do need the ability to walk in the sun. They're currently on my list of temporary allies, and once they've served their purpose, I'll move them to my Kill When an Opportunity Presents Itself list." His smile turned mocking as he swung his gaze towards me. "Surely you understand how this game is played by now?"

Tension in the room rose. Andrei's eyes had gone wolf-yellow once more, and all his focus was on Cassius. I didn't know how to de-escalate the situation because that really wasn't my forte. Plus, I very much wanted to stab Cassius right now and apologize to Elisa and Misha for killing their asshole brother later.

Elisa was pragmatic enough to understand. Misha . . . well . . . he already thought I was a monster.

Slowly, I rose to my feet. Mist swirled down my forearms, trailing through my fingers, and then my swords appeared. The magic felt a little off, almost like it had a lighter touch to it. I suspected that was because Mikhail was still running low on magic, and I made a mental note to avoid traveling through the mist until he fully recovered.

None of us were in fighting shape right now. The question was, how tapped out was Cassius? He'd definitely been wounded, but I didn't think he was as drained as the rest of us. And his ability to teleport would be obnoxious in a fight.

Especially since every muscle, joint, and bone hurt when I stood. Even my toenails hurt.

Cassius eyed my swords, his eyebrows rising with that damn smirk still on his face.

"What did you do?" Mikhail smoothly rolled to his feet to stand next to me, his sword appearing in his hand with the thinnest tendrils of mist. His fingers were clenched so tightly around the hilt that they were almost white. "I know that look. What the fuck did you do, Cass?"

"Sorry, Azuris," Cassius replied in a conversational tone. "But you really should have learned from the first time you trusted me."

A dagger sank into the wall half a second after Cassius teleported.

"Fuck!" Mikhail snarled and stalked over to rip his dagger out of the wall before turning to look down at Justina. "We need to get out of here. We'll have to try to find the othe—"

Somewhere else in the house, a door slammed open.

"Nemain! Please tell me you're here!" Lestari shouted.

My stare connected with Mikhail's, and we looked at Justina, who was still unconscious, and Magos, who hadn't reacted to anything that had happened in the last few minutes.

"Stay here," I told Stela and Andrei. The former just nodded, her brows bunched together as she watched the vampire beauty on the bed. Mikhail and I strode towards the door, but I paused in front of Magos and crouched. "I'll be right back."

No reaction.

"I'll keep him safe," Andrei promised, coming to stand next to me and laying a hand on my shoulder. "Promise."

My throat tightened, but I nodded just as Lestari burst into the room. She appeared unharmed but clearly rattled, her dark eyes wide with fear. "Izaak is coming . . . and he's bringing fae devourers with him."

I squeezed past her into the hallway. No one else was here. "Where are the others?" My gaze swung back to the witch as she stepped into the hallway. "Where is Jinx?"

A pained expression spread over her face. "Thaxea came to get us, but we only made it halfway back before some fae woman attacked us." She swallowed. "I think it's Syndra. Jinx and Vizor stayed behind and told me and Thaxea to run."

Stupid fucking grimalkin. The damn dragon could take care of himself. What had Jinx been thinking?!

I spun on my heel and sprinted for the front door, Mikhail racing after me.

"Be careful! Thaxea is activating her defenses!" Lestari warned.

The ornate wooden entrance door hung open, and I slowed, Mikhail doing the same. Perfectly framed in the doorway were two figures standing amongst the sculptures that decorated the front yard.

Izaak had traded his faded, greyish-brown robe for a black one stitched with gold. He held himself straighter, and I could have sworn that his face was a little less wrinkled. His grey hair was more of a steely grey than the lighter color it had been days ago, and those piercing green eyes seemed to laugh at me.

Kneeling on one knee in front of him with her head bowed was Thaxea. I couldn't see her face, but her hands were balled into fists at her sides, and the muscles of her back and neck were rigid.

"What did you do to her?" I stalked through the doorway and out into the yard. A full moon rose in the early evening sky, lighting everything up. I halted after a few feet when Thaxea whimpered. Mikhail stopped next to me, his eyes scanning the buildings overlooking Thaxea's house while I focused on the sorcerer.

"Once an apprentice, always an apprentice." Izaak smiled. "We may have gone our separate ways after she disappointed me, but I left safety measures in place." Thaxea let out a pained hiss, her body jerking in place for a few seconds. Izaak glanced down at her. "I wouldn't advise it, foolish child."

I had no idea what she was doing, but clearly, it was hurting her. We needed to subdue Izaak, both for Thaxea's sake and because we needed him to break the curse on Magos. Once he was taken care of, I'd open a gateway and shove everyone through it—except Mikhail—whether they wanted to go or not.

Then Mikhail and I could find Jinx and Vizor and we could get the fuck out of here. We'd have to deal with Cassius later, especially because I didn't know where he had gone off to. Maybe back to Emir.

I suspected the blood oath was the only reason the warlock wasn't here. He was still bound by it and thus would have had to warn me of any direct threats or intervene on my behalf. So he'd simply removed himself from the situation.

He had outlived his usefulness. He was definitely in the To Be Killed column. I needed to clear some space on the Murder Board anyway. It was getting too full.

"We upheld our part of the deal—you have your extra chimmeris." I pointed one of my swords at Izaak. "It's time for you to fix the curse on Magos."

The sorcerer chuckled heartily, like I'd just told the best joke ever, and a cold knot of despair formed in my gut.

"There's no fixing it," Izaak said lightly as his amusement died off. "It truly is a remarkable and elegantly crafted curse."

"You haven't even tried." Anger rolled off Mikhail in waves.

The sorcerer gave Mikhail a placating look. "The deal was that I would look at his curse and fix it if I could. And I did look at it—before you left, if you remember. The curse is woven deep into his soul. Perhaps I could've removed it in the first few days, or maybe before he drank blood and strengthened it." Izaak shrugged. "But it's too late now. That curse will follow him, even into death."

"I don't believe you," I bit out. He just didn't want to help us. There had to be someone who could unravel the damn curse. Maybe Thaxea could study it more; she had to be familiar with Izaak's work.

Izaak's gaze flicked back to me. "How many people have to

tell you that there is nothing you can do about it before you accept it?"

"There are countless realms." I flashed my fangs at Izaak. "Somebody can help us."

"And if that somebody isn't you, then there's really no reason for you to keep breathing." Mikhail took a step forward before halting, his head snapping to the pathway behind Izaak.

Syndra strolled around the corner of a redbrick building with two people on either side of her—Mariam on her left and Cassius on her right.

The rage burning through the mate bond was so hot that I was surprised I wasn't on fire. I only registered it briefly, because the bulk of my attention was on Syndra. Her arm was held out in front of her, and dangling in her grasp was Jinx.

"Did you misplace something?" Syndra's deep and melodious voice rolled over me.

Panic threatened to claw its way out of my chest because Jinx wasn't moving.

Jinx? Answer me. Please, I begged, not caring if Syndra or any of her allies had the ability to hear my thoughts.

He didn't respond with words, but I felt the barest brush of his mind against mine. Alive. He was still alive. With that knowledge, I was able to push back the panic and rage enough to think again.

"We found this too." Syndra raised her other hand, flicking her fingers forward, and some of her henchmen poured out from behind the building. Two of them dragged a bloody and beaten Vizor. "His magic was truly delicious." Syndra hummed, biting her bottom lip.

The fae dropped Vizor onto his back, and he fell like a stone, not even reacting when his head bounced off the ground. I thought I saw his chest rise and fall, but I wasn't sure. There was nothing I could do for him until I figured out how to get us out of this mess.

"Do you have it?" Izaak looked at Cassius.

"Yes," the vampire answered and held up a familiar cylinder. The blood from the hyaenir we'd collected. That's why the asshole had grabbed all the bags when we'd left the realm earlier. Fuck it all. I wanted to scream. Everything we'd gone through . . . and we had nothing to show for it.

Izaak reached over to grab the cylinder, but Cassius pulled it away and slipped it back into his pocket. "You'll get it when I can walk in the sun again. No hard feelings"—his gaze cut to me—"but I'm finding it hard to trust folks these days."

I would kill him. Slowly.

But first, we needed to survive. I scanned the warriors lined up behind Syndra. There were less than a dozen, but in our current state, that was more than enough to put both me and Mikhail down. We had no magic, and I could feel his fatigue.

And then there was Syndra. I studied the fae I'd heard so much about. She was my height, with golden blonde hair pulled back into a tight bun and lightly tanned skin. Dark brown fighting leathers wrapped her lean, muscular body. When she'd walked towards us, there'd been an arrogant swagger to her movements, but now, she stood with her weight equally distributed.

Two sword pommels poked out over her shoulders.

"Ah." She passed Jinx to Mariam and gave me a small smile. "There it is. You've finally realized just how in over your head you are."

I tried to come up with something quippy to say, but failed. Grim resignation filtered through me. My friends were counting on me, my mate was counting on me, and I had nothing left.

Syndra studied me with sharp, oceanic blue eyes. "I've got to say, this is mildly disappointing. So many people have talked you up to me. They speak your name as if you're the devil herself, but look at you." She snorted. "I've been to devourer realms that make the one you were in look like a walk in the park. You're barely standing. Hells, you're probably seeing double right now."

"Good thing I've got two swords." I forced some bravado onto my face as I grinned at her and spun them. "Want to dance?"

There was no way I could win this fight, but I didn't need to. I just needed to create a window of opportunity for Mikhail and the others to grab Jinx and Vizor. If we could get back into the house, I'd just need a minute to dredge up enough magic to open a gateway.

"Alright." Syndra reached over her shoulders and pulled her swords free. "Let's see what the fuss is about."

Her swords were made of a silver so dark, they were almost black. I started towards her, my swords raised in a defensive position. Normally, I was an aggressive fighter, but this wasn't about winning; it was about stalling until the right moment presented itself.

Unfortunately for me, Syndra was also an aggressive fighter, and she had no reason to buy time.

My right sword blocked the strike she aimed at my thigh, but my left was too slow. I let out a harsh breath as she opened a cut on my bicep.

She didn't stop to gloat or taunt; her blades became a whirlwind as she forced me to match her speed to block.

I couldn't.

More cuts opened up on my body as my movements became more and more sluggish. Syndra moved on liquid joints, her strikes beautiful and precise. It was like fighting a better version of myself—one who hadn't been beaten to hell over the last few days.

Out of the corner of my eye, I saw Mikhail dart forward to join the fight, only for him to jerk to a halt. His sword suddenly fell from his hands as he clutched his neck.

"Mikhail!" I screamed as I barely managed to dodge Syndra's attack. There was nobody around Mikhail, and I couldn't see what he was struggling against, but he gasped for air as if he were being strangled.

For a few seconds, nothing existed but the pain through the mating bond. I lurched towards him, only for a new agony to tear through me. A raspy cough slipped from me as blood dribbled from my mouth and my swords slipped from my fingers. I looked down at the shiny black sword sticking out of my abdomen.

"So disappointing," Syndra whispered in my ear.

Chapter Twenty-Two

SYNDRA YANKED the sword from my back, and I collapsed to my knees six feet from Mikhail. Whatever magic had been strangling him released its grip, and he also fell to his knees, gasping for air.

"The vampire is all yours, sorcerer," Syndra said coolly. "Mariam, see that the shifter is contained and gets enough healing to stay alive. My queen and king are still interested in her, so she can't die yet."

I dragged myself towards Mikhail, almost blacking out a few times. He grabbed me, pulling me onto his lap as his body shuddered as if it was still in pain.

"If you have no use for the dragon and grimalkin, I'll happily take them off your hands too," Izaak greedily offered.

"Sure. You can have whoever is ins—" Syndra suddenly spun around and thrust one of her swords out into the mist swirling between her and us.

It slammed against Magos' sword as he blinked into existence.

Syndra broke away and sliced at Magos' right side with one blade and at his inner thigh with her other. He blocked both strikes and slammed the pommel of his sword into her chin. Syndra's head snapped back, and she stumbled a few feet.

Blood shone on her teeth as she smiled. "Magos, I take it? The one these two are searching every realm to find a fix for?" She pointed a sword at us. "Funny, nobody mentioned you were such a talented fighter. Or gorgeous." She winked.

"Not interested," Magos said calmly.

In my peripheral vision, I thought I saw Cassius grin, but then Syndra attacked, and all I could do was watch as she and Magos danced through the sculpture garden. Swords flashed at preternatural speed. Syndra's people watched the fight with blank expressions, except for Mariam, who frowned slightly.

Izaak had backed up to stand behind the fae, leaving Thaxea in a broken heap on the ground.

Mikhail and I sparred with Magos regularly. I'd been a good fighter before I'd started training with him; I was a better one now. I considered it progress that I could hold my own against him for a few minutes, but I'd always suspected that was because he let me, not wanting to beat me down constantly.

And because Magos enjoyed being a teacher. He took pride in my getting better.

I'd seen Magos fight others before, but never a one-on-one with a fighter who had Syndra's skill. Watching Lir fight had been eye-opening. Watching Magos was breathtaking.

Syndra was a deadly whirlwind of blades. Her technique was perfect, and her balance never wavered.

Magos blocked every strike though.

Her face grew redder and redder the longer the fight went on. Then a scream of pure frustration tore from her after she'd tried a complicated move only for Magos to block one sword before twisting the other out of her grasp and tossing it aside.

"Is this a new fighting technique?" Cassius drawled from

where he leaned against a statue. "I'm not familiar with throwing one's sword away."

"Shut the fuck up!" Syndra snapped, taking a few steps away from Magos, who just stood there calmly. He didn't have a single cut on him, but Syndra was bleeding from multiple wounds. Her lip was also split, and she sported a bruise on her cheek where Magos had slammed his elbow.

"What's the matter, fae?" I let out a ragged laugh. "You seem to be struggling a bit. Need some pointers?"

"You could just walk away," Magos said evenly. "We can call it a draw."

It wasn't a draw. Everyone here knew it. The fight was tilted in Magos' favor. It was only a matter of time before he landed the hit that would put Syndra down.

She knew it too.

"How's that bloodlust, vampire?" Syndra rasped. She glanced over her shoulder at her warriors, who had remained still during the fight, before grinning at me. "Feeling thirsty?"

One of the fae warriors stepped forward. Like the others, they wore a cloak obscuring their features, but they pointed at me with slender fingers, and I arched in Mikhail's hold. It felt like someone had just shoved their hand into my stomach wound.

I screamed and slumped when the magic tore into me—and threw my blood directly at Magos. He went rigid as some of it landed on his face . . . and on his bottom lip.

As if he were in a dream, Magos touched it with his fingertips, drawing them away to look at the bright red stain. His copper eyes brightened like they were lit from within, and a darkness crept in at the edges.

"Fuck." Mikhail struggled to his feet, lifting me with him. He backed up a step towards Thaxea's house but froze when Magos' eyes snapped to us. His head moved to the side in that jerky movement of the chimmeris.

"No," I breathed out.

Magos' mist sword vanished, and he flexed his fingers as his nails hardened into black claws. Fear gripped me. That was new. What the fuck was this curse doing to him?

"Magos?" My voice trembled.

Another jerky head movement as Magos took a step towards us.

"Uncle," Mikhail said tightly. "Stop."

Black threads weaved their way through the copper as Magos focused on my neck . . . and the pulse thumping rapidly.

Slowly, Mikhail backed up another step. I could feel him straining through our bond, trying to pull on his magic, but he had no misting ability left, which meant I didn't either.

"Stop her!" Izaak shoved his way through the fae warriors, and the amused expression on Syndra's face dropped as she looked away from us to the sorcerer. He thrust a finger towards Thaxea, who was crawling on the ground. She was practically dragging herself towards a sculpture that looked like a deer. It was rearing up, branching antlers stretching towards the sky. Two legs were on the ground, and the other four were raised.

Oh, it was like the ones we'd seen in the devourer realm.

"Don't let her touch the statue!" Izaak screamed.

Syndra blinked, then darted towards the young sorcerer, but not fast enough. Thaxea slammed her palm down on the left hoof of the statue and spoke too quickly for me to understand.

The deer statue glowed faintly . . . and then came to life—and so did every other statue in the yard.

An enormous feline statue tackled Syndra while the deer bulldozed through her fae warriors. Magic erupted across the yard as the fae tried to dismantle the statues as quickly as possible. Chunks of stone flew through the air, punctuated by screams as the fae found themselves gored by antlers or crushed by stone teeth.

Thaxea staggered to her feet and grabbed Jinx from where Mariam had dropped him in the mayhem. Andrei and Stela rushed out of the house to Vizor. Andrei swung him over his shoulder while Stela guarded his back against the fae who had broken away from the statues to try to stop them.

During all of this, Mikhail and I remained perfectly still because Magos hadn't taken his eyes off us.

"Just get us inside," I rasped, fighting to stay conscious. The pitiful amount of magic I had left was trying to staunch the bleeding, but I blocked it from doing so. We needed to get out of here, which meant I had to open a gateway, and I needed every drop of magic I had left to do that.

Mikhail glanced down at my bleeding stomach, his expression dark. "I'm sorry." Then he bolted towards the door, holding me tightly against him to lessen the jostling, but every step he took was pure agony.

Lestari waited by the front door, words pouring out of her as flower petals swirled around her hands. Mikhail darted through the door, and I looked over his shoulder to make sure Magos didn't attack the witch as he followed us. He didn't even pause; nothing else existed to him but me and my blood.

We'd barely made it to the room I'd woken up in when Magos caught up to us. I screamed as strong fingers closed around my arm and yanked me from Mikhail, then threw me against the wall. *Crack.* My vision dimmed, and it was hard to think. I touched the side of my temple and pulled my fingers away. Sticky. Warm. Red.

Blood. It was like someone hit the play button, and all my thoughts unpaused just as a loud crash sounded from the other side of the room.

"Mikhail!" I screamed. My hand clutched at my chest, not

from an injury, but because of the sharp pain I'd felt through the bond. Mikhail was slumped against the wall, his head and neck at an odd angle. For a second, my heart stopped beating, but then I felt his life force.

The older vampires were, the more damage they could take, and Mikhail was one of the oldest. He would survive. I wouldn't accept anything else.

Before I could try to rise, I was jerked up and slammed against the wall, my feet dangling off the ground. Magos cocked his head as he looked at me, and fear clamped me at the movement that was so unlike him.

"Magos." His name came out broken on my lips. "Please don't do this."

For a moment, the darkness bled from his eyes, but then his gaze dropped to the blood rolling down my face, and his eyes turned solid black. I screamed as he snapped forward and his fangs ripped into my neck.

The memory of when I'd been held captive by Sebastian and he'd let vampires feed from me came flooding back. Vampires could make the feeding process feel good, but when they were in a frenzy, it was nothing but pain.

I was going to die here. Killed by one of my truest friends. A man I loved like family. The sorcerer would take Mikhail. He would be tortured and eventually killed.

Jinx. Andrei. My friends would die because I had failed them.

Deep in my soul, my magic tried to stir before collapsing. The world started to go dark, and I could barely feel the pain anymore. Just the sound of Magos snarling as he consumed my blood.

Then there were voices screaming. The potent scent of burning herbs and flowers. A sharp pain, and I fell . . . Someone caught me.

"Andrei?" I blinked rapidly, trying to focus.

"Hey, kitty cat," he said in a strained voice. "Can you open a gateway? We need to go. Now."

"I don't know." My words slurred. "Not much magic left."

"Take some of mine." He raised his head and looked at something or someone over my shoulder, worry flashing in his eyes before he looked at me again. "Can you do that? Take enough to open a gateway?"

A part of me recoiled at the idea of devouring the magic of someone I cared about, but I was so tapped out, I didn't even know if I could summon my flames.

"They're getting through!" Thaxea stepped into my view. She still had Jinx clutched to her and was staring at the wall. I blinked several more times, trying to focus, and looked around the room. Lestari knelt over Magos, who lay on the ground, unconscious. Blood covered his face—my blood—and she placed flowers on his chest while whispering.

Stela held Justina, her face bloodless but determined. Vizor and Mikhail lay on the ground at her feet. My mate was coated in blood, and his wounds were healing slowly. Too fucking slowly. I could feel the tenuous hold he had on life through our mate bond.

"Don't let me take too much." I pushed the words out.

"I trust you." Andrei looked at me with his kind hazel eyes. "You won't hurt me, Nemain."

The house shook, and a loud crash sounded from somewhere outside. "They're through the outer walls!" Thaxea announced, backing up a step.

I looked at Mikhail one last time before closing my eyes and burrowing deep into my soul, where that ever burning flame lived. It felt so faint now. Barely more than a flicker. I tried to pull it towards me, but it slid from my grasp and grew dimmer.

Please, I begged it. *Our mate will die.*

For what felt like an eternity, my magic waned until I thought it was going to go out completely. Then the spark ignited. My eyes flew open, and I raised my right hand as blue flames engulfed it. Andrei didn't hesitate. He placed his palm against mine and intertwined our fingers.

My magic didn't hesitate either.

Blue flames surged down Andrei's arm. *Don't hurt him,* I thought frantically. *We just need some of his magic.* My words were unnecessary though. The flames didn't burn Andrei's skin or clothing, but they hungrily took chunks of his magic.

A yellow glow rolled over Andrei's eyes, and he gritted his teeth, fighting to keep his wolf under control. Magic poured into me. I was so empty that even the small amount I took felt like a flood.

The house shook again.

Enough, I told my magic. The flames immediately went out. Still holding Andrei's hand, I raised my other one and concentrated. The air shimmered in the center of the room, going in and out of existence several times.

I pushed harder.

The air split, revealing a gateway, and it almost closed immediately, so I pushed more magic into it. Bright spots filled my vision, but I clung to consciousness.

"Not. Steady," I ground out. "Go. Fast."

Stela didn't hesitate; she bolted through the gateway with Justina in her arms, then came back and took Jinx from Thaxea before vanishing again. The sorcerer looked worriedly at the wall, as if she could see Syndra and her ilk fighting through whatever defenses she'd managed to raise.

Andrei unwound his fingers from mine and got up, but when he reached down to pick me up, I shook my head. "Him first." I pointed at Magos. Part of me wanted to get Mikhail out of here, but if he were awake, he would've demanded Magos go before him.

"Okay." Andrei jerked his head in a nod and quickly went over to the unconscious vampire. He and Lestari exchanged words, and then Andrei carefully picked Magos up from underneath his shoulders. Stela appeared and immediately went to help her brother, gathering up Magos' legs. The two of them carried Magos through the gateway, Lestari following them, still quietly chanting whatever spell she'd used to put him under.

The witch remained on the other side of the gateway, but Andrei and Stela returned and took Mikhail and Vizor through it. Only then did I let out a breath of relief. Safe. They were safe.

The two werewolves returned, and Andrei swept me off the ground. I flinched as the wound in my stomach, which had healed a little bit, tore open again and blood oozed out.

"Shit." Andrei winced. "Sorry."

We stepped towards the gateway, and I saw the precise moment panic flooded Thaxea's eyes. The wall behind us was ripped away, revealing the crumbled remains of the rest of the sorcerer's house and yard.

And a very pissed-off Syndra with dozens of fae warriors. Izaak was with her, looking equally pissed-off. Standing slightly off to the side was Cassius, who did a quick sweep of the room. He wore his usual mask of arrogance, but I could have sworn I saw something akin to relief in his eyes.

For a few seconds, we all looked at each other, then Thaxea, Stela, and Andrei bolted for the gateway.

Thaxea made it first, then Andrei. He whipped around to his sister, and the sharp movement almost made me pass out. I started to pull my magic from the gateway because I needed to shut it the second Stela made it through.

The gateway shimmered when Stela was a foot away, so I started to close it.

Stela suddenly stopped, her eyes wide, and then something yanked her back, as if an invisible lasso had been tossed around her.

The gateway slammed shut.

"No, no, no!" Denial rapidly sprung from my lips. I reached for my magic again to open the gateway, but as soon as I pulled on it, my body gave out, and for the second time in twelve hours, I passed out.

MY MIND STIRRED before I fully woke up. Two thoughts immediately hit me: Mikhail was alive—he wasn't next to me, but he was close—and there was something in my hand.

It took a couple of tries, but I convinced my eyes to open and look down at my hand resting on my chest, fingers curled around the object. I flipped my hand over and stared at the familiar crystal container.

The hyaenir's blood.

How did I get this? The last I'd seen it, Cassius had it in his possession. What had happened? I tried to piece everything together. He'd betrayed us. Thaxea had activated the statues. We'd escaped through a gateway . . .

"Stela." I jackhammered up into a sitting position. Pain punched me, and the crystal flew from my fingers as I wrapped a hand around my abdomen.

"Back to the land of the living and already throwing things at me," Eddie said dryly.

"We need to rescue Stela." I shoved myself up with a groan. "Where is Magos? Is he still under? What about Vizor and Jinx?" I swung my feet off the bed I'd been laid on and tried to stand, only for my legs to give out immediately.

Eddie was there in an instant. He carefully grabbed me by the waist and settled me back onto the bed before taking a seat next to me.

"Don't tell Cerri, but I just lost our bet." He tossed the cylinder in the air, letting it flip a few times before catching it. "Thought for sure you'd lose your shit when you woke and Mikhail wasn't here."

"I can feel him," I explained numbly. "He's one floor down and feels slightly better." My gaze was locked on Eddie casually tossing the hyaenir blood. "Did you put that in my hand?"

He caught the cylinder and looked at me curiously. "No. You didn't have it when you arrived and Cerri has been busy taking care of the others, so I doubt she did either, and we're the only ones here."

I'd opened the gateway to Eddie and Cerri's future home just outside the city I'd left Finn in. It'd been the safest location I could think of on the spot where our friends would find us quickly. They only lived here part time, so Eddie had set up magic sensors to alert them if anyone came to the house.

I held my hand out, and Eddie passed the cylinder to me. Cassius had definitely had it last . . .

The mystery would have to wait. I shoved it into the clean pants I now wore. The amount of times I'd now passed out and woken up in someone else's clothes was becoming disconcerting. I was mildly impressed that they'd managed to put me into a sports bra without waking me up. Magic had to have been involved. That was the only explanation.

Thaxea would need to check the blood and make sure it hadn't been tampered with, but maybe we'd somehow walked away with at least something.

Not enough. I swallowed and felt the tightness of the barely healed skin and muscles along my throat.

Magos had attacked me. What if he woke up and still wasn't himself? What if he never came back? Icy dread spread throughout my chest. I'd promised him I would fix this, and he'd believed me.

"Nemain." There was a seriousness to Eddie's voice that had me turning to meet his gaze. Burnt-orange eyes full of concern looked at me. "How bad is it?"

"Bad." I let out a humorless laugh. "I met Balor."

Eddie straightened. "As in the exiled fae king? That Balor?"

"The one and the same," I confirmed bleakly.

"How is that possible?" A deep crease formed between his dark, golden-blond eyebrows. "Did he break free?"

I shook my head. "He took advantage of the situation and made sure I ended up in a devourer realm, where the boundary between it and his realm is weak." I squeezed my eyes shut. In my mind, I could picture him perfectly. "We can't let him get free," I rasped. "He'll come for Finn. I know he will . . . and I don't know if I can stop him."

Warm fingers wrapped around mine and squeezed once before releasing. The bed dipped as Eddie rose, and I opened my eyes to find him standing in front of me.

"Then we won't let him get out." A spark rolled through Eddie's eyes, dark pupils narrowing to slits. The dragon peered at me through my friend's eyes. "You're not alone in this, Nemain." He held his hand out. "But Balor's a problem for another day. In the meantime, who are we killing?"

I grabbed his hand and let him pull me to my feet, wincing a little before releasing it. "Everyone between us and Stela." Placing one hand on Eddie's shoulder to steady myself, I gently prodded at the bandage wrapped around my midsection. It'd been a long time since I'd needed a bandage or had bruises lingering on my skin. "How long have we been here?"

"About an hour." Eddie offered me his elbow, and I swallowed my pride and took it. Falling on my ass in the hallway would be far more embarrassing than needing a little help walking.

"Good," I breathed out and started to the door with Eddie's help. "Because we need to go after Stela within the next hour."

Eddie glanced at me sideways, his brows raised. "I know you're a badass and everything, but right now, I'm fairly certain a strong wind could knock you over."

"Oh, it wouldn't have to be strong." I snorted. "But I've got an easy way to fix that. Just help me get to Mikhail because he's coming with me."

We made our way down the hallway. Eddie didn't comment on the number of times I had to pause to catch my breath. I'd have to give him the coveted best friend title for at least a week after this and just not tell Kaysea.

It took almost ten minutes for us to get downstairs because the house Eddie and Cerri were building was huge, and I'd been placed on the opposite side of the stairwell since all the other rooms on that floor hadn't been furnished yet.

Once we got down the stairs, Eddie led us through the first door on the right, which turned out to be a large bedroom.

A soft sob escaped me before I could stop it. Because at the center of the room was a canopy bed. It wasn't the light pink gauzy material around it nor Vizor snoring away that had me almost crying.

It was Jinx. Safe and sound. Sleeping at the dragon's feet.

Against the wall on a fainting couch was Justina. Considering what we'd all been through, the vampire looked surprisingly good. Her skin and hair lacked their usual luster and perfection, but she no longer looked like she was on death's door. Someone had clearly given her blood.

Across the room, Thaxea was slumped in a chair, and Andrei leaned against the wall behind her. His posture was tense, and his eyes were glowing yellow.

I stepped away from Eddie so I could perch at the end of the bed and gently run my fingers through Jinx's soft black fur. He didn't stir, but a low purr filled the room, and I smiled.

"Took several pictures of sleeping beauty." Eddie waved a hand at Vizor before shooting Cerri a hurt look. "But she wouldn't let me put a tiara on his head."

"The two of you can play your games when we don't have a house full of injured people." Cerri gave her mate a warning look before turning her gaze to me. "Mikhail is checking on Magos. Lestari still has him under, but she's trying to reach out to her coven for help because she can't continue on her own for much longer."

That cold dread threatened to rise again, but I shoved it down. Stela's rescue came first. I had to trust that Lestari and her coven could keep Magos asleep until that situation was solved.

I pet Jinx one more time before taking a deep breath and standing back up.

"How are we getting her back?" Andrei's gaze was locked on me.

"We're going to hit Syndra hard and fast. She won't expect us to attempt a rescue this quickly." I placed a hand over my bandage. "We need that element of surprise."

"You don't seem to be all that healed." Justina pushed herself up onto her elbows and frowned at me.

"I've got a plan for that." I glanced at her before returning my attention to Andrei. "Can you fetch Mikhail for me? I need him for this next part."

Andrei stalked out without a word. I pulled the crystal from my pants and tossed it to Thaxea. She caught it, but her expression still looked a little lost. Considering her entire world had just turned upside down and her home had been reduced to rubble, I supposed that was understandable.

"You got it back." She pondered the hyaenir blood. "How?"

"Details are a little murky on that." I shrugged. "Can you test it to make sure it hasn't been tampered with?" My eyes flicked to the door Andrei had vanished through. "Don't tell him yet—not until we know for sure we have good news."

"Y-yes, of course," she stammered before hesitating. "My workshop was in my home. There are things I'll need . . ."

"I've been setting up a work area on the third floor." Cerri ran her hands down the front of her dark green dress. "You're more than welcome to use that, and whatever else you need, I'm sure we can procure."

The two of them headed towards the door, but Cerri paused in front of me. "Are we sure Stela is still alive?" she asked quietly, and Justina went very still across the room.

Balor's words echoed in my mind. "*Syndra likes her toys, though she has a habit of breaking them.*"

I nodded. "At least for now, I'm confident she is, but she might be wishing she were dead. We need to get to her. Fast."

Cerri paled slightly in understanding before ushering Thaxea out of the room.

"I'm coming with you to get her back," Justina announced.

I arched an eyebrow. "Oh?"

She raised her chin. "Yes."

"Are you sure that's wise?" I cocked my head. "You might still be able to salvage your position within the Vampire Council since you were passed out when we took you. Just claim we kidnapped you and you escaped. If you do this, it's doubtful it will ever be safe for you to return."

And your child will be in even more danger. I didn't say that part. She'd gone to great lengths to keep her son a secret, so I wasn't going to acknowledge his existence out loud, even if we were in a safe location.

"The Vampire Council is no longer the safest place for me.

I will figure out a new path." She smiled wide enough to flash her fangs. "After we rescue the wolf. I've always wanted to save a damsel in distress."

I huffed a laugh. "Dare you to call Stela that to her face."

Justina's smile softened slightly, but before she could respond, Andrei and Mikhail swept into the room. Concern flashed in Mikhail's eyes and down our bond as he took in my still-bandaged state.

"Mikhail and I will be right back." Slowly, I got to my feet, refusing to lean on Mikhail, even as he hovered next to me. "I need to fix this." I waved at my broken body.

"I'll go with you," Andrei said firmly.

"No," I replied in a tone that brokered no argument.

"Why?" The word was more of a growl than anything.

"Because I'm about to slaughter a bunch of fae," I answered honestly. "They're probably going to scream for their lives and all that jazz while I'm doing it."

A golden sheen rolled over Andrei's hazel eyes. "I'm fine with it."

I looked at the wolf staring back at me. Andrei wasn't entirely himself right now. His wolf side was superseding his human side. And while the wolf might not care about the cries of the dying . . . it would haunt Andrei later.

"No," I repeated and held up a hand, cutting him off when he opened his mouth to argue. "Do not test me. We will return in fifteen minutes, and then we will rescue your sister."

The look the wolf gave me promised death. "Fifteen minutes."

"Fifteen minutes," I agreed before turning to Mikhail. "Come on, we've got to make a quick pit stop."

I opened a gateway to our apartment and stepped through, closing it as soon as Mikhail crossed over in case Andrei changed his mind and darted in. It wasn't as hard as it'd been when I'd opened one out of the sorcerer realm, but I felt the drain on my magic. Luckily, I only had to open one more after this, and I could feel my devourer magic stirring back to life.

All I needed was a spark, and then we'd be back in business.

The note Misha and Damon had dropped off was exactly where I had discarded it on the kitchen counter. I walked over and snatched it up. The paper had a slight yellow tint to it, and Tadg had marked it with his family seal. It'd come from the fae realm—likely from his home.

I loved it when the fae made it so easy to find them.

Granted, as a Tuatha Dé Danann, Tadg Soleil no doubt thought he was untouchable.

We arrived in a typical house of the upper members of the fae court, and I looked around the beautiful library. The walls were almost covered with bright blue vines, and the dirt floor told me we were on the ground level, which was confirmed when I glanced out the large arched window behind the desk and saw a garden.

Three fae lounged outside, enjoying the starry night sky.

"Elvinia lets you get away with a lot, but she probably won't be happy if you kill him." Mikhail studied the dark-haired fae, who was telling the other two a story that had them all laughing. "Although, if we remove any trace of the bodies, it'll potentially take a while to come back to us."

"We won't kill him, just his buddies." I grinned at Mikhail. "Feel free to hurt him though."

"With pleasure." A wicked smile spread across his face. He'd read the note and understood the threat.

Silently, we made our way through the house until we strolled out into the garden. "Tadg," I drawled. "Got your message. Figured I'd deliver my response in person."

Mikhail and I stopped a dozen paces from where the spoiled fae still lounged on a chaise, a glass flute of dark purple liquid casually held in one hand. Like all sidhe, Tadg leaned androgynous and was absolutely stunning. Dark chocolate brown eyes sat above a straight, narrow nose and chiseled cheekbones. His square jaw added a touch of masculinity, and he favored a more masculine way of dressing as well.

I was very familiar with his family. His parents hated mine with a passion and were constantly whispering snide comments about them. The Soleil bloodline was an old and extensive one. Tadg had three aunts and two uncles, each with children and grandchildren of their own.

There was a reason my parents hadn't wiped them out of existence despite the fact that the Soleils undermined them at any opportunity. Though I suspected when Badb and Kalen returned from whatever mission they were currently completing for Elvinia and saw the note, they might take more drastic measures.

But I didn't need my parents to fight my battles. Even if I was being targeted because of them.

"How considerate of you." Tadg didn't bother rising, nor did his two companions. I vaguely recognized both of them from some of the parties Elvinia had forced me to attend. They were sidhe but not from the Tuatha bloodlines. They'd attached themselves to Tadg to better their standing in the Unseelie Court.

A cool night breeze carried their scent to me. They were the ones who'd delivered the letter. Perfect.

"Did you need clarification or anything?" Tadg asked smugly as he sipped on the fae wine. "You don't seem as clever as your father. Perhaps you take after your mother and are a bit more dense about these things."

Mikhail chuckled, and Tadg's gaze snapped to him.

"Something funny, vampire?"

"Only that we both know you wouldn't dream of saying such a thing in front of Badb." Mikhail gave the fae an appraising look and his expression clearly said he wasn't impressed. "You'd probably piss yourself if she showed up right now."

"He definitely would," I agreed.

The amusement fled from the fae's beautiful face, and his cheeks darkened.

I gave him a breezy smile, which only enraged him further, and glanced at the blond-haired fae on his right. "Alfie, right?"

"Yes," he replied in a bored tone.

"And you're Silan?" My eyes flicked to the chestnut-haired fae, who was outright leering at Mikhail.

"The bitch knows my name. I'm honored," he mocked. "I see why you like this one. He's pretty." Silan winked at me. "I think I prefer the quiet vampire though. What was his name?"

"Damon." Alfie snapped his fingers and leaned forward in his chair. "There was something intriguing about him."

Silan smiled at me, showing off perfect white teeth. "What do you think he would do if I told him I'd spare his life and the lives of his worthless siblings if he *served* me?" He sank enough meaning into that word to make the insinuation clear.

Alfie chuckled.

"Forgive my friends. They can be a bit crude at times," Tadg gave me a condescending smile. "But in their defense, it was bad enough when your father brought his shifter mate into our court. Now you've lowered us even further with your association with vampires." He gave Mikhail an appreciative look. "Despite how pretty they are, they're still beneath us. Your parents walk the halls of our palace as if they could ever belong there. As if they're untouchable," he spat and rose to his feet, closing the distance between us until he was only a few feet away. Alfie and Silan got up to stand on either side of him. "As powerful as your parents are, they have a weakness: you. And you have many weaknesses. Just something for you to keep in mind as you figure out where you stand in the court."

I let out a dark laugh. "Oh, I'm afraid you've made quite the mistake."

Several things happened at once. Mikhail vanished into mist and reappeared behind Tadg. Before the fae could react, Mikhail summoned swords—my swords—and skewered the sidhe. Tadg screamed as Mikhail lifted him several feet off the ground.

Twin blue flames shot from me and speared Alfie and Silan in the chest. They gasped and jerked like fish on a line, and I yanked them off their feet and onto their knees in front of me. I held the flames back, not letting them do anything but keep the fae in place.

"My parents are dangerous for sure. But they have a long history with the fae queens and the court. There are reasons they hold themselves in check while sniveling cowards like you whisper behind their backs."

Tadg let out another strangled scream as some of my devourer flames flickered to life on the blades. Mikhail dropped him, letting the fae crash to the ground between his burning friends, and vanished into mist, only to blink into existence behind me. He pressed his chest against my back and wrapped an arm around my waist. Warm lips kissed my neck as he let out a slightly unhinged laugh against my skin.

I smiled at Tadg. "You should have feared us more."

The fae screamed as my flames devoured their magic. Mikhail sank his fangs into my soft flesh as magic poured into me and then into him. When Alfie and Silan stopped screaming, their lives and magic snuffed out, I let my magic take a few bites out of Tadg, although I left him alive.

Mikhail unwound the bandage on my stomach, his fingers brushing across smooth, unblemished skin, then licked the blood from my neck, sending a shiver down my spine before he stepped away. I pulled my devourer magic to me, enjoying the wild feel of brimming with magic.

I felt strong, powerful, and so fucking ready for a rematch against Syndra.

"Don't," Tadg protested weakly as he gasped for air on the ground.

Mikhail strolled over and wrenched my swords out of his back before tossing them to me. I caught them as I moved to stand on Tadg's other side and pressed the flat of my blade against the fae's throat.

"Tell me," I purred, "have I gotten my message across?"

Chapter Twenty-Three

WE HAVE A PROBLEM, Lynette signed quickly as soon as Mikhail and I stepped back through the gateway to Cerri and Eddie's house. It was rare to see Lynette rattled. She always had a serene calmness to her, but she'd been pacing when we'd arrived and was currently wringing her hands.

Fifteen minutes. I flew jerkily through the movements. *We were gone fifteen fucking minutes!*

Mikhail and I scanned the room. Vizor and Jinx were still asleep, but there was no sign of anyone else.

Is it my uncle? he asked.

Lynette shook her head. *Magos is fine, or as fine as he can be. Lestari's coven arrived to back her up. But I was downstairs when he arrived, and Finn went out to meet him before I could stop him.*

Who? I stared at Lynette. *Who is he?*

Mikhail tossed me a black shirt someone had laid on the bed, and I tugged it on, followed by a reinforced leather vest with built-in sheaths for daggers. Perfect fit. Cerri really had planned for everything.

Lynette's mouth flattened into a hard line. *Lir.*

The undeniable sound of two dragons roaring rattled the

walls. Half a thought had me vanishing into mist and reappearing outside.

Or at least that had been my intention. Instead, I found myself almost thirty feet in the air because we'd been on the second story, and in my haste, I'd miscalculated. I plummeted to the ground, trying to twist so I could land on my feet. Just as I braced myself to land on my ass, Mikhail appeared and caught me.

"Look before you leap, shifter," he chastised before setting me on my feet.

We glanced at the black dragon and the larger green dragon stalking around two figures—one big and one small. Andrei was in his wolf form and was crouched with his ears flat against his head, yellow eyes locked on Lir. I moved to stand next to him and raised my hand, pushing it out until it contacted an invisible wall.

Magic nipped at me, and I dropped my hand. It was Finn's magic. He'd set up some type of protective circle around him and Lir. I hadn't even known he could do that. Kid was full of all sorts of surprises. Even more interesting was that Eddie and Cerri couldn't get past it. Dragons were uniquely talented at passing through protective wards.

Finn furrowed his brows together, and a small patch of air rippled in front of me. Mikhail and I took a step forward, and this time, the barrier let us pass.

Whatever Finn just did, I can sense what's going on inside the barrier now, Eddie said. *Still can't get through it though.*

"What the fuck is going on?" I crossed my arms and narrowed my gaze at Finn.

"Language." His dark brown eyebrows bunched together over his two-tone eyes.

"Finneas," I said evenly, "you're gonna get a whole new lesson on language if you don't explain why you're protecting the bad guy from the pissed-off dragons."

Eddie and Cerri slammed their tails against the invisible wall as if to punctuate my point.

"He's here to help us."

I stared at Lir. There were some singed patches on his cloak, but otherwise, he appeared unharmed. He also didn't seem to pose any sort of immediate threat to Finn and made no move to close the distance between them, nor did he have any weapons out. I hoped Finn had been smart enough to also put a barrier between him and Lir, but the kid was entirely too trusting.

"Minor clarification." Lir held a hand up with his index finger raised. "I'm here to fuck over Syndra and also repay a favor. When I kill you, I'd prefer there to be no debts between us." His gaze dropped to my midsection. "My people reported on your encounter with Syndra. Although you seemed to have healed. Aside from your pride, of course."

Flames ripped down my arms, meeting the mist swirling around my hands as my swords appeared. "Drop the boundary, Finn. I'd love to have a chat with our guest."

Finn frowned at me. "You don't need swords for a chat."

I took a deep, calming breath so I wouldn't take out my frustration on Finn. "It's not safe for you to be around him."

"I want you to listen to what he has to say," he replied firmly.

"He gets his stubborn streak from you," Mikhail grumbled.

"Fine," I ground out, and my swords vanished.

"Taking orders from a child?" Lir let out a dismissive snort. "You're just everyone's bitch these days, aren't you, Nemain?"

Before I could open my mouth to say something that would definitely have Finn scolding me for language, Lir gasped and stumbled back a step, shock slapped across his face as his gaze snapped to Finn. A hint of something *other* had slipped onto Finn's usually kind face. Something dark and twisted.

"Don't speak to my mum that way," he said coldly.

Part of me wanted to cheer that Finn was standing up to someone. It was such a change from the quiet, meek child who had been lost in the fae realms years ago. Another part of me was a mixture of terrified and weirdly humbled that he'd referred to me as his mom.

Isabeau did it frequently, but mostly because she liked the look on my face. While I took responsibility for Isabeau, I didn't think she truly looked at me that way. She had Elisa, Bryn, and a handful of others. It was a village raising Isabeau because that's what she required.

But Finn was . . . Finn. He wouldn't say something he didn't mean.

Awww, Eddie whispered in my mind. *He used his scary powers to defend you and called you mom.*

Shut it. Also, can you and Cerri back off? I mentally sighed. *No eating the annoying fae for now.*

But he looks magically delicious.

Cerri lowered her head until she was at eye level with Lir. *We'll step back a bit. We can always eat him later.*

I had to hand it to Lir. The fae warrior just gave Cerri a lazy grin before she and Eddie retreated from the barrier. When Lir looked back towards me and Mikhail, the amused expression slid off his face. "The wolf is being held here." He tossed a shiny red stone onto the ground in front of me. "Syndra has a base in some backwater realm. All of her people are there."

"How many?" Mikhail asked lightly.

"Too many for a direct assault." A sly glint entered Lir's blue eyes. "Syndra likes her privacy though, especially for her prized toys. She holds them in a soundproof tower at the center of the fortress. You'll find it difficult to open a gateway inside it, and you'll never get to it from the ground, but from the sky?" He shrugged. "It's possible."

I raced through the options in my head. Assuming I

believed Lir—which I weirdly did—an outright assault was out of the question. I'd need to open a gateway somewhere outside the fortress where we could try to validate his information. Then maybe Mikhail and I could mist up by the window of the tower and drop in?

I didn't love that idea. If I miscalculated, I'd have seconds to correct my error, and while I was getting better at the whole traveling by mist thing, I wasn't sure I wanted to test my ability while free-falling. Even if I managed to land without going splat, we'd then be in the center of Syndra's stronghold and massively outnumbered.

Andrei also would not be a fan of that plan because he'd have to be left behind.

"Thanks for the intel. Debt's paid." I opened a gateway to a random spot in the human realm just outside Finn's boundary. "Come near Finn again, and I'll kill you."

Again, that arrogant, lazy grin graced Lir's face. "Sure. We're even now." He glanced at Finn. "Good seeing you, kid."

Finn chewed on his bottom lip and waved towards the gateway. Smart of him to only drop the boundary there because I definitely would have thrown a dagger at Lir.

Just out of principle.

Lir strode towards the gateway but halted and looked over his shoulder. "One more thing: you'd do well to bring the sciatháin."

"Thought we were even," I said mildly.

"You and I are." He turned and walked towards the gateway. "That's the debt I owe him."

I shut the gateway as soon as he passed through and looked down at Andrei, who stared at the spot where Lir had gone. "You need to shift back if you want to come, wolf."

Golden yellow eyes looked at me, and I fought the panic that tried to claw its way out of my chest. There wasn't a hint of the Andrei I knew in those eyes, and I wasn't entirely sure he could shift back. Or if he did, would it still be his wolf nature in charge?

What if Thaxea's fix came too late for him?

"Pup," Mikhail snapped. "Shift the fuck back."

The wolf growled at Mikhail but trotted off towards the house and disappeared through the door we'd left open.

Cerri and Eddie joined us again, both fully clothed. She cast a worried look in Andrei's direction but said nothing. Meanwhile, Eddie tapped against Finn's boundary. "You can drop it now, Finn. There's no one left for us to eat." There was more than a little disappointment in his words.

"You really need to stop eating people." I wrinkled my nose.

Eddie gave me a confused look. "What do you want me to do? Chew on them and then spit them out?"

I sighed and rubbed my forehead. "Were you able to pick up any of his thoughts?" Aside from Isabeau, Eddie was the strongest telepath I knew.

"No," he reluctantly admitted. "There's essentially a brick wall around his mind as far as defenses go. It's crude, but it gets the job done."

"My gut tells me he spoke the truth," Cerri said thoughtfully. "I don't know if he truly cares about the debt between you and him, but based on everything we've observed and heard, it seems he and Syndra are in their own pissing contest. He's using you as a battering ram against her. It just so happens to benefit us this time."

"Sigrun and Niall should be back by now. I'll check in with them and get their thoughts."

"They'll be useful if it turns out his information is accurate and we need to get into that tower," Mikhail added.

"Good." Eddie nodded in agreement. "One of them can carry me if necessary. I think I'll make Sigrun do it. Niall might drop me just to see what would happen."

"And why would she need to carry you?" I narrowed my eyes at him.

"Well, my dragon form isn't exactly gonna fit through a window, and despite how amazing I am in this form"—he waved at his body—"I can't fly."

I looked at Cerri. "Neither of you are coming. We're keeping this rescue group small." Not to mention, Vizor still lay unconscious on the bed upstairs. I couldn't handle seeing Eddie or Cerri hurt right now.

"Technically, we're not coming as part of the rescue mission; we're going for payback," Cerri said calmly, a hint of steel in her emerald green eyes. "My people are still getting situated in this new realm. It'll take months for the cities to be finished and our defenses to be up. In the meantime, we're a bit scattered. Those who followed my father are still out there —likely working with Syndra, or at least in talks with her. We cannot afford to look weak, because if we do, she's going to try to take us off the map before we can become a major player. It's what I would do." She smiled widely, showing off her pearly white teeth as her pupils flicked to vertical slits. "We are not weak, and she needs to know that if she attacks one of ours, we'll burn down her world."

"Well, given what I just did in the fae realm, I suppose I can't really argue with that tactic." I sighed. "Whatever you're planning needs to wait until we've secured Stela."

"Of course," Cerri agreed. "We can also serve as a distraction if necessary."

I didn't love that idea. We didn't have a good understanding of Syndra's magic other than she'd been strong enough to easily incapacitate Mikhail, and for all we knew, she had single-handedly taken down Vizor.

"If you see Syndra, do not engage," I said seriously.

Eddie opened his mouth, but Cerri clamped her hand over it. "Agreed."

"Where's Justina?" I ignored Eddie's grumbling against Cerri's palm. "We just need her and Andrei, then we can find Sigrun and Niall."

"I'll get her," Cerri volunteered. "I sent her down to guard the sorcerer when Lir arrived, just in case. If I see Andrei, I'll tell him to get out here too."

She dropped her hand from Eddie, gathered up her long dress, and jogged towards the house.

Eddie cocked his head, sending his blonde hair tumbling over his shoulder, and looked me over. "Well, aren't you just brimming with magic? At least someone got a tasty magic snack." He pouted again in Finn's direction. The fae child was concentrating, and I felt a sudden, strong pulse of magic that had me wincing.

"Sorry." Finn walked over to us. "I've never set up a barrier like that before, and it was difficult to dismantle without causing a blast of magic."

Awesome.

"Next time you experiment with raw magic, how about you do it somewhere not next to my house, eh?" Eddie ruffled Finn's hair.

Pink stained Finn's cheeks, even as he swatted Eddie's hand away. "Sorry. I felt him approach, and I didn't want you to eat him, so I panicked." His eyes shot to me. "It was a strategic panic though. I didn't lose control."

"No." I gave him a small smile. "I suppose you didn't."

"So I can go with you to get Stela?"

"Absolutely not," Andrei growled as he stalked out of the house. "It's too dangerous."

Finn glanced at him momentarily before focusing on me again. "I was well-behaved while you were gone, I did all the tasks assigned to me, and I never once lost control of my magic."

I pondered him. "Technically, I said I'd take you on the *next* trip."

A stubborn expression—that he'd absolutely picked up from Isabeau—stretched across his face. "Technically, the last trip you went on was to the sorcerer realm to acquire what you needed to help the werewolves and fulfill your blood debt to the warlock. While this rescue mission is related, one could argue that it has a new goal and is therefore a new trip."

"'One could argue'?" I arched an eyebrow at him.

Mikhail sighed next to me. "That's definitely Pele's influence."

"You promised," Finn said quietly.

"He's just a kid, Nemain." A muscle along Andrei's jawline tensed as he clenched his jaw.

"Yeah . . . but he's my kid." I sighed. "And I gave him my word. Besides"—a small grin played across my lips—"kid's got mad skills."

Finn blushed harder.

"You do exactly as we say, when we say it." Mikhail gave Finn a hard stare. "No arguments."

"Yes." He nodded eagerly before hesitation flashed in his eyes. "Isabea—"

"Isn't coming," I cut him off. "We already have more than enough people on this trip, and Isabeau tends to be volatile, especially around you."

I could tell he wasn't happy about that, but he didn't push me further. It probably wasn't a good parenting move to bring a ten-year-old into a realm where we were planning on breaking into the house of a dangerous and powerful fae, but a promise was a promise.

Plus, there was only so much I could do to shelter Finn. Bad people were coming for him—one of whom was his father—and I wanted him to be able to defend himself if necessary.

He needed to learn how to wield his magic in high-tension situations.

With any luck, we'd be able to sneak in with no one seeing us and find Stela. I'd open a gateway and get everyone out while Eddie and Cerri made it clear the dragons were not to be trifled with. Then we'd all have to prepare for Syndra's retaliation.

Cerri strode out of the house with Justina hot on her heels. The vampire had changed into black fighting leathers and had pulled her hair into a tight bun at the back of her head. There were an impressive number of weapons strapped to her body too.

I had to admit, it was kind of hot.

"Hopefully our lethal winged friends are back." I opened a gateway, revealing Sigrun and Niall's cottage. "If not, we'll have to go without them."

A white wolf with feathery wings landed in front of me as soon as I crossed over. "Gunnar," I greeted the Niflheim wolf. "Sigrun back?"

Ice-blue eyes looked at me for a long moment before he turned and trotted to the cottage, tucking his wings in tight.

"Friendly," Andrei commented.

We started after the wolf, only for a sixty-pound cat with dappled brown fur to appear in the air before us, jumping around as if he were landing on invisible lily pads. *Where is your lesser feline half?*

"Injured," I answered tightly. "He's resting at Cerri and Eddie's place."

Viggo leapt to the ground, blocking my path. *And you left him there undefended?*

"Lynette is with hi—"

Dog! Viggo yelled. *Get your furry ass back over here. The dumbass grimalkin got himself hurt.*

With a heavy sigh, Gunnar smoothly turned around, and

the two of them trotted through the gateway. I closed it behind them with a shake of my head, and we continued towards the cottage.

"Don't Viggo and Jinx hate each other?" Mikhail gave me a sideways glance.

"Cats." I shrugged like that one word explained everything.

When we reached the door, I raised my hand and knocked. Loudly.

"Would have thought you were the type to just walk on in," Justina commented. "Aren't they your friends?"

"Yes." I knocked again. "But one time, I walked in on them —" I looked down at Finn. "They were getting their aerobics in for the day, and Sigrun threw a hammer at my head."

"Maybe they're not home?" Finn suggested politely as I continued to pound my fist on the door.

"No, they're here," Mikhail said, tilting his head and listening. "They're coming now."

"I bet they are." Eddie chuckled, only to be smacked on the back of the head by Cerri, who pointedly looked at Finn.

The door opened, revealing a sweaty, bare-chested Niall. He blinked at all of us, his bright blue eyes taking in our weapons, and sighed before yelling over his shoulder. "Sigrun, love! Our friends are here, and I think they need us to help kill some people!"

***

"That tower fits Lir's description." Mikhail studied the spiraling building in the center of the sprawling Gothic fortress. I'd opened a gateway a safe distance from where the stone Lir had given me was from, and we'd slowly made our way closer. Currently, we were lying on our stomachs on a cliff, looking down at Syndra's stronghold.

And the army camped around it.

"And Lir wasn't wrong about us having a zero chance of direct assault," I murmured.

There had to be thousands of fae warriors milling around outside the fortress, and more on the walls and parapets. Syndra had been busy. I'd need to warn the fae queens about this, because while we'd known about the seraphim armies Lir had been building up, this was a surprise.

"How long do you think it's taken her to get this many devourer fae out of Balor's realm?" I wondered out loud.

"Decades," Niall replied grimly. "It's become easier in the last few years because the ward is weakening, but there is still a limit to how many can make it through on any given day. Maybe a dozen if they have relatively low magic. The queens have refocused their efforts on keeping the most powerful magic users in, so those like me with smaller amounts have an easier time. I'm surprised Syndra made it through, to be honest. She packs a lot of magic."

"We're aware." Mikhail grunted.

"This is a problem for another day." I raised my eyes to the sky. "We need to figure out what to do about that."

Dark clouds swirled above us . . . and something was flying in them. A lot of somethings.

They would definitely spot us making our way into the tower.

Cerri grimaced. "One of us could go up to take a look, but then we'd risk being seen."

"I'll do it," Sigrun scooted back from the ledge so she could stand. "I haven't met a fae yet who could see through my invisibility."

"Wait," Niall said suddenly, something odd in his tone. "It can't be . . ." He shoved himself off the ground and bolted into the sky.

"Damn it," Sigrun growled. "I hate it when he does that." One second, she was there, and the next, she used that nifty invisibility magic of hers and was gone from sight. I felt the whoosh of air as she took to the skies after her mate.

Those of us who remained watched the army below to see if anyone would notice Niall's sudden flight. We were about a quarter mile away, so not that close, but definitely visible. After a minute of nobody reacting, some of the tension bled out of me.

"Remember the plan, Finn?" I asked while scouring the sky, trying to get a glimpse of what was going on but seeing nothing. I mostly trusted Niall not to do something stupid, but for a five-thousand-year-old being, he had serious impulse control issues sometimes.

"Stay behind you and Mikhail," Finn repeated his orders in a calm, even tone. "You will tell me if my magic is needed. Otherwise, I'm to keep it to myself and not complain. We get to the tower and find Stela, open a gateway, everyone but you and Mikhail will leave. I will not argue. Then you two will go and get Eddie and Cerri after they do their scary dragon stuff, and the four of you get out of here." He paused. "And then we'll have a pizza party."

When he didn't say anything else, I dropped my eyes from the sky to stare at him.

He smiled slightly. "And you'll have a bottle of whiskey."

"Something's coming," Justina murmured.

My gaze snapped up to see six forms diving straight towards us from the clouds. All of us scrambled back. Finn obediently got behind Mikhail and me as we summoned our swords, his eyes a little wide but otherwise calm. Fire sprung to life and swirled around Eddie's and Cerri's hands as they watched the approaching beings while Andrei and Justina wielded daggers.

I felt the air stir in front of me before Sigrun dropped her invisibility a second later. "Niall made some new friends, or rather, met some old ones, I suppose," she said mildly.

Niall landed in front of Sigrun, his gaze immediately going to the hammer she casually held at her side. "No smashing yet, love."

"We'll see," she answered as the newcomers landed behind Niall.

Every single one of them was decked out in matte black leather and armed to the teeth. They were a mix of genders, but all of them were over six feet tall and corded with muscle. Feathery black wings identical to Niall's poked over their shoulders.

Sciatháin.

"We've come to bargain with the Unseelie Knight." One of the sciatháin broke away from the others and moved to stand next to Niall. Where Sigrun's mate was all dark, masculine beauty, this fae warrior was fair-haired and had a rugged handsomeness to him.

It took me a second to realize he was talking about me. "What are you bargaining for?"

Solemn brown eyes looked at me. "For our freedom."

"There are few sciatháin left," Niall explained. "I didn't even know Brennan and his unit had crossed over. We all served under Lir together until . . ."

"Until everything went to shit," Brennan finished for him. "Ever since, we've been bounced around to different commanders until Syndra dragged us all here."

"I don't see a collar around your necks," Justina drawled. "And you got those fancy wings. Why not just fly away?"

Brennan's light brown eyes flicked to her. "And go where? We've been locked away for thousands of years. Now we're here, but we know nothing about the other realms. The fae queens wiped out every sciatháin who didn't leave with Balor, and it seems unlikely they'll welcome us back now. We know nothing about the daemons or any of the other powers that have risen." He looked back at me. "But you . . . you were able to negotiate on Niall's behalf. You could do the same for us."

I mean, I had spoken with the fae queens about Niall . . . but Sigrun had also been standing behind me with lightning sparking off Mjölnir.

"They will ask for something in return," I warned. "The fae queens do not do things out of the kindness of their hearts."

"I'm fairly certain they don't have hearts." Brennan let out a humourless laugh. "We will not trade one master for another . . . but when the time comes, we will be willing to fight against Balor's people."

"How many of you are there?" I asked, even as I fervently tried to think of options. Getting them out of this realm would help us in this moment, but more importantly, this mattered to Niall. I'd do what I could to save the sciathàin, but even with my poor grasp of political machinations, I knew bringing them back with us would be a challenge in the courts.

Those who supported the return of Balor were getting bolder, and there were factions who didn't want the exiled fae king to return but did believe it was time for someone else to take over the throne. Both could use any deal with the sciathàin to undermine the queens.

I'd need to stash them somewhere and speak with Pele to get her take. Probably Ashling as well. She didn't have as much power as the fae queens, but as the Merfolk Queen, she still had some, and she was very good at scheming.

"There are only five hundred of us left," Brennan said evenly. "And we're all here. Camped on the other side of the fortress."

"Are you sure all of your people feel the same way as you?" Mikhail gave Brennan and the warriors behind him a calculating look.

A woman with bloodred hair spoke up. "We all stand with Brennan." She glanced at Niall. "And him."

Niall's bright blue eyes fell on me. He didn't say anything, but he didn't have to. I could see it all on his face. These were what was left of his people. He hadn't been able to save his brother, but he could save them.

We could save them.

Also, having five hundred elite-trained warriors on our side definitely wouldn't hurt.

Someone tapped my lower back, and I turned slightly to see Finn. He raised his hand and beckoned me closer with his finger. I knelt, and he whispered in my ear. "Can we please help them? No one else will."

"He . . ." The hint of fear in Brennan's voice had me rising and facing the leader of the sciatháin again. His eyes were locked on Finn. "That is Balor's creation."

Creation. Not child. Creation.

"You're going to want to choose your next words very carefully." My voice held the cold promise of violence.

Brennan shook his head, as if he were trying to shrug off a bad dream, and held up his hands. "Apologies." He leaned to the side so he could peer behind me, and I felt Finn mirror the motion so he could see as well. "I was simply surprised to see you . . ."

Finn stepped a little farther out from behind me. "Finn. My name is Finn."

"It's a pleasure to meet you, Finn."

I let some of my magic creep out, not the devourer kind but the soul-reading kind, and inhaled deeply, letting Brennan's scent wash over my tongue. He reminded me of a breezy summer day, but more importantly, I didn't feel any deception. This magic of mine wasn't foolproof, but my instincts told me Brennan was sincere.

He hadn't been expecting Finn but didn't mean him any ill will.

I looked to Sigrun, who was still warily watching the sciatháin. The ancient valkyrie wasn't quick to trust people. Maybe in a hundred years, she'd stop treating everyone like potential threats. Or a thousand.

Sensing my attention, she met my gaze.

"They'll need a place to stay while I negotiate with the fae queens."

Sigrun sighed. "Fine." She pointed her hammer at Brennan. "Do not touch my things."

A puzzled look spread over his face before his eyes widened as a gateway opened next to him, revealing the meadow surrounding Sigrun's home. "Can you get your people through here in the next fifteen minutes? Quietly?" I emphasized.

He blinked a few times before nodding. "Yes. The other fae don't like us all that much. We often go flying in large groups, so they'll pay us no mind."

"Perfect." I tilted my head as I looked at Andrei and Justina, who'd remained quiet this whole time, before looking back at Brennan. "Before you go, we could use your help with something."

Chapter Twenty-Four

"THAT WAS UNNECESSARY," Justina hissed, pushing herself up from where she'd landed on the hardwood floor of the tower after Sigrun had less than gracefully thrown her through the window.

The sciatháin had used their wings to block those on the ground and walls from seeing Sigrun, Niall, and Brennan tossing some of our group into the tower. Mikhail had managed to mist in, and I had as well, only stumbling a little on the landing.

Sigrun shrugged, unrepentant, before snatching Finn out of the air and setting him onto the ground as Niall flew away with the other sciatháin to help them get through the gateway quickly and quietly. Eddie and Cerri waited on the ledge to assist if necessary.

Finn smiled thankfully at Sigrun before peering around the open space. There were two sets of stairs on opposite sides of the room, one leading up and the other down. There was no furniture or decorations of any kind, just some chains that hung from the ceiling in the center of the room and a dark, reddish-brown stain on the floorboards beneath them.

I saw the exact moment Finn realized what it was.

"This is a bad place," he whispered.

Andrei cut me a look that said, *I told you it wasn't a good idea to bring a kid here.*

"We won't be here long, and that blood is old," I told Finn. Not really sure if that actually made it better, but at least it wasn't Stela's blood staining the floor.

"I hear people moving around upstairs." Mikhail turned to Andrei. "Do you detect any scents that could lead us to Stela?"

The plan was to split up only if we absolutely needed to so we wouldn't have to find each other when it was time to go. I hadn't tried to open a gateway inside the tower because I was paranoid Syndra would have some way of detecting it. Our goal was to find Stela, and then I'd open up a gateway outside the window. We'd have to jump through it, but hopefully it'd mean we could get in and out completely undetected.

A low growl spilled from Andrei's throat, and then his eyes turned gold. He bolted up the stairs before anyone could stop him.

"Shit." I moved to follow, only for Mikhail to hold out his arm, stopping me, his eyes locked on the stairwell on the opposite side of the room from where Andrei had dashed up.

"It's rude to enter someone's home without knocking," Syndra called out with a laugh. "We don't have that kind of friendship, Nemain."

"Finn," I said calmly. "Can you do your barrier magic again?"

My heart raced. Part of me wanted to challenge Syndra right here while I was uninjured and full of magic. I heard only one set of footsteps, so she was alone.

But for once, the more rational part of my mind was louder. Currently, she was trying to court—or beat—me into joining Balor. I didn't think she'd pass up the opportunity to grab Finn though. As much as I wanted to beat the shit out of her, we were here to get Stela back. The rematch would have to wait.

Magic charged the air, making it uncomfortable to breathe for a few seconds before I felt it solidify across the doorway. It felt similar to the way Jinx and other grimalkins manipulated raw magic. Although their use of it was limited, they could solidify magic and wield it as an invisible, weighted force. It was on such a small scale that it wasn't very powerful or dangerous.

Finn was channeling raw magic—a lot of it.

In that moment, I truly understood Finn's potential. He was only ten. At this age, most fae children were lucky if they could summon a single drop of water from a puddle. Finn was performing magic that I suspected most of the Tuatha would struggle with.

What would he be capable of in a few decades, when he really started to tap into all his magic?

Mikhail dropped his arm and held his hand out, his sword appearing in an instant. His rage burned through our bond, but wound within it was a steady reassurance. We could handle Syndra, just as we would help Finn as he grew into his power.

Alone, I might not have been able to do this, but with Mikhail by my side, I could. I summoned my blades, mist dancing across the dark silver. "Justina, find Andrei." The vampire darted up the stairs without argument. "Finn, go stand with Sigrun."

I'd pulled the valkyrie aside earlier and told her she was to protect Finn no matter what, even if that meant hauling him out of here and leaving us behind. She'd agreed to do it—after punching me in the face. Telling a valkyrie to run away from a fight apparently made them very angry.

But Finn could not be allowed to fall into Balor's hands. Both for his own sake and that of the realms.

A look over my shoulder told me Finn had obeyed and was tucked up in the stairwell that led to the levels above us. Sigrun had parked herself in front of them, her hammer glowing slightly. She couldn't use the magic within it directly against Syndra or any of the devourer fae, but she could still smash their heads in.

Syndra strolled into view and stopped on the stairwell landing, inches from Finn's barrier. "Well, this is just adorable." She tapped on it with her nails, sending a magic reverberation through the room that had me grinding my teeth. "Finn's work, I take it? The little abomination has been busy playing with magic that doesn't belong to him."

"Yes, it does."

I momentarily squeezed my eyes shut. Sigrun cursed, and I heard the rustle of her wings, but it didn't matter now. When I opened my eyes, Finn stood between me and Mikhail.

We were definitely going to have a conversation about his disobeying orders later.

"Hello there," Syndra crooned as she crouched so she was eye level with Finn.

"Finn," Mikhail growled, but when he reached for the boy, Finn slipped forward until he was directly in front of Syndra, only his barrier separating them.

"The magic is mine," Finn said quietly. "Balor already has so much. He doesn't need mine too."

"That's where you're wrong, little one." She dropped her hand from the barrier. "It's not your magic. It's his and my queen's. They put a lot of effort into permeating your soul with their magic and that of others, but it was never yours to keep." Cruel eyes slid over his shoulder to look at me and Mikhail. "You think of them as your parents, don't you?"

I gripped my swords a little tighter. We needed to get Finn the fuck away from her, but I was worried that if I grabbed him, he'd lose control over his magic, and we really couldn't afford for that barrier to fall now.

"Yes," Finn answered, and my heart beat faster. I didn't like where Syndra was going with this.

"They've definitely claimed you as theirs. Another addition to the little misfit family." She smiled, but it didn't reach her eyes as she focused on Finn again. "Do you want them to die?"

The magic around the room took on a dark, vicious edge, and I shifted on my feet while Mikhail remained perfectly still. He couldn't sense the magic, but he could no doubt feel my anxiety building through the bond.

"So many people defending a thing that's past its expiration date," Syndra continued. "They're all going to die because of you. Either defending you from us, or when you lose control of that dark inferno in your soul and kill them yourself."

"Get him out, Sigrun!" I lunged forward to grab Finn—we'd just have to deal with his magic going haywire—but I wasn't fast enough.

"No!" Finn screamed, and magic lashed out from him. The solid barrier turned into a kaleidoscope of colors before exploding outward, shards like sharp pieces of glass flying directly at Syndra.

My fingers closed around Finn's shoulders, and I hauled him back. Sigrun was there in an instant, only to be flung back as if some invisible force had sucker punched her in the gut. She flew across the room, and I heard her slam into the wall, but I couldn't afford to check on her because fragments of the barrier froze in place around Syndra.

Syndra chuckled, and the pieces rotated until they pointed at us. "Oh, Finny boy, did you think you were the only one who could play with raw magic?"

I yanked on my magic, blue flames erupting into a wall between us and Syndra a second before the shards crashed into it. Normally, when my devourer fire absorbed magic, I got an instant rush and a power boost. That didn't happen this time.

"Fuck," I hissed as some of my flames turned from crystal

blue to an oily black. I could feel her magic's corruption in my soul as it polluted mine. "What the fuck are you?"

The barrage stopped, and Syndra's musical laugh echoed around the room. I released my magic, and the flames faded, taking with them that feeling of wrongness, although I could still feel traces of it.

Finn shook next to me, and I realized he'd put up another barrier. I hoped the others had found Stela, because we desperately needed to get out of here.

Syndra held up her hand, and black flames flickered across her fingers and down her forearm. "I'm a little of this and a little of that," she answered vaguely. "Your magic is no match for mine, and we've already established that your fighting skills aren't either."

She dragged her fingertips across the new barrier, and Finn's trembling increased. More of that sickly magic poured from her, and a low whimper escaped Finn before ghostly black flames wove their way through the barrier.

It was going to fall.

"Sigrun?" I asked tensely.

"I've got him." Gold wings appeared in my peripheral vision, and then Finn was swept off his feet.

He didn't even protest, and I suspected he was on the verge of passing out. Whatever Syndra was doing to his barrier was hurting him.

The valkyrie paused. "Don't die."

"Wouldn't dream of it, friend."

She raced away and must have leapt out the window because alerts started blaring from outside. Niall might blend in with the other sciatháin, but Sigrun and her golden wings wouldn't. *Eddie.* I pushed the thought out. *Now is the time for whatever you and Cerri have planned.*

Mikhail and I had our hands full with Syndra. We couldn't handle anyone else on top of her.

On it, he replied instantly. *Niall has almost all the sciathán out.*
Rip a hole at the top of the tower. We'll be there in thirty seconds.

"Nemain!" Justina shouted from somewhere upstairs. "We found Stela, but we're still trying to break her out of the cell! We need more time!"

Fuck. Mikhail looked at me, and his lips curled into a wicked grin before he nodded and vanished into mist. He didn't leave the room, but Syndra didn't know that.

Eddie?

Yes, bestie?

Make it three minutes.

As my favorite feline shifter desires.

"You've got less than three minutes, Justina!" I shouted. "Make it fucking happen!"

"What's going to happen in three minutes?" Syndra knocked her knuckles against the barrier, and it turned opaque, with cracks forming everywhere the black flames went. "I'm guessing it has something to do with all the commotion outside. It'll be good for my people. They've been getting bored. Torturing and slowly killing whatever friends you brought with you will be great for morale."

Someone let out a high-pitched scream that was abruptly cut off.

"I think one of my friends just ate one of yours." I grinned.

An earthshaking roar made the tower tremble.

"Fucking dragons." Syndra rolled her eyes before laying her palm flat against the boundary. Black flames swirled within the invisible barrier, and the cracks grew rapidly until the entire thing fell, disintegrating into ashes. She stepped over it and into the room, drawing her swords. "I meant every word I said to the abomination, by the way. Everyone who came with you today is going to die, including that vampire mate of yours, and I'm going to make you and Finn watch."

Three minutes. I needed to stall her for three minutes, and I would make it fucking hurt.

"I'm gonna slice you cunt to throat." I bared my teeth.

"In another life, we could have been friends, or lovers." She circled around me, her steps light and balanced, and winked at me. "The latter is still an option."

She spun around and crossed her swords in front of her, blocking Mikhail's strike as he appeared in a swirl of mist. He snarled in her face as he shoved his sword harder against hers.

"Did I strike a nerve?" She cackled.

Mikhail vanished again, only to reappear and slam a fist into her temple before sliding out of her reach. We circled her, biding our time.

Syndra glanced between the two of us, a thin bead of blood trailing down her face from where Mikhail had struck. "This hardly seems fair." She raised an eyebrow at me. "Not honorable enough to fight me one-on-one, Nemain?"

"Like how you were honorable while fighting Magos?" I half snarled. "You're a sore fucking loser."

She shrugged. "How is he, by the way? Lose his mind yet?"

I launched an attack, targeting her left side while Mikhail went for her right. She laughed as she gracefully moved between us, her dark short swords swirling. All our blades moved so fast, they were practically blurs as we danced around the room to the beat of steel against steel.

This fight was definitely going better than my previous one, but despite my pent-up rage and determination, we weren't winning. Mikhail and I sported at least a dozen cuts each, whereas Syndra only had a few. This was a stalemate that was slowly turning to her advantage, and time wasn't on our side. Her reinforcements would be here soon, and then we'd be fucked.

The three minutes were up.

"The two of you are fun. I think I've changed my mind

and want you both," Syndra purred after Mikhail made a shallow cut across her abdomen. I darted forward, aiming a strike at her exposed back, only to catch an elbow to the face. Tears fell down my cheeks, and I blinked rapidly, trying to clear my eyes as my broken nose healed. Syndra slid underneath another attack from Mikhail and spun to face us both, her eyes on him with her back to the window. "Nemain doesn't want to negotiate, but what about you? If anyone could lift the curse on your uncle, it would be Balor."

"There is no future where we would trade Finn's life for any of ours," Mikhail said flatly. "My uncle would suffer for the rest of eternity before he ever sacrificed a child. That's not the type of man he is."

"Sure." A sly glint entered Syndra's eyes as she pointed one of her swords at Mikhail. "But what type of man are you? He doesn't have to know. The two of you have put up quite the fight today, but you must know that you're not going to win. Why not get something out of it? Save who you can."

I'd been alive long enough to know that, sometimes, hard decisions had to be made, ones that people would hate you for, but Mikhail was right. Giving up Finn to save his life would kill Magos faster than any curse.

More people screamed outside, and I saw fire erupt past the window. We needed to end this fight, and I'd just gotten an idea . . .

I let a little hesitation slip into my expression and glanced at Mikhail, who met my gaze with a blank stare, even as I felt fury roaring through our bond at Syndra's suggestion. "Remember what happened to Elisa? Finn didn't mean to do it, but it happened so fast, none of us could stop it." I rasped as my eyes briefly flicked to the window while I tugged faintly on Mikhail's magic.

Mikhail nodded and let his sword drop a little, then blue

flames flickered in and out of existence, as if our mating bond was acting up again. "I remember."

"He'll be the death of you both if you let him," Syndra said almost sympathetically. "He can't help what he is—chaos and destruction."

"True." I bit my lip and dismissed my swords. "But when you put it like that . . ." I grinned. "That is kind of our motto."

Mikhail flung his hand out, and blue flames poured from it. They winked out of existence as soon as they made contact with Syndra, but their purpose hadn't been to hurt her.

It'd been to blind her.

A second before the flames went out, I misted directly in front of Syndra and spun around in a roundhouse kick. My foot slammed into her chest, and she let out a harsh grunt before flying back—directly out the window.

Her expression was a mixture of anger and surprise that I cherished for half a second before sprinting for the stairwell. Mikhail raced after me. I had no doubt Syndra would figure out how to survive the fall, and then she'd be back up here with an army. We needed to be gone before then.

We ran up the spiraling stairwell just as the entire tower shook and a loud crash came from above. Mikhail and I slammed against the stone wall before continuing our sprint up the stairs until we came to an open door with Finn and the others.

The entire outer wall had been ripped away. Wind tore at us, and from here, we could see the all-out battle being waged against the dragons.

Justina hovered nearby while Andrei held Stela. She was coated in blood, her eyes swollen shut, and her legs appeared to be broken in several places. Andrei's eyes were solid gold.

Two enormous dragons flew around the tower, raining down fire on everything beneath them.

I sprinted towards the ledge and let my magic out. A

gateway ripped through the air a foot from the ledge, revealing Eddie and Cerri's home. "Let's go!"

Andrei took off at a dead run and leapt through, still holding Stela. Justina did the same. Finn waited by Sigrun, who was also holding someone in her arms. A tattered cloak obscured most of the person's body, but I glimpsed bits of dark skin covered in a layer of dirt with wounds that not only weren't healing but had begun to fester.

A helmet of dark silver covered their entire head with only small openings for their mouth and nose.

"Who is that?" Mikhail shouted over the roar of the battle raging around us.

"I don't know," Sigrun answered loudly, glancing down at Finn, who was deathly pale. "He was adamant that we couldn't leave without her."

I had a sneaking suspicion about who she could be. Syndra would be really pissed about losing both her toys.

"We'll deal with it when we're out of here!" I pointed to the gateway. "Go!"

Sigrun carried the mysterious prisoner through the gateway, and Mikhail practically threw Finn through it.

Eddie! Cerri!

The two dragons let out two more streams of fire before diving straight for the gateway. Twenty feet from it, fire rippled over their scales, and they passed through it in their human forms.

Mikhail grabbed my hand, and the two of us leapt through together, leaving Syndra's fortress burning in our wake.

"Can you get some more water and washcloths to clean her off?" Kaysea murmured to Zareen. The daemon nodded, brushing her hand down Kaysea's shoulder before getting up from where she knelt and quickly leaving the room.

We were back at Eddie and Cerri's house for now because it was safe and had plenty of room. Sigrun and Niall had returned to their realm to deal with the sciatháin, all of whom had made it over, but everyone else had come here. Once I'd seen the extent of the mystery person's injuries, I'd fetched Kaysea and Zareen.

Kaysea was a talented healer, and Zareen had some skills as well. With Cerri's knack for potion making, I had no doubt our guest was in the best possible hands.

Finn had refused to leave this room, even for a few minutes to get cleaned up. He was currently lying on the other couch in the room, stubbornly clinging to consciousness and watching Kaysea work her magic. It was like he was afraid that if he closed his eyes, the prisoner would disappear.

Lyra. The sidhe who had sacrificed everything to get him out.

A low snore came from the hallway, drawing a faint smile from me despite everything. Andrei was back in his human skin and passed out on a bed. In the other bed, Justina was carefully curled around a sleeping Stela. The worst of her injuries had been healed, and Kaysea had reset the bones in her legs, so now she just needed rest.

"I think I got it," Eddie said, his brows bunched together in concentration as he fiddled with the back of the helmet. Aside from dulling her senses, it seemed to create some type of magical void. If Eddie was right, the helmet had prevented Lyra from accessing her magic, maybe even feeling it. For a sidhe, that must have been absolute agony. It also explained why her wounds hadn't healed.

A click sounded, and then Eddie carefully pulled the helmet off her. My eyebrows crept up. She was stunning. Her face was a little gaunt, but her dark skin was unblemished.

When she wasn't half-starved, she likely had a soft face with round cheeks and full lips. Her hair had been shorn, and the helmet must have prevented the hair from growing back because there was only a thin layer of dark purple curls.

Finn jumped up from the couch, stumbled, and Mikhail caught him, guiding him over to the sofa while ensuring not to disturb Kaysea, who was healing a grotesque wound on the fae's thigh.

"She'll be okay," I assured him. "Kaysea's the best."

He didn't look entirely convinced, and I couldn't really blame him. Lyra's injuries were extensive, and she hadn't stirred once.

"What is that?" Mikhail pointed to a spot on Lyra's forearm.

I squinted at the patch of skin that was relatively clean because Kaysea had already healed a wound there. Faint purple lines marked the skin. They weren't injuries of any kind, more like a pattern . . .

"She's not pure sidhe," I murmured. "Some type of dryad?"

"Yes." Kaysea's lips pursed together, and she hovered her hand over a bowl, drawing the water up from it and running it over the gash. With each pass, the angry flesh looked a little better until it was completely closed up. The skin was a few shades lighter and slightly raised, but at least it wasn't a festering wound anymore. My mermaid friend rocked back on her heels. "My guess would be alseid."

Mikhail glanced at me.

"Nature folk," I told him. "I mean, all the fae have a close connection with nature, but the dryads form a close connection with a specific type. Rivers, meadows . . ." I studied the light purple patterns on Lyra's skin. "Alseids prefer groves."

"She was forced to wear this." Eddie held up the helmet. "And was locked away in a tower where she couldn't even see the sky, let alone her trees." He glanced at Lyra with pity. "Her own personal hell."

"And she likely believed that no one would ever come for her." We all looked at the sleeping fae. Her face was the only part of her that wasn't scarred, which meant that helmet had been placed on her long ago. Maybe the night she'd helped Finn and Luna escape.

Even asleep, her full mouth pinched at the corners. She didn't look like she was having a peaceful slumber; she looked like she was caught in a nightmare.

Slowly, Finn reached out and took her hand in his. "I'm sorry, Ly. Please wake up."

When the fae didn't react, Finn's face fell.

"It might take a while," Kaysea told him gently.

He nodded, chewing his bottom lip before looking up at me. "We'll keep her safe, right? You won't let Syndra take her back?"

"Yeah, kid." I leaned back against Mikhail, and he wrapped his arms around me. "She's one of us now."

Chapter Twenty-Five

*A*RE *you sure it shouldn't be tested more?* Iseult stared at the glass of sapphire blue liquid on the table.

It'll be okay. Andrei cupped her face briefly, and a rosy hue spread across the dragon's cheeks.

"You guys are really adorable," I said aloud while signing. "It's gross. Knock it off."

"I don't think they've stabbed each other once," Mikhail mused, his fingers casually translating for Iseult. "Can't be that serious."

Eddie grinned. "Actually, I'm pretty sure Andrei has stabbed her with somethi—"

"It's definitely ready," Thaxea cut him off.

The sorcerer had opened up more in the last month she'd been here, and we'd all learned quickly that she got very flustered over dirty jokes and double entendres. Not because she was offended, but because she'd never been around people like us before.

Violent, horny degenerates.

Since Eddie and Cerri had plenty of space, they'd offered to let her stay in their house, which she'd taken them up on.

Mostly because she'd spent most of her time in Cerri's laboratory anyway, working on a fix for Andrei. Thaxea's way of dealing with her life being turned upside down had been to throw herself completely into her work.

Given that she'd reverse engineered how she'd created the werewolves centuries ago and figured out how to correct the flaws, none of us were complaining. Even if she did sometimes randomly fall asleep at the dinner table.

I watched as Andrei wrapped his fingers around the shot glass but didn't raise it. A golden sheen rolled over his eyes— something that had been happening with increasing frequency for the past few weeks. More than once, he'd shifted into his wolf form and been unable to shift back for days.

A desperate hope wound its way through me. Despite our lighthearted joking, I desperately needed this to work; I couldn't handle another loss right now. I needed a fucking win, and those had been scarce lately.

Aside from watching Andrei struggle to control his wolf nature, I'd had to deal with the fae queens and the fallout of my deal with the sciatháin. To no one's surprise, they hadn't been happy. They'd informed me bluntly that the winged warriors weren't welcome in the fae realms and that they were my responsibility.

Truthfully, I'd been expecting more of a fight, maybe some public punishment or humiliation, but Elvinia and Áine had just seemed . . . tired. Probably because I'd told them about Mariam and that she'd been a spy for Syndra all along, and then they'd told me about two entire Tuatha families that had vanished without a trace.

They'd reluctantly gone to Ashling for answers when they'd turned up nothing in their search. The Merfolk Queen informed them—courtesy of either her magic or her extensive spy network—that the families had allied with Syndra. Had probably always been allied with her.

Cerri had suggested the sciathán relocate here. There was plenty of space in the dragon realm, and more importantly, Eddie and Vizor could monitor their thoughts. Niall believed in his people, that they truly wanted to defect and wanted a life outside of Balor's world.

But I found it difficult to trust these days.

There were other newcomers in the dragon realm too, like the werewolves who had no interest in the war against the vampires. The dragon realm was rapidly becoming a haven for those who had nowhere else to go.

Including Justina and her son.

The vampire had left for a few days after Stela had woken up and returned with a bright-eyed five-year-old boy, who had instantly hit it off with Iseult's son. Justina spent most of her days filling Cerri in about centuries of Vampire Council knowledge—when she wasn't in Stela's bed.

I was happy for all of them, even though a part of me was silently freaking out about my ever-growing list of people to protect. There had been no sign of Syndra, not a hint of what she might be plotting. We all knew she wouldn't let what had happened go, but it was hard to prepare for an attack when you had no idea where it would come from or who it would be directed at.

Lir had been conspicuously absent as well. Only Emir had been easy to monitor. He'd moved most of his warlocks into vampire strongholds; Cassius was frequently spotted with him —in sunlight.

An arm wrapped around my waist. Mikhail tugged me to his side, and I leaned into his warmth.

Magos was awake. The witches had only been able to keep him under for a few days. He was himself again, or at least, that's what Lestari said.

I wouldn't know, because he'd refused to see me or Mikhail.

Hazel eyes looked across the table at me. Andrei gave me a

lopsided grin before slamming the potion back in one shot, then he placed the glass back on the table, sliding it forward a few inches. His eyes were shut.

Stela leaned forward where she was perched on Justina's knee, her gaze locked on her brother.

I was pretty sure I had stopped breathing. "Andrei?"

After a few beats of weighted silence, he opened his eyes. Hazel . . . flecked with gold.

"It worked," he breathed out. "The wolf is . . . not gone . . . but no longer pressing on my every thought. I can still feel the instincts, but they're my instincts."

Cerri hadn't even finished translating before Iseult threw her arms around Andrei's neck.

"By my estimates, it'll take two to three days to fully settle," Thaxea reminded him and us. She'd given everyone a twenty-minute lecture before placing the glass on the table. "We should wait a week to monitor for any unexpected side effects —not that I think there will be any, but better safe than sorry— and then we can do the next group."

Despite Stela's hopes about getting superpowers, Thaxea's fix would just correct the imbalance some werewolves suffered from. While they'd get increased speed and strength in their human forms, that was the extent of it.

The only major known side effect was that their children would be born werewolves, not just potential werewolves who could be turned. The sorcerer hypothesized that it was possible those werewolf children could have additional abilities if they had something other than human in their bloodline, but it was impossible to know.

Iseult stepped back so Stela could hug her brother. Happy tears rolled down her cheeks as they embraced. I let out a relieved breath. Finally. Something went right.

"This calls for more shots!" Eddie set a bunch of empty shot glasses on the table.

"Shocking." Justina rolled her eyes before snatching a glass and holding it out for Cerri to fill.

Andrei untangled himself from Stela's arms and rose to stand in front of me. He glanced over my shoulder at Mikhail. "Are you going to stab me if I hug her?"

"Would that stop you?" Mikhail asked with a touch of amusement.

"Nope." Andrei grinned.

Mikhail laughed and dropped his arms from around me. "I'm going to get some whiskey before Justina and Stela drink it all."

Andrei and I stepped back a few feet as the raucous chatter grew louder. Clearly, I wasn't the only one who'd desperately needed some good news.

"Nemain." Andrei looked at me. Despite the flecks of gold in his eyes, it was him. Just my sweet-natured werewolf. "I don't even know how to thank you for thi—oof!"

He wheezed as I wrapped my arms around him and squeezed. "If you tell anyone I voluntarily hugged you, it's not Mikhail you'll have to worry about stabbing you."

He wound his arms around my back and hugged me. "Your secret is safe with me, kitty cat."

"He's still not ready to see you," Lestari announced as she stopped a few feet from me. After several rounds of drinks, I'd quietly snuck out when more of the werewolves had shown up to celebrate, knowing Andrei was in good company. As thrilled as I was that he was okay, I wasn't in the mood for a party.

But he deserved it.

I should have gone back to my apartment, but I couldn't seem to stop myself from inflicting more pain on my soul, which was why I was sitting on a half-built stone wall around a tall stone building. No one lived in this city yet, the infrastructure was still being built, but some of the houses had been finished so those working on getting everything up and running had somewhere to stay.

Lestari's coven was temporarily living in the house next door. It'd been heavily warded to keep vampires from entering, per Magos' request.

"I'm actually here to speak with you." Briefly, I looked up at a window on the top floor, where I thought I saw a tall, broad figure standing, but there was no one there now. I dropped my gaze back to Lestari. "I wanted to thank you and your coven for everything that you've done. I know the dragons have been welcoming to you, but if you ever need anything from me, it's yours."

"From witch hunter to witch protector?" She arched a dark brow. "Quite the change."

I shrugged. "Don't get me wrong, I'm still happy to hunt any witches who ally themselves with Emir and the warlocks."

"Any witches who make that choice deserve their fate." She smoothed her hands over the pale pink kameez she wore. "How is the fae woman you rescued?"

"Hasn't woken up." I sighed. "We moved her to our apartment yesterday. Both Finn and Luna want to stay close to her, and it's easier if she's in our apartment. For now, she's in Magos' room, but when he returns, we'll have to figure something else out."

Lestari didn't comment on my belief that Magos would return home, but her expression turned sympathetic, and I couldn't handle it. Half a thought from me had a gateway opening, and I stood. "When he's ready to talk, please let me know," I rasped.

"Of course," she said softly.

I stepped into my apartment and closed the gateway. My head fell back, and I stared up at the ceiling.

Did it not work?

I dropped my head back down to find Jinx sitting on the kitchen island, looking at me. Both he and Vizor had thankfully recovered in just over a week.

"Did what not work?" I walked over to the espresso machine and started stabbing at buttons.

Thaxea's fix for Andrei. He leapt onto the counter next to the machine and pawed at a button. *This one.*

"Thanks," I mumbled, pushing the button and sighing with contentment as the aroma of espresso filled the air. "And it did work. Andrei is gonna be fine."

Then why do you look like someone just told you all the whiskey in the world is gone and never coming back?

I stared at the dark espresso dripping into the cup, my eyes burning a little. "Magos still won't see me." I wiped at my eyes roughly and turned, leaning my hip against the counter. "How's Sleeping Beauty?"

Golden eyes studied me for a long moment before Jinx allowed the topic change.

Still asleep. Luna's curled up with her now. The kids are downstairs having a movie night. Something about robot dinosaurs. His whiskers twitched as he wrinkled his nose. Jinx was not a fan of anything with loud noises. *Isabeau has compiled a long list of reasons why you should take her to that devourer realm, by the way.*

"Shocking." I snorted.

Once the chaos of getting Stela back and dealing with the fallout of that had died down, we'd filled the vamp brats in on everything we'd seen in the devourer realm. Naturally, Isabeau had latched on to the dinosaur-like monsters and had been very persistent about going there.

She was still spending time in the death realm, working on our secret project, and I was fairly certain Cian was giving her pointers to strengthen her case, because recently, she'd gone into guilt-tripping territory. And that was something my brother excelled at.

The machine made a beep, and I reached out to pick up my cup, only for mist to swirl and Mikhail to snatch it first. "It's like you read my mind." He took a sip and let out an appreciative sound. "Delicious."

"I hate you." I shoved him out of the way and made another cup. "Kids are downstairs watching a movie. I was going to go check on them."

Plus, a couple of hours of watching a dumb action movie sounded really nice right about now.

Enjoy that. Jinx leapt off the counter and trotted down the hallway. *I'll be sleeping. If you wake me when you come back upstairs, I'll give you bad luck for a week.*

"Pretty sure I wouldn't notice," I muttered.

Mikhail let out a raspy laugh, and we made our way to the downstairs apartment.

"Just in time," Elisa called out as we entered. She balanced a bowl overflowing with popcorn in one hand and two boxes of pizza in the other. "We're just about to start the next movie."

"Still dinosaurs?" Mikhail grabbed the bowl and plopped down on the couch with it. Finn and Isabeau sat up from where they'd been lying on the floor and fell on it like wolves on an injured deer.

"Yep." Elisa set the boxes onto the coffee table and grabbed a slice of pepperoni before settling next to Bryn. "No robots in this one though. I think sea monsters?"

"Sea monsters!" Isabeau raised a fist in the air, sending popcorn everywhere.

"We need to train Hannibal to clean up after her." Bryn sighed.

"Alright." I settled on the couch next to Mikhail, then

picked up some stray pieces of popcorn and tossed them into my mouth. "Let the sea monster versus dinosaur movie begin!"

"Actually, I think they're friends," Finn said. "Or at least . . ." He trailed off as Elisa's phone made a persistent whistle.

"Pele." Elisa frowned and leaned forward, grabbing her phone. "She's supposed to be preparing for some big meeting . . ." Her eyes widened at whatever the message said. "Bo, hand me the remote."

For once, Isabeau didn't argue; she just passed the slim remote to Elisa, and the vampire frantically mashed buttons while pointing it at the TV. The dinosaur movie vanished and was replaced by a news channel doing a live stream.

"This isn't a hoax!" A young brunette human woman pointed hysterically at something off camera. "They arrived twenty minutes ago, and the authorities are here to . . . contain the situation? Or talk to them?" She looked frantically at the camera. "What the fuck are you supposed to do with angels?"

I went still as the camera turned and we saw what the reporter had been pointing at.

Hundreds of seraphim lined up in neat rows, gleaming gold armor shining against brilliant white wings. One of them stepped forward and removed his helmet as he slowly walked towards several people, who looked like members of the human military.

He held up his hands in a calm, nonthreatening manner. "We are not here to harm you." His voice was smooth and reassuring. "Once upon a time, we protected humans from the monsters of the night, but we were locked away by those who wanted to take your world for their own."

"Get fucked," I breathed out.

"A war is coming." He turned, as if he knew exactly where the camera was. "There are monsters amongst you, preying on the innocent, heralding your doom, but have no fear . . . we will keep you safe."

Epilogue

SHE LOOKED at the dead daemon on the floor. Blood pooled underneath them, staining the brand new floors. Having to deal with an assassination attempt tonight was annoying enough, but she'd really liked those floors. They'd been half the reason she'd rented this place.

The other half being that nobody knew about it. Not her overprotective father. Not her stabby shifter girlfriend. Not the retired vampire assassin who was determined to keep her safe because of said shifter girlfriend—who just happened to be his mate.

Was Nemain her girlfriend? They'd never really put a title on their relationship.

They just . . . were. A smile stretched across her lips. Nemain drove her nuts sometimes but, godsdamn, did she love her.

Asmodeus didn't know about this place either.

The smile faded.

Blood touched her designer heels. She frowned and backed up a step. This was the fifth assassination attempt in the last two weeks but the first in this apartment.

She'd known they'd track her down eventually, but she'd really wanted a night off from disposing of bodies.

It brought her a little bit of joy that those trying to prevent her rise to power were getting increasingly frustrated. They kept sending assassins after her. And she kept quietly killing them off and removing any trace of their existence.

It was exhausting doing this all on her own, but it was how the game was played. She had to prove she was worthy of taking her father's place as leader of the Daemon Assembly.

And that meant being ruthless and cunning. But kind of low-key about it. Daemons respected underhandedness more than overt power displays.

Mostly. *"There is a time and a place for everything, my dear,"* her father's words echoed in her mind.

She sighed. It was currently the time to hack a body apart.

"Shame about the floor," a masculine voice said smoothly.

She forced her expression to remain blank and did her best to slow her heartbeat that was going a mile a minute.

The wards around this place were no joke. She'd put them up herself and had deliberately included weak spots for the assassins to exploit.

It was possible for someone very powerful to force their way through them, but she would have felt that.

She looked at the vampire standing six feet away from her. His dark brows were raised as he stared at the body.

Smoothly, she pulled the curved dagger from the hidden harness at the small of her back.

"Not here to kill you." The vampire held up his hands. A charming smile graced his lips.

He was gorgeous. Dark hair and eyes. Perfectly smooth, olive-toned skin. Chiseled cheekbones and a strong jawline. She could see how that smile opened doors for him.

Unfortunately for him, he wasn't her type.

"Cassius." She held up a hand, and bright orange flames

tinted with red surged between her fingers. "You picked a strange way to die. As you can see, I don't really care much for uninvited guests. And definitely not vampires who betrayed those I cared about."

"I see Nemain filled you in on our little trip to the sorcerer realm." The grin morphed into a smirk. "I figured she would still be a little miffed about that, even though I did give her an apology gift. It's why I'm here and not there. I figured you would be more open to negotiation."

She studied him, flames weaving between her fingers.

The vampire was correct in his assumption. Nemain had informed her on how things had gone in the sorcerer realm. Not good. That's how they'd gone. Epically not good. Technically, they'd accomplished most of what they'd wanted to. That stupidly happy werewolf pup who hung around Nemain had gotten his cure. And the werewolves in general were better off.

But Magos was still fucked. More fucked, she supposed.

The vampire before her had played a role in everything going to hell. Him possibly being Elisa and Misha's older brother wouldn't keep Nemain from killing him on sight.

Brutally.

Any amount of patience or refrain Nemain possessed was gone at the moment. The shifter wasn't handling Magos' continuous downward spiral very well on top of everything else.

Cassius was well aware of this. Why had he risked coming here?

"The apology gift." She lowered her hand and let the flames wink out. "You're referring to the hyaenir blood that somehow ended up in Nemain's hand?"

Curiosity flickered through her mind. Nemain had told her that too. How Cassius had taken the crystal filled with the blood needed to help the werewolves . . . but Nemain had woken with the crystal in her hand.

Nobody had an answer for how it got there.

Teleportation usually only worked on the individual gifted with it. At most, they could take another person with them; they couldn't teleport someone or something without them going along for the ride. But Nemain would have smelled Cassius if he'd been in that room.

"Does your Vampire Council know just how rare your gift is?" She cocked her head. "Or are there other vampires capable of teleporting objects?"

"I am one of a kind, as far as I know." He gave her that devilish smile again. When she continued to stare at him flatly, he just chuckled. "You really have it bad for that pretty daemon, don't you? The one who used to work for you? What's their name? Asmodeus?"

"Speak their name again," I said lightly, "and I'll fillet the skin from your bones and burn it in front of you."

"Kinky." He waved at the body. "Would you like any help?"

"Why are you here?"

For a moment, the vampire's mask slipped, and he just looked like someone who knew nothing good awaited him but who was resigned to his fate.

"I didn't want to betray Nemain. She's more than a little terrifying, and I actually like having all my organs inside my body." He rubbed his face. "And Mikhail . . . I didn't want to hurt him."

"Again," she said coldly. "You didn't want to hurt him again."

His mask slid back into place, and he gave her a knowing look. "Don't lecture me, daemon. We both know you haven't risen to where you are without stepping on people along the way."

"Never those who mattered." She shrugged. It really had always been that simple for her. She wanted the best for the daemons as a whole, but when it came down to individuals . . .

there were very few she genuinely cared about. She'd never toyed with people's emotions though. Not in the way Cassius had with Mikhail's.

Cassius looked away. "The Vampire Council was onto Justina, and they were suspicious of me as well. By appearing to betray the others, I've maintained my seat on the Council for now. And furthermore, the faction that has Nemain in their sights considers me a loyal asset."

"It's my understanding that the Council came very close to kidnapping Justina's son." She narrowed her eyes at him. Regardless of how she felt about vampires, kids were always off limits. No matter what games they played, daemons never used children as pawns. It was one of the few rules they all agreed to.

The vampires felt otherwise.

Dark eyes swung back to me. "They were exactly three minutes too late because someone tipped off Justina and she moved up her plans." The muscles along Cassius' jaw feathered as he clenched and unclenched. "They would have been thirteen minutes too late if it hadn't been necessary for me to go through multiple people to ensure Justina got the information she needed. Because she's also feeling rather murderous towards me these days."

"You're very good at pissing off the women in your life," she drawled. "Have you ever considered that it's a *you* problem?"

He didn't rise to her bait. Instead, he glanced at the body on the floor before meeting her gaze again.

"Everyone always says they'll be the villain to protect those they care about. But they're not the villain. Not really. The vampire kids who turned their backs on Nemain can't even fathom what true villainy is." Again, that desolation flashed across his face. "It's being hated by those you care about.

Knowing that if you die . . . they won't care. Maybe they'd even celebrate it."

"So you've come here to, what?" She tilted her head. "Tell me the sob story about how you're just the misunderstood villain? Would you like a tissue?"

He scoffed. "I came here because I need to be able to funnel information to Nemain in a way that won't get me dead."

In a blink, he teleported to stand right in front of her. Flames surged over her skin, but he made no move to attack her, so she held her ground and waited.

The vampire leaned forward slightly. "You've survived multiple assasination attempts. I'm sure there are more I don't know about. You are alone. No one is guarding your back, because politically, you need to stand on your own two feet. I get that. But we both know you're also doing it because you won't risk the lives of those you love."

"Your point?" she said evenly, giving nothing away.

He gave her a charming smile. "You don't care about me. Risk my life; I'll help keep you alive." He teleported back across the room. "And no one will ever know."

"In exchange for passing along your messages to Nemain?" She arched a brow.

"No." He shook his head. "For lying to Nemain about where you got your information from. Because we both know she won't trust anything I say."

Something in her gut twisted. She'd withheld information from Nemain before, especially when the shifter had spiraled while trying to get revenge after Myrna's death, but she'd never lied to her.

"How far are you willing to go?" the vampire pushed. "What will you do to protect her? And the daemon I'm not allowed to name?"

"Careful," she hissed.

"I know about the title you've left behind," he taunted. "The mantle your mother bore and you picked up after she died. Just as I know your original name. You cast both of them aside over the last few centuries." Another blink, and he teleported closer to the dead daemon on the floor and knelt, swiping his hand through the blood. The vampire stepped over the body, holding out his hand. "You used to love bargains back then. So make a bargain with me now, Lucifer the Morning Star."

Want to read chapters from Mikhail's POV?

I'm working my way through the books and rewriting some chapters from Mikhail's POV! You can read all the existing ones and get the new ones delivered right to your inbox!

Newsletter subscribers also get the short story of how Nemain and Kaysea met. Hint, it involves a kidnapped kelpie… and Nemain talking a lot of shit.

Visit www.maddoxgreyauthor.com to get your bonus goodies!

Acknowledgments

So…how we doing? I know that ending got a little wild there.

But we're entering the home stretch! Things are going to heat up, in more ways than one, in Pele's book. And then we have the final three books of the series!

Sorry in advance for being mean to Magos but know that it hurts me too. I adore my perfect barista and knight in shining armor.

Also let's not forget that book 11 will be his book. I'm going y'all an entire book of Magos! So you can't be mad at me. Them's the rules.

A massive thank you for everyone who has supported me with this series. I know it's a little unconventional but I'm having so much fun writing it and it means a lot that it resonates with so many people.

As always, it would be incredibly appreciated if you could leave an honest review on Goodreads or whichever platform you prefer. Reviews are super important for authors and we really appreciate it when y'all take the time to leave one! Plus, it helps other readers find us :)

Lost Legacies Guide

CHARACTERS:

Bryn - newbie valkyrie; her soul is bonded with Finn's and she is his guardian

Cerridwn - dragon, sweetheart of Eddie; daughter of the dragon who rules their realm

Cian - feline shifter with necromantic magic; twin brother of Nemain; has a strained relationship with her but still loves her fiercely

Damon - teenage vampire on the run from the Vampire Council

Dante - necromancer, incredibly powerful and in a long-term relationship with Nemain's brother Cian

Eddie - a dragon who owns and runs a shop of magical oddities and supplies

Elisa - oldest of the teenage vampire runaways

Emir - leader of the Warlock Circle

Finn - fae child of the exiled fae king Balor; a prophecy about him says he will bring about the end of the realms

Isabeau - child vampire that the teenage vampires take care of and treat as a younger sister

Jinx - a fae cat known as a grimalkin, him and Nemain have been together since she was born; he's grumpy and has the ability to inflict bad luck on others

Kaysea - mermaid princess and bestie of Nemain; Myrna was her twin sister; older brother Connor is very protective of her

Lir - fae devourer hybrid, serves as the right-hand of the exiled fae king, Balor

Luna - another grimalkin (because the only thing better than one cat is two cats); unlike Jinx she is sweet and cuddly

Magos - old vampire warrior, his past is a bit of a mystery but he's loyal to Nemain and their relationship is similar to that of a an uncle/niece despite not being related

Mikhail - former vampire assassin of the Vampire Council; nephew of Magos

Misha - part of the teenage vampire group, looks very similar to Elisa but they don't know for sure if they're actually related, either way they consider each other brother & sister

Nemain - feline shifter and fae hybrid with devourer magic; all around freak of nature; raised by Macha and Nevin who she only learned recently were actually her aunt and uncle; biological parents are Badb and Kalen

Niall - fae devourer hybrid who fought Nemain and lost, but she chose to spare his life

Pele - daemon who runs the local tavern, The Inferno; close friends with Nemain who she has been in an ongoing casual poly relationship with for centuries

Sigrun - valkyrie, exiled from her people after the events of Ragnarok; has a wolf companion named Gunnar and a magical cat named Viggo

REALMS:

*Note, this is not an extensive list of all the realms because there are many. Only those relevant to the story are mentioned.

Human Realm - the modern world that humans are familiar with; most humans are completely unaware that their realm is one of many or that magical beings walk amongst them

Meenri - the main realm controlled by the daemons after they fled their original home realm

Acleonia - the new realm for the dragons after the events of A Shift in Ashes

Fae Realms

Mag Ildathach - belongs to the Seelie Court; name means multi-colored plains

Mag Mell - belongs to neither the Seelie or the Unseelie; like all death realms it is difficult to fully comprehend or travel in without necromantic magic; currently where Dante & Cian call home

Tír fo Thuinn - despite being referred to as a realm, this is actually a territory that stretches across all the fae realms, it is the dominion of the sea fae, all the oceans and seas belong to them

Tír na mBeo - only realm shared by the Unseelie & Seelie Queens

Fallen Realms

Kanima - former realm of the feline shifters; this is where Nemain's parents were born; it fell to devourers and the survivors fled to the human realm

Cerulle - former realm of Magos and Mikhail; also fell to devourers; survivors fled to the human realm and were later killed during the vampire and werewolf war

About the Author

Maddox Grey is a queer nonbinary elder millennial who still remembers vividly what it was like to be emotionally damaged by the season two finale of Buffy the Vampire Slayer.

They write morally grey characters who fall for equally unhinged morally grey love interests. And the banter flows as fast as the action in the stories they craft.

When they're not putting their characters through hell, Maddox is playing video games, reading smut, burying their nose in comic books, or hiding behind a pillow while they watch horror movies.

To get regular email updates about new releases and other announcements, be sure to sign up for the newsletter on maddoxgreyauthor.com

facebook.com/maddoxgrey.author

instagram.com/maddoxgrey.author

tiktok.com/@greymalkinpress